FIXED

Enjoy the ride.

Paddy Head

FIXED

PADDY HEAD

Dedicated to the heart and courage
of the Thoroughbred
and to my good friend and
fellow pioneer woman jockey,
Denise Boudrot Hopkins

MAIDEN VOYAGE

The chestnut filly wheeled on her hind legs. Andy tipped dangerously in the saddle and grabbed for mane to stay aboard. "Whoa, girl, take it easy."

She turned the horse back in the direction of the starting gate. The gate handler continued his approach, leather lead strap in hand. The filly tensed, ready to bolt.

"It's alright, just walk right in there. There's nothing to be afraid of." Andy kept her voice low and soothing, gently stroking the filly's neck.

A sudden clanging in the starting gate drew the filly's attention as a jockey called out for assistance. The handler quickly slipped the leather strap into her bridle.

Andy took a deep breath as he led them into the narrow, padded stall.

The filly tossed her head impatiently as the handler climbed up on the ledge beside them. The latches closed behind her as he removed the strap and held the bridle firmly.

Andy quickly reached up to her helmet and pulled the layered sets of goggles down over her eyes.

"Last horse coming in!" the starter's voice called from his stand beside the gate.

"Get tied on," the handler instructed her.

Andy twined the fingers of her left hand in the mane and pressed her right hand against the filly's neck. She looked straight ahead at the track.

A loud clang reverberated through the metal stalls as a

horse thrashed against the sides.

"Hold it, boss!" a jockey shouted.

The handler pulled the filly's head to the side as she jumped forward. Andy was thrown up against the padded bar. Instinctively, she pushed herself back into the saddle and reset her feet in the stirrups. The moment the handler straightened the filly's head, the latches sprang open.

Andy let out a shout of encouragement as she reached forward with the filly's thrust. The track was clear in front for a brief second. A horse appeared on either side of her, so close their jockeys' boots pressed against hers.

She shouted once more, scrubbing the filly's neck with both hands until she pulled away from the two horses. Suddenly, a horse cut across her path, his heels throwing dirt in her direction. Her breath caught in her throat as the clods hit her face, cutting into her cheeks like hundreds of sharp needles. She angled in to avoid the dirt but more horses joined the leader, forming an impenetrable wall in front of her.

A horse moved up on the inside rail and she took a position beside him.

The dirt clung to her goggles as they galloped along the backstretch, her vision narrowing with every stride. Andy reached up and carefully peeled the top layer off. Just as she dropped it around her neck, the tiring horse directly in front of her slowed suddenly, his heels inches away from her filly's front legs. Andy pulled the filly out to avoid the deadly entanglement that would bring her horse down.

"Damn!" she cursed under her breath, now three horses wide going into the sweeping turn. The horses on the inside rail gained a length on her as they straightened out for the homestretch.

Andy looked straight ahead. Her path to the wire was unimpeded. She sent the filly forward at full gallop. A sound like thunder roared in her ears as the bettors cheered on their favourites. Andy reached out with every stride, her face buried in the filly's mane. The thunder reached a crescendo as she slipped under the wire.

All tension dissipated from her body and with it, the last of her energy. She gasped for air as she stood up in the stirrups and looked around. One horse was in front of her, the rest of the field behind.

"We almost got there," she cried out, glancing over her shoulder as several horses galloped by.

The jockeys called out congratulations or complaints to each other. Two of them were arguing over who had shut off who at the quarter pole.

"Hey Angel, good win!" someone called out.

Andy looked over at Angel Cordero, one of New York's leading jockeys. His smile seemed to stretch from ear to ear as he turned his horse around.

Andy's joy reached exhilaration when she realized she had beaten several of the finest jockeys in North America. She now felt like one of them.

She turned the filly around and galloped back along the homestretch. As she neared the unsaddling area, she reined the filly down to a walk.

The groom reached for the reins. "Hey, girl, you almost got there."

"How far behind was I?" she asked.

"Angel got you by half a length. One more stride, you'd have caught him at the wire."

"If I hadn't been caught behind that horse, I'm sure I would have won. That cost me the race."

"Yeah, that was a pisser." He glanced over at the mutual board. "It's gonna be one hell of a payoff. Wish I had the perfecta."

"Why? What were my odds?"

"You were thirty-to-one, girl."

"No way, this filly's too good to go off at thirty-to-one."

"It's not the horse they didn't have any confidence in," he told her as she dismounted. "Your first two races, you finished off the board. The bettors aren't gonna believe in you till you win a race."

"That'll be next time," she assured him as she unbuckled the girths and pulled off the tiny leather saddle. The lead weights unbalanced her and she staggered backwards. The tack weighed a mere ten pounds but it felt more like fifty.

"I know who's going to have a good sleep tonight," Jake said as he led the filly away. "Sweet dreams, girl."

Andy carried her tack over to the scales and watched the needle register a hundred and fourteen pounds, two pounds more than her pre-race weight. Neither her helmet nor the dirt collected during the race had been factored in beforehand.

The clerk of scales nodded and she gratefully handed her tack over to the valet and stepped off the scale.

"Have a little trouble out there?" Barry Locke, the trainer, asked her as they walked across the saddling paddock.

"That horse in front of me backed up so fast, I almost went down," she replied. Barry Locke smiled. "That's racing luck for you. You made up a ton of ground in the home-stretch, Andy, nobody could have done any better."

"We'll be the ones in the winner's circle next time," she said confidently.

The smile vanished from the trainer's face. "I need to talk to you about that. This isn't easy for me to say, Andy, believe me." He looked away, his eyes not meeting hers. "But some-thing's come up with Mr. Raglan. Any other owner, I'd say no, but Raglan pretty much fills my barn. I can't afford to lose him."

"What's wrong with Mr. Raglan?"

Barry shook his head. "It's nothing you did. It's his son, Darrin."

"What about Darrin?" She had been galloping every morning for the past six months with Darrin Raglan, teach-ing him how to balance a horse and keep them in rhythm. "Isn't he happy with what we're doing? I thought Darrin was coming along really well."

"Yep, so well he thinks he'd make a great jockey."

"What? Darrin, a jockey?"

Andy shook her head slowly in disbelief. She'd noticed Darrin had been losing weight lately but she thought his bout of flu during the winter had caused it. It was suddenly clear to her that his weight loss was intentional.

"I have to take his contract," Barry said. "I have no choice in the matter."

"But, Mr. Locke, Darrin's not ready to ride races. He needs another year of experience. He's only been in the starting gate a couple of times. And he can't switch sticks. Every time he tries to switch the whip over into his left hand, he drops it."

Barry sighed, frustration obvious in his voice. "The kid's got it into his head that he's ready. I told Mr. Raglan he needed more experience but after he watched him in the workout with you this morning, he thinks he's ready. But listen, the kid's tall for a jockey, he's going to have a tough time keeping his weight down. I'll call you back here if he can't cut it."

"What do you mean, call me back?" she asked confused.

"I've spoken to a trainer in Boston and he's interested in taking your contract," he told her.

"But I don't want to leave New York. This is where I live. I want to ride here at Belmont."

"Of course you do but all of the big stables here have their apprentice jockeys. The competition is tough at Belmont. It's different at Suffolk Downs, the girls do great there. Denise Boudrot won the leading jockey title a couple of years ago, back in '74. So I talked to Emmett Gibbons, the leading trainer. If you ride for him, you've got a good chance of winning the jockey title this year."

"I don't know anybody in Boston," she insisted.

"You won't have any trouble making friends. It'll feel like home before you know it. You get your name in the record books at Suffolk and you can come back to New York and pick your mounts."

Andy's mind was numb, her surroundings taking on a surreal aspect.

"I know this is hitting you hard. It's lousy timing but Raglan just sprang it on me last night. I didn't want to tell you this morning, not before your first race." He looked down at her, his eyes as apologetic as his tone. "You've just proved you're a hell of a good jockey, Andrea Crowley. With or without my help, you've got a great future ahead of you."

THE SMILING OYSTER

Mickey wrapped his jacket tighter around him as he approached the door. The weather was unseasonably cold for late April in Boston. Heavy fog was predicted later in the night. He wanted to get his business done quickly and get home before the grey blanket obscured the city.

He walked by the sign, *The Smiling Oyster serving the finest seafood in New England* without a glance and pushed open the heavy oak door. A blast of warm air greeted him as he stepped into the restaurant. He welcomed the warmth but not the odour of fried, greasy food.

Matt Durgan waved at him from behind the bar. "Ey, Mickey, what'll it be?"

Matt filled several positions at The Smiling Oyster, cook, bartender and bouncer. A semi-pro wrestler throughout his twenties, at the age of forty but he could still bring down the younger men. His skills as a chef however left much to be desired.

It was well past the dinner hour and only a few tables were occupied. Most of the customers sat at the bar. Mickey recognized their faces. They were all connected in some way to Boston's notorious Winter Hill Gang.

Operating out of a garage in the Winter Hill section of Somerville, the gang was led by Howie Winter and his second-in-command, James 'Whitey' Bulger. Like several other establishments in the area, *The Smiling Oyster* was under the 'protection' of the gang, whose henchmen often came by to see that their rules were being enforced. Mickey didn't want to be here when they paid their nightly visit.

Long ago, Michael Seamus Amato had learned the art of survival. Mercilessly taunted throughout his early childhood, he learned to outrun the bullies of the streets of his native South Boston. Affectionately called 'Southie' by its proud Irish population, it was a training ground for both professional boxers and future gangsters. Mickey's fleetness of foot eventually led to a tenth place finish in the 1965 Boston Marathon. Not only fleet of foot, Mickey's intelligence made him an astute chess player and keen observer of humanity. As a child Mickey was 'church mouse poor' and so quiet that he earned the appellation Mickey the Mouse. Mickey's epiphany came that Marathon day, when he noticed the respectful looks he received from the Southie crowd. At seventeen, he realized respect was the prize he craved.

Abhorring violence, he learned to use his brain to command respect from people whose methods were primitive, direct and effective. Yet as an adult, here he was, employed by Anthony 'Pony' Cantoni—mobster, race fixer, killer. The irony of his position did not elude him. As always, when meeting with Pony, he must keep his wits about him. One slip could bring his life to a sudden and violent end.

"So, what can I do you for, Mickey?" Matt spoke with the Boston accent characteristic of much of eastern Massachusetts, his 'for' sounding more like 'foah'.

"What'll it be? Glenlivet?" Matt pointed to the bottle of single malt scotch over the bar.

"Business first." Mickey's tone was as brisk as his walk. He knew he wasn't missing out on anything. The bottle over the bar had been filled with a cheap brand of Scotch from the corner package store. When Matt offered the bottle under the bar, that would be worth accepting.

"They're in the back room," Matt said before turning his attention back to wiping the bar.

Mickey headed to the back of the building. A shadowed

hallway ended at a closed door. Muffled but angry voices emanated from within the room. He turned the knob, slipping in quietly. The tension in the room made his skin prickle. A whale of a man sat in a chair that looked dangerously close to collapsing. Even seated, Anthony Cantoni towered over the little man who stood before him. Another man sat with his back to Mickey, his chair tipped forward and balancing on the front two legs. Mickey recognized the short cropped hair of Tommy Flaherty.

"Weasel, you fucking retard, you've really fucked up this time!" Pony bellowed.

"Yeah, fucked up good this time," Tommy echoed, his chair slamming down onto all four legs.

Pony's heavy breathing added menace to the interrogation. He pounded the billy club he was holding into the palm of his hand and the little man jumped.

Mickey stepped back further into the shadows. Wally 'the weasel' Malloy had obviously screwed up badly. The jockey's sharply chiselled features, close set eyes and thin lips were pinched even more than usual, making him appear much like his namesake. Sweat dripped from his forehead and along the back of his neck. An odour of fear permeated the room, similar to the stench of a ferret. Wally the Ferret would be closer to the truth, Mickey thought, but 'weasel' definitely had a more sinister ring to it.

"You telling me you couldn't get a coupla' no talent pinheads to take five C notes and give their horses an easy ride?" Pony demanded in his nasal slur. "The fucking retards would rather get dirt thrown in their face for a lousy thirty bucks?"

"Gees, Pony, we've got a couple of new kids in the room. They're wet behind the ears." Wally paced around in a tight circle, his eyes directed at the floor. He turned to the left, just like on the racetrack.

"Tell us something we haven't heard," Tommy demanded. "I've got a bunch of greenhorns at Suffolk, but I keep them in line. So what's your problem?"

"These kids don't know their ass from their elbow. They sure as hell don't know where the horse's ass is!"

"I know where it is, standin' right in front of me." Pony laughed loudly at his own joke.

Wally made a feeble attempt to laugh, knowing how much Pony liked people to appreciate his jokes but his face was a contortion of pain.

"When are you gonna' come through for me, Weasel?" Pony demanded. "I can't keep carrying you. You want me to break down like those sorry ass nags you ride?"

Mickey almost laughed aloud at the idea of three hundred and fifty pound Pony running around the track with Wally on his shoulders.

"Dammit, Weasel, look at me!" Pony bellowed.

Mickey could feel the power of the big man's voice vibrating through the wooden planks of the floor. Wally froze in his tracks, his head spinning in Pony's direction, his eye level shifting from the floor to Pony's chest.

Wally never made eye contact. The eyes were the windows to the soul and Wally had sold his a long time ago.

"I got ya the kid from Florida, Smartalex. He's on the payroll, so how come he's not doing his job?" Pony demanded.

Mickey recognized the nickname for Alex Munsey, an apprentice rider on the Rhode Island circuit who'd been pretty hot in the standings last year.

"The kid was great when we put him on the lead. Mural and I knew how to take care of our mounts and let Smartalex go to the front. But then the savvy bettors caught on and started betting him." Wally was back to his left-handed pacing as his voice took on his famous 'weasel whine'. "So you told me to switch to plan B. Okay, we get the kid on a nag that couldn't outrun my grandma in army boots. The smart bettors think we got him set up for a big one so they start laying down their bets. Before you know it, he's almost the favourite. It couldn't be any better for us. I've got the legitimate mount and they're not even looking at him. Gives me odds as long as a telephone number. Money in the bank, right?"

Wally's pacing became so frantic Mickey was getting dizzy watching him.

"But the kid likes getting his picture taken so much he rides the hair off his horse and nips me at the wire."

Pony bellowed like a raging bull as he heaved himself up. He swung the billy club and caught Wally on the side of the head. The little man fell to his knees, blood running down his cheek.

Mickey couldn't believe Wally would be so stupid. It was bad enough screwing up in the first place but now he was riling Pony even more with a blow-by-blow replay. The old jockey must have landed on his head too many times.

Tommy quickly stepped in between the two men. A successful middleweight boxer, Tommy could defend himself with his fists but this situation called for his other skill, mediation. He rolled his shoulder muscles to ease his tension as he turned towards Pony.

"We've got a big one going down tomorrow, Pony," he said in a quick but neutral tone. "We need the little asshole in one piece. He screws up again, you tear him apart limb from limb and I'll dispose of the parts."

Pony's grunt turned into a low growl as he lowered himself back down into the chair. The groaning of the wooden legs made Mickey close his eyes. If the chair collapsed, Tommy and Wally together couldn't lift the man back to his feet.

They had yet to notice Mickey.

"Get your sorry ass over here and gimme the numbers for tomorrow's fifth," Pony demanded. "I wanna see if ya got it straight."

Wally jumped to his feet, wiping the blood from his face with his sleeve. His survival instinct finally kicked in and he positioned himself between Pony and the door.

Tommy took a folded white envelope out of his gym bag and dangled it like a carrot. "What's the numbers, Wally?"

"Six, two, three," Wally rattled off.

"Six isn't the longest shot in the race," Pony countered.

"No, but he'll be at least twelve-to-one. He hasn't won a race since JC was born. He's sound and he's got Mural on him. 'The Mule' can move any horse up ten lengths with his whip." Wally spoke at a rapid fire pace. "The number two has got a lot of closing speed. One of the old timers is on him, Lyle. His car is going to be repossessed tomorrow unless he can make a payment. He'll make sure he's right behind Mural at the wire."

"Lyle screws up tomorrow, he won't have to worry about his wheels. He'll be ridin' around in a hearse, compliments of the Winter Hill Gang."

Even Tommy laughed at that image.

"And the third horse in my trifecta?" Pony demanded, pointing the club in Wally's direction.

"That's me. I know exactly where to be at the wire."

Wally's eyes were glued to the little white envelope, his bonus for arranging the deal. It was a full week's worth of blow.

As a certified accountant, Mickey knew that Wally was living well beyond his annual earnings. His rare winning ride wouldn't cover his rent let alone his habit. But there were no cheques or bank statements to alert the IRS. All of Pony's bonuses were paid in cash. The bills barely touched Wally's palms before disappearing into the coffers of his drug dealer. The transition was so quick Mickey was certain Wally couldn't tell you which president's face was on the hundred dollar bills Pony handed out.

"No screwing up this time," Tommy warned.

"Fuck it up tonight, ya spend the rest of your life shining shoes in the grandstand," Pony threatened him. "And get Smartalex back in line. He's ridin' the favourite in the last race. He's gotta finish off the board."

"Right," Wally agreed.

"The kid comes through, he's back on the payroll. So now

it's all your show." Pony laughed uproariously at his play on words.

Wally didn't make the connection between his third place finish and 'show' but it brought a smile to Mickey's face. As Pony's puns went, it wasn't a bad one.

Tommy opened the folded envelope and dumped half of the cocaine on the table. He folded the envelope up again and threw the package at Wally. "Get your ducks in a row and you get the rest of it."

Wally squatted down, his eyes never leaving the billy club. "It'll go like clockwork," he promised, grabbing the envelope and scuttling across the room. Without so much as a glance at Mickey, he slithered out the door.

"Hey, 'Class Act', how ya doin'?" Pony greeted him as he leaned back in the wooden chair until its legs creaked in protest.

The sound set Mickey's nerves on edge and he started fiddling with the strap of his leather briefcase. He knew Pony always seized the mental advantage and suddenly realized the creaking of the tortured chair was a ploy to make him uneasy.

Mickey took a quick breath, to settle his nerves. He lifted a file out of his briefcase. "Month's end for The Smiling Oyster, a.k.a., *Pony Cantoni Racefixing Limited.*"

Pony roared. Mickey had used that line every week in the three years he had worked for Pony and it was like the big man was hearing it for the first time.

"Your 'Special Edition'," Mickey said, handing him the file that contained not only the accounts for the restaurant but all income and payoffs for his illegal endeavours. He placed a second, more sanitised, version on the table beside the creaky chair.

Pony took out a pair of glasses and read the figures. He took his time studying the columns of figures in both versions, finally nodding in satisfaction. "I like your cookin' better than Matt's."

Another burst of laughter. Tommy joined in the laughter but Mickey just nodded. He had long ago cultivated a persona of the serious accountant and it relieved him of that duty. As far as the crew was concerned, he cared only for numbers and balance sheets and had no sense of humour.

Pony handed the first folder back to Mickey. "File it."

Mickey walked to the stone fireplace on the far wall and slowly fed the sheets one at a time into the fire. There would be no paper trail for the IRS to get their hands on.

Anthony Cantoni filed an income tax return faithfully every year, a lesson learned from Al Capone's mistake. All legitimate expenses and income from the restaurant were in the ledger. Listed as employees of the Smiling Oyster were Matt Durgan, head chef, bartender and bouncer, Cheri Connery, his girlfriend, as waitress, Tommy Flaherty as short order cook and bouncer and Michael Amato, bookkeeper. All very legit.

"Tommy and me got some business to do now, Mick."

Mickey almost sighed in relief at his cue to leave.

"Grab a shot on the way out," Pony offered. "Tell Matt to give ya the good stuff, on me."

Mickey backed slowly towards the door as if he were leaving the presence of the Queen of England. In Her Majesty's case it was a sign of respect. With Pony it was sheer survival.

NEW ENGLAND HOSPITALITY

A ndy shivered. A sense of dread penetrated deeper into her bones than the New England fog. She could see her hand in front of her but it was impossible to see her feet, a mere sixty inches away. The urge to turn around and head back to New York was overwhelming.

The guard shack appeared in front of her. Whether she liked it or not, she was here, in Boston. It wasn't forever, she reminded herself, just one racing season. Win some races and she'd be on her way back to New York.

She knocked on the door of the guard shack and waited several seconds before it opened a crack. Light and heat streamed out.

"Yeah?"

The voice was anything but friendly.

"My name is Andrea Crowley. I'm expected at Emmett Gibbons' barn."

The security guard picked up a clipboard and scanned the names. "Ya ain't on my list."

She reached into the back pocket of her jeans and pulled out her New York jockey's license, handing it to him.

"This is fine in New York," he said, "but it doesn't work here."

She counted to three. Though she had inherited her father's gift for gab she also had her mother's quick temper.

21

"I'm here to ride for Gibbons' stable. I'm his new apprentice jockey."

"Okay, but you'll need to get a Suffolk license today. Tell Emmett to arrange it." The security guard handed her back the little plastic ID card and shut the door.

Andy shoved the card into her back pocket and turned on her heels. "Welcome to Suffolk Downs," she muttered.

She found herself on a wide paved road. Unlike the complex set-up of Belmont Park, the barns were arranged in a simple pattern on either side of the road. The dense fog obscured the number plate on each barn.

Without warning, a man cut across her path. Andy skidded to a halt to avoid a collision. Dressed entirely in black, he was barely perceptible even from a few inches. He stared down at her, his eyes as dark as his clothes. Without a word, he disappeared into the fog.

"This is the famous New England hospitality?" she sighed. "I'm not impressed."

The clip clop of hooves sounded behind her. A horse and rider took shape from about three feet away, the horse's hot breath condensed into little wisps of steam.

"Hello," she said, catching the rider's attention. "Can you direct me to Emmett Gibbons' barn?"

"Yeah, I'd take you there but I'm kinda busy," the rider replied. The voice sounded male but helmet and goggles obscured any facial features. "I'll give you directions but it'll cost you a cup of coffee."

Definitely male. It was a pick up but at least it was friendly.

"You've got it," she promised.

"Barn 7," he said as his horse broke into a trot. "I take mine with milk and two sugars."

Horse and rider disappeared. Andy made her way along the road until she found barn 7. As she stepped into the lighted shed row, the barn was alive with activity, horses going and coming from the track. Hotwalkers cooled out the horses that had already had their exercise. When she entered the shed row, none of the humans paid any attention to her but she was immediately assessed by the horses. Some eyed her with friendly interest, others pinned their ears. A big bay horse lunged at her from over the front webbing of his stall, his teeth snapping dangerously close to her ear.

"You must be related to the security guard," she said, ducking out of the way.

The predominant colours in the narrow shed row were orange and blue. Feed buckets were blue, water buckets were orange and the nylon webbings clipped to the front of each stall were a combination of both.

"Come on, Riva, get your big mug down here and take a bite of this yummy bit."

Andy followed the voice and found a stocky woman standing in a stall and tacking up a horse.

"Is this Emmett Gibbons' barn?"

"It sure as hell is." The groom took her eye off the big colt for a second to look Andy over. "What do you need, jock?"

Andy was pleased to be recognized as a jockey. Women had only acquired that right in 1969 when Olympic rider, Kathy Kusner, took the racing commission to court. Kathy won the battle for women to have a jockey's license but the racetrack has its own unwritten code of justice. There would be many incidents before a woman would actually ride a race.

Now, in the spring of '76, the male riders were no longer boycotting the women but female jockeys were still a rare species. Trainers were creative in their reasons for not giving a woman a leg up. Andy had heard every excuse in the book. *'I'm not prejudiced against women, I just don't want to see you get hurt.' 'As soon as I have a well mannered horse, I'll put you on.' 'I'd love to give you a mount but my owner won't ride women'.* And her favourite, *'If I put you on a horse, my wife will think I'm sleeping with you.'*

She put that all aside. This was a new day, a new beginning.

"I'm Andy Crowley."

"Yeah and I'm Mustang," the groom replied as she adjusted the bridle.

Andy turned her attention to the horse, a tall bay colt. "Nice looking horse. What's his name?"

"Riva Ridge."

Another strike out. Riva Ridge had won the 1972 Kentucky Derby. He was now standing at stud in Kentucky. The message was clear. It was none of her business. A lot of trainers were secretive when it came to the registered name of their horses. They didn't want the rider to spread the word around on how the horse was training.

Andy shivered but not from the cold. She believed strongly in omens. If the security guard and this crude, belligerent woman were a premonition of what was to come, she came to the wrong racetrack.

"I'm the apprentice jockey from Barry Locke's barn in New York."

"And I'm the head groom for the leading trainer at Suffolk Downs," she retorted, as though it were a contest.

"My horse ready?" a voice called out from the end of the shed row.

"What took you so long!" Mustang yelled back at an ear-splitting level. "What do you think this is, Eddie, some kind of resort? You're not on vacation. Get your ass down here so we can get our quota out to the track."

"In this pea soup, I'll be lucky to find the end of the shed row, never mind the racetrack."

A man appeared through the fog, his step light, almost carefree. At about five foot four, he was trim and muscled, probably tipping the scales at 118 pounds. Definitely a jockey, Andy decided.

"Intelligent people are still snuggled up under a warm blanket," he said, his bright blue eyes twinkling. "Not galloping around in the mud and fog."

As he stepped up beside the horse, he suddenly noticed Andy.

"Hey, Mustang, where's your manners? Are you going to introduce me to this lovely young woman?"

"Well excuse me," Mustang said in an exaggerated drawl. "I never did finish that course in etiquette. This here is Sandy, from New York. And this is Eddie Flaherty who's about to be fired because he can't get here on time."

Eddie held his hand out. "Pleased to meet you, Sandy."

Andy shook his hand. "The name is Andy, Andy Crowley."

"Ah. And what county would you be comin' from?" he said in a perfect Irish lilt.

"My father came from county Cork but I was born in New York."

"The Flahertys hail from county Clare, just a stone's throw away."

"Save the chit chat for the break. Come on, let's get this nag on the track before Emmett fires me. I may look like a lady of leisure but I really do need this job."

"I think you're just fooling us, Mustang. Any woman with a wardrobe like yours can't be poor. I've never seen so many beautifully tailored tee-shirts," he teased as she hoisted him up into the saddle.

In spite of the dampness, Mustang wore a thin, form fitted tee-shirt. "Just keep your mind on what you're doing. Emmett wants an easy two mile gallop." She turned to Andy. "Follow along behind him and he'll take you to the track. Emmett's in the trainers' stand."

Andy had to quicken her pace to keep up to the excitable colt as he pranced out of the stall. "Hey, Eddie, what can you tell me about Emmett?"

"You'll size him up pretty quick," Eddie replied. "You're from New York, huh? I rode a few races at Finger Lakes. Is that where you've been riding?"

"No, Belmont. I went to Finger Lakes first. Everyone told me women had a better chance at a smaller track."

"Free advice usually isn't worth much," he laughed. "So what happened?"

"First day there, a trainer put me up on a horse that ran off for three miles. It would have been four if the outrider hadn't pulled me up. The second horse bucked me off and bolted out the gap. Made me seriously consider other career options, let me tell you." The muscles in her left shoulder throbbed as she recounted the incident. She shook her arm, to loosen the joint and banish the memory. "But my stubbornness kicked in. I decided to do it the right way. I went to Belmont Park and learned how to handle a racehorse properly. I figured if I rode horses that were worth a lot of money, I'd be safer. Trainers don't play childish pranks with horses that are worth hundreds of thousands of dollars. That's how I ended up in Barry Locke's stable."

"Couldn't make it at the cheap track, so you went to the big Apple." Eddie smiled down at her. "I like your attitude."

Andy wasn't so sure about that. "Thanks but it didn't work out."

"The politics at Suffolk are simpler than in New York," he informed her.

"That's good to hear."

"I said simpler," he reiterated, "not easier."

"If I wanted easy, I would have gone to university and become a lawyer, like my mother wanted."

Eddie laughed. "You're going to do just fine here."

The pavement gave way to soft dirt and Andy knew they were headed onto the racetrack. The horse snorted and reared up on his hind legs. Eddie sat in the saddle as comfortable as the Lone Ranger.

"I've got to go now," he said as casually as if he was about to ride through the park. "There's the trainers' stand. You'll find Emmett in there."

In a flash, horse and rider disappeared into the fog. Andy listened to the beat of the horse's hooves in the dirt until they faded into the distance. Eddie's vote of confidence lifted her spirits as she walked towards the enclosed trainers' stand, ready to meet her new contract holder.

CAN'T CUT IT
IN NEW YORK

Tendrils of fog swirled around her as Andy walked toward the trainers' stand. She opened the door and stepped in, closing it quickly to keep the chill out of the semi-heated room.

The man in black stood nearest the door. She quickly made her way to the other end of the room. There was something about him that made her uneasy. She hoped he wasn't Emmett Gibbons.

Two other men stood peering out the window as they tried to identify the horses galloping by. In appearance, the two men were diametrically opposed. The shorter one wore a stained windbreaker and jeans that were a size too large and held up over his skinny hips with a stirrup leather fashioned as a belt. On his head was a battered Red Sox baseball cap.

The taller man wore grey slacks, a tailored jacket and rimless glasses that gave him a studious air. He reminded Andy of the pictures she'd seen of Tom Smith, the trainer of Seabiscuit. She prayed this was Emmett Gibbons.

A horse approached the turn. Andy felt the rumbling of hooves before she saw a sleek bay horse appear, his black mane flying. He tossed his head high in the air, breaking the rider's hold on the reins and rushed off into the homestretch.

"Looks like your Kentucky colt is eager to get to the races," the man in the baseball cap remarked.

The Tom Smith lookalike clicked a stopwatch. Pushing his glasses up on his forehead, he held the clock close to his eyes. "God dammit! I told him to gallop a two minute mile. He's done the first half in 48 seconds. What's he trying to do, break the track record?"

The man in black glared at the trainer before leaving the room.

"Your star owner doesn't look too happy, Emmett," the shorter man remarked, adjusting the baseball cap on his head. "That new rider of yours looks awfully young. You sure he's old enough to tell time?"

"Knock it off, Pete. It's not like your rider's Willie Shoemaker."

Andy smiled. She had the right trainer. "Mr. Gibbons?"

He turned to her as he stuffed the watch in his pocket.

"I'm Andy Crowley."

His look was as blank as Mustang's had been.

"I'm the apprentice from New York. Barry Locke spoke to you."

He didn't appear any more enlightened.

"You're looking for a bug rider," she explained, using the more common racetrack term in the hope it would jog his memory.

"*Was*," he stated simply. "Past tense."

He turned back to the window as another horse galloped by.

"That one's mine," Pete remarked.

Emmett turned towards the door. " I'm done here."

Confusion turned to anger when Andy realized he was about to leave. "Excuse me, Mr. Gibbons, I believe we had a deal. I've come all the way from New York to be your stable apprentice."

"Someone else showed up," Emmett said, glancing over his shoulder. "He's got a good seat on a horse and he's a lightweight, he can tack a hundred and four."

"I can tack a hundred and two without starving myself.

I can handle any kind of horse," she insisted. "And I won't break track records in a morning gallop, only in a race."

Emmett shrugged his shoulders. "I can't help you, miss. Like I said, I've got my rider. Besides, I can't be expected to help every bug rider who can't cut it in New York. "

"I did cut it in New York. It was just bad timing."

But Emmett didn't hear her as he stepped out and shut the door firmly behind him.

"Oh my God, what am I doing in a place like this!" she seethed.

"Temper, temper," the man named Pete warned her. "Don't judge us all by Emmett Gibbons."

Andy stared at the wall, not trusting herself to speak.

"I know Barry Locke, he's got an eye for a good rider. But he usually brings them in from Puerto Rico. How did you manage to slip in?"

She turned to face him. "I galloped for him in the morning. When I beat his other riders in the workouts, I got his attention. But I'm not getting anybody's attention around here."

"You've got mine," he told her. "So what happened in New York?"

"The son of Barry's wealthiest owner decided he wanted to be a jockey."

Pete nodded. "And the father owns fifty horses in the barn, right?"

"Forty-three." Her anger slowly dissolved. At least one trainer here seemed to be understand Andy's situation.

"Sounds like you've got some ability but you're going to have to toughen up. There's a lot of assholes in this game. Guys like Gibbons have had too much success. It makes them forget where they came from." He took his cap off and ran his fingers through his thick, dark hair. "Not that failure helps much either."

"I know about that one," she agreed.

Pete shook his head . "No, you don't. You're just getting started."

A shout caught their attention. A grey horse bolted across the track and hit the outside rail, his shoulder dipping dangerously over the railing as he slid to his knees. The rider shouted again as he was hurled to the ground. The horse scrambled to his feet and galloped off into the fog.

"There's a horse who'll be needing a new rider tomorrow," Pete remarked as the exercise boy cursed in the horse's direction. "Are you interested?"

"Absolutely not!' she exclaimed.

Andy could handle a nervous horse, or an inexperienced one, but she didn't want to deal with the rogues.

"Do you think you have enough experience to spot the crazies? Somehow, you don't strike me as someone who grew up on the racetrack."

"No, I didn't," she admitted. "Far from it. My father is a history professor and my mother teaches law."

A low whistle escaped from his lips. "So how did you end up on the racetrack?"

"My uncle Michael. He always wanted to own a racehorse but he couldn't afford one. He had to be satisfied with betting on them. On my twelfth birthday, he brought me to Belmont. The moment I set eyes on the horses parading in the post, I knew I would become a jockey. Uncle Michael was the only one who took me seriously. He offered to pay for my riding lessons. My parents weren't too thrilled but as long as I kept my school marks up, they went along with it."

"No racing in your lineage, on either the dam or sire side?"

"Great grandfather Crowley trained steeplechasers in Ireland. No horsemen or women on the dam's side," she said with a grin.

Pete looked her up and down. She was the right size and weight for an apprentice jockey. He saw intelligence in her blue eyes and sensed she was a quick thinker. "Good thing you chose flat racing over steeplechasing. You're too light to ride over the jumps. Can you really tack a hundred and two?"

"With my light saddle. But to be honest, I prefer using my heavier saddle, the five pounder."

Pete laughed. "You call a five pound saddle heavy? My western saddle weights fifty pounds."

"I'll borrow it when I ride the steeplechasers," she replied.

Pete laughed. He took his cap off and ran his fingers through his hair once again. "Like Emmett said, my rider isn't Shoemaker, not weight-wise anyway. I could really use a light rider. I don't have any New York stakes horses but I've got some hard knockers."

"I'll gallop them for free," she promised.

"Won't do either one of us any good if you starve to death." Pete plunked his cap back on his head in a decisive movement. "Come by my barn tomorrow morning and I'll give you a leg up on a couple of horses, see how you get along with them. I don't have enough stock to get you into the jocks' room every day but I can get you going. I know a few other trainers who could use a light rider, not to mention an honest one."

"Thank you," she said earnestly. "I really appreciate it."

Pete headed towards the door. "Do you need a place to stay?"

Andy froze in mid-step. Pay back time.

"I've got a room, over on Revere beach," she replied, her words coming out in a rush. "It's fine for now, a roof over my head. As soon as I get going, I'll find a better place."

"I'm not hitting on you," he assured her with a shake of his head. "My wife would have me for breakfast. She's bigger than me and ten times meaner."

"Sorry," Andy apologized as they stepped out the door. "It comes with the job, I guess."

"Yeah, I'm sure you're hit on a hundred times a day. I'm asking because my groom is new here, came from England a couple of months ago. She's looking for a roommate."

"I'd definitely be interested. My room isn't Buckingham

Palace, that's for sure."

She'd spent the night in an Arctic sleeping bag spread out over a lumpy mattress. The attic room she'd rented was like a deep freeze. The bathroom was one floor down at the end of the hall and was shared by four other rooms.

The sun peeked through at that moment and Pete hurried to catch up to a stocky chestnut horse. He listened intently as the rider told him about the horse's gallop.

Not so classy on the outside, Andy thought, as she watched him walk away, but pure class on the inside.

CHARLIE'S WELCOME

Andy, as usual, was up well before the sun. She appeared at the guard shack once again, still without a Suffolk Down's license. The guard opened the door and stood on the step, towering over her. His name tag said simply 'Howie'.

"Good morning, Howie," she said in a cheerful tone, handing him her New York license. She was fully prepared to use her Irish charm this morning.

"Emmett didn't get you a license?"

She was about to tell him she'd be riding for Pete when she realized she didn't know his last name. There had to be a dozen Petes in the barn area. She wasn't going to score any points with Howie by telling him she was going to Pete's barn.

"You want me to take the question back and give you an easier one?" Howie said with a smirk.

Andy had all the patience in the world with horses but very little with people. She took a deep breath to remind herself to be civil.

"You sure this is you?" Howie demanded, pointing to the photograph on her ID.

When the picture was taken a few months ago, her sandy coloured hair was shoulder length. It was now cut in a layered fashion, just below her ears.

"I've had a hair cut," she replied, struggling to hold her temper in check while figuring out the best way to handle this. She decided to go with the idea that Emmett hadn't had time to get her a license. "Emmett Gibbons is a busy man," she said.

Howie folded his arms across his chest and leaned back on his heels. "Too busy to get his new little bug rider a license?"

"Oh, go ahead and page him!" she snapped. "Ask the leading trainer to drop whatever he's doing and come all the way down here to sign me in."

Howie glared down at her from his elevated stance as Andy held her ground. Finally, his arms fell to his sides.

"Get your license this morning or it's your last day at Suffolk."

"My last day," she muttered, "wouldn't that be a blessing!"

She walked down the main road, stopping at the first barn to ask if anyone knew a trainer named Pete. She was informed there were three Petes; Pete Wilson in barn 5, Mackenzie in barn 8 and Kingsley in barn 9. Andy jogged to barn 5. Pete Wilson was a tall Oklahoman. She quickly made her way to barn 8. A large sign mounted on the wall proclaimed it to be AM stables. The colours were red, blue and white, with the initials AM painted in a white star in the center. It looked much like the flag of Texas.

The feed tubs were blue with red rims, the water buckets red with blue rims. In the doorway of each stall hung a nylon webbing in red, white and blue. Several horses leaned their chests against the webbing and looked out, watching the activity. The grooms wore baseball caps with the initials AM and had matching jackets. This was one classy outfit. Andy's spirits rose tremendously.

The horses that had already been to the track were being led around the shed row as they cooled out. Half a dozen grooms cleaned stalls, brushed horses or legged an exercise rider up into the saddle. What first appeared as chaos was actually an orderly system of horses going or coming from the racetrack.

Andy inspected the horses that were led by. They were

full of energy, even after a morning gallop. The blankets they wore were embroidered with the names of stakes races and championships. Things were looking up. This barn smelled of success.

She checked her watch. Twenty minutes after five. This really was the AM stable. The track had been open for training barely twenty minutes and already several horses had been exercised. A tall man in a Stetson stopped to let his horse drink from a bucket hanging on a post.

"Where can I find Pete Mackenzie?" Andy asked.

"You'll find him on the other side, m'am," he replied in a soft Texan drawl before leading his horse in that direction. Andy followed behind him. She couldn't believe her eyes when she reached the other side of the barn. A yellow and burgundy sign displayed the initials PM.

Was this somebody's idea of a joke?

As the initials implied, the two sides of the barn were as different as night and day. In the PM barn, the stall door webbings were a faded yellow, the feed buckets an indistinguishable shade of brownish red. Activity was slower, with no sense of urgency or clockwork. A horse was led out of the stall right in front of her and she gasped when she saw his left front leg. He had a bow that would make Robin Hood proud. She'd never seen a bowed tendon that big, not on a horse that was still in training.

The big dark horse halted in his tracks and stared at her. Andy instinctively corrected her posture as though being assessed by a drill sergeant. Intelligence shone in the horse's eyes. He had what racetrackers' called 'the look of eagles'.

"Come along, your Highness, your chariot awaits," his groom said in a distinct English accent.

The horse turned away and Andy wondered if she had passed inspection. Unlike the other horses that were prancing nervously and tossing their heads, the big gelding walked slowly and sedately with his groom. A chestnut gelding from the AM barn dragged his hotwalker dangerously close to the big horse's hind end.

"Hey, come on, move that big caboose before we run you over," the young man complained.

The woman looked back over her shoulder. "Button your lip and wait your turn, you little blighter, his Highness gives way to no one."

They didn't hurry their pace. At the end of the barn they took a right turn while the other horses turned left. The groom attached the horse's halter to the arm of an automatic walker and switched the motor on. The big gelding stood stock still, surveying his surroundings as the machine groaned in protest.

"Bloody hell, Heckler," she chided him. "If you burn out the motor on this old machine, you'll have to race every week to pay for it, won't you? Get along now."

The horse moved forward at a leisurely stroll and the groom turned towards the barn.

"Oh, hello. Sorry, I didn't see you there," she greeted Andy.

There was a friendliness to her tone that Andy responded to immediately. "Is this Pete Mackenzie's barn?"

The groom nodded.

"I think he's the one I'm looking for. Is he short and skinny with sandy brown hair, looks like an ex-jock?"

The woman laughed. "A jockey? Pete's a dear man and he's great with horses—but only with his two feet planted firmly on the ground. He does have sandy hair, though."

"Good, I've got the right barn. I'm Andrea Crowley, known mostly as Andy."

The groom held out her hand. "I'm Charlotte Middleton, known mostly as Charlie. Won't we make a great team."

Charlie turned to a large chalkboard mounted on the wall. She marked a 'W' next to the first name on a list, The Heckler. Above the list was the name 'Incandescent' printed in large letters.

"Incandescent, I like that name," Andy said, reading the

board. "Must be a brilliant horse."

"That's the definition, is it? Brilliant?"

"It means white-hot, electrifying. With a name like that, it must be a hell of a horse. That's the mount I want."

"Sorry to disappoint you but that's not a horse. It's Pete's word game. Every once in awhile, he'll write a word on the board. The first person to put it in a sentence gets a free lunch."

She thought about it for a few moments before writing. "*The man of my dreams is tall and dark and has an incandescent charm.*" She turned to Andy. "It can be used that way, can it?"

"It's grammatically correct, but good luck finding him."

"I'm a hopeless dreamer." Charlie smiled as she put the chalk down. "We do make a great team. I'll split lunch with you."

"Put in a good word for me with the trainer's wife and I'll consider the favour paid. I hear she's a tough one."

"She gives the orders but Pete is the one with the training skills," Charlie agreed. "I think down deep, she's really a softie."

Andy followed Charlie to a stall in the middle of the shed row. Charlie slipped a halter on over a horse's head and clipped her to a tie chained to the wall.

"Who is that amazing horse that you just put on the walker?"

"That would be The Heckler. The old codger is still racing at the ripe age of seven. But don't call him old to his face. When he's on the track, he thinks he's still a two year old." Charlie began brushing the chestnut filly.

"That bowed tendon doesn't bother him?"

"It's cold and tight. And he knows his way around the track."

"I guess so, at his age. He's been around longer than I have, that's for sure. How long have you been on the racetrack?"

"Two months. Well, sixty-three days to be exact," Charlie

replied, suddenly losing the rhythm of her brushing.

Andy sensed a deep sadness. "Are you homesick?"

"No, it's not home that I miss." Charlie lifted her chin and began brushing vigorously. "It's a whole new world for me, a strange one but I'm in the land of opportunity, aren't I?"

"Yeah, if you're willing to fight for it," Andy said.

"You've got that right. The racetrack is a lot rougher then I thought it would be. I'm trying to develop the right attitude." She stopped brushing and leaned against the wall, affecting a devil-may-care attitude. "Ah, forgit aboot it."

Andy couldn't hold back a laugh. Charlie's imitation of a New York gangster came across more like a Southern redneck.

"Okay, my American accent sucks but I have yet to hear a Yankee do a half decent British accent."

"It's hard to talk with a stiff upper lip," Andy teased.

"After awhile, you get the hang of it."

Andy felt relaxed for the first time since setting foot in Boston. Already, this woman seemed like an old friend.

She looked up and down the shed row. The colours changed from burgundy and yellow to black and green about half way down. The last three stalls were pink and black. "Seems like there's a few different stables on this side of the barn. How many horses does Pete have?"

"He's got thirteen in all but he was only allotted eight stalls."

"Why didn't he get thirteen?"

Charlie shrugged her shoulders. "Dear Pete breaks the golden rule, *never fall in love with a racehorse*. He loves his horses dearly so their welfare comes first. That doesn't put him in the top ten trainers' list."

"I see," Andy said with a nod. "He doesn't win enough races to warrant more stalls."

"Right. Cal Dowell is the official stall man here. He's a nice enough chap but he says he doesn't have any choice when it comes to allotting stalls. I suppose he's got a point. If he doesn't give the winning trainers the most stalls, he'll be replaced with someone who will, won't he?"

Andy grimaced. "I suppose so." She glanced at the black and green colours beginning in the next stall. "Who's next to you?"

"That's Carla Wynett, more commonly called Carla Whynot. She'll try anything with her horses to get a win. And the three stalls at the end belong to Harley Spencer, or Big Spender."

"Is that true or are you being sarcastic?"

"His two horses cost more than all of Pete's put together."

"Does he run them in the big stakes races?"

"He put one of them in a stakes last fall but 'run' isn't exactly what I'd call it. The horse was beaten forty-five lengths."

"What about Pete's stable? Does he have any stakes horses?"

"Pete calls them 'blue plate specials'. He runs his horses where he thinks they can win but he hates losing them. He's a nervous wreck before every race."

"So all of his horses are claimers?"

"I believe that's what they're called but I really don't understand this crazy system. Why does Pete have to run his horses in races where other trainers can buy them?"

"To make the competition fair," Andy replied. "At least, that's the idea. Think about it, if there was no risk involved, a trainer could run a five thousand dollar horse in a two thousand dollar claiming race and win every time. But if he knows another trainer can put in a claim and walk away with the horse for the bargain price of two thousand dollars, then he'll think twice about it."

"What if you don't want to lose your horse for any price?" Charlie insisted.

"Then you have to run them in allowance races. There's no claiming price but the competition is a lot tougher." Andy looked over at the big gelding on the mechanical hotwalker. "What does The Heckler run for?"

"The bottom, two thousand," Charlie replied. "But none of these horses started off that way. Each and every one of them has the heart of a champion."

"Lots of heart is great but what about their legs? The Heckler has the biggest bow I've ever seen."

"He bowed at the age of four," Charlie informed her. "He's been running for three years with it so it can't be a problem. When Pete enters his horses in a race, their legs are just fine. He won't take any chances." She pointed to the chestnut filly she'd just finished grooming. "This little filly has legs of steel but her lungs give her trouble. Pete knows how to keep them clear but he can't run her as often as the others."

Charlie waved her on as she walked to the next stall.

"This is Miss Lili Marlene. Must have been named by a Marlene Dietrich fan."

"If she's half as feisty as her name sake, she's got to be a winner." Andy looked the dark bay filly over. She was barely fifteen hands high, sleek and muscled.

In the next stall was a slender, white faced grey filly. "Here's our hope for the future, a two year old filly."

Andy walked into the stall to assess the youngster.

"She's just here for the week to get used to the commotion of the racetrack and school in the starting gate. Then she's going back to the farm. Pete has a half mile track there. He'll bring her along slowly."

"What's her name?"

"It's a weird one. But she was already named when Pete bought her at the yearling auction. Black's Home Law. Who would give a horse that name?"

"A lawyer. Black's Law dictionary is a standard textbook for law students. My mother teaches law so I'm familiar with the book." She began rubbing the filly's withers and smiled as she leaned her head into Andy's chest. "So Pete starts his gate training early. I like that. Horses are more relaxed in there when they have lots of time to get used to it. They can't race until they've been okayed from the gate so the sooner you get them in, the better."

"Our Pete is never in a hurry when it comes to his horses," Charlie assured her. "And here's another of our old fellas, Tim B Quiet. Do you think somebody had a chatty little boy?"

"Or husband," Andy said with a grin, looking the horse over. "He's very handsome."

"And famous. Tim B Quiet holds the track record at Narragansett Park for a mile and seventy yards. Back in his youth, he covered the distance in one minute and forty seconds."

"Good for you, fella," Andy congratulated him. She stepped back and looked down the shed row. "You certainly have some real characters in your stable."

"Hey, Charlie, ya got that hoss ready?" a voice called out as a horse and rider appeared in the shed row. "Did that bug rider show up?"

Andy looked over her shoulder in the direction of the voice. "Holy crow, there's someone who takes rhoticity to a whole new level."

"She takes what to what?" Charlie asked. "I'm going to have to carry a dictionary to understand what you're saying."

"It's the Boston accent, they don't pronounce their 'r's' ". She looked over in the direction of the voice. "Is that Pete's wife?"

Charlie nodded. "That's Candace. You definitely want to stay on her good side. If Candace ain't happy, ain't nobody happy." Charlie's American accent was quite good when she used that expression. "She's not as tough as she sounds but one word of warning; don't ever call her Candy. Believe me, she's not that sweet."

FIRST IMPRESSIONS

Andy followed behind Charlie as she carried the saddle and bridle towards a stall.

"How tall are you? Six feet?"

"Seventeen hands," Charlie replied. "It's my full bodied, curvaceous figure that gives you the impression I'm an Amazon."

Andy mentally calculated four inches per hand. "Five foot eight. That's tall."

"I'd say you're pony size, fourteen two hands."

"Close. I'm fifteen hands, about her size," she said, pointing to Miss Lili Marlene.

"Perfect height for a jockey," Charlie remarked, "and a good match for Lili. I'll have her tacked up in a jiff and you'll be on your way."

Pete's wife, Candace, approached the stall from the opposite direction. She had a no-nonsense expression about her as she strode purposefully towards them. Andy guessed her height to be just over sixteen hands. Where Charlie had curves, Candace had straight lines. The expression 'skinny as a beanpole' could have been coined for her.

"So you're the bug rider from New York." Her gaze travelled quickly over Andy, taking in the polished boots, the neatly ironed pants and shirt, the tailored jacket. "Lookit the crease in those jeans. Amazing."

Andy knew this woman's assessment was integral to her acceptance into this racing stable. She wasn't sure if the comment was a compliment or if Candace was insinuating that she was anal. Whichever it was, first impressions were important. Racetrackers had a tendency to believe in the infallibility of their own judgement.

Andy had to make an impression on this woman but she wasn't certain just what approach to take. A little boasting would insinuate confidence, an important quality in a jockey, but too much was a sign of arrogance. None at all meant the jockey was timid, or 'chicken shit' as the vernacular went. The boundaries between categories weren't clearly defined and Andy didn't know how she should respond to the 'not-so-sweet' Candace.

Without waiting for a response, Candace walked by her into the stall and ran her hands over the horse's front legs. The filly's slight frame gave her the appearance of an over-grown greyhound. She couldn't have weighed more than nine hundred pounds, saddle included. She pawed the ground, anxious to go.

Andy turned her attention to the tack. The saddle was in good shape and the bridle was freshly cleaned. This side of the barn didn't have the polished look of the AM stables but it was much like its trainer, Pete Mackenzie, ragged on the outside, pure class inside. One thing Andy had learned, if the equipment had seen better days, so had the horses.

She noticed the rubber snaffle in the filly's mouth, the kindest of bits. Normally, that would mean the horse was easy to control and didn't need a stronger bit. In this case, it could be a test to see if the new jockey had the strength and the smarts to keep a tough horse under control. The filly stood quietly and seemed sensible but stall behaviour could be totally different from a horse's attitude out on the track.

"I want ya to take this filly twice around and don't go pulling her up at the wire."

Andy was surprised by the instruction. "Why would I pull her up at the wire?"

"Cause you want to hurry up and get to the next hoss."

"What next horse?" Andy joked.

"Right, I forgot, you're new here."

"Even if I had a dozen horses lined up, I wouldn't rush. I may be in a hurry to get on a horse but I'm never in a hurry to get off." Andy stepped close to the horse and rubbed her face. "How do you do, pretty girl."

"Ya always introduce yourself to the hoss?" Candace asked.

"Of course. Wouldn't you want an introduction before someone jumped on your back?"

"Anyone wants to jump on my back, they'd need a helluva lot more than a 'hi, how are you'," Candace said, hoisting her up into the saddle with enough force to throw her into the next stall. "Man, you're wicked light!"

Andy straightened herself in the saddle and collected the reins. She measured them to her preferred length and tied a knot in the end of the leathers as she moved out of the stall. There wasn't a lot of bulk to the filly or a feeling of great power but she was light on her feet, as quick and agile as a cat. Her walk was long and fluid as they headed down the shed row and out onto the cement walkway leading to the track. Andy heard a horse jogging on the cement and Candace appeared beside her on a big buckskin gelding.

"That's your stable pony, huh? What's his name?"

"Bucky."

"I hope he got that name because of his colour and not because of his behaviour."

"Bucky's a real gentleman. But don't let his relaxed attitude fool you. He's got a real turn 'a foot. He can burn rubber when he needs to."

When they neared the gap where Eddie's horse had disappeared into the fog the previous morning, the sound of pounding hooves greeted them. A set of three horses breezed by. Lili pranced excitedly. The cat was ready to spring.

"Just ease her into a gallop," Candace instructed her, heading in the opposite direction. "Let her stretch out the last sixteenth."

"Yes, ma'am," Andy said, as eager as Lili to get going. It had been three days since she was on the back of a racehorse and she could hardly wait to get into full stride.

"Easy, now, easy," she said in a soothing tone, trying to calm both of them. The filly tried to gallop but Andy held her in at a trot. "There's plenty of time to run. We've got a couple of miles to go so let's save a little for the last sixteenth, just like we were told."

The gap led onto the homestretch and Andy kept the eager filly at a trot for the first quarter of a mile. When they had passed the wire and were headed into the clubhouse turn, several horses galloped by in full stride. Lili bolted forward, trying to join them. Andy didn't fight with her, knowing intuitively that this filly would resent any kind of a strong hold. She used a give and take motion, her wrists stretching like rubber bands to allow a little leeway but not enough for the filly to get into full stride. By the time they reached the first turn, Lili's muscles were warmed up and there was a looseness in her stride. Andy let her slip easily into a gallop. The filly was eager to show just what she was capable of, but this wasn't the time for it.

"The boss says an easy couple of rounds and then you can turn it on," Andy told her. "Let's just enjoy the scenery for now."

Lili put her head down but kept a snug hold on the bit, ready for action. Andy had the reins bridged together and braced against the filly's neck, causing her to pull against herself. Even the strongest exercise rider couldn't hold back a thousand pound racehorse with just their biceps. Once the reins were set against the horse's neck, there was no changing them. A horse could read the rider much quicker than a rider could read the horse. A split second of vulnerability or indecision and the horse took charge. There was no time for thinking in this game, only reacting.

Normally, Andy was relaxed in the saddle but this was

a test. People were watching her and judging her, deciding whether she was good enough to become their stable jockey. Somehow, she had to put that out of her mind and do what she did best—ride.

She took a deep breath and expelled it slowly, feeling the tension dissipate. Lili responded immediately, relaxing her neck and releasing her frantic hold on the bit. Andy's body moved easily with the filly's rhythm. As they galloped around the turn and into the homestretch, Lili's stride lengthened, covering more ground with less energy. Her action was smooth and effortless. She changed leads on cue for the turn and they began their second round. When they entered the homestretch again, Andy looked for the black and white pole that marked the final sixteenth of a mile. She crouched slightly and Lili immediately launched forward, almost at full stride. There was at least one more gear, but Andy didn't ask for it. Not today.

They throttled down when they entered the backstretch and the filly eased slowly back to a trot, pulling up near the outside fence. They stood there, catching their breath and watching the activity. Riders sang to their mounts or chatted with each other as they galloped by.

"You may be small but you're one heck of a racehorse, all heart," Andy complimented her horse, running her hand along her neck. "Thank you for making my first gallop such a pleasant experience."

Lili was invigorated from her gallop and arched her neck proudly as they enjoyed a long, leisurely trot back. Pete was standing beside Candace and Bucky at the gap. Candace gave her a nod, Pete a big smile. Andy felt confident she had passed the test.

"I've never seen the filly gallop like that," Pete said, patting the filly's shoulder and Andy's leg simultaneously. "Smooth as silk. I swear her feet barely touched the dirt."

"She's an amazing horse," Andy agreed. "Changes her leads like clockwork, lengthens her stride the moment you ask her to. She's a real professional."

"She's all heart but she never gets to show it," Candace complained, nudging Bucky up beside the slender racehorse. "We want to get her in light but hell, the bug riders round here take one look at her size and think they're gonna get creamed. Last kid took her to the middle of the track, ran twenty lengths more than anybody else. She still finished third. Hell, I'd ride her and let her run but she'd have to carry full weight."

Andy wasn't quite sure what she had just heard. "You ride races? You're a jockey?"

Irritation was on her face and in her voice when Candace replied. "You bet I am. Why should you midgets have all the fun?"

"I didn't mean to sound insulting but it's just, well, you're pretty tall for a jockey." She glanced sideways at Candace, looking her quickly up and down. "What do you tack?"

"A hundred and sixteen."

"Yeah, sure, if you don't eat for two weeks," Pete remarked.

Andy knew all jockeys weren't as small as she was, but the only tall one she'd ridden with was Robin Smith in New York. Robin was close to five foot seven, but had a small frame. Candace was what the foxhunting people would call a middleweight hunter.

"You've got all my light mounts," Pete assured Andy.

"Yeah, both of them," Candice said with a smirk. "She'll need more than two hosses to ride. Hell, she'll need a dozen mounts just to stay fit. We sure as hell ain't got a dozen hosses."

"We've got eight here and five more at the farm. That gives us a baker's dozen," Pete argued.

"And a couple of those hosses are oldies, Pete, they ain't going to last forever."

"We've got yearlings. They'll be ready to go next year."

"Don't count your chickens till they're okayed from the

gate."

Andy laughed at the image of a bunch of chickens flying out of the starting gate. Obviously, Candace could give any saying a racetrack twist.

"You gallop horses for practically every trainer on the grounds," Pete was saying to his wife. "Why don't you take Andy around and introduce her, get her on a few horses. Give this kid a chance and she'll make history. She's got what it takes."

Andy hadn't expected that much of a compliment. It was a real boost to her confidence.

"Yeah, sure, but we've gotta hustle. I got a bunch of hosses lined up and waiting. Gotta get to ole man Morris' barn."

"Don't start with Morris. He uses bug riders just so he can get his galloping done for free." Pete turned to Andy. "Whatever you do, don't agree to his terms. If you finish worse than third in a race, he wants you to give him the jock's fee back."

Andy was stunned. She'd never heard that before.

Suffolk Downs was certainly turning into an adventure.

CONTRACTS

Mickey shivered in the early morning chill as he walked towards the track kitchen. He needed more fat on his bones to keep him warm. He remembered all the early mornings back in high school when he was running the streets of Southie before sunrise, preparing for the marathon. He had looked forward to the days when he could sleep in, but the racetrack demanded the same early schedule.

Suddenly, he heard a squeal. A horse appeared out of the dark, playfully bucking. The rider barely moved in the saddle.

"Easy, Lili, save it for the race!" The woman's voice carried a hint of laughter.

These jockeys had nerves of steel, he thought to himself, the female ones included. Mickey was familiar with the few woman jockeys here at Suffolk, but he didn't recognize this one. Pete Mackenzie walked along behind the horse while his wife Candace rode their stable pony.

It looked like Pete had found himself another jockey. She was a lot lighter than his wife. Candace had some real ability when it came to riding races, but her weight was a problem. Pete could never get his horses in under a hundred and twenty pounds unless he switched to one of the apprentice jockeys.

Mickey had briefly considered Pete as trainer for M&M Stables. The man had talent but he got too emotional about his horses. He would never have lasted with Pony.

Mickey followed them from a slight distance, curious about the horse. He was always on the lookout for a good claim. Many of Pete's horses were previous allowance and stakes winners that had dropped into the claiming ranks due to age or injuries. No one would get any more run out of his horses than Pete and they were always worth betting. The horses Pete sent out before dark were the ones he wanted to keep under wraps. The girl had called the horse Lili. That would be easy enough to check out.

He watched as the girl dismounted. Racetrack etiquette demanded that you never set foot in another trainer's shed row without being invited. Mickey had a good view of the barn from the front steps of the kitchen. He waited until the groom began hot walking the horse around the barn. The filly was small in stature but well muscled and light on her feet. If Lili was part of her registered name, and not just a pet name, he should be able to find a past performance record in the *Daily Racing Form*.

He watched the filly come around the shed row, still squealing and bucking. He'd do his homework on her, but not until he had his coffee.

"Lili, keep your feet on the ground," Charlie pleaded as the filly pranced. "Andy, I don't think you blew her out far enough!"

Andy ducked into the tack room to avoid the flying heels. "You'd better have a race picked out for her, Pete. She's ready to go."

"I'm waiting for the perfect conditions," Pete informed her. "She's sitting on a win. I don't want to blow it."

"Hurry up or *I* won't be sitting on her," Andy said with a laugh.

"Bartie Fartie promised to write us a race this week," Candace replied, hanging a bridle up on the wall.

"Bartie Fartie?" Andy repeated. "Is that really the racing secretary's name?"

"Bart Farley," Pete told her. "He writes races for Emmett Gibbons at the drop of a hat, and even for Arley Mitchell, but not for Pete Mackenzie."

"Is Arley Mitchell AM stables?"

"Yeah, that's him," Candace informed her. "I don't mind Arley winning a few, he's the real thing, knows a hoss inside and out. But Emmett? Hell, he wins on everybody else's training. He claims a hoss, runs him back in a couple of weeks and makes a score."

"He became leading trainer just by claiming?" Andy found that hard to believe.

"You've got to be pretty sharp when it comes to claiming," Pete informed her. "Emmett keeps his eyes open and he's got some owners with pockets as deep as an Arab Sheikh. One of them went to Kentucky last fall and bought a well bred colt."

Andy whistled. "That one must have deep pockets alright."

"Naw, the guy's connected."

"You mean he comes from a rich family?"

"It's a family alright but not the kind you're thinking of. He's a wiseguy."

"A wiseguy?" Andy repeated.

"You know, like in the movie, *The Godfather* ."

Andy was stunned. "That can't be possible. Barry Locke would never send me here to ride for Emmett if he was in the mafia!"

"That's just Candace's over-active imagination. She sees cosa nostra everwhere. It was bad enough after *The Godfather,* but it got even worse after *The Godfather II*."

"I don't know if Emmett's connected. I don't think he's got the smarts but some of his owners sure look like wiseguys," Candace said. "Take a good look at them in the winner's circle. They could be extras in that Godfather movie."

Andy laughed. Though she'd been born in New York City, she'd never been to little Italy or Hell's Kitchen and had no personal knowledge of the mafia. She had gone to the cinema to see the original Godfather, but the sequel had sounded too violent for her. Besides, she liked movies with happy endings.

"You are kidding, aren't you? Please tell me the mafia

doesn't have anything to do with racing here at Suffolk."

"Naw, we send them all to Rhode Island," Candace said with a wink. "When ya ride at Gansett, ya better have eyes in the back of your helmet."

Andy was becoming so accustomed to Candace's accent that her mind automatically put the r's in the right place. But it was going to take longer to get used to the idea of rubbing elbows with the mob.

"They not only ride rough, they party pretty hard too. Look at the article in the Globe."

Andy picked up the paper lying next to the coffee machine. It was open on page three.

'*Leading Apprentice Jockey Found Dead*' was the heading.

"Oh my God," she muttered as she continued to read.

Alex Munsey, leading apprentice at Narragansett Park in 1975, was found dead in his Pawtucket apartment early yesterday morning after a night of celebration. Several grams of cocaine were found in the apartment and are now being analyzed for content. Sergeant George Denkin of the Pawtucket Police Department is in charge of the investigation. Sergeant Denkin stated he believed the cause of death was an accidental overdose. "According to the jockeys that I've interviewed, Alex was known to be a bit of a party animal," Sergeant Denkin said. "Especially when he was on a winning streak. He hadn't been visiting the winner's circle much over the past month, but did it in style in the final race of last night's card. He invited everyone in the jockeys' room to a celebration at his apartment. Seems most of them took him up on it."

The article went on to say that several of the jockeys were asked for their opinions of Alex, but only one of them was willing to speak to the press. A journeyman jockey by the name of Wally Malloy gave a quote. "*Alex was a good kid, but success went to his head. You see this kinda thing a lot with bug boys. One minute they haven't got two dimes to rub together and then all of a sudden they've got money to burn. Alex was partying pretty hard, lots of booze and drugs. He was an accident waiting to happen."*

She put the paper down and shook her head. "If I didn't regret leaving New York before, I sure do now."

"Hey, ya gotta meet some of the people here before ya start thinking like that. Come on, jock, there's trainers to talk to and hosses to ride. I got a list of all the guys who could use you." Candace plunked her helmet on her head, tucked her whip into the back of her pants and strode down the shed row. She tapped her head, inferring that the list was memorized. "Let me do the talking. I know how these guys think, what they want to hear and what they don't want to hear."

Andy had to jog to keep up with her. "Ever thought about being a jockey's agent? You could make some serious money, with the right rider of course. And you could eat all you want."

"I tell you what, start making a few thousand a week and I'll take twenty percent, no problem. Right now, I'd starve to death if I was your agent." Candace shrugged as they walked around the barn to the AM stables. "Course, then I'd make the weight."

"But if you were an agent, weight wouldn't be a concern." Andy reminded her.

"Exactly, so do as I say and we'll both get rich."

The shed row was quiet. The hotwalkers were gone and only a couple of grooms remained.

"Hey, Arlie, I got someone for ya to meet!"

A head poked out of a stall. "You sure don't need a blowhorn, Candace. I swear, I could hear you if I was forty acres away."

"There ya are. Arley, meet Andy, our new bug rider."

Arley was down on his knees in the deep straw, rubbing a horse's leg.

"I'd like to shake your hand, Miss Andy, but I don't think you'd truly appreciate this liniment, not this early in the morning, anyway." He smiled in her direction. "I believe we met briefly this morning. Pleased to meet you officially."

Andy had a better look at the Texan with the white Stetson. She couldn't help but notice how handsome he was with his deep brown eyes and sandy blond hair peeking out below his hat. His western shirt and jeans were clean and pressed. Though he was too tall to be a jockey, he looked trim and fit enough to ride a race.

"You've missed all the action this morning," he said as he briskly massaged the horse's tendons. "I have all my horses galloped before the break. After that, the city folk come out and all hell breaks loose. I like to have a clear track when my horses work." He glanced at his watch. "Look at that time, almost seven. No wonder I'm feeling a little narrow at the equator."

Andy looked confused.

"That means he's hungry," Candace said, familiar with Arlie's lingo.

"Sure am. I believe it's almost time to get on the outside of six or seven hot biscuits."

"He's going to the cook shack for breakfast," Candace continued her translation.

It felt odd to Andy to have Candace translating.

"My boy and I do most of our galloping but I'd be happy to leg you up when I need to burn the breeze."

"That means—"

"A workout," Andy said. "I've got that one figured out. Narrow at the equator would have taken a lot longer."

"Okay, we're off," Candace announced. "We'll be by first thing tomorrow."

"I'll be here," Arley said.

Candace took off like a quarter horse out of the gate and Andy ran to catch up.

"Now, listen, most 'a the trainers here at Suffolk ship horses to Narragansett Park in Rhode Island. Can't always get the right race conditions here. You'll be riding afternoons at Suffolk and nights in Rhode Island so you won't be getting a lot of sleep, 'specially if you ride the last race at 'Gansett. That'd be at eleven or even midnight. The warm-up there can take a long time if the bettors are slow getting to the betting windows. We were on the track for twenty-five minutes one night. Way I hear it, the starter doesn't call the horses to the gate till he gets the green light from the penthouse. Gotta be some serious betting before the race starts."

Andy was certain Candace was making this up, but decided to go along with it. "That sounds like fun."

"If ya like to celebrate after the last race, you won't get any sleep at all. Some of the jocks show up in the morning still drunk." She glanced over at Andy. "Ya don't look like the partying type."

"I can cut loose once in awhile, but not after a day of racing."

"That's good to hear. Now, we're going to ole man Morris' barn. The ole man's got his own way of doing things. If he decides to ride ya, he'll want ya to give him the jock's fee back if you finish worse than third."

Andy lifted her hands to either side of her head and shook it. "I'm either dreaming or I've just fallen down the rabbit hole."

FORTUNE HUNTER

Candace made an abrupt left turn into a dark shed row. "Let me do the talkin'. When ya get to know these guys, you'll know what ya can say, what ya can't say and if ya give a damn." Candace waved at someone half way down the barn. "Mornin' Mr. Morris. Ya got that big guy ready?"

A man who looked to be somewhere in his nineties walked unsteadily towards them, cane in hand. The cane was swinging in the air more than it was on the ground. The horses leaped back into their stalls as he passed.

"What the hell ya doin' coming here so damn late!"

The old man could have been Candace's uncle. He had the same accent and impatient way of speaking.

"The sun ain't even up yet," Candace retorted. "I want ya to meet the new bug rider from New York. This is Andy. She's light and she can ride the hair off any hoss."

"Never mind your damn bug rider. I've had a horse ready for an hour. I want you to ride the hell out of him. Work him a half mile. And don't pamper him. This lazy son of a bitch wants to drag his ass in the morning."

Andy had to resist covering her ears. Profanity was not something she was used to, not until she came to the track. She was often criticized for using big words by the back-stretch workers, but she wasn't about to replace them with the more popular four lettered words.

"Tan his hide if you have to. I want a black letter workout."

This surprised Andy even more. A black letter workout was the fastest workout of the day. It would be printed in the *Daily Racing Form* in bold black letters and stand out amongst the slower works. Most trainers didn't want to draw that kind of attention to their horses, especially if they ran in a claiming race.

"Is he deliberately trying to lose the horse?" Andy asked in a low voice.

"Naw, it's just the old man's way of giving the other trainers the finger," Candace said at her usual full volume.

Andy looked nervously in Morris' direction. "Are you this rude with everyone?"

"Don't sweat it, he's as deaf as a pitchfork."

Andy had second thoughts about Candace as an agent.

A groom appeared in the aisle leading a chestnut stallion. The horse's coat was dull, but he was well muscled and fit. Andy noticed how gentle he was with the groom. Instead of snapping and biting like a lot of stallions, the horse gently took a hold of the groom's sleeve.

Andy was stunned by the terrible condition of the tack. The saddle on the horse's back was a vintage variety, with a hard, solid seat. The newer saddles were made of softer leather and a lighter tree, making it more comfortable for both horse and rider. This saddle looked like it came from Man O' War's era and hadn't been cleaned since that famous horse had run his last race in 1920. The bridle hadn't seen any oil for some time either. The knot tied at the end of the reins was set in a petrified lump. There would be no changing the length of these reins.

The old groom legged Candace up onto the horse and once again, Andy had to jog to keep up.

"Aren't you afraid the tack will fall apart?"

"I usually bring my own, but I forgot. Must've had other things on my mind."

"Great, now it'll be my fault if you fall off and break your neck."

"I'll be fine," Candace assured her. "You ever galloped a horse from Chile?"

Andy shook her head.

"Old Fortune Hunter and I will show ya how it's done."

"Old? How old is he?" Andy asked.

"Seven, same as Heckler and Tim."

Andy made some mental calculations. "That makes him twenty-nine in human years."

"How do ya figure that?"

"It's a very old method. You take the age of the horse, in this case seven, subtract four, multiply by three and add twenty. Voila, you have the horse's age in human years."

"It'd take me a donkey's age to figure that out. I never was any good at math," Candace admitted, "But I got the race-track figured out. There's eight poles, all different colours so you don't get confused. The mile, half mile and quarter mile poles are red and white, the eighth poles are green and white, the sixteenths are black and white. But most important, you gotta know where the wire is. And you gotta get there first."

"You certainly have that right," Andy admitted. "When did you quit school?"

"Soon as I realized I was making more money galloping hosses than my teachers were making trying to teach dumbasses like me. That would've been around grade six."

"Grade six?" Andy had never met anyone who hadn't made it through elementary school. "Did you ever regret it?"

"Naw, this is where I belong." She looked down at Andy. "I'll bet ya went to college."

"I tried university but I couldn't stop thinking about the horses," Andy admitted. "I quit after my second year."

"Funny, you don't look like a quitter."

"I'm not, if it's something I really want. Leaving university was my way of getting back on track." She smiled up at Candace. "Pun intended."

"Pun intended," Candace repeated. "Hey, that'd make a great name for a racehoss."

Andy smiled. "Yes, it would."

"I don't usually get along with the educated type, but you've got the right attitude."

"Thanks." Andy accepted that as a vote of confidence. She stroked the horse's shoulder. "So how old is old man Morris?"

Candace shrugged. "No one knows. This hoss has papers, but the ole man doesn't. He's not much for shooting the breeze so I've never asked him, but he's gotta be in his eighties, maybe nineties. He's not the best trainer on the grounds, but his hosses will jump up and run a big one every once in awhile. Always worth a couple of bucks on the nose, just in case."

Candace lifted the side flap of the saddle and pulled the girth tighter. "In Chile they gallop without a saddle, so that's what he's used to, but it's against the rules to gallop bareback here." Candace let her legs dangle along the horse's sides. "I'll just ride him like this till he's warmed up. Then I'll shove my feet in the stirrups and stand up."

"This'll be fun to watch."

Andy avoided the trainers' stand, not wanting to run into Emmett and stood near the outside rail. She watched as Fortune Hunter cantered onto the track. Candace sat comfortably on his back, her legs still dangling. She rode like this for the first half a mile. When the horse began picking up speed, she shoved her feet in the stirrups and stood up. Andy had never seen anything like it. As horse and rider neared the red and white half mile pole, Candace crouched low over the horse's withers, her arms and legs folding into a neat package. As they flew around the turn, Andy admired Candace's style. She rode smoothly, not handicapped in any way by her long legs. She didn't know if it was a black letter workout but but it was certainly a sharp one.

She waited at the gap until they returned and jogged off the track.

"Holy crow, that's some kind of fancy riding, Candace.

I'm impressed."

"You've got to do a little trick ridin'with some of these hosses," Candace informed her. "They got their own funny habits but it doesn't mean they can't win a race or two."

"What do you do with this horse in a race? You can't come out of the gate without your stirrups."

"Naw, when it comes to a race, he's all business. And he's got some wicked speed coming outta the gate. The rider rates him just right on the front end, he'll go all the way. But if a hoss looks him in the eye coming down the homestretch, he'll spit the bit. Ya gotta keep his head in front."

"He's an intriguing horse, that's for sure. I'd love to ride him in a race, but I don't know if I could ride for old man Morris, not with his strange terms."

"Beggars can't be choosers," Candace warned her. "Besides, if I'm going to be your agent, I'll pick the hosses and you concentrate on riding."

Andy was beginning to regret the whole idea. If Candace booked her mounts, they would probably spend more time arguing over trainers than planning race strategy. She had as much control over her career here as she did in New York.

She sighed deeply. Maybe it was time to let go of the reins and just leave it all up to the fates.

BOUNCING BESSIE

"Hey, Cecil, come out, come out wherever ya are!"

"Jesus, Candace, I'm right here, not in China!" Cecil replied from several feet behind her. "I have Big Burch ready for you."

"Hey, Cecil, I want ya to meet Andy, my new bug rider."

"How do you do," Andy greeted him, shaking hands with a man a couple of inches taller than herself and not much heavier. He looked more like a jockey than a trainer. She wanted to ask him about his background, but she had promised Candace she wouldn't speak until spoken to. Even her parents had never demanded that.

Cecil's English accent was different than Charlie's. Andy assumed he came from another part of England.

"Who else you got going this morning?" Candace asked.

"Just Bessie." The prim Englishman wiped his hands on a towel. His thick woollen pullover and jeans didn't have a speck of dirt on them. It was hard to believe he'd just been handling a horse.

"How about sending them out in a set?" Candace suggested. "Andy can get on Bessie. She's just in from New York and she's got some wicked talent."

Cecil looked her over, his expression neither critical nor friendly. Professional is how Andy would assess him.

"From where in New York, Finger Lakes?"

"Belmont Park," she replied. "I rode for Barry Locke."

Cecil nodded, but his demeanour was still hard to read.

"What brings you to Boston?"

"Barry had to take on an owner's son as apprentice. Left me out in the cold." Andy shivered to make her point.

"I could certainly use an apprentice," he said. "If you've got Candace's seal of approval, you've got mine. I'll see about getting Bessie tacked up."

He headed off to the tack room at the end of the shed row.

Candace gave her the thumbs up. "So you see, we have some classy trainers here, not just gyps like ole man Morris."

A woman stepped out of the tack room carrying a saddle and bridle. "Hi, I'm Marion," she introduced herself to Andy. "My husband tells me you're our new bug rider."

Marion's jeans had fresh manure stains on the knees and straw was stuck to the elbows of her sweatshirt. Andy suddenly understood why Cecil looked so clean. "Pleased to meet you," Andy said with a smile.

"Have you met Bessie?"

"No, not yet." Andy followed Marion along the aisle until she ducked under the webbing into a stall. A big black mare turned to face them, her brown eyes soft and friendly. Her coat gleamed.

"Hello gorgeous girl," Andy greeted her, offering her hand for the horse to sniff. She looked the mare over quickly, her gaze following the line of her neck and over her sloping shoulder. Everything looked good until she got to her ankles.

"Look like two bags of marbles, don't they?" Marion said, noticing her gaze. "She had some filling in her ankles as a two year old. The trainer put a blister on her and the ankles swelled up, like they're supposed to, but they never came back to normal. Knocked her out of the top level competition that she was bred to run for. A real shame for that trainer, but a bargain for us. We couldn't have afforded her if she was unblemished."

"What's her breeding?"

"She's by Ribot's Fling, an up and coming stallion by Ribot."

"Classy bloodlines," Andy remarked. "How old is she?"

"Four. We bought her last summer as a three year old, but we decided to take our time getting her fit. We wanted to make sure her ankles were cold and set." She nodded towards them. "Go ahead and feel them."

Andy squatted down and ran her hands over the left ankle and then the right. "They're ice cold."

"They bother the jockeys more than they bother her. You can decide after you gallop her if you think she's sound enough," Marion suggested. "She takes her time warming up, but when she's ready to go, take a hold. She's a tough one."

Andy rubbed the mare's jowl and the big horse leaned into her, enjoying the touch. She liked her already.

"I think you two are going to get along just fine," Marion said with a smile.

"Come on, girls, you can have tea during the break!" Cecil called out. "The track will be closed before we get there."

Marion slipped the bridle on and legged Andy up into the saddle.

"Bessie has class alright, but no speed," Marion said in parting. "The longer the distance, the better she runs."

Andy and Bessie caught up to Candace.

"Hey, jock, you look good on that hoss," Candace said as they headed out onto the road. "Bessie needs a rider with a clock in her head. We've got a few savvy jocks here, they know how to get out front and slow the pace down. Bessie comes from behind so you've got to know what kind of fractions the leaders are cutting and make your move at the right time. Ya wait too long, you ain't gonna catch them."

"Is she ready to race?"

"Yeah, she's fit alright but Cecil's waiting for Bartie to write him a good distance race. Bartie writes a lotta races at a mile and seventy yards and a mile and a sixteenth, but ya gotta get down on your knees and beg for a mile and an eighth."

Candace shortened her reins and bridged them together in her hands, ready to take a strong hold of her horse. "Remember, you've gotta sit still on this mare till she's warmed up and ready, especially in a race. It's the hardest thing for a jock to do."

"What? Hard to judge the right moment to make your move?"

"Nah, hard to sit still. Most jocks are jumping up and down on the hoss, swinging their whip. Take a lesson from George Woolf. He was called the Iceman because he could sit chilly forever, didn't make a move till the right moment. And that man could hand ride, pick a horse up and put 'em across the wire first."

"If I know my horse has only got a short run, I'll wait till hell freezes over before I make my move."

"Yeah, I saw ya sitting real quiet on Lili. Hell of a lot better than Benito Gallo. We put him on Lili last year. She was the best hoss in the race, but Benito was all over her, couldn't sit still a moment. Little pinhead couldn't ride a hoss in a boxcar with both doors shut!"

"I take it Benito isn't your favourite apprentice. What about Emmett's boy, Billy Feagin?"

"Billy got to Emmett a day before ya and that's the only reason he's the bug rider for the barn. Ya mark my word, he ain't gonna last long. Kid's got big feet and hands, he ain't finished growing. Sides, ya could ride circles around Billy and it won't take Emmett long to see it. You'll be riding for him in no time."

"I don't think I want to ride for that jerk," Andy said.

"Hey, Candace, who's your friend?" a petite woman called over as she trotted by in the opposite direction.

"Hi, Deni, this is Andy Crowley, our new bug rider."

Andy recognized Denise Boudrot from her many pictures in the Daily Racing Form.

"Hi, Denise, nice to finally meet you."

"Hi to you too, Andy. I'll see you in the jocks' room."

"You'll want to listen to whatever that girl tells you," Candace informed her. "Ya follow her advice and ya could be leading rider before the meet's over."

"I'm all ears," Andy remarked as they entered the gap.

Bessie picked up the bit and trotted off. Candace's horse snorted like a Brahma bull. She took a short hold of the reins, the muscles in her arms already straining.

"We might have to get into a gallop pretty quick," Candace warned her. "This guy's wicked strong. He's a sprinter, not a router and he doesn't have any use for farting around."

They were into a gallop within the first quarter of a mile. Even though she wasn't warmed up yet, Bessie's stride was big enough that she could keep up with the headstrong Big Burch. Candace wasn't talking anymore, all of her concentration was needed to keep the horse under control.

"You're one hell of a strong woman, Candace. If I was on that horse, we'd have completed two laps already."

"So ya telling me I need to be ya agent and ya exercise rider?" Candace said between clenched teeth.

"You're hired. We'll shake on it later."

In the second round, they let their mounts move out a little, but Candace still had to keep a strong hold on her horse to keep him from reaching racing speed. She sighed in relief when they finally pulled up.

"Problem with galloping these tough ones is they build up my appetite. A twelve ounce steak and baked potato would go down real nice about now." She looked over at Andy and held out her hand. "We can shake on it now. I'll be ya agent and exercise rider, but it'll be unofficial for awhile. I'm not ready to hang up my racing boots just yet. I'll get ya some mounts, but I'll still ride once in awhile."

Andy took Candace's hand. "Tell you what, get me a horse with just an ounce of talent and I'll get them into the winner's circle."

THE MOUSE
AND THE PONY

Mickey was still breathing hard from his two mile run, the distance between his office and The Smiling Oyster.

"Hey marathon man, how're ya doing?" Pony greeted him in a relaxed, almost cordial manner.

"Miller time," Tommy said, slapping Mickey on the shoulder. "You want a beer, Pony?"

"Naw, gimme a whisky, and none of that crap above the bar." He leaned back until the old wooden chair creaked. "And bring me them numbers. I wanna hear six, two, three."

Tommy looked at his watch. "Race won't be going off for another hour."

"Yeah, that's right," Pony replied as though he had been testing him. "Bring some Scotch for Mick, the best."

Mickey would normally refuse alcohol with the quip that he didn't 'drink and run' but when you did business with Pony Cantoni or Whitey Bulger, you did it their way. With Pony, you drank, with Whitey, you didn't. Mickey despised the violent nature and greed of both men, but he respected their power.

"Tommy's a good guy, but he ain't got your smarts, Mick," Pony said in a confidential tone as the door closed.

Mickey was wary of the compliment. It didn't take a genius to make the honour roll in Pony's gang. Mickey was the only one in the crew who had finished high school. His

Italian father had little use for schooling, but his Irish mother believed strongly in education. She was determined someone in the family would get to university.

Mickey didn't make it to the Ivy League, but he'd studied in night school to become an accountant. His real schooling came from watching people. He had what he called a PhD in PA, 'paying attention'. He made it a vocation to study people's body language, taking note of their vocal tone, their facial expressions and how they reacted. From childhood, he'd studied different forms of aggression, what methods of intimidation the bullies used, which ones worked and which ones didn't. He also studied the victims' stance and mannerisms, their lack of eye contact and how quickly they acquiesced. He long ago came to the conclusion that the victim drew the bully rather than the other way around.

"I'm making my traveling money tonight, Mick."

Mickey gave Pony his full attention. Pony's race fixing business went clear across the country—almost. He had yet to crack California. His winning percentage was second to none. Pony claimed that he won ninety-nine percent of his races, which was a slight exaggeration but the figures proved that he was very successful. Pony knew how to handle the trainers and jockeys, when to use a light touch and when to go to the whip.

A couple of years ago, Pony had bought some racehorses so he could have more control over his bets. But the Thoroughbred Racing Protective Bureau, or TRPB as it was referred to, had noticed his horses' erratic performances and barred him from all the New England tracks. As far as the TRPB knew, Anthony Cantoni had been running a one man operation which they'd nipped in the bud. Mickey was certain if they knew just how extensive his business was, they would call in the FBI.

"By the way, ya done a good job with Perry the Pencil. I knew he was holding back on me. How'd ya get him to come clean, Mick? Ya rough him a bit?" Pony laughed at the thought of Mickey beating up on someone, but his laughter wasn't as hearty as usual. The big man was obviously waning.

"Perry's better with words than numbers," Mickey replied. "He miscalculated the odds on that last perfecta. It was an honest mistake. He'll run everything by me before he turns it over to Tommy."

"Good thing he ain't handing out the payoffs."

Mickey nodded. His cousin, Perry, was his shadow. As kids, he followed Mickey everywhere. They graduated from high school the same year. Mickey had earned an MBA degree while Perry, a lover of literature, tried to write the great American novel. Though he managed to sell a few articles to magazines, eight years later he was still trying to convince a publisher to pick up his manuscript.

Meanwhile, he worked in Mickey's accounting office. At first Perry had been an asset. His organizational skills and filing techniques made the office run smoothly. He could make conversation with clients and drew in new business. But that was when A&M Accounting was totally legit. Now that Mickey was doing Pony's books, his cousin had become a liability. He now had the responsibility not only of protecting himself, but keeping Perry safe.

"Sure glad I told Tommy to make all the payoffs himself."

Mickey nodded though Pony's memory was inaccurate. Pony had wanted him to hand out the payoffs directly but Mickey knew his talents were limited to creative accounting not strong arming a bunch of bookmakers.

"At least I got one guy knows how to take care 'a business," Pony said with a sigh. He was doing his best to get Mickey to fall for the soft touch.

The door opened and Tommy appeared with a tray of drinks and bags of nuts, pretzels and candies. Pony attacked the food, shoving it into his mouth by the fistful. Tommy handed Mickey a double scotch. Mickey held the glass up in toast as Tommy opened a bottle of Miller.

"You want me to stay?" Tommy asked. Ever the devoted flunky, he was at Pony's beck and call, twenty-four hours a day.

Pony nodded. "Tommy's got a fish on the line," he told Mickey, his mouth full of pretzels. "Ain't that right?"

"Yeah, I've got a big shot who wants to get into the racing game, a real neophyte."

"You've been hanging around them rich fuckers too much," Pony grumbled. "Enough with the big words, will ya?"

Mickey had to smile over that one. The only reading Pony did was the *Daily Racing Form*. Though Tommy had been forced to leave school to help support his family, he was an avid reader. He and Mickey had grown up two blocks apart in Southie and had attended the same schools. When Mickey was working his way through the accounting course, he tutored Tommy so he could get his high school certificate. To return the favour, Tommy got him into Pony's crew. Now, almost a decade later, Mickey wasn't so sure that had been a favour.

"Sorry, Pony," Tommy apologized. "This guy is a bit of a fancy talker. I've been acting the part to convince him to throw some of his money our way."

"One of them new-vooh rich huh?" Pony said with a grin.

Mickey's facial expression remained blank as he held back a smirk. Pony's attempt at foreign languages was more laughable than his jokes.

"The guy wants to impress his friends," Tommy continued. "And nothing impresses them more than getting their picture in the winner's circle."

Pony had polished off the food and was fully revived. "He thinks if he spends a lotta money, he'll get himself a Mass 'Cap winner, huh?"

The Massachusetts Handicap was the biggest race of the season. It had enough prestige to draw horses from around the country, including Seabiscuit back in the '30's.

Pony reached for another of the half dozen glasses of whiskey. Tommy had returned prepared. He knew his boss' habits well.

"And we got just the horse to sell him, right?"

"You bet we do."

Mickey spilled his Scotch as he plunked it down on the table. The remark had thrown him off balance. Where were they going with this?

"That two year old we bought at the auction, he's shaping up pretty good, right?" Pony asked before downing a shot. "Ya like the way he's training, Mick?"

Mickey pulled his thoughts together. Selling the Kentucky colt had not been part of the plan. "So far, so good," he said, keeping his tone even to hide his confusion. "But it's early. Anything can happen with two year olds."

"Not bucking shins, is he?"

Mickey shook his head. The condition is similar to shin splints on a human athlete. "His shins are as cold as ice. Sheehan's remedy is doing its magic."

"Good boy, ya' been using your nonno's liniment, huh?"

Mickey nodded. His grandfather's special liniment worked wonders to keep a horse's shins and tendons tight. He was the only one who knew Broedy Sheehan's blend of ingredients.

"Emmett's listening to you, ain't he?"

"He leaves the leg work to me."

"He's treating his big owner with respect, right? "

Mickey nodded. "Absolutely."

"For a skinny guy, Mick, you pack a big wallop." Pony's laugh was back to full volume. "You got the leading trainer eating out 'a ya hand and ya got M&A's Laundromat doin' a booming business."

It took some effort for Mickey to smile. He failed to appreciate the metaphor of his business as a laundromat. As far as he was concerned, Pony did the money laundering, he simply rearranged a few numbers. Last year, the IRS had done an audit of M&A Accounting. A lot of questions had been asked about The Smiling Oyster account, but no irregularities could be found.

Right after the audit, M&M Stables had been created. Mickey had been itching to get into the racehorse business and see if he had acquired any of his grandfather's talents. He used the initials from his nickname, Mickey the Mouse, rather than his official name as it had a better ring to it. But his ownership of the racing stable was as much of an illusion as the Smiling Oyster accounts. Pony ran the show. His choice of trainer was Emmett Gibbons. Mickey thought Arley Mitchell was the best trainer on the grounds but the tall Texan was the independent type. He was not only horse savvy, he was good at reading people. It wouldn't take him long to catch onto their game. Emmett on the other hand only paid attention to the *Daily Racing Form*. He was perfect for the job.

"I hear my colt is the best looking horse in the barn."

Mickey suspected this was Pony's way of reminding him he had spies everywhere. He liked to think he could spot them, but he could never be absolutely certain. The only one he was sure about was Eddie Flaherty, Tommy's twin brother. Tommy brought lots of information from the jockeys' room.

"You keep riding him," Pony said. " Emmett, I mean, not the horses."

Mickey gave him a slight smile. Even a man without a sense of humour would be expected to acknowledge that one.

It seemed only natural that the grandson of a trainer from the early days of Suffolk Downs would want to get into the racing business so Mickey was the perfect foil for Pony. M&M Stables had begun with cheaper claiming horses. Emmett Gibbons wasn't known for his talent in developing young horses, he was a claiming whiz. Emmett had a knack for knowing when horses were running below their price. He claimed several horses for them at the lower claiming level and ran them back at a higher price. The horses usually won, especially when Pony's jockeys were involved, and within two years, M&M Stables had accumulated a nice bankroll.

The last horse that Emmett had claimed for them hadn't been successful. The gelding bowed his tendon during a morning workout. Pony ordered Mickey to destroy the horse but Mickey had other ideas. He moved the gelding to a boarding stable just outside Boston. He blended his grandfather's special liniment and put it on the horse every day. For months, he massaged the injured deep flexor tendon. The ingredients in the liniment reduced the swelling, but as grandpa had taught him many years ago, the true healing came from his hands. Within three months the horse was a hundred percent sound.

It was this experience that had convinced Mickey he had his grandfather's touch. Now, he was eager to test his skills with a good quality horse.

"Ya must be learning a lot hanging around the barns every day," Pony said.

If Mickey didn't know better, he'd think Pony was reading his mind. But the big man didn't read thoughts, only body language, and Mickey wasn't giving anything away.

"So, that horse ready to run? The two year old races'll be starting soon."

"It's still early in the season, he's only had a couple of workouts, short ones," Mickey replied, stalling for time. He should have been prepared for this. Pony changed his mind more often than his underwear.

"He's been at the track, what, thirty, forty days?" Pony insisted. "He's gotta be ready."

"Forty days is fine for an experienced horse," Mickey insisted. "But not a two year old. I laid the basic foundation on him at the training center over the winter, but it won't do to rush him into a race."

Mickey should have remembered Pony's sole interest was the mutual window not the thrill of developing a young horse. Pony didn't go to the barn every day, he didn't brush the colt and pick his feet, he didn't watch him prance onto the racetrack at the break of dawn. And he certainly didn't thrill to the sight of the colt pulling effortlessly away from the other horses.

At that moment, Mickey realized he was thinking more like a trainer than a mafia accountant.

"Hey, Mick, come on, think a little faster. When can we run this horse?"

Mickey was usually way ahead of Pony, but this curve ball had thrown him off stride.

"I didn't know we were planning to sell the colt," he said, keeping a tight rein on his disappointment. He tried to make it sound like it was his misunderstanding rather than Pony's change of plan. No one disagreed with Pony, at least not to his face.

"That crooked leg, did the blacksmith fix him up?"

"Yes, he balanced the heel. The leg's straighter, but we've got to strengthen the tendons slowly. That's why we have to take our time."

Sweat formed under his collar. He had never lied to Pony before. It was true that the colt needed time to adjust to the new angle, but that had been achieved weeks ago. His muscle and wind had been developed at the training center, but he wasn't at peak physical fitness. Neither his body nor his mind was ready for a race. The colt was nervous and could be difficult to ride. He had to settle and build some confidence. To achieve that, Mickey had to find the right rider.

"Give him a few days to get it figured out, then we blow him out and put him in the first two year old race of the season."

The finality of Pony's order hit like a fist. Mickey's fingers tightened on his glass as he lifted it to his lips and drained the Scotch. The alcohol burned its way down his throat. For a moment, he thought he was going to break out in a fit of coughing. He busied himself shuffling through some papers in his leather case until the sensation subsided and he could compose himself. "I'll breeze him at the end of the week. Then I'll know for sure if he's ready."

Tommy handed Mickey a piece of paper with a name and phone number on it. "This is the guy, Mark Rodale. Let him come out one morning and watch a gallop. We don't want the guy to lose interest. When the horse is ready to run, make sure he burns up the track. It'll impress the pants off the guy. And believe me, he wears some pretty impressive pants."

Mickey shoved the paper into his pocket.

"Yeah, we dangle the chump on the line, let him watch the horse gallop. When he wins his first race, we reel the chump in for big bucks."

Pony reached for the candies and held them out to Mickey. The M&M's were part of Pony's ritual, his juvenile sense of humour. Mickey hated the candies, but took a small handful and put a couple in his mouth.

"My name isn't to be mentioned. But ya know that, Mick. Last thing we want is the TRPB sniffing around."

Mickey nodded.

"When the deal goes through, ya get your usual twenty percent," Pony assured him before emptying the bowl of candies into his mouth.

The crunching sound of Pony's jaws made Mickey nauseous.

"It'll be the biggest twenty percent ya ever had," he continued when he was almost finished chewing. "Your washing machine'll be real busy."

Mickey glanced at the paper again. The price of the horse was in the six figures. That put Mickey's percentage in the five figures. For the first time, the financial windfall failed to give him a buzz.

ROLLS ROYCE OR VOLKSWAGEN

"Wipe that frown off your face. I'm not going to be an agent for a cry baby."

Andy couldn't believe Candace had brought her to Emmett Gibbons' barn.

"Why are we here? Emmett won't give me any mounts." Her voice sounded petulant, but she couldn't help it. The last thing she wanted to do was beg for a mount from this arrogant trainer.

"He's not your favourite, I know that, but he didn't get to be leading trainer by running a bunch of dogs. Listen to me." Candace took a hold of Andy by the shoulders and looked her straight in the eyes. "His bug rider will get sick or hurt or he'll show up one morning drunk. Emmett'll need someone who can tack a hundred and nothing and you'll be sitting there right under his nose."

Andy's injured pride couldn't heal that quickly. "As soon as he sees me, he'll kick me out of the barn. He called me a 'no talent' who couldn't cut it in New York.

"Hell, that was twenty-four hours ago. He's forgotten you by now."

"Well isn't that a wonderful recommendation!"

Emmett strode out of the tack room with Mustang at his heels.

"I want three sets in a row,' he told her, "beginning with

the colts. The fillies come last."

"I'll bet they do," Andy muttered.

Candace elbowed her in the ribs. "Shush, I do the talking."

"Come on, the first set should have been out there by now," Mustang hollered. "Let's get a move on. Al, get that bridle on, pronto!"

Emmett strode by, giving Candace a quick nod. "We'll get one ready for you, Candace."

Andy glared at the trainer's backside. "This isn't a stable, it's a factory."

"Yeah? Well, even a Rolls Royce is made in a factory," Candace reminded her.

"So is a Volkswagen," Andy retorted.

"Win a few races with the Volkswagens and you get to ride the Rolls," Candace said with a grin as she went after Emmett.

"Where the hell is Randy?" Emmett shouted. "We've had his horse tacked up for twenty minutes."

"Ya need a rider?" Candace said, right on cue. "I've got a helluva good bug rider here. She can horseback and she's light to boot."

Emmett glanced in Andy's direction. "Okay, she can get on Randy's horse. Ringo, Digger, mount up, you're heading out." He strode off down the shed row.

"You've got to remember how Randy got his name," Candace said as she caught up to Emmett. "I'll bet he's riding right now, but not on a hoss. Not that you've got anything to worry about. My bug rider's good. She'll be here whenever you want her."

Three horses were led out into the aisle. Exercise boys were legged up onto a roan coloured horse and a bay. Andy walked towards a well muscled chestnut gelding and gave his neck a pat.

"You like?" the young Mexican groom asked her.

"Yes, he's a nice looking horse." Andy smiled at the young groom. "What's your name?"

"Alonzo. You call me Al." His grin spread from ear to ear.

Andy was certain the boy couldn't be more than fifteen years old. He was a couple of inches shorter than her and several pounds lighter.

"Hello Al," she greeted him. "What's this horse's name?"

"They no tell me his name," Al replied. "The...what you call it...the propietario?"

"Propietario?" Andy played with the word in her mind. "Sounds like proprietor in English. Maybe you mean owner."

"Si, the owner, he no keep the caballo..." he struggled to find the English words. "... mucho dias. He have new caballo soon."

"Okay, I know caballo means horse," she replied. "And buenos dias means good day. So, you're telling me the owner doesn't keep his horses very many days, right?"

"Si," Al said with a nod, not looking very happy about the situation. He pointed in the direction of a man standing nearby. "That hombre, he the propietario."

"In English," Andy demanded, letting him do the work this time.

"He the... owner."

"Very good." She looked over in the direction he was pointing. The man in black stood at the end of the shed row.

"Oh my God, it's him." She took a hold of the reins. "Quick, give me a leg up before he comes out. That man gives me the willies."

Al hoisted her up. "What that, the willies?"

"You won't find that word in the dictionary," she replied, slipping her feet into the stirrups. "What's the owner's name?"

"He have funny name. Like a leetle animal, it crawl around. You know, it eat the cheese. Moose?"

"I don't think a moose would eat cheese and it's certainly not little," she said, with a laugh. "I think you mean mouse, but that doesn't make any sense. Why would that man be called a mouse?" She glanced in the owner's direction once more. "I'll admit he has a rodent look about him but I wouldn't want to be the one to tell him."

"Rowdant?" Al was confused.

"Ro-dent," she repeated, enunciating clearly. "Tell you what, I'll get us both an English Spanish dictionary. You learn English and I'll study Spanish."

"Si, I learn English and then the trainers, they want to put me on their horses. One day, I ride, just like Braulio Baeza." He squatted down into racing position and imitated Baeza. "Keep practicing, Al. You'll get there one day."

The horses were moving down the aisle and Andy jogged after them, passing the strange man in black. His dark eyes scanned her before inspecting his horse.

When she caught up to Candace, she nodded over her shoulder in his direction. "Who's Mr. Sleazy? Is he one of the wiseguys you were talking about?"

"That's Mickey the Mouse," Candace told her. "He's a bookkeeper from Southie. Used to be big into claiming, but he hasn't been taking too many lately. Spent all his money in Kentucky last year at the sales. Bought himself a nice colt, but I hear he's not training too good. Mickey'll probably be dipping back into the claiming box soon."

Andy looked down at the chestnut gelding she was riding. "Is this one of his claimers?"

Candace nodded. "Yeah, he grabbed him from Carla Whynot. She dropped the gelding down five thousand bucks to win a quick one. Backfired, though, he finished second and she lost him."

Her horse yanked against the bit and Candace quickly gathered up her reins. "Got another tough one here. I'll catch up to ya later."

Candace jogged onto the track and Andy lined up with the two other colts. The exercise riders introduced themselves as Ringo and Digger. Ringo had a constant grin on his face and looked like he was stoned. Digger seemed edgy, as nervous as Ringo was relaxed. When they broke into a gallop, Ringo's colt bucked, flipping him forward onto the horse's neck. He laughed as he pushed himself back into the saddle and picked up the reins. Andy was impressed, especially when he broke into song, his voice clear and melodious.

"*They're gonna put me in the movies, they're gonna make a big star out of me, we'll make a film about a man that's sad and lonely, and all I have to do is act naturally.*"

"Shut up, Ringo!" Digger shouted as his horse pulled at the bit. He yanked roughly on the reins, jabbing the horse's mouth. Ringo remained silent as they tried to synchronize their horses' strides. When they were galloping in rhythm, he sang in a quieter voice.

"*Yesterday, all my troubles seemed so far away, now it looks like they're here to stay, oh I believe in yesterday.*"

Andy recognized Ringo as the rider who had given her directions to Emmett's barn the morning she arrived. She thoroughly enjoyed both his riding ability and his singing. She would gallop with him any time, but she could do without Digger.

Her horse seemed to be struggling to keep up to the other horses. The gelding was willing enough, but she could feel a weakness in his left hind leg. When he was leading with his right leg, he was strong, but when he switched to his left lead on the turn, his stride shortened.

When they pulled up, she stood him quietly on the outside rail, letting him relax for a few moments. Digger spun his horse around and jogged off.

"I haven't got all day to wait for you guys," he grumbled in parting.

Andy turned to Ringo who seemed content to wait with her. "I owe you a coffee. Milk and two sugars."

He looked at her in confusion.

"You gave me directions to Gibbon's barn the morning I arrived."

"Man, you've got some kind of a memory if you can remember that."

"I worked in a cafe all through high school." she informed him. "You don't seem to be in as much a hurry as Digger."

"He kinda likes to make the moola," Ringo said with a grin. "That's how he got his name, Gold Digger."

"I see. And you got your name from the Beatles' drummer, right?"

"Yeah, but it's legit. My name's Richard Skyler."

Andy held out her hand. "Pleased to meet you, Richard Skyler. I'm Andrea Crowley."

"My pleasure, man." Ringo smiled as he shook her hand.

"So, do you have anything else in common with the Beatles?"

"Lots, man. I play a mean set of drums. Not too bad on the guitar, either."

"And you're very humble about it," Andy said with a laugh.

"You've got to sing your own praises around here. No one else is going to do it for you."

"That's the truth. They're a rough bunch here." She turned her horse around and headed to the outside of the track. "Do you know anything about the owner of this horse? Is he really called Mickey the Mouse?"

"That's what most people call him, but I call him the Candy Man. He's really generous with the bonuses. You want to stay on his good side, man."

"Mickey the Mouse, the Candy Man. He sure has enough cognomens."

"Cognomens," Ringo repeated. "What's that mean, nickname?"

"Yeah," Andy replied. "Sorry. I'm not trying to show off or anything , it's just that I grew up on college campuses. My mother was a stickler for proper vocabulary. I never had a chance to talk like a normal kid when I was growing up.""

"Hey man, don't apologize. I like learning new words. Tell you what, you improve my vocabulary, I'll teach you the lyrics to every Beatle song ever made."

"You've got yourself a deal."

Ringo's horse tossed his head and broke into a gallop in his excitement to get going. Andy followed him at a more sedate pace until they came to the gap and reined down to a walk. Digger was headed out on his next mount before they reached the shed row.

The man with all the nicknames was waiting for her. She glanced down at him as she rode up beside him.

"How did he feel to you?" he asked.

His voice took her completely by surprise. She had expected a gravelly gangster voice, something like Marlon Brando in the *Godfather*. Instead, Mickey the Mouse had the melodic voice of a tenor.

"He's a very willing horse," she assured him, "but his left hind leg is weak."

Mickey's eyebrows lifted as he nodded slowly. "You're very observant. No other rider has mentioned that."

Alonzo appeared from the tack room with a halter and held the horse while she dismounted.

Anxious to get back to Pete's barn, she immediately headed off down the shed row.

"Wait a moment!" Mickey called to her.

She froze in her steps. The last thing she wanted to do was spend another minute in Gibbons' barn.

"I have another horse for you to gallop."

She was about to tell him she was needed in Pete's barn when his groom led a sleek bay colt out of his stall. The horse exuded power as he walked towards her, his coat gleaming, his large dark eyes alert. She knew instinctively this was the Kentucky bred horse Candace had mentioned.

"My God, he's magnificent," she said, touching his well muscled shoulder.

"Si, magnifico," Al agreed. "And he very...listo."

That one had her stumped. "Do you mean listless?"

Al shrugged his shoulders, insinuating he didn't know what that word meant. Andy went into pantomime, slumping her shoulders, looking tired and sluggish.

Al shook his head. He pretended he was reading a book.

"Interested, a good student," she said, trying to figure out what he meant. "Oh, I know, you mean smart."

He nodded enthusiastically. "Si, he very smart."

Andy laughed. "We'd make a great team in charades."

"Charhades? What is that?"

"Oh, it's a silly game, but fun." She glanced down the shed row. The owner was waiting. "We'd better get a move on."

Al legged her up into the saddle. "You like this caballo. He good horse, the best."

She smiled down at him. "I like his looks, but I'll let you know what I think of his ability after we gallop."

KEEPING OPTIONS OPEN

Mickey watched as the two horses headed onto the track. Ringo's horse was on the inside and his colt was on the outside. No, he reminded himself, not *his* colt, Pony's colt. Mickey had as little control over the colt's fate as he had over his own. When you sign a deal with the devil, he thought bitterly.

Whoever he belonged to, this horse was special. He might even be as good as his sire, Round Table . A sensation in the '50's, Round Table won stakes races on both surfaces, dirt and turf. The stallion had retired as the all time money earner and his success carried on in the breeding shed. In '72, he was leading sire of the year.

Mickey knew good breeding and conformation didn't necessarily guarantee a great racehorse. Only time would tell if he had chosen a stakes horse or a claimer, but he felt in his gut this horse was the real deal. Claimers, like the gelding the girl had just galloped, were useful horses but there was a quality missing. This colt had the look of eagles.

The two horses picked up a trot. Mickey studied the action of the colt's front legs. His slightly crooked leg was now straight and strong, but Mickey was still using it as an excuse to delay Pony's sale. He was giving himself time to put together an airtight plan to foil the deal, but he had to do it in a way that wouldn't rile Pony. Going against Pony's wishes wasn't something you did and lived to talk about.

Mickey used grandpa Sheehan's liniment faithfully

every day, rubbing it onto the colt's legs. He also used his grandfather's training regimen, trotting the colt up and down hills at the training centre when he first started under saddle. Grandpa had taught him this was the best way to build muscles and lung capacity. The cooling down period was as important as the warm-up, not only to prevent lactic acid build-up but also to assess the horse's fitness level. The shorter the period of recovery, the fitter the horse.

At the training center, Mickey had access to riders who were patient with young inexperienced horses, who would take their time with them. Here at the racetrack, the riders had a different mentality. Most of them wanted to get on as many horses as possible in the four hours that the track was open for morning exercise.

Mickey watched as the colt tossed his head nervously. Though he showed moments of brilliance, his nerves were still interfering with his progress. The girl didn't jab him in the mouth like Billy Feagin did whenever he acted up. Though big and strong, the colt was sensitive and over-reacted to harsh handling. Mickey liked the way the girl rode the gelding. He was especially impressed when she'd noticed the weakness in his hind leg. Maybe she would find the key to getting the colt to relax.

The horses jogged along the stretch and broke into a gallop on the far turn. The only fault he could find with the colt, aside from his nerves, was his name—Dundurn Dancer. To Mickey's ear, it wasn't the name of a Triple Crown winner. He had requested a change of name with The Jockey Club, the organization that registered all Thoroughbreds before they could be entered in a race. He had sent in a new name and hoped it would be approved.

Conformation was the foundation of a good racehorse, but there was something else that Mickey felt was as import-ant—attitude. Seabiscuit, the famous horse from the '30's, had plenty of it. Even with a small build and crooked legs he'd become one of the all time greats.

As the horses galloped into the backstretch, the colt suddenly veered out towards the outside rail, spooking when the inside horse brushed his flanks. Rather than slap him with the whip as Feagin had done, the girl touched him gently on the neck and brought him back towards the center of the track. She had remained perfectly balanced in the saddle throughout the spook which seemed to give the colt as much confidence as the gentle pat.

Mickey watched how she handled him for the second mile gallop. When he came around the turn again, the colt's stride was rhythmic and fluid as he steered a straight course.

Mickey sighed in relief. He had found the rider who could gallop the colt in the mornings and bring him to peak condition. Then he would decide which of their jockeys would ride him.

He would keep his options open for the jockey who would ride this potential champion. He looked quickly around to make sure none of Pony's spies were watching. A groom stood nearby but his attention was focused on a horse jogging back on the outside rail.

He waited until the colt had safely pulled up and was headed back before returning to the barn. Alonzo had just finished cooling out the gelding and was waiting for the colt's return. M&M Stables' horses had originally been groomed by Mustang. Emmett claimed she was his best groom. Mickey didn't agree. She groomed and bandaged horses to perfection, but there was no nurturing in her attitude. She was as brusque and coarse with the horses as she was with people. Mickey also sensed she wasn't who she said she was. The uncouth attitude was real but he was certain she'd been planted there as one of Pony's spies.

When Alonzo had arrived four months ago with his cousin, Armando, Emmett had hired them and Mickey gave the younger groom his three claimers to rub. By the time the colt arrived in mid March, he was satisfied enough with the boy to give him the colt. Emmett argued that Al was too inexperienced to be handling a good horse, but as far as Mickey was concerned, that played in his favour. The boy had no preconceived ideas on how to do the job and was eager to please. He knocked himself out to do whatever Mickey asked. He naturally had a good touch with horses and talked to the colt constantly in Spanish, telling him he would win the Kentucky Derby. Mickey would never admit this to anyone, but he believed horses understood what people said to them.

The girl rode into the shed row. She leaned close to the colt's ear and whispered to him. Mickey liked that touch.

Suddenly, a pencil thin man rushed into the barn, spooking the horse. The colt leaped sideways and reared. The girl barely moved in the saddle and had the horse settled within seconds.

"Perry, how many times have I told you to move slowly when you're around horses?" Mickey reprimanded his cousin. "You could have injured that colt. He almost went through the roof!"

"Sorry," Perry apologized, "but I'm the one who should be jumping through the roof." He adjusted his thick glasses and peered owlishly at the horses nearby. Mustang was leading a horse around the shed row and stopped behind the colt.

"Are you gonna get off that horse sometime today?" she demanded of Andy who blocked her path.

"Which one is yours?" Perry asked, pointing to the horse Mustang was leading. "The orange one?"

"For God sakes, Perry, horses aren't orange." Mickey hoped no one had overheard his ignorant cousin. "You've been around the stables long enough to know that's called a chestnut."

Andy dismounted and Alonzo quickly led the colt into his stall. Mustang pulled sharply on the lead shank to get her horse moving again.

Andy walked over to Mickey. "Thank you, Mr..." she

hesitated, realizing she didn't know his real name.

"Amato," he informed her. "Mickey Amato."

"That's a very special horse you have, Mr Amato. I like your gelding too, but that bay colt is something else, he's in a different category."

Andy was surprised when he handed her some money. Normally, the galloping fee was for exercise riders. Jockeys were expected to gallop free of charge in the hope they would ride the horse in a race.

Obviously there was little hope of that. Mr Amato was paying her off. She glanced at the bill as she walked out of the shed row. Ten dollars. Nice, she thought, but nowhere near ten percent of what that horse would win.

NEVER SQUEEZE
THE LEMON DRY

"Stop playing the flunky," Mickey said irritably. "Act normal."

Perry had opened the door for his cousin, as was his habit, but Mickey was especially irritable today. "Yeah, sure, if I could figure out what normal is," he replied, shutting the door behind him.

They welcomed the warmth of the enclosed trainers' stand. The raw, spring air was heavy with moisture. If the temperature dropped a few more degrees, it would be snowing. Mickey stood next to Emmett, paying little attention to the chatter of the other trainers. The talk was mostly gossip, who was screwing who, both in the bedroom and at the mutual windows.

Mickey nodded in Emmett's direction, his demeanour polite rather than friendly. He had little respect for the man. Emmett's language wasn't offensive in the way Mustang's was, but he was generally clueless. His one talent was reading the past performance charts in *The Daily Racing Form*. The first year that Emmett had trained for M&M Stables, Mickey had learned from him how to study the *Form* and find a good claim. It had been an educational year and Mickey was grateful for the knowledge, but he had nothing else to learn from Emmett. The man had only a working knowledge of conformation and breeding and he wasn't a hands-on trainer. He hired experienced grooms and left that work to them. The man was born with a horseshoe up his ass when it came to claiming, but that's where it ended. And Lady Luck tended to be a fickle companion.

It was Emmett's arrogance that made him the perfect foil for Pony's scam. As long as he believed his expertise at claiming was responsible for all his wins, Mickey could keep using him as the front man. There wasn't another trainer on the grounds that fit their plan so perfectly.

"This mare is ready," Emmett remarked as a set of horses approached the turn. Perry watched as three horses galloped by and wondered which one Emmett was referring to. Try as he might, he couldn't differentiate one horse from another. The difference in colour was obvious but aside from that, they all looked the same to him. And they were all too big. Perry would follow his cousin anywhere, except into a horse's stall.

Mickey, on the other hand, had no trouble spotting the horse Emmett was referring to, the bay mare ridden by Ringo. She had been the most recent claim for M&M Stables at five thousand dollars. Mickey was determined to run her back for the same price. The horse was still 'in jail' as the racetrack vernacular went. For thirty days after a claim, the horse would have to run at a higher claiming price. Mickey had instructed Emmett to wait out the thirty day period and run her back for the same price. It would look like they wanted to lose her. The serious bettors would think there was something wrong with her, giving her higher odds. Meanwhile, he was giving her some short, quick workouts to put more speed in her. He would instruct the jockey to send her to the lead. With the help of Pony's crew, the mare would score an easy win. And more importantly, Mickey would score points with Pony.

As fickle as Lady Luck was, Pony's favours could change at the drop of a hat. Tommy was Pony's number one lieutenant with his direct connection to the jockeys. Mickey, on the other hand, could easily be replaced by another accountant. Creating M&M Stables had been his first step in becoming an active player. By developing his training skills, he could hone the horses and increase their chances of winning. Horses were more reliable than jockeys as far as Mickey was concerned. If his claimers returned to the winner's circle in their next race, Mickey would become an indispensible part of the crew.

That had been his original plan. And then the Kentucky colt had come along. His mind drifted back to the colt's gallop, his long, effortless stride. Though claiming horses were the bread and butter of the industry and the mainstay of Pony's gambling, Mickey was now finding it impossible to focus on them.

"There's a perfect race for her, non-winners of two in a lifetime," Emmett said, breaking into Mickey's reverie. "She's out of jail now."

"Five thousand, non-winners of two," Mickey repeated, bringing himself back to the business at hand. "Enter her."

"How did the colt gallop this morning?" Emmett asked. "Is he ready for a workout?"

Mickey's expression remained stoic. "Soon."

Emmett shrugged. "I think we missed the best buy of the sale when we lost the bid on the Bold Ruler colt. Bold Ruler's by Nearctic. I've done well with the Nearctic line."

Mickey almost scoffed. "As well as Horatio Luro?" he commented drily, referring to the well known Argentine horseman. Luro, or the Grand Senor as he was called, had trained some of the best racehorses this century. The only thing Emmett had in common with the famous trainer was a knack for claiming. Early in his career, Luro had claimed a horse named Princequillo for twenty-five hundred dollars. Unlike Emmett, the Grand Senor didn't plan a quick flip. He patiently brought the horse along and turned him into one of the legends of horseracing. Luro coined the phrase, '*never squeeze the lemon dry*'.

When Emmett was finished with a horse, only the rind was left.

"Well, the Round Table colts are doing okay," Emmett admitted. "It'll depend on how that leg of his holds up. Doesn't look too strong to me."

Mickey clenched his jaw in an attempt to control himself. Perry stepped between the two men, aware of his cousin's body language. He was relieved when Emmett moved closer to the window to watch the horses, giving them some much needed space.

Mickey no longer noticed the horses or anyone else in the room. He sensed his grandfather turning over in his grave.

Broedy Sheehan had given his life to horse racing. As a fifteen year old, he'd ridden horses at the Curragh, Ireland's most famous racetrack. A racing spill had left him with a broken back at the ripe age of seventeen, threatening to paralyze him for life. Through sheer will, he got up on his feet but never back in the saddle. After emmigrating to New England in the mid forties, Broedy Sheehan began at the bottom again, walking hots and rubbing horses at Suffolk Downs. By the fifties, he had become assistant trainer to Will Ricci, leading trainer at Suffolk Downs throughout the fifties. An old timer, Will had been training since the track opened in 1935. But by the fifties, he had become a raging alcoholic, plastered by eight o'clock in the morning. His assistant trainer held the stable together and carried on the duties of training.

Mickey had come to the track every weekend with his grandfather from age five until fifteen. He was walking hots by the time he was seven and riding the horses around the shed row by age ten. As a boy, he idolized his grandfather, but as a teenager, he began to grasp the politics of the backstretch. He saw his grandfather as Will's lackey, doing all the work and receiving none of the credit.

Ricci's name was in the records book and in the local racing hall of fame, but there wasn't a single mention of Broedy Sheehan. Owners brought their horses because of Ricci's fame, but it was Broedy who did the training. Broedy's hands brushed the horse's coats until they gleamed and rubbed their legs with his special liniment.

To add insult to injury, the old man wasn't even well paid for his tireless work. His weekly pay was a pittance. One of the few Irishmen who didn't drink, he always turned his salary over to his wife, Mavis. It had been barely enough to feed and clothe their three children, but Broedy hardly noticed. He could tell you minute details about any of the horses under his care, but he couldn't tell you the age of his three daughters. It was a small family for an Irish Catholic. This was mostly due to the fact that Broedy spent more nights sleeping in the tack room than at home with his wife. The arrangement seemed to suit both of them.

Mickey felt someone nudge his elbow. He looked over to see Perry holding out a pack of gum. Perry didn't have any talent for reading a horse but he could quickly tune in to people's feelings. As calm and cool as Mickey was in his accounting business, the horses had a different effect on him.

"Here, Mickey, have a Juicy Fruit."

Mickey unwrapped a stick of gum and shoved it in his mouth.

THE HOUSE
ON ELM STREET

Andy never had a good sense of direction, but since arriving in Boston, she had none at all. The city was a maze of one-way streets and dead ends that defied logic. She'd been driving in circles for what seemed like hours before finally finding Elm Street.

"It does exist!" she cried out in relief. She wasn't talking to herself this time, but to her cat, Dolly Button. The grey tabby meowed in response. "I know, I should have listened to you when you told me to turn right. I can't help it, I'm used to turning left."

She found the address Charlie had given her and angled her Volvo over to the curb. "Oh my God, look at that house, it's amazing. How in the world did Charlie find it?"

Andy recognized the architecture as Gothic Revival. The house had to be close to a hundred years old. She stepped out of the car and glanced up and down the street. Elm Street was right out of a weekly television show, shady trees, children and dogs playing in the front yards. For a moment, she thought she'd walked into a scene from *Father Knows Best*.

After two weeks of living on Revere Beach it was a relief to think she could spend her evenings relaxing on the porch in an old rocking chair, sipping a beer and enjoying the scenery. Nights on the beach belonged to the drug dealers. A moonlight stroll wasn't recommended unless you were trying to make a score.

"I'll check the house out first, make sure it's suitable for us," she said to Dolly Button, closing the door before the cat could escape. "Then we'll see if it passes your approval."

The front door to the house opened just as she reached the pathway leading to the front steps. Two golden retrievers rushed out and galloped down the stairs. "Rupert, Jasper, sit!" Charlie commanded.

The dogs screeched to a halt and sat down barely a foot away, staring up at Andy anxiously, tails sweeping the walkway.

"I'm impressed," Andy exclaimed, leaning down to give each dog a pat. "What good boys you are."

"Somebody around here has to take orders," Charlie said from the top of the stairs, "and it's certainly not me."

Andy looked up at the stately house once again. She'd made a trip to Britain with her parents when she was twelve years old and was familiar with the cathedrals and castles that Gothic Revival imitated. Her eye ran over the steeply pitched roof and cross gables, the windows on the top floor with their pointed arches. She skipped up the stairs, the dogs at her heels and held her arms out, as if measuring the porch. "Just what I've always wanted, a wraparound porch. Do you have a rocking chair?"

Charlie nodded. "I'm re-varnishing a couple of rocking chairs that I found at the thrift store."

"How did you find this amazing place?"

"It's a long, sad story," Charlie replied, opening the door.

"With a good ending. This neighbourhood is right out of a Norman Rockwell painting."

"During the day, maybe, but you wouldn't want to be walking to the corner call box after dark."

"Call box?"

"Yes. You'll want to make your calls during the day."

"Oh, you mean phone booth," Andy said, finally clueing in. "You mean, you don't have a telephone?"

"We'll need to win a dozen races before I can afford that." Charlie led the way in. "This lovely heritage house is draughty and the radiators only work when they feel like it. But there's plenty of rooms and the rent is fair, if two people are paying it."

"Just tell me one thing," Andy asked. "Do you have hot water?"

"That I have. The hot water tank hasn't let me down yet."

"Great. I can hardly wait to have a long, hot shower."

Charlie shook her head. "Better make that a bath. This house was built before showers were all the fad."

"You're kidding?" Andy hadn't had a bath since she was a child.

"I'm afraid not. Come on, I'll give you the royal tour."

A small vestibule with a coat rack and boot tray led to an open, spacious living room that was sparsely furnished.

"Welcome to my parlour," Charlie said, her voice echoing off the walls.

Andy looked around the parlour. A beautiful stone fireplace was the centre of attraction. Vying for attention was a magnificent cow skin rug set up in front of the fireplace.

"An heirloom," Charlie explained, following Andy's gaze. "A gift from my great aunt Edith."

The only other piece of furniture in the room was an old, friendly couch facing the fireplace, its floral pattern faded from years of use. Several novels were spread out on the couch.

"That's my nightly entertainment, watching the fire and reading a book. Can't afford a telly. When we've had a good week at the races, Pete takes us to the pizza parlour and the cinema. Have you seen *Harry and Walter go to New York?*"

Andy shook her head. "No, but I loved *Silver Streak*."

"At least we both like comedies."

"Yeah, we get enough suspense and tragedy on the race-track." Andy remarked.

"The kitchen is right through here." Charlie led her

through a doorway into a spacious kitchen.

"The rooms in these old houses are so big. And look at these ceilings." Andy stretched up as if she could touch the ceiling that was a good twelve feet high. "It's like a palace."

"And cost as much to heat as a palace. I hope you have an eiderdown. I turn the radiators down at night to cut down on the heating bill."

"Compared to my room on Revere Beach, this place feels balmy."

The furnishings in the kitchen were also sparse. A card table with a lacy white tablecloth and two folding chairs were set up in the corner.

"Who's your interior decorator?" Andy asked with a grin. "She has very eclectic tastes."

"Her name is Charlotte Fliss Middleton." Charlie took a bow. "I had some help from the previous tenants. They left this heirloom kitchen table behind."

Andy laughed. "They must have had a very small car if a folding table didn't fit in."

"The refrigerator and stove came with the house otherwise I'd be cooking on a hot plate and keeping the veggies in an ice chest." She walked over to the sideboard next to the sink. "I have a toaster, a kettle and a tea pot, all from the Salvation Army."

"Good, at least we can have breakfast, the most important meal of the day."

"So I've been told. I've no idea, really. I can't eat till noon."

"You're kidding? By then you've been up at least seven hours."

"Oh God, don't remind me!" Charlie filled the kettle. "Tea?"

"Sure. Do you have Earl Grey?"

Charlie shook her head. "Just the cheapest tea I could find. When we win a race, we can splurge on more exotic teas. I hear there are some lovely tea shops in Boston."

"Considering the history of tea in Boston, I'm surprised it isn't banned," Andy said with a grin. "I don't suppose your tea is from the British East India Company."

"No. I believe they went out of business not long after the famous tea party."

"That's right, the company folded in 1857."

Charlie looked suitably impressed. "You actually know the date? "

"My father read history books to me from the day I was born. I can't tell you a thing about fairytales, but I'm a whiz at historical facts and dates. I know the history of Boston like the back of my hand. I'll take you on a tour one day."

"I love tours," Charlie said. "Did your dad teach you about the racetrack too?"

"Are you kidding? Secretariat to him means someone who maintains records for international organizations, not a triple crown winner. I have my uncle Michael to thank for introducing me to the racetrack."

"So you and your uncle are the black sheep of the family?"

Andy thought about that for a moment. "I think we're more grey sheep. I was never a rebel, I didn't want to draw that kind of attention. I just quietly did my own thing. My parents were expecting a Harvard graduate and I ran off to the racetrack so they've pinned their hopes on my younger brother, Adam. Poor kid. He's a real people pleaser, he's in for a tough time."

"Can't be tougher than your life," Charlie said as she put the kettle on the burner. "I mean the work is hard enough but the Godawful hours! Up before dawn!"

"Not an early riser, huh? What brought you to the track?"

"The same reason I came to America," she said with a deep sigh.

"Oh, oh! I suspect a man had something to do with it."

"A man? No, an arsehole, an arrogant prig."

"Was this arrogant prig a trainer?"

"He called himself a trainer, but no one else did. The

best he could do was assistant trainer to Carmel Dixon. The woman has a mouth on her like you wouldn't believe, something my dear Simon seemed to enjoy."

"He likes women who swear?"

"No. He likes women who are good with their mouth."

It took Andy a few seconds to get it. "Oh, I see."

"So did I, unfortunately." The whistling kettle interrupted their conversation and Charlie poured the hot water into the teapot. " I opened the door to the tack room and there they were. It was a sickening sight."

Andy winced. "Was that when you dumped him?"

"He dumped me! Can you believe that! He acted like I was the one at fault. Threw the house keys at me and said he was moving out. Just like that!"

"What a jerk!" Andy gasped. "That's unbelievable."

"I'm sure you're a lot smarter when it comes to men. Where's your boyfriend, in New York?"

Andy shrugged her shoulders. "I had a boyfriend in high school, David Henderson. Great guy, I really liked him, but he wanted to get married when we graduated. It was the last thing on my mind but he was such a nice guy, it wasn't easy. Breaking up with David was the hardest thing I've ever had to do." Andy hesitated for a moment. "Second hardest thing. Breaking out of the starting gate for the first time goes to the top of the list."

"You mean you haven't had a boyfriend since high school?"

Andy couldn't tell if her tone was one of surprise or suspicion.

"No serious relationships," she said. "I've had a few flings, but if the guy even starts thinking serious, I'm gone. Racing comes first."

Charlie sighed. "I wish I had your discipline."

"So how do you handle it when you run into this jerk, Simon?"

"No chance of that happening. He's back in England. His

pride wouldn't let him play second fiddle to anyone, especially a woman." Charlie reached into the cupboard for two mismatched mugs. "Do you take yours white or black?"

"With milk, no sugar."

Charlie poured the tea and handed Andy a mug. "Bring it with you and we'll continue the tour."

They headed up the stairs. There were four doors on each side of the hall with a bathroom at the end. Charlie led her into the first room to the right.

Unlike the living room, their voices would not echo in this room. Canvasses were arranged all around the room, some set up on easels with others leaning against the walls or properly framed and hung. In the centre of the room was a life-sized sculpt of a dog that could have been Jasper or Rupert. The smell of paint stung the air, and other odours that Andy didn't recognize. Paint cans, jam jars and other sundry containers held brushes, paint, varnish and tools that she couldn't indentify. Two rocking chairs, freshly varnished, were drying next to the radiators.

"What is an artist doing rubbing horses at the track?" Andy asked.

"She's making money to pay for her artist's supplies, not to mention a roof over head," Charlie answered. "And she gets her hands on the magnificent animals that she likes to paint."

"My God, that's The Heckler, isn't it?" Andy exclaimed, staring at one of the completed canvases.

"Well, isn't that encouraging, you recognized him right away. I've captured him then, have I?"

"It's not just his presence you've captured, his spirit shines through." Andy slapped Charlie on the back. "You're one hell of an artist, Charlie. I mean it, you're really good."

"Thank you," Charlie said, a tinge of shyness in her tone.

Andy studied the other canvasses, several of them half finished and then inspected the paintings that were framed. One was a pencil drawing of a pony.

"I love this pony drawing, it has so much character. Even though I've never met him, I know exactly what the little rascal was like. This is one of your best."

"Alfred would be pleased to hear it."

"Alfred?"

"Alfred Munnings."

Andy gasped. "You have an original Munnings? How in the world did you afford it?"

"It was free." Charlie stepped closer and smiled as she looked at the drawing. "I met him when I was five years old. We're both from Dedham, you see, Dedham, England, not Massachusetts. My father did some work around Alfred's place and I went along with him one day. Mr Munnings drew that for me, to keep me quiet, I suspect. He wasn't an endearing man."

"Really?" Andy looked at the drawing for several more seconds. "Good artist, though."

She followed Charlie back out into the hallway.

"The room on this same side of the hall is for storage, in case you need to store something. I've got some boxes and a couple of trunks in there, but there's plenty of space left over. The bedroom next to the loo is mine and then there's this one."

Charlie opened the door and led the way in. The hot water radiators pinged loudly.

"I thought I'd warm it up a little. I swear there were icicles inside the windows when I moved here back in December."

Andy looked around at the faded pink walls with yellow trim. On closer inspection, the trim was meant to be white but had yellowed over the years.

"What do you think? Do you like it?"

"Like it? I love it!" Andy spread her arms out and twirled. "The Heckler and Miss Lili Marlene could move in here with me and I'd still have plenty of room."

"I wish I could supply you with furnishings but that's not possible at the moment. You'll need a bed and a bureau, not to mention some sheets, blankets, and pillows."

"Have pillow, will travel," Andy announced dramatically. "I have my pillow in the car."

"The car," Charlie repeated. "Oh, what blessed words those are. I've had to beg, plead and almost sell my body to get a lift to the track every day."

"Life is looking up, for both of us." Andy reached into her jacket pocket and took out a sheet of paper. "Look at the overnight. I'm named on two horses."

Charlie looked at the overnight sheet. All of the next day's races were listed. Most of the horses had jockeys named on them, but a few were open.

"Has Candace tried to pick up some of the open horses for you?"

"Oh, yes, my new agent was right on it, but no luck. The trainers are waiting to see how I ride."

"What about the fifth race? I see Denise Boudrot is named on two horses."

"Denise's agent gives Barbara Smith second call. He wants to watch me too. But I've got Bouncing Bessie for Cecil in the first race and Miss Lili Marlene for Pete in the third. It's a good start."

Charlie smiled. "Move over, Willy Shoemaker, here comes Andrea Crowley."

Andy put her hand in the other jacket pocket and pulled out some bills. "Here's my first month's rent. I'll grab my sleeping bag and suitcase and I'm moved in."

Charlie smiled. "I like a woman who makes quick decisions."

Jasper and Rupert came bounding into the bedroom, tails wagging.

A look of doubt suddenly shadowed Andy's eyes. "Wait a minute, there's one more opinion that's needed."

She skipped down the stairs and out the front door returning in minutes with a suitcase in one hand and her tabby cat tucked under the other arm. "Dolly, meet Jasper and Rupert. Boys, this is Dolly Button."

She dropped the case and held the cat in both arms as the dogs eyed her with keen interest.

"Manners, boys." Charlie took a hold of the dogs. "They're very good with the neighbour's cat, but he doesn't come in the house. There may be some adjustment time needed."

"I thought so," Andy said, looking around the empty room. "Okay, Dolly, we're off to the Salvation Army. Time to buy a bookcase."

"Wouldn't you want a bureau first?"

"I have more books than clothes. They can stay in the suitcase. And Dolly can use the top shelf, for safety." She hugged the cat. "You get to choose it, Dolly. You'll be using it as much as I do."

THEY'RE OFF!

Andy parked her car in the jockeys' lot. Looking over the battered mid-sixties models of Toyotas, Chevelles, Ramblers and Valiants, she estimated many of the jockeys at Suffolk Downs were struggling to make a living. Her '67 Volvo fit right in. Like the others it looked jaded next to a shiny new Gran Torino. That one had to belong to one of the top jockeys.

As she stepped out of the car, she noticed two men leaning against a station wagon. One of them was Eddie Flaherty, the jockey she'd met on her first day in Boston. They seemed to be having an argument. When the other man turned in her direction, she almost gasped. He was a carbon copy of Eddie. There was no mistaking them as brothers. They had identical facial features though the other man wore his hair shorter and was at least thirty pounds heavier. Even with the extra weight, he wasn't fat by any means, it was all muscle. Seeing the two men side by side, Andy realized how dehydrated Eddie was from 'doing light'. Keeping his weight down to a hundred and fifteen pounds must have been a challenge.

The brother paced back and forth like a soldier on parade. He moved like a trained fighter. The crew cut and the erect posture all spoke of military training. Andy wondered if he was a Vietnam veteran. His mouth was moving as fast as his feet while Eddie stood with his arms crossed. Whatever the brother was saying, Eddie definitely didn't agree as he threw his hands in the air and walked away.

"I need this!" his brother yelled, but Eddie disappeared amongst the cars.

"Sibling rivalry," Andy muttered as she pulled an old army duffle bag out of the backseat, one she'd found at the Salvation Army. Dolly button had chosen the biggest and ugliest bookcase in the store. Andy tried to interest her in a newer, lighter model but the cat kept going back to the old one. When she jumped up on it and curled up to sleep, the decision was final. She had also invested in some free weights, five and ten pounders along with track pants. She had been jogging every morning since her race in New York, determined to be a lot fitter than she'd been for her first race.

Andy walked across the lot to the grandstand and then followed the sign for the jockeys' room. Opening the door, she stepped into a large, open room bustling with activity. Valets cleaned tack, whistling contentedly or shouting to someone across the room. Jockeys competed with each other at pool or ping pong while three of them sat at a small round table playing cards. They were all in varying stages of undress. One jockey walked by naked. He took a quick backward glance when he noticed Andy.

"Hey, whadda you doin' in here?"

Andy managed to keep her eyes at chest level in spite of her curiosity.

A valet stepped between them. "Cover yourself up, Pedro," he said before turning to Andy.

"You're new here," he said, stating the obvious.

Andy read the name on his shirt.

"Yes, Johnny, this is my first day. Looks like I've come to the wrong jocks' room."

"I'll show you the way to the girls' quarters," he offered.

She fell in step behind him.

"Cover up boys, lady coming through!" he called out.

A young jockey whose baby face made him look under legal age quickly grabbed a towel and covered himself as they passed.

"Good for you, Benito. At least you don't need to show off."

The other jockeys laughed while the young Benito blushed.

"Which jockeys do you valet for?" she asked Johnny.

"I've got Carlo Gessani, Eddie Flaherty, Aidan Odahl and the one who was trying to impress you, Pedro Vargas."

"I've seen their names in the *Racing Form*. All top riders."

"My boys do okay," he replied, opening a door at the opposite end of the room. They stepped out into a short hallway.

"You'll have to walk through the outdoor saddling paddock to get to the girls' room." He pointed to a door marked *Women Jockeys Only*.

"Thanks. Sorry for disturbing the guys."

"Gave you a chance to size up the competition."

They both laughed.

"Thanks, Johnny, you've been very helpful."

"No problem. Darrell is the girls' valet. He'll be by in a few minutes."

Andy made her way to the *Women Jockeys Only* door and walked in. The ambience was totally different. The room was small and cramped with no space for recreational activities. To the left were cubicles that held piles of clothing; jeans, shirts, socks and shoes. Beside them, neatly folded, were stacks of thin nylon racing breeches and tee-shirts. Each cubicle had a name tag: Denise Boudrot, Barbara Smith, Candace Mackenzie, and at floor level, an empty cubicle was assigned to Andrea Crowley.

She knew where she was in the hierarchy.

Andy dumped her duffle bag on the floor and went off to check the rest of the women's quarters. The main room had a card table, a TV mounted on the wall, two chairs and a loveseat. She walked up a couple of steps and found herself in a bathroom with a sink, two toilet cubicles and a shower.

She glanced at the mirror where her smiling image greeted her. "Welcome," she whispered.

Back in the main room, she found another door and opened it slowly. It took her several seconds to adjust to the blackness within. Two sets of bunk beds held three sleeping bodies. One of the top bunks was empty.

She closed the door. She didn't need a nap today.

She picked up the *Daily Racing Form*, the racetrackers' bible. In newspaper format, the *Form*, as it was usually called, began with articles covering the racing news across the country. Andy went directly to the section that listed all of the days' races at Suffolk Downs.

This section gave the breakdown of past performances on each horse in the ten races. She looked at the first race and found the name of her mount, Bouncing Bessie. The big black mare with the ankles like bags of marbles had only run five races in her life. She had won her first race, or broken her maiden as the jargon went, at Aqueduct Park in New York at a distance of a mile and an eighth. Her last race was five months ago on September 8, 1975. The chart showed her positions at the half mile pole, the quarter pole and the finish wire. Bessie was last and second to last most of the way, but closed considerably in the homestretch to be beaten only a few lengths.

Andy turned to the third race and looked for her second mount, Miss Lili Marlene. The filly had been ridden by bug riders the previous year, mostly Juan Estevez. Benito Gallo had ridden her twice. According to her past performance, Lili liked to run just a few lengths off the pace and close down the stretch. Benito had won on her once.

The main door flew open and a human whirlwind rushed in with arms embracing an impressive load of helmets and goggles.

"Hey, you must be Andrea Crowley," he explained. "I'm Darrell, your valet. The guys get to choose their valet, but I'm the one who takes care of all the women."

"I'm sure you take good care of all the women," Andy said.

When he had assigned the goggles and helmets to the appropriate cubicles, he held out his hand and she shook it.

"Pleased to meet you, Darrell."

His hand shake was as energetic as his entrance.

"This your gear?" he asked, picking up the duffle bag before she could answer. "I'll get it all organized. Your cubicle is marked. Anything you want from the kitchen, I'll be taking orders as soon as I get back. It'll go on your tab and you pay up every week when you get your cheque. "

He opened the door to the bedroom and switched on the light. "Wakey, wakey, rise and shine!" he called out, shattering both the darkness and the silence.

Andy heard moans and a couple of swear words.

"Put together your orders," he called over his shoulder as he strode out into the hall. "I'll be back in five."

The door slammed shut and the room was left quiet once again. Three women stumbled out of the bedroom, each of them wearing tee shirts and underwear.

"You're here," Candace said after blinking a few times. "Thought maybe ya got lost somewhere."

"I took a roundabout route through the men's quarters. They certainly don't stand on ceremony in there."

"Get a peek at anyone?" Candace asked. " I hear Farrell King's well hung."

"I don't know, they weren't carrying ID."

Candace laughed. "I'm sure ya gave them a thrill."

"Hey, nice to finally see you in the jocks' room."

"Thanks, Denise. Tell me, what was it like to make history? I was thrilled to read about you back in '74 when you won the jockey title here."

"When it was over, it was great," Denise said, her Boston accent a little softer than Candace's. "Ninety-four wins in ninety-two days. I wouldn't want to do it again. It was wicked tough. I didn't even weigh a hundred pounds by the end of the year."

"Oh, oh, I'm only a hundred pounds now. Wonder what

I'll be at the end of the year?"

"You'll look like me," Barbara Smith remarked as she followed behind Denise.

Andy looked Barbara over from head to foot. Even for a
jockey, she was skinny.

"What do you weigh?"

"Ninety-four, and that's after a big meal," Barbara
replied, stretching and yawning. "So why'd you come here
from New York?"

"Not by choice," Andy admitted. "No offense, but I'd
still be in New York if I didn't get pushed out by an owner's
son."

"Them's the breaks," Barbara said, making her way into
the bathroom.

The door opened and Darrell came in, his arms loaded
with racing boots which he deftly slid into the cubicles.

"Okay, who's eating?"

Barbara ordered eggs and bacon and Denise ordered
spaghetti.

"Spaghetti for breakfast?" Andy couldn't believe it.

"Pasta, the food for athletes," Denise mimicked a television commercial. "Besides, I need to be a little heavier now
that I'm not an apprentice. I don't get the five pound weight
allowance like you do. If I'm too light, I've got to carry lead.
Trainers don't like you to carry a lot of dead weight."

"I can hardly wait," Andy said with a sigh. "I love Italian
food."

Candace called her order out from the bathroom, a clubhouse sandwich.

"Spaghetti for Deni, breakfast special for Barbara and a
salad for Candace, no dressing." He turned to Andy. "Anything for you?"

"Orange juice please." Andy didn't eat before a race. She
experienced a slump in energy right after a meal and she
needed to be physically and mentally sharp.

"Everyone has to be at films today, to see who gets busted

for yesterday's races," Darrell called out over his shoulder as he headed out the door. "Stewards' orders."

"Shit!"

Andy looked over to see who had sworn. Barbara obviously wasn't impressed.

"Is that usual, to call all the jockeys to films?" Andy asked.

"They're going to give us another lecture on cleaning up our act," Denise said. "There's been some rough riding out there."

"If ya get any cleaner, Deni, you'll squeak," Candace teased.

"If the guys want to play some games out there, they don't talk to me about it," Denise said as she strode by on her way to the cubicles.

"Yeah, they just put you little bantam weights on the lead." Candace shook her head before pulling on a clean tee shirt. "Guess they figure ya don't have the strength to hold a horse back."

The door flew open and Darrell appeared with the orders. He placed the tray on the card table. "Chow down, girls. You've got twenty minutes before you weigh in. Then it's film time."

"Get the popcorn ready," Barbara said sarcastically as she turned the TV on.

Andy expected to see the day's handicapping odds on the screen but instead, a soap opera came on.

"You girls watch soap opera!" she exclaimed in disbelief.

"Yeah, *All My Children*," Denise replied. "I never miss it."

"Don't know why you'd wanna watch it on TV," Candace remarked. "We got enough of it around here."

"Watching other people screw up their lives takes our mind off our own messes," Barbara said, picking up her plate and settling down in front of the television.

In twenty minutes, on the dot, Darrell appeared and led the girls into the men's quarters where the clerk of scales waited.

"Morning ladies," Gerry Marinick greeted them. "Let's start with the newcomer, Andrea Crowley."

Andy stepped up on the scale and watched the needle bounce back and forth, finally settling on one hundred pounds. Moans and curses erupted through the little group of men who had gathered to watch.

"Hey, Carlo, come see this," one of the guys called out. "She weighs as much as your left leg!"

Carlo Gessani strolled over and looked at the scale. He resembled a wrestler more than a jockey, muscled from head to toe. "I wouldn' be gloatin', Farrell. You ain't weighed that low since the day you was born."

Gerry checked the list on his clipboard. "You're carrying a hundred and ten on your first mount, one twelve on your second. Do you have a heavy saddle?"

"I have a five pounder."

"The five pounder it'll be, with extra lead." He glanced over the girls. "Okay, let's give the scale a bit of a shock. You're next Candace."

Candace stepped up. Unlike Andy, she faced away from the needle.

"Six ounces lighter and you'd almost make it," Gerry said, jotting down her weight at one hundred nineteen and a half. "Your horse is in at one twenty so even with your postage stamp saddle, you'll be two pounds over."

"No way, I'll only be one pound over."

"You're going to ride bareback, are you?" Gerry asked. "With your saddle, girths and your real boots, not those cheaters you're wearing, you're two pounds over."

Andy looked down at Candace's feet. The paper thin boots she wore were basically weightless. Heavy jockeys used them to weigh in hoping to shave a few ounces off. The genuine racing boots were made of leather or vinyl and though they were light, they obviously weren't light enough for Candace.

"Gimme a break, Gerry, this trainer hates it when a jock's

overweight. He won't ride me back, even if I win."

"You know I can't do that, Candace." He looked at the next in line. "Okay, Barbara, you're up."

More moans erupted from the men when Barbara stepped on the scale. She was a mere ninety-six pounds.

"We'll use a cavalry saddle for you," Gerry joked. "Even your twelve-pounder will need lead today."

Denise was only four pounds heavier than Andy, even with a stomach full of pasta. She'd be carrying lead on several of her mounts.

"Girls coming through," Darrell yelled out as he led them to an open door at the far end of the room. "Enjoy the movies, girls. I hear Farrell's starring today."

FUN AT FILMS

Chaos erupted. Jockeys whooped and hollered as the horses broke from the gate.

"Silence! That's enough! Sit down!" The cacophony slowly ebbed as Eddie Flaherty stared them down from the front of the room. "Okay, let's have a little order here."

Andy had never experienced anything quite like this. There had been an occasional display of emotion during the daily film reviews when she was in New York but nothing like this. She sat at the back of the room, content to be an observer in the drama unfolding around her.

Two jockeys were involved in a claim of foul in the third race, Juan Estevez on the number five horse and Farrell Kohler on the six horse. There had been some interference coming out of the starting gate. Juan had finished third in the race and Farrell, who'd finished well out of contention, had claimed foul on him.

The replay began with the pan shot, showing the action from the side view. When the gate opened, Farrell's horse fell to his knees. Andy winced at the sight while most of the men yelled and cursed. Farrell leaped to his feet, waving at the screen.

"See that, he knocked my horse clear to his knees! Show the head-on and you'll see!"

"Sit down, Farrell," Eddie ordered him. "The stewards are running this show, not you."

Eddie turned in the direction of the men seated at the far

side of the room.

"We'll view the head-on next," Arthur Healey announced, picking up the receiver on the phone. "Don, give us the head-on."

"You got it," the voice of Don Cress replied from the video room high in the media tower.

Andy turned her attention to the stewards. Arthur Healey was one of the track's three stewards, or 'three blind mice' as the jockeys liked to call them. They were seated behind a wide table that acted much like a protective moat separating them from the fray. Of the triumvirate of stewards, Arthur was the only one who seemed to be taking an active interest in the proceedings.

Andy was thankful she hadn't ridden in the previous century before cameras were used on the racetrack. Back then, race riding was much like a cavalry battle. Jockeys waged war with each other, shutting horses off or pushing them over the rail, anything to get an advantage. Grabbing a saddle cloth, hitting a jockey in the face with a whip and or knocking their foot out of the stirrup were common tactics. It would be one rider's testimony against the other when the stewards tried to decide who was at fault.

Andy's gaze fell on one of the jockeys at the back of the room, Don Meade Jr. This man had a real racing pedigree. His father, Don Meade Sr. had been involved in one of the most notorious stretch battles in the history of the Kentucky Derby.

In the running of the 1933 Derby, Don Meade Sr. was on a colt prophetically named Head Play and Herb Fisher had the mount on Broker's Tip. As the two horses ran head and head to the wire, Don and Herb battled it out, grabbing and shoving at each other. Herb eventually won both the fight and the race.

Such blatant tactics came to an end when cameras were strategically placed around the racetrack. A jockey's every move was captured on film. Anyone who incited such violence today would be fined and suspended, possibly for life. Modern day methods of interfering with another jockey during a race had to be much more subtle.

The proceedings were interrupted when the door opened and a jockey entered, naked except for a towel wrapped around his waist.

"Carlo, you're late," Arthur said. "And we would appreciate it if you dressed appropriately for films."

"I've got another pound to go," he said, wiping the sweat from his forehead with a small towel.

Carlo's face was pale and drawn. Obviously, he'd dropped several pounds already in the sweat box. Andy would watch out for him out on the track. The dehydration would affect his reflexes.

She turned back to the TV screen as the head-on view began. She watched closely when the gate opened. Twelve horses lunged from the narrow iron stalls. The number five horse veered sharply to the right colliding with the six horse and knocking him to his knees. Farrell was flipped forward onto the horse's neck. Miraculously, the horse scrambled back to his feet, lifting his head and throwing Farrell back into the saddle.

"You son of a bitch, you did that on purpose!" Farrell yelled rushing at Juan. The young Peruvian apprentice shook his head frantically.

"No...no, not me...the horse, he break like that."

Eddie stepped between them, firmly planting his hands on Farrell's chest.

"Cut it out!" he ordered him. "Calm down, Farrell, or you'll be the one looking at a suspension. Now get back to your seat!"

Farrell made a few threatening noises before returning to his chair.

"Juan," one of the other stewards said, "next time you make a ninety degree turn, put your signal light on."

A couple of jockeys laughed but Andy had heard most of them talking amongst themselves before films began. The general consensus was that it was time for Juan to have a short holiday.

The steward who had made the remark was Dick Trumball, or Tinballs as he was called by everyone on the backside. The man looked to be in his eighties. He was the head steward and had been for several decades. Andy couldn't believe he was acting so unprofessionally.

As the film rewound, the horses on the screen ran backwards into the gate and the latches closed. The picture froze until the film ran forward. The gate opened and the two horses collided once again. While Farrell's horse struggled to get back to his feet, Juan's horse accelerated and joined the leaders at the head of the pack.

Most of the jockeys leaped to their feet, protesting the reckless ride. The Spanish voices were at the highest pitch, followed by a French Canadian jockey who spoke half in French and half in English. The locals sat back and watched, seemingly entertained by the commotion. All except Eddie Flaherty.

Eddie was the Jockeys' Guild representative. His job was to act as liaison between the jockeys and the stewards, but he also acted as referee between the riders, preventing them from coming to blows.

Andy sighed. It seemed the film room could be as dangerous as the racetrack. She looked around the room to see where the other girls were. Denise Boudrot was sitting off to her right, sharing a joke with a tall, blond haired jockey who wore a tee shirt with the name L Brady. She assumed it was Liam Brady, a name she'd seen in the *Form*. Barbara Smith was having a private conversation with Yves LeBlanc, the French Canadian jockey who'd moved here from Montreal back in 1973 when the Blue Bonnets Racetrack had closed their Thoroughbred meet. Yves' dark eyes and scowl made him look like he was permanently angry, even when he was laughing, as he was at the moment. Candace was at the back of the room, leaning against the wall, enjoying the scene.

"Quiet!" a voice cut into the roar.

Arthur was taking control again.

Andy glanced over at the stewards sitting at the table. These three men had as much authority over the racetrack as the pope had over the Catholic Church. Like the pope, they often thought they were infallible. A jockey who was given a suspension could ask for a hearing, but decisions were rarely overturned on appeal.

Dick Trumball had turned his focus to the Boston Globe business section. Andy suspected he had already made his decision.

The third steward, John Baxter, sat quietly and simply nodded approval to whatever Arthur said. Like herself, he seemed to be more of an observer than a participant.

Arthur Healy was the only fully active steward. He left the safety of his chair and walked around the table, bravely facing the line of fire.

"Juan, what was happening with your horse in the gate?"

Andy noted that Arthur kept his tone neutral, making it sound like a question, not an accusation. Juan seemed to relax a little and present his case in a more confident tone.

"My horse, he was leaning on the gate, he crush my foot. I show you the bruise."

"That's okay, just tell me what happened when the latches opened."

"The gate man, he try to put his head straight but the gate, she open. He come out like that. I no can stop him."

"Run the head-on one more time," Arthur called out towards the phone receiver and Don started the film again.

Andy had her eyes glued to the number five stall. When the latches opened, she could see the horse leaning on the side of the gate. His head was turned towards the gate handler who stood on the narrow ledge beside him. As the horse launched out, he swerved to the right and collided with Farrell.

"I see what Juan's saying," Eddie said. "The handler is trying to straighten him out but instead, he throws the horse off balance. There was nothing Juan could do."

The jockeys shouted their opinions, some in favour and some against Juan. Arthur held his hands up in the air.

"Okay, okay, we've seen enough. Let's move on."

The next race came up on the screen at the half mile pole. A pan shot showed a horse a length in front of the pack. They rounded the turn and headed into the homestretch. The action suddenly switched camera angles. The jockey in second place stood up in the saddle and pulled back on the reins.

"Liam, what happened?" Arthur asked.

"She came right over on me. I almost clipped heels."

"There's enough room for a Mack truck in there," Candace exclaimed.

"Time to take your damn driver's license away if you think a Mack truck could get through that!" Liam complained.

"Okay, that's enough," Arthur warned them.

The screen went blank for several moments before the action picked up again, this time from the head-on view. It was impossible to tell how far ahead the front horse was from this angle, but the path of each horse was more obvious. Candace was two horses wide off the rail. Another horse on the outside of her. Liam was behind her, right on the rail. As the horses switched to their left lead, the horse on the outside drifted in and forced Candace's horse in.

"Carlo, looks to me like your horse set the whole thing off," Arthur said.

Andy glanced over at him. Carlo shrugged his shoulders, but didn't say anything.

"Okay, there was some shifting of lanes here," Arthur announced. "Your horse drifted in, Candace, but it looks like you had no control over the matter."

"If Liam isn't running up my heels, it's no problem at all. He's the one should lose his license." Candace pretended she was playing a guitar and started to sing, *Give me forty acres and I'll turn this rig around.*

"That's enough, Candace, spare us the sarcasm," Arthur warned her.

A few of the jockeys began singing along with her, but Eddie shut them down before they could get out of hand.

"Listen to me, it's dangerous enough out there," Arthur lectured them. "You've got to pay attention to what you're doing. We expect you to ride to win, but you don't have to kill anyone to get there. Start using your head more than your whip."

Andy liked that concept. And she definitely liked this steward. He had some class, which seemed to be sadly missing around here.

There was nothing to look at in the remaining races and they were all excused. As the jockeys left, Arthur instructed Eddie to wait outside the door with Juan.

"Are they going to give Juan a suspension?"Andy asked Candace as Darrell led them back across the room.

"Naw, they'll just tell him to lift some weights and build up his strength. Ya pretty much gotta kill someone to get days here."

They entered the women's quarters and started to get ready to ride. Only Barbara didn't have a mount in the first race.

Candace put on a set of yellow and burgundy silks. Andy's silks were white with a blue diagonal stripe. She slipped into them, running her hands over the smooth, shining richness of the material. Most modern day silks were made of nylon, but Cecil's were real satin. Cecil Elwood was definitely a man of exquisite taste.

"Bessie hasn't got speed, but she's got a hellava late kick. Make sure ya got room down the stretch," Candace coached her. "She'll start running at the sixteenth pole."

"And what about your horse?" Andy asked.

"Tim and I'll be way ahead 'a ya, at least for the first half mile. But he'll be short 'a air today. It's been a long winter."

"A long, cold winter," Andy said with a sigh, "but spring is here. A new racing season is upon us."

CONTACT SPORT

A ndy walked up the stairs and into the saddling paddock. "Good luck, kid," Candace said as she headed towards the number eight stall. "Show them how it's done."

A full field of twelve horses had been entered in the race and the little oval surrounding the saddling paddock was heavy with traffic. Several of the fillies pranced and kicked up their heels in anticipation of the upcoming race. Andy made her way to the number five stall where Cecil was waiting for her.

"This isn't her distance," he said without preamble. "It takes her half a mile to get warmed up, but there aren't any world beaters in this race. You can certainly get part of it."

Andy nodded. She had no illusions about winning a sprint race on a distance horse but she had to impress the trainers somehow with this initial ride. She looked over at the big black mare. Her head was up, her eyes alert, but she walked calmly.

"Riders up!" the paddock judge called out.

Marion led the filly into the stall and Cecil hoisted Andy up.

"Good luck," he wished her.

"You'll be warming up without a pony horse," Marion told her as she led the filly towards the track. "She doesn't need one."

Andy was glad to hear it. She preferred to warm up alone. It could be uncomfortable warming up with a pony horse beside you, crushing your foot between the two horses.

Bessie walked quietly throughout the post parade in front of the stands, but took a strong hold as soon as the warm up began. Andy bridged her reins together and set them against the filly's neck, keeping a tight hold on her. She galloped all the way down the backstretch.

"That's far enough," the outrider called out as she passed him. He looked ready to sprint after her if she went any further.

"It's okay, Harry, looks like she's got her horse under control," Eddie called out from close behind her.

"Just stay where I can see you," Harry warned her.

Andy understood that the outrider's job was to keep the horses in a confined area so they wouldn't run off. But Bessie needed a long warm up if she was to have any speed at all coming out of the gate. She turned the filly around and set off at a gallop clockwise along the backstretch, picking up speed until she was half way around the clubhouse turn.

"Pull that horse up!" the second outrider yelled at her. Like sentries, the two outriders were positioned at each end of the warm-up area, ready to catch any runoffs.

Andy pulled up, satisfied that Bessie had two good gallops. She set her off at a trot to keep her muscles loose and ready for action. Within minutes, the starter called the jockeys to line up for the gate.

Andy stayed at a safe distance behind the number four horse who was bucking and rearing. Both the jockey and the pony rider had their hands full trying to control the horse. One of the gate crew took the fractious horse immediately into the gate. Andy could feel Bessie's heart rate accelerating and she stroked her neck gently.

"You'll be fine," she spoke softly as a handler slipped a leather strap on the bridle and guided her into the padded stall. He climbed up on the narrow ledge beside her.

"You want me to hold her?" he asked.

"No, she's fine," Andy informed him.

He jumped out over the back latch and went to help the other handlers. Bessie looked around, but stood quietly. Andy pulled her goggles down over her eyes, removing the saran wrap that had kept the plastic goggles clean throughout the warm-up. She had kept her nerves at bay while focusing on the warm-up, but it suddenly struck her just how important this race was. This one ride would either launch her career or kill it.

"Hey, Andy, have you got speed?" Denise asked from the stall to her right.

"No, none at all."

"Too bad. You'll want to stay away from Juan, he might take you out."

Andy turned her attention to the young Peruvian jockey on the other side. His hands gripped the reins hard enough to turn his knuckles white. Arthur Healey's warning was having the opposite effect of what he had tried to achieve. The young man was a nervous wreck.

"Hey, Juan, don't worry, your horse looks good," she assured him. "Just take a deep breath and relax. You'll break nice and straight."

Juan didn't look reassured, but he had taken her attention off her own nervousness.

"Last horse coming in," the starter, Bertram Michaels, warned them. "Get tied on, riders."

Andy bridged both reins in her left hand about half way up the horse's neck and twined a finger in the mane. She rested her right hand against the horse's neck, whip ready to be cocked after the break. Her left foot was slightly forward, her right foot back, to keep her balanced should her horse duck left or right. Her eyes were straight ahead as the rest of the world faded from her senses.

The latches sprang open. The horse's haunches dropped as she lunged forward. Andy reached out along her neck, expelling her breath as she yelled out encouragement to her horse.

Her break was straight and clean, but Juan's horse bumped her shoulder and Bessie lost her momentum. By the time she got back into stride, she was in last place. The dirt hit her at full force, stinging her cheeks and clinging to her goggles but she wasn't going to make the mistake of pulling to the outside this time. She swung over to the inside rail. She would save as much ground as possible.

Within a quarter of a mile, the top pair of goggles was completely covered in dirt. She had to pull them down. Holding the reins and whip in her left hand, she reached up and peeled the top layer of goggles off, letting it drop around her neck. Her vision was momentarily clear. She angled Bessie between the haunches of the two horses directly in front of her and the onslaught of dirt lessened slightly.

The incident at the break had unsettled Bessie and she was running with her head high, causing her to climb with her front legs.

"Easy, girl, easy," Andy soothed her, slowing the motion of her hands and body to encourage the filly to settle into stride. By the time they reached the turn, Bessie was in a more comfortable rhythm and changed leads smoothly. As they rounded the turn and headed into the home stretch, her head came down and her stride lengthened.

Andy had been so intent on saving ground after their bad break that she hadn't given any thought to Candace's advice to keep a clear path for the stretch run. She looked for daylight between the horses in front, but they were glued together. Several horses blocked her on the outside. Suddenly, one of the front horses drifted out, a sliver of daylight appeared. Andy set her sight on the small opening and chirped to Bessie. The filly surged ahead, squeezing into the narrow space. Andy touched boots with the jockeys on either side of her as she galloped through.

Eddie looked over at her from the outside. "Go for it, jock!" he called out to her.

"Hey, watch it!" Farrell Kohler screamed from inside her.

He swung his whip up in the air and lashed back, cracking it squarely across Andy's kneecap.

Pain shot through her body like a bolt of lightning. Her eyes watered beneath the goggles, distorting her vision. Between the dirt, the tears and the pain, she couldn't see where she was going. Determined, she buried her face in her horse's mane and rode with all her might. Jockeys all around her shouted and whistled. She heard Denise's voice call out to her horse somewhere in front. Andy used her whip twice to encourage Bessie and went to a hand ride for the final strides.

When the frantic sounds died out and Bessie's stride shortened, she knew they were past the wire. When she picked her head up, she was somewhere in the middle of the pack. The leaders were only a couple of lengths in front of her.

"Hey, you've got guts, kid," Eddie called over. "Not too many jocks want to ride blind."

Andy was surprised that he'd noticed what she was doing. Obviously, the jockeys were watching her as intently as the trainers.

She pulled the rest of her goggles down around her neck as she stood up in the stirrups, her legs strong beneath her. The cool air was a relief to both her eyes and her lungs. She spat dirt out of her mouth as she tried to catch her breath. She didn't know if it was the exertion from the race or the pain in her leg that had left her so winded.

"I didn't know horseracing was considered a contact sport," she called over to Eddie. "They do everything but tackle you around here."

"You've got to make a statement," he advised her. "Let the guys know they can't push you around. Looks to me like you'll have no trouble doing that."

They galloped back to the unsaddling area side by side. When Andy pulled up, she looked up towards the tower high above the grandstand. Custom had it that you waved your whip to the stewards to let them know all was well. If she didn't wave, it meant she would be claiming foul. As much as she'd love to claim foul on Farrell, it wouldn't bode well for her. She needed to make friends with her fellow jockeys, not enemies. She held her whip up in salute before tossing it to a waiting valet. He caught it in midair and stuck it in his back pocket.

Cecil and Marion were both there to greet her. She hoped they wouldn't be disappointed in their horse. Bessie had run just as they predicted but it was more the rider they were watching than the horse.

Cecil had an unreadable expression on his face, but Marion was smiling.

"Perfect," she said as Andy leaped from the saddle. "She ran even better than we expected."

"It was a little rough coming out of the gate," Andy said.

"Ran into traffic in the stretch?" Cecil asked.

"When I found myself last, I wanted to save as much ground as possible," Andy explained as she unbuckled the girths. "I knew I'd be getting some run at the end and I hoped I could get through on the rail, but no such luck. If I'd been able to get through right after the turn, we would have hit the board."

"You were beaten less than three lengths," Marion said, patting the mare. "That's the closest she's ever been in a sprint. Don't you worry, we'll do more than hit the board next time."

Andy felt instant relief. She'd passed the test. She pulled her saddle off the filly's back and gave her a pat. "You're even classier than I thought, Bessie. I can hardly wait till our next race."

Cecil nodded and strode off with his wife as she led the filly away.

On her way to the scale room, Andy stopped to look at the group gathered in the winner's circle. The groom, owner and trainer were smiling, but Denise had the biggest smile of all. There wasn't a speck of dirt on her face. Obviously, she had been just where she liked to be, in front all the way.

Andy weighed in and handed her tack to a valet. Instead of heading back to the jockeys' room, she sauntered over to the winner's circle, now empty. She stood right where Denise had posed for her picture and looked out over the track and infield.

"Nice view," she said with quiet determination.

NO SURE WINNER

Mickey glanced at his program. The next race was a four thousand dollar claimer for fillies and mares, three years old and upward, non-winners of a race since December 15, 1975.The number nine horse, Miss Imp, had won a race on December 13 at Hialeah Park in Florida. With Carlo Gessani in the irons, she was the favourite.

The old racetrack adage echoed in his mind, *there's no such thing as a sure winner.* Everyone knew that, everyone except Pony Cantoni.

Mickey looked over the names of the jockeys. Carlo's horse was five-to-two, a favourite that would sadly disappoint today. Pedro Vargas's mount was ten-to-one. The plan was for Pedro to finish second as the bottom horse in the perfecta. Vargas had resisted Pony's offers for several months but had recently come on board when he needed to pay off his girlfriend's credit card.

Mickey's eyes travelled to the rider on the number seven horse. An asterisk was next to the name Juan Estevez, denoting that he was an apprentice. This asterisk had led to the popular racetrack term, bug rider. His mount was five-to-one on the program and would be at higher odds by the time they reached the starting gate. If Juan didn't have a propensity for being disqualified, he would be the one on the lead today. But his riding was too erratic. Carlo and Pedro would see to it that he finished off the board. The jockey who would win the race had no idea what kind of help he would get. Benito

Gallo, on a twelve-to-one shot, would go wire to wire. This was the first time Pony had ever used a jockey who wasn't in the loop. And it had been Mickey's idea.

Mickey felt a nudge at his elbow and turned to see his cousin standing beside him. Perry patted his pocket to signal that his bets had been made. In order not to draw attention, they made smaller bets at several different windows. Pony's serious wagers were being made in Las Vegas and with a few local bookies, but the payoffs right here at Suffolk Downs would cover a large part of their expenses.

A light perspiration broke out on Mickey's forehead as the jockeys appeared in the saddling paddock. He suddenly had doubts. What had made him step up to the plate like this? If something went wrong...

He quickly put that thought out of his head.

He watched Benito shake hands with the trainer and owner. The eighteen year old Panamanian was a natural light-weight. At four feet eleven inches, he barely tipped the scales at a hundred pounds. He had ridden eighty races last year and four of them were winners. The rules regarding appren-tices stated that they became journeymen one year after their fifth win. The clock would start ticking after his next winner.

Mickey fervently prayed that fifth win would be today. He tried to calm his nerves by reminding himself that the lightweight jockey was very successful on front runners. Main opinion was that the horse ran off with him, but Mickey knew better. A horse couldn't run full speed from gate to wire, they had to be rated. Unlike Carlo and Pedro, Benito didn't have the physical brawn to hold a horse back, but he didn't interfere with the horse's rhythm. He allowed their natural speed to come through. Of course his win today wouldn't be a hundred percent natural, but that didn't take anything away from his ability.

Apprentice jockeys weren't as easy to influence as the older ones. They still had dreams of becoming the next Shoe-maker or Baeza. Like Alex Munsey, a little success could turn their heads. Mickey knew Alex's death was no accident. He wasn't privy to any of the details, but he had been there when Pony gave his instructions to Wally concerning Alex's ride. The apprentice had gone against those orders by winning the race. It wasn't the first time Pony had given the word to eliminate someone and it wouldn't be the last, but Mickey fervently hoped he wouldn't be next on the list.

Mickey watched Benito chat amiably with the owner. Though it was proving difficult to bring an apprentice willingly under Pony's influence, it was impossible to keep them out of the wagering. A lot of trainers used apprentices, or bug riders as they were called, to keep the weight off their horses. If Pony's boys tried to stop every bug rider from winning, it would raise a red flag. But when the apprentice was on a speed horse, like Benito was today, the boys could let him get a clear lead and see to it that the horses coming from behind ran into traffic.

Mickey was familiar with the records and riding styles of all the Suffolk Downs jockeys, all except the new girl, Andrea Crowley. She was the dark horse.

Her mount, Miss Lili Marlene, was at eight-to-one odds on the morning program. She would climb higher by post time. The seasoned bettors knew that the trainer, Pete Mackenzie, didn't normally go all out for a win on the first race of the year. Pete didn't have the killer instinct. He would tell the jockey to go easy on the horse and the odds would reflect that.

Mickey knew the girl had talent after watching her gallop his horses in the morning, but a good seat on a horse didn't necessarily translate into a winning ride. Too many other factors were involved in a race. His binoculars had been on her from the gate to the wire in the first race. Her mount, Bouncing Bessie, was a route horse running in a sprint. The girl had ridden every inch of the final sixteenth, winding her way fearlessly through the pack. She'd only been beaten three lengths. If any other jockey was on the horse, the margin would have been closer to a city block. The older jockeys wouldn't have put that much effort into the ride and the less experienced apprentices wouldn't have been able to rouse the mare enough to get her that close.

The girl had the right attitude, but it would take the trainers awhile to catch on. In the meantime, she would be riding long shots. That could work in nicely with Pony's perfectas and trifectas. Mickey could see the girl had more talent than either Benito or Juan. When the trainers recognized her ability, she might become the year's hot apprentice, maybe even leading jockey like Denise Boudrot had a couple of years ago. If that happened, she would no longer be useful to the Cantoni crew. But for now, everything hinged on this race.

Alex Munsey's independent thinking had cost him his life and brought ominous losses to *Pony Cantoni Race Fixing Ltd.* Whitey Bulger had paid a visit to The Smiling Oyster last night. Mickey hadn't been invited to the meeting in the back room, but he had a good look at Tommy when he came out. The ex-boxer looked like he'd been through twelve rounds and lost every one. Cantoni's crew was hurting.

Mickey watched the horses circling the paddock. He took a good look at the number six horse. It wasn't so much the horse that caught his attention as the jockey, Eddie Flaherty. The horse was from the Kingsley Stables, a barn that was second only to Emmett Gibbons in the number of horses. Kingsley didn't have as many winners per year as Gibbons but was close enough to stay on the top five trainers' list. Mickey wondered how Eddie was able to satisfy both his brother Tommy and the trainer, Pete Kingsley. Either he came up with creative excuses when he lost or he was sharing his percentage with Pete Kingsley. Mickey didn't know. Tommy warned him never to speak to Eddie.

He turned his attention to the other horses. Two scratches had narrowed the field to ten horses. The girl's mount, Miss Lili Marlene, was the smallest horse in the field. Even the groom was taller than the filly. It looked like a stiff wind would blow the little horse over but Mickey never judged a horse by its size. Big, beautiful horses lost races and scrawny little horses won. Unlike a halter class at a horse show, correct conformation and size didn't guarantee a win.

To the naked eye, Carlo's horse looked like a winner. The filly had spent the winter in Florida and looked fit and ready. A glance at the tote board informed Mickey most of the bettors agreed. The horse was now seven-to-five. Pedro's horse was second favourite at two-to-one. Benito was a healthy twelve-to-one. It would be a very nice payoff, if all went according to plan.

Mickey paced along the fence looking the jockeys over as they came into the saddling paddock. Carlo's face was pale and drawn. He'd obviously pulled a few pounds in the sweat box this morning, but his legs looked strong. He wasn't buckling at the knees, not yet. He'd fade after a few rides and probably take off his mount in the last race. Pedro had his business-as-usual demeanour. He looked neither right nor left, but walked straight to the number three stall as though he were wearing blinkers.

Aidan Odahl walked by and Mickey studied him closely. The tall, slim jockey shifted from left foot to right, tapping his thigh with his whip while the trainer gave him instructions. The man was as jittery as a colt breaking out of the gate for the first time. Aidan had a habit that was second only to the Weasel's. It was called on occasionally when the boys needed some help. Carlo gave him his instructions and he usually managed to carry them through. But he wasn't needed today.

The girl came out, limping slightly. Something must have happened in the first race. It didn't dampen her enthusiasm in any way. She high-fived the groom and started talking to her horse like they were planning their strategy together. Pete Mackenzie nervously fiddled with the saddle and girths before checking the bridle. He didn't stop talking until the paddock judge called for riders up.

Benito was first to be legged up into the saddle. The kid had no problem with weight unless you considered the eight pounds of lead in the saddle cloth a detriment. Many trainers believed that live weight was easier for a racehorse to carry than lead weight. Mickey didn't necessarily agree. If the rider kept his weight over the horse's centre of balance, it was an advantage, but not all jockeys knew exactly where that centre was.

Mickey got a good look at the horses as they pranced onto the track and were handed over to the pony riders for the warm-up. Miss Lili Marlene was turned loose on the track by herself.

"See you in the winner's circle!" the groom called out.

"Not if we can help it," Perry said aloud.

Mickey jabbed him in the ribs with his elbow. Perry exhaled in pain.

"Watch what you say!" Mickey looked around quickly to make sure no one had overheard. Satisfied that no one was paying attention to them, he watched the girl gallop off towards the backstretch. He didn't want her anywhere near the winner's circle today, but he didn't wish her any harm.

Andrea Crowley was a future investment.

ROUGH RIDING
AT SUFFOLK

The starting gate shook wildly. Andy grabbed mane and turned Lili's head sideways.

"Not yet, Lili," she said as a handler struggled to get the thrashing horse under control.

Suddenly, another horse reared.

"Rider down!" a handler called out urgently as the jockey was thrown out over the back latch onto the track.

"Sonamabitch! The fucking horse is a lunatic!" the fallen rider yelled, jumping to his feet.

Andy glanced over. Carlo was the one who had been thrown. He wasn't injured, but the incident would likely throw him off his game. She smiled. One fewer horse to beat and the favourite at that.

She quickly looked the field over. She had memorized the colour of silks each jockey wore so she would know exactly where everyone was. It was integral to her strategy to know where the speed horses were and when the come- from-behind horses were making their move.

"Okay, riders, get tied on," Bertram warned them. "Last horse coming in!"

Andy set her hands and positioned her filly, bringing her hind legs well under her. The latches opened and Lili sprang forward like a cat on the hunt. Andy was at the front of the pack. Suddenly, she was thrown out of the saddle. A jockey's foot had hooked her leg. With the stirrup lost, she tipped over the filly's shoulder, her head ominously close to the dark earth and the pounding hooves. She clung to Lili's neck desperately. It took all her strength to push herself back up. Her left foot miraculously slipped back into the stirrup.

A flash of blue and green silks crossed her path, the dirt from the horse's heels hitting her in the face.

"Bastard!" she swore. "You'll get yours, Pedro!"

She grabbed hold of the reins and organized herself. She'd lost any chance at a good position and had to reassess her situation. Most of the horses were in front of her, but the rail was open. She angled over and took the inside position once again to save ground. She was at least seven lengths behind the leaders.

Pete had instructed her to let the filly run on her own. He didn't want her to overexert herself in her first race of the year. But Lili was as upset about her position as Andy was and tugged at the bit.

"We'll get our chance, Lili, just be patient."

Andy studied the horses in front of her. Carlo's black and green silks were just ahead of her on the inside rail. Benito was in the lead, standing tall in the stirrups to slow his horse down. In spite of his effort, Andy judged the pace to be very fast. Benito wouldn't be able to carry that kind of speed all the way to the wire.

Just to the outside of Carlo was Pedro's blue and green silks. He was the one to beat, she was sure of it. She wouldn't let him get too far in front of her. If she could get Lili's head in front before the sixteenth pole, she could beat him to the wire.

As they neared the turn, Andy angled Lili out slightly to give her enough room to switch to her left lead without hitting the rail. The filly switched smoothly and tugged even harder at the bit, eager to pick up the pace. But there was nowhere to go. Andy held the reins tightly, holding her back.

"Not yet, Lili, not yet," she muttered.

When they entered the homestretch, Andy prayed for room to get through. Carlo had his mount glued to the rail and Pedro was still beside him. Andy started to angle out when a horse appeared beside her, blocking her way out.

"Shit!" she swore between clenched teeth, pulling back on the reins when she wanted to turn her loose.

Benito's horse was fading in front, but neither Carlo nor Pedro were closing any ground on him.

"Hey, jock, let me out!" she screamed.

The horse stayed glued to her side. She looked over and recognized Eddie Flaherty.

"Eddie, let me out!" she pleaded.

He kept his gaze straight ahead.

"Dammit, Eddie, if you're not going anywhere, let me out!"

Eddie ignored her and kept his horse glued to her side.

Pedro had gained half a length on Carlo's horse who was still on the rail, but Eddie shadowed her movement and she couldn't get out. Benito's horse was fading badly out front even though he'd gone to the whip. Lili was pulling hard on the bit, her front legs coming dangerously close to Pedro's hind heels.

"To hell with this!" she swore, angling Lili out and taking Eddie with her.

"Hey, jock!" he hollered. "Take a hold of your horse!"

"You take a hold!" she yelled. "I'm getting the hell out of here!"

Lili surged forward the moment her path was clear. Within two strides, she was a neck behind Pedro. His whip suddenly flew into action. Andy didn't care if her knee came under attack again, she was determined to catch him. She urged Lili forward with every fibre of her being, scrubbing her neck with her hands, calling out encouragement. They closed on Pedro with every stride and passed the wire nose-to-nose.

Benito's exhausted horse had somehow managed to hang on by half a length.

Pedro glared at her as they stood up in their stirrups. "What the fuck you tryin' to prove!" he yelled. He spit a wad of dirt at her, but the wind carried it harmlessly away.

"I'm trying to win a damn race!" she retorted. "Maybe if you moved a little sooner, you'd be headed to the winner's circle."

"Shut the fuck up!" he screamed.

Andy was startled by his rage. She'd had disagreements with jockeys before, but had never encountered this kind of anger. Pedro veered his horse towards her, but Lili instinctively ducked away. Before he could come at her again, another horse galloped up between them.

"Something going on here?" Eddie asked.

"Fucking bitch can't keep her horse straight!" Pedro lied.

"Maybe you should head straight back yourself," Eddie advised him as they pulled their horses up to a walk.

Pedro yanked his horse around and galloped off. Eddie turned to Andy. "Where did you finish?"

"Too close to call," she replied, "But I could have won it easily if you'd gotten out of my way."

"All's fair in horse racing," he remarked, nodding in the direction of Pedro's receding back. "I'd stay out of his way if I were you."

She galloped back towards the unsaddling area, noticing Mickey sitting on bench in the grandstand. She smiled at him, but he didn't smile back.

Mickey's heart was racing faster than the horses in the stretch run. His gaze was fixed on the tote board. The photo sign was flashing.

Perry patted his shoulder. "I'm sure Pedro got there ahead of her."

Unable to speak, Mickey pointed in the direction of the girl who was dismounting, nodding his head up and down. Perry understood the sign language—go and listen. He moved quickly over to the fence to be within hearing distance.

"You were in tight quarters down the stretch," the trainer

said, his tone more one of worry than regret. "Did you clip heels?"

"Almost, but I managed to get out," she replied, "not soon enough to win, though. Damn it, we could have caught them!"

"Coulda, shoulda," Pete remarked as he inspected the horse's legs. "You're both back safe, that's all that matters. Luck just wasn't on our side this time."

"Luck had nothing to do with it. It's all the other jockeys, they're out to get me."

"First day at school is always rough."

"There's rough and then there's rough. I've got to let these guys know they can't push me around like this."

"Maybe, but you'll need a bigger horse than Lili to do that." Pete patted her on the shoulder. "And I've got just the horse for the job. I'll bring him in from the farm. You'll love Bruiser."

Andy's face broke out in a smile. "Bruiser? I love him already."

Perry spun on his heels and headed off towards Mickey, eager to relate what he'd just heard. Suddenly, the grandstand erupted in hoots and hollers. The results were flashed on the tote board.

"You did it, Mickey!" Perry yelled excitedly, slapping him on the back. "You pulled it off!"

Mickey took a long, deep breath and exhaled slowly.

"Too close for comfort," he said. "There's going to be some changes in our jockeys, that's for sure."

LIFE AT SUFFOLK DOWNS

"Charlie, come on, we've got to go." Andy stood in the hallway, her ear pressed to the bedroom door. "You up?"

All was silent. She opened the door. "Hey, Charlie, come on, up and at 'em."

A groan was the first sign of life.

"Time to rise and shine."

"Can't be. It's still dark."

Andy turned on the bedside lamp. "Not anymore."

Charlie yanked the blankets up over her head. "It isn't morning, it's the middle of the night!"

"Hey, you want to get up when normal people get up then go and work at the Gillette factory. They're always looking for people."

"Oh God," Charlie moaned. "You were so nice the first day. What happened? "

"I was on my best behaviour. This is the real me." Andy stood over the bed, her hands on her hips. "Look, I'm sorry, I don't mean to take my frustration out on you but honestly, we've got to get a move on."

Charlie slowly came out from under the blanket. "Tea ready?"

"Ya wanna drink tea, go ta Boston haw-boor." Andy failed miserably at mimicking Candace's accent, but it brought a smile to Charlie's face.

"Stick to your Ivy League accent," Charlie advised her,

sitting up and planting both feet on the cold floor. "How can you be so awake at this time of the morning?"

"It's my metabolism, I guess."

"Ridiculous! Nobody wakes up this early by choice." She yawned. "It doesn't make sense. How did the daughter of a history and a law professor end up on the racetrack?"

"Without their consent."

Charlie stretched. "Which one of them is the mean one that you take after?"

"Probably my mother, she isn't as popular as my dad. Everyone loves him."

"Maybe it's time you took after him." Charlie fell back onto the bed, her head slapping against the pillow. Andy yanked the blanket off and dropped it on the floor.

"I'll bring your coffee out to the car. See you there."

Twenty minutes later Andy had both dogs in the back seat and Charlie's steaming cup of coffee on the dashboard. She was about to go back in the house to raise a ruckus when Charlie appeared. She settled into her seat and didn't say another a word until she'd had several sips of coffee.

"Have your parents come to the track to watch you race?" Charlie asked, picking up the conversation as if there hadn't been a twenty minute interval.

"Are you kidding, they've never set foot on a racetrack in their lives."

"Where do they live?"

"In Syracuse, New York. "

"Have you invited them to Suffolk Downs?"

Andy laughed scornfully. "Wouldn't that be a treat, come and watch your daughter being massacred by a bunch of hooligans. That would really impress them."

The old Volvo was in a parking space that was tightly hemmed in. Andy inched back until she touched the bumper of the car behind. Charlie's coffee spilled into her lap.

"Sorry," Andy apologized. She waited for Charlie to take a few more gulps. "Ready?"

"With this jolt of caffeine, I probably don't need a ride. I could run all the way to the track."

"Great idea. And when you're able to run to the track and back home, you'll be ready for the Boston Marathon."

"And wouldn't I look cute in those tights they wear. I don't think they make them in my size." She took another gulp of coffee. "Of course, after running thirty miles a day for weeks, I'd have no problem fitting into them."

Andy put the car in gear. "And, we're off!"

Her imitation of Jim Hannon, the track announcer, was about as good as her imitation of Candace.

"You didn't do any theatre at school, did you?" Charlie commented.

"No, I was more interested in basketball."

Charlie almost choked on her coffee. "You're pulling my leg, you didn't play basketball."

"Did so. I could pretty much go through everyone's legs. And I had a mean hook shot. I won high scorer in our finals one year." She glanced over at Charlie. "Why are you so interested in my extracurricular activities?"

"Well, think about it, a jockey's career isn't very long. Even if you ride for another twenty years that puts you in your forties when you retire. What will you do then?"

"Obviously I don't have an acting career waiting for me," Andy said with a grin.

"Maybe I'll join the NBA."

"Come on, be serious."

"You've got me retired before I've even won my first race." Andy screeched to a halt at a red light and the few remaining drops of coffee spilled over.

"Wonderful, I'm up for barely thirty minutes and already I'm a mess."

"Don't worry, it'll blend in with the manure stains," Andy quipped. "I think I'd better concentrate on my driving or neither one of us will make it to old age."

"To be continued," Charlie said, wiping the coffee from

her jeans.

Traffic was light at this early hour of the morning and they arrived at the track well before five.

"Hey, sleepy head," Pete greeted his groom. "Where've you been? The day's half over."

"Sorry, boss, I think I'm still on Greenwich time." Charlie grabbed a pitchfork and a plastic tub and dragged it into a stall.

"I've never been able to figure out why wheelbarrows aren't allowed on the backstretch," Andy remarked. "It would make cleaning stalls a lot easier."

"Too dangerous," Pete replied. "Ever seen a horse get his legs tangled up in a wheelbarrow?"

"Naw, that's not how come," Candace said, throwing a western saddle up on Buck, the pony horse. "It's all because of ole man Morris. Back in his younger days, the ole man was a real gambler. They use to have a mutual window in the cook shack, so the grooms could bet their horses. But ole man Morris knew the skinny on all the races and he was taking his winnings out in a wheelbarrow. So they banned the damned things."

"Yeah, and if you believe that, I've got a Triple Crown winner here to sell you," Pete said, leading a stocky horse out of a stall. "Andy, meet Bruiser."

Andy walked slowly around the horse, inspecting him from every angle. She whistled long and low. "Well, hello Bruiser, am I glad to make your acquaintance."

The gelding was built like a Sherman tank, with a massive shoulder and hind end, good strong legs and a neck like a stallion.

"His registered name is Calling All Hands. Bred by a mariner I think."

"He certainly looks like he could handle himself in a sailor's bar." Andy patted his neck and the horse turned to look at her. His eyes were a soft brown, belying his macho appearance. "Does he actually fit into the starting gate?"

"How he goes into the gate doesn't matter as much as how he comes out." Pete touched the horse on the chest and he nodded his head as if to say yes. "This horse will go anywhere you put him. He'll go through the eye of a needle if you ask him. He's fearless."

"Holy crow!" Andy admired the horse even more. "He's built like a quarter horse. Is he a sprinter?"

"Yes and no."

Andy looked confused.

"He runs in little sprints. He'll give you a good kick out of the gate so you can get into position, then he'll take a breather. About half way down the backstretch, he'll give you another kick, get back into contention. He'll have one more kick down the stretch, but it's less than a sixteenth of a mile. You make your move too soon, you run out of gas."

"So this horse is all about strategy and timing?"

"Strategy, timing and a lot of luck," Pete agreed, legging her up into the saddle. "But Bruiser's first mission of the year isn't so much about winning as getting a message across to the boys."

Andy smiled down at Pete. "A message they won't forget."

"It might be just a single ride, though. He's Candace's favourite mount."

"Like I said, I'm not ready to hang up my tack. But I'll get ya other winners, don't ya worry."

Pete held up the condition book. "There's a race for Bruiser on Friday. Let's get out to the track and see how the two of you get along."

Pete followed her around the shed row. "Just play with him a little, get used to his way of going. Let him have a little spurt down the backstretch and again just passed the sixteenth pole. You'll get a feel for how far he wants to run, how much he's got to give you."

When they reached the track, no other horse and rider was in sight.

"Perfect," Pete said with a wave. "No one's going to know

about your secret weapon. Have your seat belt on when you ask him to go."

Andy jogged the big gelding down the homestretch. His movement wasn't what she would call free and easy but he was strong and sound. When he went into a gallop, she felt like she had something solid beneath her. He listened to her like a well trained ranch horse, responding to her every command. By the time she had completed the warm-up, he was ready. She turned him loose at the five-eighths pole and he accelerated like he was coming out of the gate. The moment she took a hold, he came back to her and they coasted around the turn and into the stretch. She watched the sixteenth pole slip by. After several strides, she chirped to him and his acceleration was even stronger.

"Amazing!" she called out as the wind whistled by her ears and made her eyes water. The moment she stood up in the stirrups, he relaxed, coming back to a slow hand gallop. "Bruiser, you are one fine horse."

She began the trek back along the outside rail when another horse appeared on the freshly harrowed track.

"Aren't you the early bird," Eddie Flaherty called out to her as he galloped by.

She glanced over at the big chestnut horse he was on.

"And what kind of secret training is he doing?" she muttered into the wind.

MICKEY PITCHES
THE SALE

Mickey watched the tractor move off the racetrack. He dug his toe into the surface. The freshly harrowed sand and loam spread out before him like a perfectly rolled carpet. The mid-morning break was just finishing. At eight o'clock sharp every morning the racetrack was harrowed in anticipation of the work-outs that would take place. A well groomed track made for a smoother, safer footing and the later hour suited many of the owners who liked to watch their horses work.

Some of the trainers preferred to train under the secrecy of darkness. Mickey often hid in a secluded corner of the grandstand, stop watch in hand. He had clocked several horses the past few mornings hoping to discover a good claim. The blistering workouts before daylight wouldn't be listed in the *Daily Racing Form*. The clocker didn't arrive that early.

There were a couple of workouts that had caught Mickey's eye. He'd done his research and knew their names. Cal, the official stall man at Suffolk Downs, was happy to supply the names on each trainer's list of horses, as long as a few bills greased his palm.

The horse that had caught Mickey's attention earlier that morning hadn't done a spectacular workout. Pete Mackenzie had sent the first horse out on the track at five am sharp. The New York girl was in the saddle. She had galloped the horse in an unusual way, giving him what looked like short wind sprints. Pete was up to something and Mickey figured he could make good use of it. The only way to derail the sale of the colt was to distract Pony with another payoff. If his pockets were full, Pony would forget about the sale at least for the time being.

Mickey looked over towards the grandstand. A man stood near the finish wire. Though he was almost a quarter of a mile away, Mickey had no trouble spotting him. Tommy's high roller, Mark Rodale, had what could only be called eclectic tastes. He wore a sports jacket of blue, green and orange plaid, a salmon coloured shirt and a green felt fedora. Several fat cigars peeked out of his top breast pocket. Not that Mickey could see the cigars from this distance but an earthy, peppery odour of smoke still clung to his nostrils just from standing next to the man for a mere ten minutes.

In that short time he'd learned Mr Rodale made his money in Vegas. Not from rolling dice at the black jack tables but from owning the tables. The man kept his cards close to his chest. Rodale was more the type to ask questions than to answer them. Mickey sensed he wasn't the neophyte that Tommy thought he was, but rather a shrewd, if not totally honest, businessman who was eager to get into horse racing. Rodale had done his homework. He knew how much Mickey had paid for the colt at the Kentucky auction and that the crooked leg had been the reason for the low price.

Tommy's claim that the leg was a hundred percent sound hadn't totally convinced Rodale, especially with the six figure price they were asking. That was Mickey's ace in the hole. He planned on making good use of that doubt to negate the sale. But he had to play his hand cautiously.

He turned away from the track and walked the short distance to Emmett's barn. Several horses were being led around the shed row, tacked up and awaiting their riders.

Mickey inspected the leggy bay colt that Alonzo was leading. Pony's price was a bargain. The colt looked like a million bucks.

When Alonzo halted the horse next to one of the exercise riders, Mickey shook his head.

"Where's the girl?" he called over to him.

Alonzo looked confused. "Chica?"

"The girl who rode him the last time. Where is she?"

Mustang appeared seemingly from thin air. "The broad from New York? She just came that one day with Candace. She's not one of our regular riders."

"She is now," Mickey said firmly. "I want her on this horse."

Mustang opened her mouth, ready to argue, but seemed to think better of it.

"Ringo!" she hollered, spinning on her heels. "Where's Sandy?"

Ringo stepped out of the tack room, coffee cup in hand. He shrugged his shoulders. "I don't know, in Mackenzie's barn, I guess."

"Well, get her in this barn," Mustang ordered. "We need her."

Mickey motioned to Ringo and handed him a five dollar bill. "Get her here as quickly as you can. I want to be the first one out on the track after the break."

"No problem, man." Ringo moved off with a smile, stashing the bill in his back pocket. He crossed the road to Mackenzie's barn.

"*Help, I need somebody,*" he sang out in full voice as he entered the barn, "*not just anybody!* Sandy Andy!"

Andy's head popped out of the middle stall. "I've got a couple of horses to get on here, Ringo, then I'll be over."

Ringo shook his head. "Won't do. The Candy Man wants you, pronto. Come on, it'll be well worth your while, believe me. Like I said, he's the generous type."

"I'll be there as soon as I'm done."

"Who wants her?" Candace asked as she strode down the aisle.

"The big owner wants her."

Candace tossed Andy her helmet. "Get ya skinny ass over to Emmett's barn. I'll gallop Tim."

"What, I'm supposed to drop everything and waltz over there whenever the big trainer calls?"

"When his top owner calls, ya run."

Andy glared at Candace. "I need a better reason than that."

"Cause ya want the best hosses on the grounds so ya can win a lot of races and get ya ass back to New York."

Andy plunked her helmet on her head. "Alright, I'll do it but I don't have to like it."

"We'd better hurry," Ringo advised her, "he wants to be the first to cut up the track."

Even when Ringo was hurrying, he moved at a turtle's pace. Andy had to slow down to match his stride. That was okay with her, she wasn't in any hurry.

"I think maybe this guy's sweet on you," Ringo said, giving her his puppy dog grin. "I mean, he's kinda eerie but he's loaded. Slips us a tenner when his horses have a good workout, more when they win. Give him a big smile, Sandy Andy, he's worth it."

"I'll save my smiles for the guys who deserve it." She turned and gave Ringo a big grin.

He giggled.

Andy was so surprised to hear a man giggle that she giggled back, which surprised her even more. But her mood turned serious when they entered the barn. Mickey Amato was tapping his foot impatiently, his face an unreadable mask. He waved to Alonzo who led the horse over to Andy.

"The proprietor—the owner, he want you ride his horse."

Andy forgot about her anger when she recognized the bay colt. "Okay, give me a leg up, Al, before Mr Sleazy comes over."

Al hoisted her up and she rode the horse along the aisle. As she passed Mickey, he took a hold of the horse's reins.

"He's going to breeze this morning," he explained in a brisk, business like tone. "I don't want to break any records. You can wave the whip to keep him focused, but don't touch him with it. I just want him to stretch his legs for a quarter of a mile."

He was walking beside her, his stride as long as the colt's. Only when they reached the gap and the colt began to prance did she pull ahead of him.

For the second time that day, Andy rode onto a perfectly harrowed track. There was no one in front of her as she trotted down the stretch and passed the wire. She released her hold slightly and allowed the colt to break into a gallop. Without another horse to keep him company, his attention wandered and he travelled a meandering course from side to side. The only way to get him to steer a straight path would be to pick up the pace but Mr. Amato had been very clear about that. He didn't want a fast workout, just a breeze.

Andy understood the importance of protecting not only the young horse's legs, but his mind. Too many fast workouts would make the colt speed crazy. The most important lesson a racehorse had to learn was how to run in a relaxed state of mind. Unlike a car, horses didn't come with gears and a brake. A fit racehorse was inclined to go from first gear to overdrive in a fraction of a second.

As she completed a mile warm-up, the colt became bored with the slow pace. He bucked in his impatience to go faster. When she wouldn't let him accelerate, he bucked again.

"Alright, we can move out a little bit but this isn't a race. Let's just keep it under control."

She released the reins by a couple of inches and prayed the exuberant colt wouldn't run off. She kept him in the middle of the track. The inside track was for speed work, the middle for galloping and the outside for pulling up. The colt stretched out his legs, his stride covering the ground effort-lessly. Andy had never felt such a smooth acceleration. As she headed into the turn, she angled over towards the inside rail.

The colt knew immediately what this meant.

In his excitement to run, he began climbing with his front legs. His energy was going up instead of forward. Andy bent lower and spoke to him. "Easy, now, big boy, settle down. Just reach out nice and easy, that's all I want."

The colt lowered his head in response to her soothing tone, his stride lengthening as they glided down the home-stretch. His stride was so smooth it felt like he was barely out of a gallop, but Andy knew they were covering the ground quickly. Instead of asking for more speed, she closed her hands on the reins and kept him at a steady rhythm.

This colt would one day break a record, she was certain of that, but not today.

BRUISER

Andy walked across the saddling paddock and looked the horses over as they were led around the small oval. Given the choice of any of the twelve horses in the race, she would pick her mount, Calling All Hands. He looked spectacular. She glanced over at the tote board. The bettors disagreed with her. They had him at thirty-five -to-one.

"I don't need to give you a lot of instructions," Pete said as she joined him in the saddling stall. "You know what you need to do. Just come back in one piece, both of you."

"I won't put your horse at risk," she promised.

"Or yourself," he added as he legged her up into the saddle. "The race is a mile and seventy yards. You've got the first turn and the backstretch to make your statement. Behave yourself in the homestretch. It'll be too obvious."

"We'll take care of it, don't worry."

Andy patted Bruiser as Charlie led him towards the track.

"You're not going to go bonkers out there, are you?" she asked, looking up at Andy with a worried expression.

"I won't do anything stupid, like put somebody in the hospital. I just need to make my point." She looked around at the other jockeys as they mounted up. "I guess it mean's I'll be on vacation for a few days but it'll be worth it."

"Look on the bright side. You'll have lots of time to decorate your room."

Andy filed in behind the number four horse when Charlie released her. As they paraded past the grandstand, she studied the competition. Several horses were covered with sweat even before the warm-up began. As was her habit, she memorised the silks of the riders she wanted to keep tabs on. Carlo wore red silks with green and yellow sleeves, Pedro was in black with a white vertical stripe and Eddie, fittingly, wore green. These were the three men that she wanted to impress the most. Benito was in white with blue hooped sleeves. She wanted to recognize him simply to stay out of his way. Farrell Kohler was in blue with green diamonds. He was known to lock you in on the rail or take you wide to get the advantage. She would definitely steer clear of him.

The jockey on the number ten horse was someone she'd read about, but hadn't met until today. Leo Valente was well into his fifties. He'd been riding at Suffolk Downs since the early forties. He'd ridden some top stakes horses in his halcyon days, but his career had tailed off a decade ago. He still rode for some of the older trainers but his mounts were sporadic. Andy figured he would know all the old tricks, having ridden in the era of George Wolf and Red Pollard, but when she'd asked around, she was told he was a gentleman.

"If Leo's beside you, you've got nothing to worry about," Denise had assured her.

Leo was not on Andy's hit list.

"Okay, Bruiser, let's warm up," she said to her horse. "You'll need to move forwards, backwards or sideways at a moment's notice so let's get you nice and limber."

She galloped by the clubhouse where Mickey watched her closely. He'd thought Pete was planning an early win with this experienced horse and had planned to make a big bet until Perry insisted this was a revenge ride that he heard about in the conversation the girl had with Mackenzie after her first day of racing. It made sense. The girl had to get across to the boys that she meant business. Calling All Hands was big enough and experienced enough to help her make a statement. The conditions of the race weren't ideal for this particular horse. He wasn't a fast sprinter, but neither did he have the endurance for a distance race. Seven furlongs was his speciality and yet here he was going a mile and seventy yards.

Mickey put his high powered binoculars on the girl as she was led into the starting gate.

Andy was the first one in. She tried to relax while the other horses were loaded. She took several deep breaths, exhaling slowly to calm her racing pulse.

It suddenly struck her that this was a bad idea. What had she been thinking? She didn't know how to shut riders off or keep them boxed in. She'd never been taught those kinds of tactics. If she attempted such dangerous techniques she would be putting everyone at risk.

"Last horse coming in. Get tied on, riders!"

Bertram's voice brought her attention back in focus. She got into position.

The gate opened. Bruiser hesitated and then launched himself from the gate. The horses on either side of her broke quickly and narrowed the gap between them. Bruiser slowed his stride.

"Son of a bitch!" she swore as the outside horse took the position she wanted.

She settled in behind Eddie and Pedro. They both had a hold on their horses. She sensed they were deliberately setting a slow pace in the hope that they would have some reserve for the homestretch.

"To hell with that!" she muttered.

She swung to the outside. She was now in the unenviable position of three horses wide going into the first turn, not a strategic move if she were trying to win the race. As a tactical move, she was now in a position to implement her plan.

Closing in on the horse directly inside her, she touched Eddie's boot with her own. His horse moved away from her, closing in on Pedro.

"Hey!" Pedro yelled. "It's gettin' tight in here! Lay off me!"

A horse loomed up on the outside of Andy. She couldn't believe someone would go four horses wide and lose all that ground. She glanced over and saw that it was Farrell. Whatever his reason for being there, it was an opportunity she wasn't about to miss. The moment he settled into stride beside her, she swung Bruiser out and bumped his horse's shoulder. The contact sent him even wider. He lost several more lengths and slipped back out of her view.

She put her focus on the horses in front. Leo Valente was directly in front of her with Benito in his favourite position on the lead. The French Canadian jockey, Yves LeBlanc, was at Benito's heels. They were both setting an extremely slow pace. Pedro and Eddie were caught in a traffic jam. She held her position and kept them locked in well into the backstretch.

Pedro screamed again, ordering Eddie to give him some room. Andy decided her point had been made and moved on. She clucked to Bruiser and he gave her a burst of speed. As she moved along the outside, Eddie and Pedro made their way through on the inside, moving in tandem with her as all three of them passed Leo. Within a few strides, they were three abreast again with Leo behind them.

Pedro and Eddie were looking for an opportunity to catch up to the leaders and force a faster pace but there was no daylight between Benito and Yves. Andy could feel Eddie staring at her, but she refused to acknowledge him. She kept her eyes straight ahead. When his boot touched hers, she knew he would try to force her wide and slip through to join the leaders.

She held Bruiser steady. The powerful gelding wasn't intimidated by physical contact and leaned in against Eddie's horse. He wasn't going anywhere.

An angry voice called out from behind. "Come on, ass-holes, if you're not going anywhere, get out of the way!"

She glanced under her arm and saw that Carlo was directly behind Eddie. Leo was blocking his outside path.

"I think you're the one who isn't going anywhere, Carlo," she shouted back at him.

Benito's horse in the lead tired dramatically and lost ground, causing a traffic jam behind him. The sound of heels clipping competed with the screams of jockeys.

"I'm goin' down, let me out!" Pedro hollered.

"Give me a break!" Eddie yelled in unison.

Andy immediately pulled out. Before Eddie could move, Carlo rushed up to take her position. Pedro and Eddie were standing straight up in the stirrup, hauling back on the reins and screaming at the top of their lungs. If either of their horses' front legs tangled with the lethal heels in front, they would flip.

"Back off, Carlo!" she yelled. "You're going to kill them!"

"Shut up bitch!"

With that, Carlo swept passed her to join the leaders. She stayed out in the middle of the track. Eddie swerved his horse out and Pedro followed, just as his horse touched the heels in front and stumbled.

Pedro managed to keep his horse up, but faded to the back of the pack.

It wasn't time for her to make her second move, but she couldn't let Carlo get away. She slapped Bruiser on the shoulder and he spurted forward, drawing up beside Carlo as they entered the final turn. Yves had taken over the lead and was a couple of lengths ahead. She steered Bruiser sharply to the left and bounced Carlo off the rail.

"What the fuck ya tryin' to prove?" Carlo snarled in her direction.

She hit him again, just to make her point. He swung at her with his whip, but Andy ducked away. She kept Carlo in tight against the rail, her eyes on Yves' horse as they entered the home stretch. Just before the sixteenth pole, the leader's stride shortened almost as quickly as Benito's horse had done. She kept Carlo tucked in with nowhere to go.

The horses that had been trailing the field suddenly made

their move. A jockey's shrill whistle sounded behind her as Eddie caught up. Andy asked Bruiser for one last attempt, slapping his hindquarters with her whip. The courageous gelding gave her a burst of speed, joining the late closers as they bore down on the wire.

In the last few strides, she recognized a voice directly behind her. It was Farrell hollering at his horse and trying desperately to make up the ground he'd lost on the first turn. She glanced under her arm and saw him creeping up on her outside. She cocked her whip and got it in position. She didn't know if she had the accuracy to make contact, but she'd give it a try.

His horse appeared in her peripheral vision. He was at Bruiser's haunches, inching forward slowly. When his head was just up past her boot, she took aim and swung back with full force. She heard the smack as she came into contact with something harder than horseflesh.

Farrell's holler turned into a scream of pain.

"Eureka!" she called out as she crossed the wire.

She decided it would be a good idea to keep her distance from the other jockeys as she pulled up. The sound of galloping hooves behind put her on alert. Carlo ducked in as he passed, hitting Bruiser even harder than she had hit him. Andy lost her stirrups, but managed to stay aboard.

"You can dish it out, but you can't take it, huh?" she called out after him, putting her feet back in the stirrups before heading off to the unsaddling area.

Pete was waiting for her, his face a mask of worry. "Any wounds?" He looked his horse over quickly.

"Bruiser's fine," she assured him. "Me too."

When he'd finished his inspection, he looked up at her and smiled. "Congratulations, you're now one of the boys."

Andy slipped out of the saddle and landed squarely on her feet. "I don't ever want to ride like that again."

A buzz went through the grandstand as bettors threw tickets on the ground or whooped excitedly. She turned to the tote board and saw her number in third position.

"You've got to be kidding. We hit the board?"

Immediately, her number began flashing.

Jim Hannon's voice came over the PA system. "There is a steward's inquiry into the running of the third race. Please hold all tickets until it is made official."

"Was there anyone you didn't interfere with?" Pete asked.

"Yeah, the guys that finished first and second. I couldn't catch them."

Andy pulled her saddle off and headed to the scales. Carlo made a lunge at her, but the clerk of scales stepped between them.

"Back off, Carlo," Gerry said firmly. "Go wait in line."

Several jockeys were queued in front of the phone. It was a direct line to the stewards' room up in the towers. Pedro was shouting into the phone in Spanish with Farrell waiting impatiently behind him, rubbing his knee. Andy kept her distance. The stewards would catch up to her soon enough.

She walked quickly across the saddling paddock. Someone caught her eye and she glanced over to the clubhouse. Mickey Amato nodded in her direction. It was the first time she'd seen him smile.

PONY'S CELEBRATION

Mickey walked along the darkened street until he found the place he had been looking for, the Back Side Restaurant. Though this was one of Pony's favourite haunts, Mickey had never been here. Unfamiliar with the town of Dedham, he had taken several wrong turns on the drive from South Boston.

He welcomed the warmth inside the restaurant as he stepped out of the raw spring air. It was past the dinner hour and too early for the night crowd though a couple of guys at a nearby table were well into their cups, loudly proclaiming their allegiance to the Boston Red Sox.

"This would be a good time to shut up!" a voice boomed from across the room. Mickey was as startled as the two baseball fans. He looked over to a corner booth deep in the shadows of the dimly lit room and recognized Pony's back. The man seated beside him continued, "That's better!"

The voice carried enough authority to silence the fans. Mickey instinctively stepped back out of view as he scanned the faces at Pony's table. He had no problem identifying the man who sat directly across the table from Pony. Whitey Bulger. Hard bodied and fit, his signature blond hair swept back, he sat with an arm casually spread out along the seat back. His piercing blue eyes were focused on Pony.

Mickey knew he wouldn't be welcomed at the table, which was fine with him. He discreetly made his way across the room and ordered a scotch. A long mirror several feet above the bar made it possible for him to watch what was going on behind him.

"Hey, Mickey, there you are." Tommy slapped him on the back hard enough to knock the glass out of his hand. "Come on, bring your drink and we'll grab a table. They've got great steaks here."

He followed Tommy to a table in the middle of the room.

"Everything okay with Pony?" Mickey asked.

"More than okay," Tommy said with a grin. "The payoff has made for a lot of happy people."

Just as they sat down, Pony lumbered over. "There he is, the man 'a the hour. Hey, class act, why aren't ya drinking champagne? Time to celebrate."

Pony waved to the bartender. "Hey, Norm, bring us a bottle 'a that Mott 'an Candone."

"Not so sure we have the French stuff, but I'll bring ya what we got."

"Yeah, bring the best ya got." Pony slapped the table with gusto. "Who'd 'a thought you'd be the big handicapper, Mick. Your nonno could train a hoss better'n anybody, but he never went near the windows. Against his religion. "

Broedy Sheehan would be turning over in his grave if he knew what his grandson was doing, Mickey thought grimly.

The bartender appeared with a bottle and three champagne glasses. He held it up for Pony to read the label.

"Cook's," Pony said, nodding with satisfaction. "Ya, I like that. We cooked us a good one, didn't we?"

Tommy and the bartender laughed appreciatively. Mickey forced a smile. Sparkling wines gave him a headache. He hoped he could make it home before it started.

When the bartender popped the cork, Whitey and his crew leaped out of their chairs.

"Friendly fire," Pony called over with a laugh.

Whitey didn't look amused. He scowled at the bartender who quickly filled the glasses and left the bottle on the table.

"To Mick," Pony said, holding up his glass. "I knew ya

had it in ya."

Tommy and Pony drained their glasses.

"Tommy says the other boys rode good but Pedro almost blew it," Pony said as he refilled his glass. "He says some broad just about caught him at the wire. That the way it went down?"

Mickey took a sip of champagne, giving himself time to consider his reply. He had to steer this conversation in the right direction.

"Last thing I need is another bug rider messin' up my perfecta." Pony complained.

"I wanted to talk to you about that," Mickey said, his plan taking solid shape in his mind.

"I knew ya'd have a plan. Told Tommy ya'd know what to do." He drained his glass again. "So what do we do to get rid of the broad?"

Mickey wasn't comfortable with his new role as strategist for *Anthony Cantoni Race Fixing Ltd*. He needed to tread carefully, promise only what he knew he could deliver.

"I've been watching this girl apprentice since she arrived from New York," he explained. "She's from Barry Locke's stable. He's a top trainer and only hires the best so I knew she had some talent."

"If she's so good, why'd he dump her?" Pony demanded.

"From what I've heard, his top owner had a son who wanted to ride. He had to let her go, even if he didn't want to."

"Ah, gees, I'm gonna cry. Boo hoo!" Pony pretended to wipe away the tears. Tommy laughed along with him, but Mickey continued.

"I didn't know if she could adapt to the Boston style of riding. The boys tested her pretty good, but the girl didn't back off. Instead, she got herself a Sherman tank and gave them even better than she got."

Pony sat up a little straighter. Mickey had his attention.

"Believe me, this girl's got guts. And talent. She gets

horses to run and she puts them through holes that aren't even there. And the horses love her, they'll give her everything they've got."

Pony rubbed his hands together, greedy with anticipation. "And she's hungry, right? We put her on the payroll?"

Mickey shook his head. "The last thing we need is another Smartalex. All bug riders think they're the next Shoemaker, their heads full of glory and riches. It's the has-beens that'll take a bribe, but they won't take any risks. This girl will." He leaned in closer, to make his point. "She just about beat us on a long shot, even with the boys trying to hold her back. So why don't we get them to clear her path? She'll break her maiden by a city block."

Pony slammed a fist down onto the table, rattling the glasses. "What the hell ya telling me, the broad hasn't even won a race?"

Pony's tantrum drew the attention of the gangsters. A glare from Whitey acted as a warning.

Mickey drained his glass as Pony finished the bottle of champagne.

"She hasn't won because our boys have done everything they could to mess her up. Even with them in the way, she rides right into the photo finish." He turned to Tommy. "She kept your brother in his place today."

"She stopped Eddie?" Tommy asked in disbelief.

"She gave him a taste of his own medicine," Mickey said with an emphatic nod. "On a long shot. Even the bettors figured she didn't have a shot."

Pony was back to rubbing his hands. "This is sounding better and better. If ya think she's got the goods, we'll give her a test run."

"Sounds good," Tommy agreed, "but first, I've got a good one coming up. Carlo and Pedro are on board."

Mickey shook his head. "Don't count on it, Tommy. Looks like Carlo is going on vacation. He had some issues with the girl, got a little hot under the collar."

"Sonamabitch!" Pony yelled.

Tommy shook his head. "Don't worry about a thing, Pony, I'll bring in the Rhode Island boys. They'll get the job done."

Mickey marvelled at Tommy's bravado. His whole plan had been shot down in an instant and he barely even blinked. Getting his Rhode Island boys on the horses would be no easy feat. The Boston trainers preferred their own riders.

"And what about your chicken shit fratello?" Pony demanded. "Eddie can't be letting a broad push him around."

"He'll take care of her," Tommy promised.

Pony swung back to Mickey. "Okay, Mick, we get this one down and then we try the broad, break her maiden and make a killing."

Mickey nodded as he sat back in his chair and relaxed. Someone had joined Whitey's table and distracted him from their business.

"Ya talked to this high roller, this Rodale? He ready with the cash?" Pony demanded.

Mickey cautioned himself to tread carefully. The last thing he wanted to do was rile Pony.

"Mr Rodale isn't as much of a chump as he seemed to be."

The glare this time came from Tommy. "What are you talking about? Have you met the guy? You've seen his suits?"

Mickey nodded, keeping his voice calm. "The guy's eccentric alright, but he's done his homework. He's not convinced the colt is a hundred percent sound."

Pony glared at Tommy. "I thought ya told him the crooked leg was all fixed?"

"I did," Tommy assured him. "He sure looked convinced to me."

"He probably was at the time, but he's been asking around. He knew what we paid for the colt at the auction. Naturally, he's suspicious of the six figure price we're asking, especially when the horse hasn't raced." Mickey felt the big man's rage building. "I brought the colt out on the track and gave him a good breeze, good enough to keep Rodale nibbling at the bait," he added quickly.

Pony fidgeted in his chair, but the explosion was stemmed. Mickey jumped in. "It'll give us time to consider our options with the colt."

"What are you talking about, options? Ya got someone else, wants to pay more?" Pony drummed the table top with his fingers.

"Not exactly, but listen, Pony, I think we've got the best colt on the grounds. This is the horse that could take us to Kentucky."

Pony's laugh could be heard clear across the room. Mickey quickly glanced over at the corner table. Whitey was tightening his grip on the tie while the man's lips turned blue.

"Come on, Mick, ya been drinking ya bathwater or what?"

Mickey reached into his pocket and took out a stopwatch, handing it to Tommy.

"Twenty-three ," Tommy read. "Decent for a quarter of a mile workout, but nothing special."

Mickey shook his head. "That wasn't a workout, it was just a gallop. I told the girl to keep him under wraps. He was barely striding out."

Tommy handed the stopwatch to Pony.

"Come on, Mick, a fast gallop in the morning don't mean nothing," Pony insisted. "He could be just another morning glory."

"This colt is the real thing." Mickey squared his shoulders to back up his boast. "Are you sure you want to sell Rodale the next Kentucky Derby winner?"

For once, Pony didn't laugh. "This the hoss talking or the bubbly?"

"There's only one way to find out." Mickey took a condition book out of his pocket and held it up. "We put him in a race and let him show us just what kind of horse he really is."

LOST CHIVALRY

"It would have been nice to keep the show money." Pete sighed as he hung up a bridle.

Andy paced around the small tack room. "Surely they won't give me days. You've got to kill someone to get a suspension around here. Isn't that what you said, Candace?"

"Yeah, or knock the hell out of half the hosses in the race," Candace said with a smirk. "Ya got your message across. That's all that matters."

"I got my message across alright but just how will the boys will take it? Are they thinking, 'Don't mess with Andy Crowley,' or is more like, "Kill the bitch!'"

"Carlo and Pedro will have some new respect for your riding skills," Pete assured her, "but they won't want you interfering with their little plans."

"Yeah, ya still need eyes in the back of your helmet," Candace advised her.

"Damn it, if it's so obvious these guys are playing games, why doesn't somebody do something about it?" Andy demanded.

"You should know the answer to that," Pete replied. "Your mother teaches law."

Andy expelled her breath in a long sigh. "Evidence."

"Exactly. Come up with solid evidence and those boys are out for life."

"I'm here to ride races, Pete, not play Columbo." She

turned an empty water bucket over and sat on it.

"If ya can't beat 'em..." Candace said.

"No way!" Andy exclaimed. "I'm not becoming one of them. I'll pack my tack and find another racetrack before I'll ride like a kamikaze pilot again."

"You've got to remember, some of us started riding on the fair grounds. Whips weren't just for hitting hosses, we used them to defend ourselves." Candace gave her a big grin. "Farrell was still howling this morning. Said he had to ice his knee all night."

Andy stomped her foot on the floor in agitation. "Those kinds of tactics may work at the fairs, but this is the A circuit—at least it's supposed to be."

"Yeah, okay, some of the guys need to smarten up, but being nice won't get ya anywhere. Look at Leo Valente, he's a nice guy. Sure don't get him a lot of rides."

Andy slumped back against the wall. "Somebody's got to clean this place up."

"That would be The Lone Ranger?" Charlie suggested as she stepped into the tack room and joined the conversation.

"Without the mask." Andy suddenly sat up straight, her expression changing. "I know just the man. Arthur Healey."

"Give me a break," Candace protested. "The stewards are nothing but a bunch of fucking retards. They don't have the balls!"

"Tinballs isn't exactly living up to his name, I agree, Mr Healey is showing some courage."

"Naw, he's just making noise. Tinballs calls the shots."

"Dick Trumball doesn't take any shots at all," Andy insisted. "For God's sake, he's reading the Boston Globe while the replays are going on. He doesn't give a damn what's happening out there on the racetrack."

"They're not going to replace him. He's been head steward since the track opened."

"Not quite," Pete corrected her. "Suffolk Downs opened in 1935. Trumball didn't become a steward until1950, the year he turned his business over to his son."

"What kind of business did he have?" Charlie asked.

"A meat packing plant," Pete replied.

Charlie winced. "Not exactly an ideal background for a racing steward."

"He probably came to the track to get more business," Andy suggested.

Pete shook his head. "He doesn't deal in horse meat. If he did, he'd send the carcasses to his foxhunting club."

"Foxhunting?" Andy had a sudden realization. "Okay, now I see how he got the position, he's connected. For all we know, he may have been a good steward back in the fifties, but it's the seventies, time for him to retire."

"Get used to it, Andy. On the track, ya'll rub elbows with—"

"Yeah, yeah, I've heard that one. You'll rub elbows with royalty on one side and the scum of the earth on the other."

"There's an awful lot in between the two," Charlie reminded them.

"Absolutely," Pete agreed as he poured a cup of coffee from an old, battered percolator. "That's the wonderful thing about the racetrack, you meet people from all walks of life. There's Mavis Morehead, the trainer just on the other side of the road. She's a nurse by profession. She works the night-shift at Malden Memorial and then comes here to condition her horses when her shift ends."

Andy looked over at Candace. "How come you haven't introduced me to her?"

"Mavis uses a needle in the barn even better than at the hospital."

"Okay, we'll skip her."

"And there's George Finnigan, a retired schoolteacher," Pete continued.

"I'll bet he has smart horses," Charlie quipped.

"He's only got two hosses and they're just like the juvenile delinquents he used to teach," Candace insisted.

"Okay, Candace, I defer to your judgement when it comes to choosing trainers, but I don't agree with your fairground riding techniques. Pedro actually knocked my foot out of the stirrup when we broke from the gate."

"That's an old one." Candace couldn't hold back a chuckle.

"That might be amusing in a 1950's movie, but not in real life. How about using strategy and riding skills? Can't anybody here do that?"

"Leo Valente's doing it and look what it gets him, one or two mounts a week."

"Listen you're both right. Saying please and thank you won't get you to the wire first, Andy, but neither will flipping a rider out of the saddle." Pete filled a cup with coffee and handed it to Andy. "You don't have to kill somebody to get into the winner's circle, but you've got to take a shot here and there."

"I can't use the tricks Pedro and Carlo use. I'm not built that way."

"Ya did a fine job yesterday." Candace remarked.

"That was a once in a lifetime ride. If I got my message across, it was worth it, but I'm not going to ride like that every day. And I won't have to if somebody cleans this place up. My money is on Arthur Healey to get the job done."

"Mr. Healey will need support if he's going to clean this place up," Charlie suggested. "Even the Lone Ranger had Tonto."

"Nobody's galloping in to clean up Dodge. Just roll with the punches, Andy, ya gotta give as good as ya get. Tinballs is wearing the badge and the only way he's leaving Dodge is in a pine box." Candace picked up her grooming kit and walked out to the shed row.

Pete looked at his watch. "Looks like it's time for you to get to the jockeys' room. You're probably the star attraction at films today. Don't let your Irish temper get the better of you, Andy. Stay cool."

Andy grabbed her helmet. "Right. Three deep breaths before I speak."

"I'll walk you to the grandstand," Charlie offered as she followed her out the door. They both stroked the horses as they passed their stalls.

"I have to admit, I've never liked westerns," Charlie remarked. "They're all about drought, starving cattle and gunfights at dawn."

"I watched them because they had horses," Andy told her. "I was always more interested in Silver than the Lone Ranger."

"Then maybe we need to change our theme. Instead of stampedes and shoot outs, how about some chivalry?"

Andy smiled as her mind conjured up images of knights in shining armour. "That's a great idea. Instead of Dodge City, we could have Camelot."

"Wouldn't you rather rub elbows with the Knights of the Round Table than Jesse James and his gang?"

"You bet." Her imagination was in full swing. "I can see it now. When the starting gate opens, it'll be ladies first."

"That might be asking a little too much," Charlie chuckled.

"You're right. That's not what the concept of the round table was about anyway. It was all about equality. I'm not asking for any special favours, just honest competition."

"We would have to start by having a Knighting ceremony."

Andy imagined the jockeys in armour and chain mail rather than silks. "Sir Eddie Flaherty, Sir Liam Brady." She thought about that for a moment. "Maybe, but Sir Carlo Gessani and Sir Pedro Vargas? It doesn't fit, even in my imagination."

"They're the dark knights," Charlie insisted. "Every fable has its villains."

They had reached the saddling paddock, empty at this early hour.

"Okay, keep the image of chivalry in your mind

throughout the films. If you get a suspension, accept your penance graciously."

Andy turned to her and bowed. "Yes, noble advisor. I'll do my best."

She tried to whistle as she walked across the paddock. She'd been practicing for days, hoping to reach Eddie's pitch, but hadn't come close.

As she was about to walk down the steps leading to the jockeys' room, she had a sudden flash. She spun on her heels.

"Hey Charlie!" she called out, running back across the paddock. "Camelot is perfect!"

"Why?" Charlie asked.

Andy beamed with excitement. "We have our Arthur!"

A NEW ERA

An electric energy filled the air. Andy had never seen so many jockeys in one room. Even the ones who didn't have a mount that day had come to watch the replays.

She noticed Leo Valente standing at the back of the room. His mannerisms and his attire were from a previous era. He wore grey flannel pants, a white shirt and tie with a blue and grey checked vest. He nodded politely when the stewards entered the room.

Arthur jostled his way through the crowd with John Baxter close at his heels. The door closed without any sign of Dick Trumball.

When he reached the table, Arthur held his hands up in the air and called for silence. He was barely heard over the chaos. He slammed the book he was carrying down on the table. "Everybody sit down and be quiet!"

His voice powered over the din. The jockeys began taking their seats and within seconds, the room quieted. Andy sat at the back with Candace.

"I have an important announcement to make," Arthur said, moving to the front of the room as Baxter took his place behind the table. "I'm afraid I have some shocking and rather sad news to report. If I could have your attention."

He waited until the scraping of chairs had quieted and he was sure everyone was paying attention.

"At a very early hour this morning, our head steward, Dick Trumball, suffered a fatal heart attack."

A buzz swept through the room, hitting Andy at the same time that the information sank in.

"Oh my God!" she exclaimed.

"I told ya he'd go out in a box," Candace said, nudging her with her elbow. "What are ya looking so surprised about? Ya said yourself it was time for the old guy to retire."

"Retire, yes, but not die."A wave of guilt flooded her senses. "You don't think it happened while we were talking about him, do you?"

"Your attention please," Arthur called out. The jockeys continued to talk excitedly amongst themselves.

"Silence!"

There was a new tone of authority to Arthur's voice. The chatter receded.

"Would you all stand, please," Arthur directed them in a quieter tone. "We will give a minute of silence in honour of Mr. Trumball."

Everyone stood. Andy closed her eyes and tried to focus on inward stillness, but her imagination went into full gallop. The Knights of the Round Table were in armour, galloping their steeds across the battlefield. The enemy were throwing down their arms. Carlo and Pedro were on their knees, begging for mercy.

"You can take your seats now," Arthur instructed them.

Andy opened her eyes. Arthur somehow looked taller.

"I have been appointed the new head steward," he announced. "Before we begin the replays, I would like to say a few words."

The newly appointed head steward took a step forward, scanning the faces in the front row, meeting their eyes with a steady gaze. "I don't care for the calibre of riding that has been going on around here. Many of you look more like rodeo cowboys than professional jockeys." His focus moved to the back row and the jockeys leaning against the wall. "But that's about to change."

Andy sat up straight, literally on the edge of her seat.

"I expect to see good, clean riding, no more wild west show. Every one of you will employ strategy and professional tactics from now on. Mr. Baxter and I will be watching your every move, from gate to wire. Any and all infractions will be dealt with severely. If you want to shut off another rider, carry them wide or slam them against the rail, be prepared to take a vacation." His eyes swept the room. "A long one."

A pin dropped at that moment would have startled everyone in the room. Arthur strode across the room and sat down beside Mr Baxter. He picked up the phone receiver and asked Don to play the first race.

"Welcome to Camelot," Andy said with a big smile.

"What?" Candace asked.

"I'll explain later."

The television screen sprang to life as the horses from yesterday's first race appeared in the starting gate. Andy's smile faded. Her dream was about to become a nightmare. The first race was Bruiser's race.

She slumped in her chair. King Arthur had ascended the throne one day too early.

The gate opened and twelve horses lunged out of the gate. Carlo's horse ducked to the left and hit Andy. A collective gasp was heard as she tipped over her horse's shoulder.

"What in the world was going on there, Carlo?" Arthur demanded.

"Her horse came into my path," Carlo insisted.

"I think your compass is off, Carlo." Arthur picked up the receiver. "Don, run that again."

The film rewound and all eyes were on Carlo as he swerved left out of the gate and collided with Andy.

"This is a perfect example of the rodeo riding I referred to," Arthur stated adamantly. "For God's sake, it's dangerous enough out there. You've got each other's lives in your hands!"

"I can't help it if my horse leans on the gate when he breaks," Carlo insisted. "What am I supposed to do, hold up a thousand pounds?"

"That's exactly what you're supposed to do," Arthur told him. "Hold your horse up and keep him on a straight path."

"What, I'm Hercules now?" Carlo had never agreed with a steward's assessment and wasn't about to start now.

"Okay, Don, keep the film rolling," Arthur said into the phone.

The horses galloped into the first turn and Andy held her breath. Farrell went wide and came up beside her when his horse suddenly veered out.

"What was happening there, Farrell?"

Farrell looked over at Arthur, shaking his head. Andy could see by the look on his face that he was confused.

"I don't know, I was in a good position and then my horse started to bolt. I couldn't straighten him out till we got to the middle of the track. Completely lost my position by then."

From the angle of the camera, it wasn't obvious that Bruiser had bumped him. Farrell was obviously so accustomed to rough riding he didn't recognize a deliberate hit. Andy expelled her breath.

The backstretch camera picked up the action and Andy spotted herself on the outside passing Leo's horse. Eddie and Pedro were passing him on the inside. As Eddie came up alongside Leo's horse, they made contact.

"Run that last eighth of a mile again, Don. I want to see what's happening."

A closer look at the film showed Pedro's horse ducked out and pushed Eddie into Leo.

"Nothing serious," Leo said when Arthur looked in his direction.

Benito's horse tired on the front end and the traffic jam began.

"What's happening here?" Arthur demanded.

"My horse, he died, like that!" Benito snapped his fingers to make his point.

"I had nowhere to go," Eddie explained, cringing as he

saw himself standing up in the stirrups.

"Damn broad's making it tight for us," Pedro yelled, pointing at Andy.

"You will call each other by name," Arthur insisted.

On the screen, Andy could be seen angling out to make room for the horses who were trapped behind the tiring leader. Immediately, Carlo drove his horse up from behind, jamming Eddie and Pedro in once again.

"Carlo, what are you doing driving up in there?" Arthur demanded. "You know Eddie and Pedro are in trouble."

"How the hell do I know, I'm behind the action. A hole opens up, I go for it."

"We were hollering loud enough to wake the dead!" Eddie exclaimed.

"I'm not out there to babysit," Carlo snapped. "I'm supposed to be riding a damn race!"

Eddie and Pedro were still standing up in their stirrups as Benito's horse continued to back up. Only when Carlo passed them were they able to swing out and avoid colliding with the exhausted leader.

Carlo was catching up to Yves who had taken over the lead. Andy was accelerating on the extreme outside.

The camera angle switched as the horses entered the turn. Andy caught up to Carlo. The moment she came abreast, Bruiser ducked in and hit Carlo's horse. Pedro laughed while other jockeys hooted in satisfaction.

"What was your horse ducking from?" Arthur asked. Before Andy could answer, Bruiser hit Carlo's horse again. Cheers erupted.

Arthur slammed his hand down on the table, calling for silence. It was several seconds before order was restored and the film ran the action again from the half mile pole. They watched as Carlo kept Eddie and Pedro in tight quarters before moving ahead with Andy in chase.

"I understand a horse ducking in when something spooks him," Arthur said, "but twice?"

Laughter rippled through the room, along with comments like, 'dumb son of a bitch' and 'serves him right'.

Andy cringed when she saw how obvious her actions were.

"The dumb bitch couldn't control her horse, she was all over me!" Carlo yelled.

"Any more name calling and you're out of the room," Arthur warned him.

There was silence as the action continued into the home-stretch. Yves' horse was tiring and Carlo was stuck behind him with Andy just to his outside. The horses coming from behind were spread out across the track. Farrell came up on the outside of Andy as she was driving her horse forward. He suddenly jumped up in the saddle.

"What was that all about?" Arthur demanded.

"The stupid bit—" Farrell caught himself. "Andy hit me with her whip."

Arthur turned to Andy, a questioning look on his face.

"I was reaching back to hit my horse," she said as innocently as she could. "Farrell must have got too close."

The television screen faded to black while Don prepared to show the head-on.

The jockeys reverted to familiar behaviour, whooping and hollering as the head-on angle exposed all the rough riding that was going on throughout the race. As the horses slipped under the wire, Andy was seen swinging her whip back just as Farrell came up beside her.

"The film doesn't show conclusively if Andy's whip touched you, Farrell," Arthur said as the screen went blank. "I'd like to think you weren't grandstanding for us. You've done that a few times in the past."

"Grandstanding, huh?" Farrell leaped up from his chair and dropped his breeches. A purple bruise spread from his kneecap to half way down his shin.

Candace nudged Andy. "Don't admit a thing."

"Okay, Farrell, you've made your point," Eddie assured

him. "Pull those breeches up."

Several more races were under scrutiny but the action was fairly benign compared to the first race. When the films were finished, Arthur asked Carlo and Andy to wait outside the room while he conferred with John Baxter.

All the jockeys walked out together. No one spoke to Carlo as he stood in the hallway, awaiting the stewards' verdict.

Andy took her place outside the door. Several jockeys slapped her on the back and wished her good luck. She tried to get her thoughts in order.

So here it is, she thought to herself, what I've been praying for. The new era is here, Arthur is in charge. He will bring law and order to Suffolk Downs.

And Andy Crowley will be the first casualty.

HAPPY HOLIDAY

Andy stood in the hallway awaiting judgement. Eddie Flaherty was having words with Carlo. The agitated jockey didn't seem to agree with his plan of action. *Fucking idiots* and *stupid sons of bitches* seemed to be Carlo's opinion of both the other jockeys in the race and the two stewards. After a terse lecture from Eddie, Carlo waved his arms and turned his back to lean against the wall.

Eddie walked over to Andy, scratching his head in frustration.

"Okay," he said, taking a deep breath. "What would you like me to say on your behalf?"

"Guilty as charged."

He grabbed her elbow and took her out of earshot of Carlo.

"Never admit guilt!" he said adamantly.

"What are you talking about? It's obvious, it was right up there on the screen."

"Do you want to give up your career?"

She stared at him in disbelief. "No way, they wouldn't do that."

"You admit you deliberately hit another jockey, put his life at risk, they can and *will* suspend you for life."

Andy was stunned. "But...I didn't put his life at risk. Not like what he did to you and Pedro on the backstretch. You almost clipped heels and went down."

"So you're a vigilante now? What Carlo did to me is my

business, not yours. I can take care of that." Eddie released her elbow but his eyes bore into her. "Whatever your intentions were, you tell the stewards it was unavoidable. Your horse ducked in, you couldn't control him."

"Is this advice from the representative of the Jockeys' Guild?"

"This is advice from a jockey with many more years of experience than you've had. *Never* admit guilt. For God's sake, you should know that, your mother's a lawyer. That's what she'd tell you."

"My mother told me to get a university degree."

"Okay, mothers aren't always right," Eddie admitted, a smile lightening the tone of his voice. "My mother wanted me to be a priest."

Andy had to laugh at that one. "Okay, so it's best if I don't admit intent, but the evidence is right there on film."

"Right, *what* happened is on film, but not *why* it happened. Your horse touched Carlo, yes, but maybe something was wrong. Maybe he got stepped on in the gate, maybe the bit slipped. If you go in there and admit you clobbered him on purpose, the stewards have to take appropriate action." He leaned back against the wall, but kept his eyes directed at her. "Especially a newly appointed head steward who's trying to make a name for himself."

"Don't remind me," she sighed. "I've been waiting for the day Arthur took over and now I'm his first suspension."

"Just answer the questions asked," Eddie said. "Keep it simple, don't offer extra information and *don't* try to explain. That'll just get you into more trouble." He tapped her on the shoulder to make his point. "And *never* admit guilt."

"My God, I feel like a criminal about to go on trial and everyone knows I'm guilty." Andy shook her head as if trying to wake up from a nightmare. "It won't work, Eddie, I'm a terrible liar."

"It's not lying, it's just omitting the truth."

"This is unbelievable," she sighed. "I won't be able to

look them in the eye."

"I'll do most of the talking," he assured her. "And one other thing. Do you remember what Arthur said to Farrell about grandstanding? That's what you have to learn to do."

"I didn't understand what that was all about," she admitted. "I must have missed the 'grandstanding lesson' when I was learning to ride."

"Going on your performance yesterday, you're a fast learner," Eddie said with a grin. "When you clobbered Carlo, you should have stood up in your stirrups and made it look like your horse was lugging in. Then stand up again when he ducked in the second time. That way, it looks like you're making an effort to control him. If you hit the board, your number will come down, but you won't get a suspension."

Andy couldn't believe what she was hearing. "This is what the Jockey's Guild hired you to do, teach jockeys how to get away with murder?"

"They've hired me to give you the benefit of my years of experience," he replied. "That's exactly what I'm doing."

"I'll bet you started riding on the fair circuit, didn't you?"

"Yes. And watching your ride yesterday, anyone would think you were still on the fair grounds."

Andy held her arms up in the air. "Touché."

The door opened and John Baxter motioned them in.

Eddie gave her one last look.

She nodded. "I'll follow your lead."

Eddie strode confidently across the room, Andy at his heels. Arthur looked up as they stood before him.

"Quite an eventful day at the races yesterday, wouldn't you say?" he remarked.

"Yes sir, but not as eventful as this morning," Eddie replied. "Congratulations on your appointment, though I'm sure you would have preferred to accept the position under different circumstances."

"Yes, I would have appreciated happier circumstances." Arthur shuffled some of the papers in front of him to get down to business. "Mr Baxter and I have discussed the first race and your actions, Andrea. You seemed to have some trouble controlling your horse."

"This horse, Calling All Hands, is a bit of an eccentric runner," Eddie said.

"I'm familiar with the horse's past performances," Arthur said. "He seems to run in short spurts rather than a steady rhythm, but normally he runs straight. Did he come back sore after the race?"

"No, sir, he didn't," Andy replied.

"Pete Mackenzie is the trainer, I see. I believe he's also your contract holder, is he not?" Arthur asked, looking up at her.

She tried to avoid direct eye contact and looked over his left shoulder. "Yes, sir, he is."

"So you've galloped this horse in the morning."

"Yes, I breezed him just before the race. He seemed—"

Eddie stepped on her toe to remind her to avoid explanation.

"He seemed okay," she said simply.

"He was sound?" Arthur asked.

"Oh, yes, sir. Pete would never run a sore horse."

"I'm sure he wouldn't," Arthur agreed, "but something could have happened in the race."

"She pulled up sharply out of the gate when Carlo crossed her path," Eddie remarked.

Andy couldn't believe this was actually happening. It sounded like the stewards and the Jockey's Guild representative were both trying to give her a way out. Emotions warred within her. She didn't want a suspension, but how could Arthur lead them into a new era, bring law and order to Suffolk Downs, if he let her get away with blatantly reckless riding?

"Andy hasn't been at Suffolk very long," Eddie continued. "This track has sharper turns than Belmont Park. It takes some getting used to."

The dilemma continued as Andy bit down on the side of her mouth to keep from giving evidence against herself.

"We could use a New York trained jockey here," Arthur said as her gaze finally met his. "I've been watching you ride, Andrea. You're very talented. I have no doubt that you will do well at any racetrack in the country and I'm glad you chose Suffolk Downs. I'm sure you will be too, after you serve your suspension."

John Baxter nodded agreement.

"You are suspended for three racing days, beginning tomorrow," Arthur announced.

The battle of emotions dissipated as she let out a sigh.

"Yes, sir," she replied.

Eddie nodded as she glanced at him before retreating towards the door. A three day suspension she could survive, especially if it meant the jockeys would treat her more respectfully upon her return.

When she stepped out, Carlo was waiting his turn. She held the door open for him.

"Welcome to Camelot," she said as he strode by.

LET SLEEPING DOGS LIE

Andy made her way through the darkness, Charlie close at her heels.

"These are ridiculous hours."

"Getting up early has all kinds of advantages, Charlie."

"Is that so. Name one?"

"You get to see the sunrise." Andy looked up at the dark sky. "In about half an hour."

"Even the sun has sense enough to sleep in."

"Morning, girls," Pete greeted them as they walked into the shed row. "There's a twenty minute delay. The maintenance crew is still harrowing the track. Come on, I'll buy you coffee."

They followed him to the track kitchen, welcoming the light and warmth of the crowded room. It seemed everyone was huddled in here while they waited for the track to open.

"I'll get the coffees. Find a table. And here, take this. It's yesterday's edition of the Globe. I haven't had time to read it yet."

Andy and Charlie found the last empty table and sat down. Charlie didn't seem to be in the mood for chatting so Andy opened the paper.

"*It makes us or it mars us, think on that,*" she read aloud. "A journalist with a background in Shakespeare. Othello, I think."

Andy glanced over the article.

"Well, don't keep me in suspense," Charlie remarked.

"Read the rest of it."

Andy spread the paper out on the table and began reading. "*It has long been wondered why children raised by the same parents can choose totally different paths in life. This couldn't be more apparent than with the Bulger brothers, James and William. Raised in the first public housing project, the Old Harbor tenements in South Boston, the Bulger brothers have travelled in different directions since adolescence. Every morning Billy staggered up Logan Way under the heavy weight of a book bag on his way to Boston College High School while older brother James, more commonly known as Whitey, roamed Mercer Street where gangs flexed their muscles in constant battle. (Note of caution, never call him Whitey to his face. He has a keen dislike of the appellation.) While Billy carved out a political career, Whitey robbed banks. In 1956, he was arrested and sent to jail for a decade. Meanwhile, his younger brother became a state representative.*

"I thought my brother and I were different, but we're almost twins compared to these two," Andy remarked, before continuing to read the article.

"*A couple of years ago, in October of '74, the brothers seemed to switch sides during the desegregation bussing fiasco in South Boston. When anti-bussing protestors were arrested outside a neighborhood school, Billy went face to face with police commissioner, Robert DiGracia, accusing him of using Gestapo troopers and overreacting to the protestors. Meanwhile, Whitey played the incongruous role of peacemaker, trying to bring calm to the streets of Southie.*

But despite their profound differences, the brothers remain simpatico. They share an incisive intelligence and drive that puts them at the top of their divergent worlds. But then again, maybe not so divergent. In his last interview, Billy may have been speaking for both of them when he referred to himself as just another redneck mick from South Boston'.

Andy shook her head as she looked up from the paper.

"Boston has really changed since the Puritans first landed. I wonder what our forefathers would think of this?"

"They couldn't foresee the potato famine in Ireland, could they?" Charlie remarked. "By the sounds of it, most of those Irish immigrants settled in South Boston."

"Break's over," Pete informed them. "The coffee will have to wait. Come on, let's get tacked up."

They followed him to the barn where Candace was waiting. She plunked Andy's helmet on her head and spun her around. "Ya needed on the other side of the barn. Arley's got a horse tacked. Go."

Candace's shove propelled Andy on her way. She walked around to the AM side of the barn. Arley Mitchell nodded at her, tipping his cowboy hat.

"Mornin' Miss Andy," he said before leading a horse out of a stall. He stood the gelding in front of her, ready for her inspection.

"He looks fabulous," Andy said, running her hand along the bay gelding's neck and shoulder.

"Raised him myself," Arley told her. "This here is a horse that's good to ride the river with."

Andy wasn't sure if that meant the horse was dependable or if he liked to run in the mud, but either way, she liked him. He had a strong sloping shoulder and hind quarters to match. Her gaze slid downwards past his knees.

"Don't worry about that ankle, it's just a little bit of arthritis."

The gelding's left front ankle was slightly bigger than the right, but compared to Bouncing Bessie, he looked whistle clean.

"What's his name?" she asked, letting the horse sniff her hand.

"Charming The Judge." Arley reached up and took a hold of the gelding's ear, tugging it playfully. The horse leaned into him, rubbing against his shoulder.

She smiled. "I sure could have used your help a few

days ago. The judge wasn't charmed at all with my ride on Bruiser."

"I hear Mr. Healey is all horns and rattles these days."

Andy laughed. She loved the Texan's creative language. Arley's phrases drew images that had her imagination running wild.

"Your five days are up already?"

"I had a three day suspension. I'm cleared to ride today. It was Carlo who got five. It was a fair ruling, for both of us. I have to give Mr Healey credit. He was almost apologetic about giving me a suspension."

"In Texas, we'd say he's got a hair in his butter."

Even Andy's imagination couldn't figure that one out.

"Means Mr. Healey has himself a real delicate situation," Arley explained. "Way I hear it, the track president, Mr. Connell, has told him to lighten up on the reins, not rake so hard with the spurs, if you know what I mean."

"But Arthur can't back off, he's just starting to get his point across."

"Don't get me wrong," Arley said in his slow drawl. "I understand his bounty hunter mentality. Dodge needed to be cleaned up, but he's got so many jockeys behind bars, we're not goin' to have enough riders left to carry out a whole day's card. He's handed out four more suspensions in the last couple of days."

"When Trumball was head steward, a jockey's licence was a licence to kill. Arthur is backing up his words with action." She was determined in her defence. "And there's certainly enough jockeys available. What about Leo Valente ? He's got years of experience."

"That he does. And he's a real gentleman. But that's not always what you want out there on the track. Don't get me wrong, most trainers don't want a jock to take foolish risks. We've got a lot invested in these beautiful creatures, but we've got to pay the bills. There's foolhardy risks and there's calculated risks. Leo doesn't seem to want to take either."

Arley legged Andy up into the saddle.

"Poor Leo. It's hard to stay in sharp and competitive when you only ride a few races a week. If he could ride more, I'm sure Leo the Lion would rise again."

"You just may have a point there, Miss Andy. I'd be pleased to see the old Lion again. I'd even use him myself."

Andy suddenly had a misgiving. "I haven't talked myself out of a mount, have I?"

"You surely haven't. You've got all my light rides. That agent of yours is one convincin' woman. You could find yourself ridin' every race soon." He strolled along beside the horse as they headed out to the track. "Just a light jog for the old fella. That's all he needs today. He might be a little stiff in the joints when he starts, but he'll warm up out of it. And don't you worry, he'll be ready to fire for you tomorrow."

"Old fella? How old is he?"

"He's eight, but he's still got some years left in him."

"I see he's in the last race on the card. Is six furlongs his distance?"

"He can sprint and he can go long. He'll break quick enough to get a good position, then you wait till the last sixteenth. That's where he kicks in. Used to be a pretty classy horse back in his younger days, but four thousand claiming is where he can win now without runnin' himself into the ground. This fella doesn't owe me a dime. I tried to put him in semi-retirement last year and used him as a stable pony. He kept outrunnin' the two year olds so I figured he wasn't ready to hang up his racin' plates."

"We'll know for sure tomorrow," she said, tying her knot at the end of the reins. "Say, Arley, do you know anything about George Krikorian, the new steward?"

"Way I hear it, him and Mr. Healey chewed tobacco from the same plug."

Andy winced. She didn't find that image appealing. Healey and Krikorian were obviously good friends.

"I believe they went to school together," Arley said.

"Sheriff Healey has found his faithful deputy."

"That's good, he needs all the help he can get."

"He may need a whole posse to clean this place up."

As they went by Emmet's barn, Andy noticed Mickey watching her. His tall, slender figure was clad in a black leather jacket and perfectly creased slacks. Dark, intense eyes studied Andy from beneath the peak of a black baseball cap. His expression was neutral but alert.

"Do you know anything about that guy?" she asked Arley. "The man in black."

Arley glanced over. "Seen him in the clubhouse a few times. I know he's got some horses with Emmet, but I don't pay much mind to other people's business. Keep pretty much to my own side of the fence," he admitted. "You want to know what's going on in town, ask your friend, Candace. She's a veritable encyclopaedia, that woman."

"Strangely enough, she doesn't know much about Mickey the Mouse."

Arley wiped his forehead with the sleeve of his shirt and straightened his Stetson. "If Candace can't dig it up, then it's better off stayin' buried. You just keep your mind on what you do best, Miss Andy, and let sleepin' dogs lie."

"He gives me the creeps. I'd steer clear of him completely but he's got a fabulous Kentucky bred colt."

"Well, then, that's all you need to know about him."

Mickey waited until they had passed by the barn before unobtrusively making his way to the grandstand. Standing out of sight, he put the binoculars to his eyes and studied the horse's action. His stride was good for an old veteran. There was definitely another win or two left in him.

PLAY IT AGAIN, DON

Andy watched the race replay with fascination. The race was even more of a fiasco than her race on Bruiser had been. On the first turn, Yves LeBlanc had taken Donny Meade wide while hitting his horse left handed. Now, in the backstretch, Eddie Flaherty was in trouble. In an attempt to save ground for the final turn, Eddie had pulled his horse over, safely clearing the horse directly beside him, but he didn't see Farrell who was moving with a great burst of speed on the inside rail. Farrell's horse clipped heels with Eddie's and stumbled badly. Gasps of horror reverberated around the room.

The jockey colony was much diminished. Pedro, Carlo, Liam, and the two bug riders, Juan and Benito, were all serving suspensions.

Arthur, John Baxter and the new steward, George Krikorian watched the film closely. Arthur asked Don to play it again. They had disqualified Eddie's horse from the win position right after the race and placed him behind Farrell's horse who had finished sixth.

"I looked over and the rail was clear. So I dropped in and suddenly I heard him screaming," Eddie said as the film rewound.

"He almost killed me!" Farrell yelled. "My whole life passed before my eyes!"

"That must have taken all of three seconds," Candace remarked to the amusement of her fellow riders.

Even the stolid faces of the stewards lightened over that crack.

"Your guardian angel was working overtime, Farrell," Arthur remarked as he watched the scene again. "Your horse had an unusual burst of speed and Liam's horse blocked Eddie's view. He didn't have a chance to see you."

"If it's any consolation, Farrell, I came out of the race worse than you did," Eddie told him. "I lost the win and I lost the mount. I told the trainer it was an honest mistake, but he won't put me back on the horse."

Andy watched as they ran the film one more time. It might have been a mistake on Eddie's part, but the jury was still out on the 'honest' part as far as she was concerned. Eddie seemed to play his own games.

The screen went black and the jockeys filed out of the film room.

"Merde," Yves LeBlanc mumbled, punching the wall as he took his place outside the door. "I only touch the horse and they take me down."

"I'll admit we're all getting a little gun shy," Eddie agreed. "But you were careless, Yves. You knew your horse was lugging out and yet you kept hitting him left handed."

"I cannot hit my horse with my right hand," Yves insisted. "There's no room."

"That's the stewards' point, Yves. There was no room because you were taking Donny's horse out wide."

Eddie stopped just outside the door to wait with Yves while the stewards conferred. "It was your own fault for not paying attention. You've got some days coming. Just keep your mouth shut and accept it. Lose your temper in there and they'll double it."

"Merde!"

"Eddie," Andy called over to him. "You're going to be on the carpet too. Who's going to represent you?"

"I have to represent myself unless I think the judgement's unfair. Then I can call in another rep from the Guild." He looked at her curiously. "You want the job?"

"With my temper?" she said with a laugh. "You'd be ruled off for life."

"Yves is right," Denise said as they made their way back to the women's quarters. "We're all getting so nervous out there, we're making stupid mistakes."

"It's pathetic to think that trying to ride cleanly is making everyone nervous," Andy remarked.

"Race riding is hard enough," Barbara Smith remarked. "Why make it tougher on us?"

"I think Arthur's trying to make it *safer* for us," Andy insisted.

"Well, it's not working," Candace insisted. "Half our jocks are in jail and now the thugs from Rhode Island are moving in."

Andy picked up the program and flipped through the pages. The Rhode Island jockeys were in several races but so was Leo Valente. "Look at this, Leo's got four mounts today."

"That's more than he's had all year," Denise remarked. "Leo the Lamb."

"Give the guy a break. I mean, when you only ride a few races a week, it's hard to stay physically fit, never mind keep your wits about you."

"If the trainers ain't using him, there's a reason," Candace insisted. "Leo's been around a long time, had a lot of spills. Must have broken most of the bones in his body. Gotta make the old Lion a bit skittish."

"Discretion is the better part of valour," Andy stated.

Candace laughed. "You've got a real classy way of saying he's chicken shit."

"That's not what I'm saying," Andy argued. "Leo uses strategy instead of bullying and reckless intimidation. I'll tell you one thing, I'd rather ride with Leo than most of the other guys around here."

"Me too," Candace agreed. "Hell, I'd win every race!"

"Only when you can make the weight," Denise reminded her.

"Weight's not our biggest problem when we're riding with the Rhode Island boys," Candace warned them. "Better have eyes in the back and the sides of your helmet."

Andy put down the program and picked up *Daily Racing Form*. "Is Wally Malloy from Narragansett? He's next to me in the gate in the first race."

"Yeah, he's from 'Gansett. Hardly ever see him riding here," Denise replied.

"If he's from 'Gansett, why is he riding one of Emmett Gibbon's horses?" she asked.

Andy looked over the horse's past performance record. "He's one of Mickey Amato's claimers. I wonder if it's the gelding with the weak hind leg?"

"You'll know after the race," Candace assured her.

"Someone named Mural Allen is on my other side."

"Holy shit, you're between Wally the Weasel and Mural the Mule?" Barbara exclaimed. "You're in trouble, girl."

"Wally the Weasel, Mural the Mule," Andy repeated. "Who gave them the cute names? The media?"

"Ain't nothing cute about those guys," Candace assured her. "Ya think Carlo's rough? He's a pussycat next to them."

"Sure glad I'm not in that race," Barbara said as she turned on the TV.

"Don't get anywhere near Mural's whip," Denise advised her. "If he hits you, you'll wake up in the hospital and you won't remember what happened."

"Here we go again," Andy sighed, pulling on her silks. "Wave after wave of barbarians."

She went into the empty bedroom to have a few minutes of solitude. Listening to the horror stories was setting her nerves on edge. She wasn't about to be intimidated by the jockeys from Rhode Island. The stewards would be scrutinizing their every move. Of course, if they did anything wrong, penalties were handed out after the fact. That thought didn't offer her much consolation.

When the PA announced it was time for riders out, she took her ritual three breaths and made the sign of the cross. It had been many years since she'd done that, but at the moment it seemed appropriate.

She walked out of the room with quick, sure steps, her stride belying her nervousness. When she saw her Judge standing calmly in the saddling stall, the tall Texan beside him, confidence began bubbling up from deep inside her. Arley stood with his arm over the gelding's neck, man and horse quietly sizing up the competition.

"Whoo-ey, I've never seen so many strangers in town," he remarked in his Texas drawl. He nodded towards the jockey in the next stall. "Now there's a man been raised on sour milk."

Andy looked around the wall that separated the stalls and saw a dark haired, dark eyed jockey with a scowl on his face.

"Mural the Mule," she said in a low voice. "I've been advised to stay out of his reach."

She glanced over on the other side at Wally Malloy. "Wally the Weasel doesn't look too nasty. I think I'll lean in his direction."

"I tell you what, why don't you just ease real slow out of the gate and let the boys fight it out between them. When they've finished hammering each other, you'll be ready to run." He legged her up into the saddle. "When in doubt, let the Judge make the decision."

"Sounds like a plan, Arley."

"He likes a little blowout in the warm-up," he instructed her. "Let him roll for a sixteenth of a mile down the backstretch. Don't worry, he'll come back for the askin'."

It was an unusual request, but Andy trusted Arley's judgement. He'd known the horse all his life. If he said to turn him loose, that's what she would do.

During the post parade, she memorized Mural and Wally's colours so she could steer clear of the Rhode Island boys.

Both of their horses looked like they'd been through some tough battles. Mural's horse had ankles even bigger than Bouncing Bessie's and Wally's horse was as thin as a greyhound. It wasn't the horse she had galloped.

When she began the warm-up, Judge didn't take much of a hold on the bit. Without any pressure on the reins, Andy had to twine a finger in his mane to help keep herself balanced. After a quarter of a mile, he picked up the bit. When she was in the backstretch, he tugged hard.

"Okay, here goes," she said, releasing her hold. He took off like a Quarter horse breaking from the gate. He felt like a runaway and she had a moment of regret, but after a sixteenth of a mile, just as Arley promised, the big gelding slowed down. She took a hold of him and he broke into a trot.

"You give me that down the homestretch and we'll be the ones kicking like a mule," she said, really excited about her chances in this race. She headed to the gate full of confidence. Settled into the number four stall, she pulled her goggles down over her eyes and prepared for the job ahead.

"You got speed?"

The question came from the inside stall. She turned to Mural. The smirk seemed to be a permanent facial expression.

"Plenty," she said, not bothering to add that she was saving it for the homestretch.

"Last horse coming in!"

Mural yanked his horse's head straight and chirped to him.

The horse in the number two stall thrashed against the gate and Judge threw his head up, ready to break.

"You stupid son of a bitch!" Liam yelled from the two hole. "You trying to get me killed?"

Clucking or chirping was strictly forbidden in the starting gate as it could easily instigate pandemonium amongst the tense, alert horses. Andy was sure a jockey of Mural's experience would be aware of this, but she wasn't about to be the one to reprimand the snarling jockey. She set her focus straight ahead, ready for the break.

The latches opened and she let her body follow Judge's movement. She had the sensation of moving in slow motion as the powerful head and neck stretched out in between her arms. She supported him with her legs, but she didn't ask him to hurry. In that precise moment, Mural cut sharply to the right. No doubt, he expected her to break beside him. Instead, he collided with Wally's horse who had also swerved in her direction. The two jockeys collided with each other so hard they were both thrown off balance. Wally lost a stirrup and tipped over his horse's right shoulder. He grabbed for mane and pulled himself back into the saddle, sliding his foot into the stirrup.

Mural sent his horse off after the pack and Andy headed for the inside rail. Wally followed behind Mural. Andy watched as the rest of the jockeys fought for position. She was surprised to see Eddie pull in beside her. He obviously had a slow break too.

She coasted down the backstretch, gauging the action in front. The leaders were setting good fractions, but it wasn't a blistering speed. The field was tightly packed. Andy knew she was well within striking distance, barely five lengths back from the leaders.

Leo was directly in front of her on the rail. Mural was on the outside of him, a quarter of a length in front. Wally was at Mural's boot and still pushing his horse to keep in contention. Two bug riders, including Emmett's whiz kid, Billy Feagin, were outside of them.

Mural was gaining ground, but slowly. Andy sensed he wanted the rail, but he couldn't get clear of Leo. He yelled at him to take back but Leo held firm. He was riding like the lion of old and wasn't about to concede his position to Mural.

As they neared the turn, Mural whipped his horse mercilessly, but could only gain three quarters of a length. Suddenly, without warning, he cut in to the rail. The deadly sound of horse shoes scraping reached her ears. Leo's horse threw his head high in the air as his legs tangled with the hind legs of Mural's horse. The old rider stood up straight in the stirrups before completely disappearing from her view. His horse cart wheeled, catapulting Leo over the inside rail.

"Jesus!" Eddie screamed.

Andy stood up in the stirrups. The fallen horse was directly in her path. Eddie was trying desperately to swing out, but horses had rushed up from behind and blocked his escape. There was no way out.

She let the reins slide through her hands, giving Judge his freedom. The gelding brought his hind end under him and dropped his head and neck. He was going to jump the fallen horse. A stationary object at this speed was difficult enough, but to clear a rolling horse seemed impossible. And yet it was their only option.

Andy struggled to stay balanced as the muscular horse catapulted himself into the air. She bent forward with his thrust, reaching out over his outstretched neck. His speed carried them through the air in a powerful arc. He touched down on his two front legs and Andy expelled her breath. Just then, his hind legs tangled with the horse beneath him. Andy gripped the reins with all her might, determined to hold a thousand pound horse up on his feet.

Judge was as determined as she was to stay upright. He swung his head high to the side to regain his balance. His legs buckled momentarily, but then found solid ground. Andy fell heavily into the saddle, the reins flapping uselessly in her hands. Instinct took over as she gripped with her calves and chirped to Judge, telling him to keep running. Several horses had passed her but miraculously, they were still in the competition.

Andy shortened the reins and pushed herself up into racing position. Perched over his withers once again, she glided along the inside rail and into the turn. Several horses had gone wide to avoid catastrophe and were out past the middle of the track. She quickly gained on them as they entered the homestretch.

"Andy the Antelope!" Eddie cried out as she galloped past him.

The horses were spread across the track in front of her. She studied the silks and saw Mural blocked behind the leaders.

"Okay, Judge, if you've got anything left, we're about to use it."

She was closing in on Mural's horse when a sliver of daylight opened between the front runners. She couldn't get there before him.

The enticing hole beckoned, but Mural didn't make a move. She glanced over as she gained on him, but he seemed to be weighing his options.

There was no hesitation on her part. "Go!" she screamed to Judge, sending him into the narrow opening. Her boots scraped the horses on either side as they jostled for the lead. Burying her head in his flying mane, Andy asked Judge for every last bit of strength, giving all she could to help him.

She didn't pick her head up until she was several strides past the wire. Three horses ran abreast with her, the jockeys spitting dirt and chattering excitedly at the same time. Grateful to be alive, each thanked their chosen god for saving their lives.

"Jesus, Mary and Joseph, that's as close as it gets," Eddie called over. "You owe that horse your life. And mine too. I thought you were going to climb over me to get out!"

"I saw it all from behind," Billy Feagin said. "Holy shit, that horse can fly! Even in a steeplechase, the jumps aren't moving!"

"I knew that bastard Mural was up to something," Liam called from the middle of the track. "He tried to get my horse to dump me in the gate!"

"It was worth hanging on," Eddie replied. "Nice win Liam."

Frantic voices suddenly got their attention. The gate crew stood on the track, waving their arms and yelling at the jockeys to pull their horses up. Andy brought Judge to a halt and looked down the backstretch. Leo was limping slowly towards the ambulance. His horse lay still on the track.

All energy suddenly drained from her body, a delayed reaction. She dug her knees into the saddle to hold herself up as she galloped back to the unsaddling area. Arley ran to meet her, as pale as his white cowboy hat.

"God damn, I've never seen anything like it!" His face shone with admiration. He looked from his horse to Andy then back to the Judge.

"You can't say I don't follow instructions," she remarked, feeling giddy in her relief.

Arley's colour was slowly coming back, but now he looked puzzled.

"Your parting instructions," she reminded him. " 'When in doubt, let The Judge make the decision'."

Arley laughed. "I think what happened out there must have been a mutual decision. You took good care of Judge, and he took good care of you." He stroked the horse affectionately. "That jump was befitting the Grand National. It made Beecher's Brook look like a hurdle."

Andy dismounted and threw her arms around the horse's neck. "You're the best, Judge."

A hand reached in suddenly and took a hold of the horse's bridle. "I hate to break up this party."

Startled, they both looked into the face of the paddock judge. His tone was apologetic. "I'm sorry to have to tell you this, Arley, but your horse has been claimed."

Andy gasped. "No, that can't be!"

Arley put a hand on her shoulder, his voice tight with emotion. "I know you're just doing your job, Bob," he said to the paddock judge.

Arley stepped back as the paddock judge clipped a numbered tag onto the bridle.

"You've been a good old warrior, Judge," Arley said to the horse, reaching up to tug on his ear. The gelding rubbed his shoulder affectionately. "I guess somebody else thinks you're a good horse too."

Andy couldn't stand to see Judge taken away. She ran quickly to the scales, choking on her tears.

HORSE WITH A MISSION

The tears wouldn't stop. Every time she thought she was under control, a fresh torrent erupted. Why hadn't she listened to her parents and stayed in university.

"Don't be ridiculous," Andy chided herself, grabbing a tissue and wiping her face. "You knew it wouldn't be easy."

She'd known about the physical dangers and faced many of them already in her short career. But no one had mentioned the gut wrenching emotional pain of horses breaking down or being yanked away in a claim. How would Arley deal with it? The empty stall would remind him every morning that Judge was gone.

Don't fall in love with racehorses. Yes, she'd been told that, many times.

"Easy to say," she muttered, blowing her nose.

She heard the other women leave the room to go out to the saddling paddock. She had hidden away in the darkened bedroom, but now she would have the main room to herself.

"Okay, Andrea Crowley, pull yourself together. This is the life of a jockey. Get used to it!"

She took a deep breath and left the bedroom. Somehow, she had to get used to this emotional roller coaster if she wanted to be successful.

"But still, who would want to claim Judge?" she demanded, grabbing a set of silks. "He's an old, arthritic gelding running for four thousand dollars claiming. What use is he to anybody except Arley?"

She thrust her arm into the sleeve as she continued to demand answers. "Judge has been with him his entire life. No one knows him or cares for him the way Arley does and no one will ever get him to run better. For God's sake, even when he had to jump a fallen horse, he still finished fifth!"

She shook her head vigorously. "Enough is enough, Andy. Get your mind on the next race. The Heckler needs your full attention!"

She picked up the *Form* and stared at it. She had already committed the names of all the horses and jockeys to memory, but she read their names one more time. Mural was in the race, but without his buddy, Wally. His horse had the worst past performance record of all the horses. Even with the Mule's kick, she was sure he didn't have a chance.

She tossed the paper onto the table and practised her whistling. Her volume was nowhere near Eddie's. Pounding hooves and the whistling wind created at forty miles an hour would obscure it like a tiny voice in a hurricane.

Darrell rushed into the room with the silks for the later races. "Leo's okay," he announced. "No serious injury. Thank God he was thrown into the infield and not run over by half the field."

"They've done x-rays?"

"Yeah, nothing's broken."

"And his horse?" she asked tentatively.

Darrell shook his head. "Died instantly, broken neck."

Andy shuddered. That was the part of racing she would never get used to.

"What was all the shouting about in the jocks' room?" she asked. "Sounded like there was a fight after the race."

"A couple of the guys decided to take justice into their own hands. They should know better than to take the Mule on. Liam got the worst of it. Got himself a shiner before we could tear them apart." Darrell hung up the brightly coloured silks. "Arthur came down from the stewards' tower to talk to Mural. Sounded like he wanted to rule him off, right there, but of course he can't. Has to be a film review first."

"He'll only get a five day suspension, but he should be charged with attempted manslaughter. That was deliberate on his part, he knew Leo would go down!"

The starting bell pierced the silence.

"They're off!" Jim Hannon announced.

Andy came back to the present and focused on the TV screen. The horses had broken cleanly from the gate. All went well down the backstretch and into the turn. At the head of the homestretch, Barbara was in front and Andy cheered loudly for her. She saw Denise coming through on the inside and cheered for her too. Suddenly a third horse appeared in the middle of the track with a dramatic rush and beat them at the wire. Andy seized the program. The winner was the number ten horse ridden by Mural Alan.

"Shit!" she swore loudly. "Is there no justice in this world?"

Muttering and swearing, she grabbed a pillow off the bed and punched it as she paced around the room. "Whoever said crime doesn't pay was an idiot!" she demanded.

She threw the pillow back on the bed and went to her cubicle to get ready for the next race. Just as she pulled her boots on, the door opened and Denise and Barbara came in, chatting excitedly about the race.

"If I'd gotten through five strides earlier, I'd of nailed him," Denise said.

"If I didn't have to hustle my horse to get in front of Mural out of the gate, I would have had more left," Barbara complained.

Andy didn't want to get distracted and stepped out into the hallway to await the call to the paddock. She focused on her strategy for the next race. Closing her eyes, she rode the race in her mind. The gate opened and she broke cleanly, but last. She envisaged horses in front of her, blocking her path. She waited patiently until the turn and let The Heckler go wide. No saving ground on the rail—he wouldn't pass a horse from the inside. She visualized several horses in front of her and swung her whip back to give him one crack on the flanks and then went to a furious hand ride.

"And it's Andy Crowley by a neck!" Eddie called out as he slid up beside her, flicking his head in imitation of a horse.

"I won that one by a length," she informed him as they walked out to the paddock together.

"Good luck," he said to her with a grin. "I hope you finish second."

"Look out for my dirt," she replied, heading for the number six stall.

Pete looked anything but calm. He was twitching like a live wire.

"I didn't see your first race, but I hear you saved yourself from total destruction," he said, speaking in one rapid staccato burst.

"The Judge saved us both. He can be a grand prix jumper when his racing career is over." She caught herself. "That is, if his new owner knows how to take care of him. Do you know who claimed him?"

"Nope. The scuttlebutt hasn't hit the airwaves yet. Might take till the fifth race."

"Better be someone who appreciates him," she said adamantly.

Pete didn't hear her. He was shifting his weight from one foot to the other as he looked for his horse.

"I'm getting seasick watching you, Pete."

"Sorry." He leaned his shoulder against the wall to keep himself still. "Listen, Andy, six furlongs isn't The Heckler's distance. It'll take him that long to get warmed up, but this race is just to get him primed for a longer distance. He'll be in a mile and seventy yards next time. Don't worry when you find yourself last from the gate. He knows where the home-stretch is, even if it comes up early. That's where he does his running. No matter where you are, stay on the outside, don't go to the rail."

Andy had never seen a trainer this nervous. She knew exactly how The Heckler liked to run. They'd been over it several times in the morning, but she listened patiently.

"He won't pass a horse on the inside. Don't forget that. Hit him once at the head of the stretch and then put the whip away and hand ride. The tighter you pull on the reins, the faster he'll go."

Mercifully, the paddock judge called for riders up. The Heckler dragged Charlie into the saddling stall.

"Oh my God, he's as nervous as you are," she remarked to Pete as he quickly legged her up. "Does he always get this excited before a race?"

Pete shook his head. "It's not the race that has him riled up, it's the timing. It's out of synch."

He ran beside her as The Heckler continued to drag Charlie.

"When he's in his distance and conditions, it's always the last race of the day. Bart likes to use a two thousand dollar claimer for the last perfecta. The cheaper horses are harder to handicap, they're not as consistent as the allowance horses. Spreads the bets across the board more."

"Weird!"

"Well, that's Bart's story and he's sticking to it."

"His Highness does not like to have his routine changed," Charlie gasped as she was dragged literally off her feet. "He knows it's a short race and he wants to start now!"

"I got him!" Candace called out as she spurred Bucky into action and grabbed the reins.

The moment Heckler saw the buckskin horse, he settled down. Candace slipped a leather strap through the side of the bit and let him walk quietly beside her.

"Your attention please," Jim Hannon's voice announced over the PA system, "There has been a rider change in this race. The number four horse, Phantom Pilot, will now be ridden by Wally Malloy."

Candace groaned. "God damn it, those boys from Rhode

Island are at it again!"

"What do you mean?" Andy asked, alert to the tension in Candace's voice.

"Wally's got himself on ole man Morris' horse. Something's going down here and it ain't gonna be in our favour." She looked Andy straight in the eye. "Don't be a hero. Ya saw what happened to Leo. He's lucky to be alive. I know ya hate Mural's guts right now, but don't use this hoss to get back at him."

"I wouldn't put The Heckler at risk to get back at anybody," Andy insisted.

"Okay, just ride your race and don't pay no mind to them. Remember, Heckler isn't gonna pass on the inside rail. And you've got to let him ease out a little on the turn, takes the pressure off that bowed tendon. This hoss has got some years left in him and he doesn't want to spend them carting kids around at 4H, he wants to be a racehoss."

Andy looked over at Wally who was just behind his buddy Mural in the post position. "Surely Mural won't pull anymore stunts. Arthur came down to give him a warning. And what good would it do him anyway, they'll take his number down just like they did in the first race. I'll bet he gets a hefty fine along with his suspension."

"Won't do you any good if you're in the hospital. Just steer clear of him. Stay in the middle of the track if you have to. That's where Heckler likes to run anyway." Candace looked over at Mural on the number two horse. "Now listen, Heckler doesn't have any speed, but he's real nervous in the gate. He's got to have a handler with him."

"I prefer to be alone in there."

Candace shook her head. "Not with this hoss, he needs someone to hold his head. Don't worry, we got one of the gate crew, Jake, who always handles him. He'll take good care of ya."

The warm-up was more about settling the Heckler and getting focused on the race ahead than loosening up muscles.

By the time they approached the gate the only thing on Andy's mind was her strategy. She would keep clear of all the other jockeys and run her own race on the outside. Even though it wasn't the Heckler's favourite distance, she felt she could hit the board and make Pete some money.

They filed in behind the starting gate and one of the assistant starters walked towards them.

"What the hell!" Candace muttered.

"What's wrong?"

"Who is this guy?" Candace nodded in the direction of the handler who was approaching them.

"He's not Jake?" Andy was instantly alarmed.

"Watch yourself," Candace called over as the handler took a hold of the reins.

Andy's heart rate soared as the stranger led her into the narrow stall. He climbed up onto the narrow ledge and turned the horse's head into his chest, holding him there. He kept his eyes averted and Andy couldn't read him at all. She wanted him to turn the horse loose and leave her alone, but if The Heckler was as nervous in the gate as Candace said, that would be a disaster. In desperation, she found herself praying to her guardian angel.

"Last rider coming in!"

She heard the latches closing behind the final horse. The Heckler's head was still sideways.

"Hold it boss!" she yelled.

It was the first time she had called out to the starter. He took notice.

"Number six, get that horse's head straight!" he ordered the assistant.

The gate handler slowly pushed Heckler's head into a straight position. The moment he was set, the latches opened. The Heckler's hind end dropped as he prepared to launch forward. Andy crouched low to go with him. Suddenly, she realized she was going up not forward. The Heckler was standing on his hind legs. He pawed the air with his front feet as he struggled to keep his balance. Horse and rider teetered precariously. Andy gripped mane. The slightest touch on the reins would pull the horse over backwards.

As suddenly as he had gone up, The Heckler tipped forward. His front feet had barely touched the dirt when he lunged forward into full gallop. Andy was sitting in the saddle, her weight bouncing on his back. She quickly gathered herself and stood up in racing position.

"Easy, boy, easy," she called out to him. "It's all over, Heckler, this isn't our race. Let's just have an easy gallop and save it for the next one."

The Heckler was running all out to catch the field of horses. Andy looked down at his leg. The yellow bandage that supported the bowed tendon was firmly in place, but if he carried on at this speed, he could easily injure it again.

"Settle down, big boy, this is where you take back and run easy, remember? We're still in the backstretch."

But the Heckler was a horse with a mission. The more she tried to hold him back, the faster he went. The best thing to do was to hold him together and support him as much as she could.

The turn loomed ahead and though there was no one directly inside her, she stayed out towards the middle of the track as instructed. The Heckler changed leads without slowing down. To Andy's amazement, they caught up to the pack half way around the turn in spite of the fact that they were five horses wide. At the head of the stretch, Heckler changed back to his outside lead. She remembered her instructions and tapped him once with the whip, but he didn't need any encouragement from her. He continued passing horses on his own initiative.

Fuelled by his rage, The Heckler was giving all that he had. The old warrior passed several tiring horses and took on the stretch runners. Andy looked to the inside and saw two frustrated bug riders blocked in on the rail. Liam was on the lead, his whip making certain his horse didn't slow down and Mural and Wally were tucked in behind him, hemming in the two apprentices.

When The Heckler pulled up beside them, Wally swore loudly and swung his whip out in her direction.

Andy stayed clear as she began seriously hand riding. She was delighted to ruin their little game.

The Heckler continued in his mission as Wally and Mural screamed, whipping their horses mercilessly. A roar rose from the grandstand as a blanket of horses thundered under the wire.

KICKED BY A MULE

Andy stood up in the saddle, weak kneed from her strenuous ride. She reined The Heckler up slowly, bringing him to a smooth halt. Together, horse and rider stood motionless, regaining their breath.

Wally galloped by, his weasel-like features contorted into a painful grimace. Directly behind him, Mural yanked his horse to a halt. Pulling viciously on the reins, he spun the horse around and glared at Andy. Without warning, he spat at her. A wad of dirt and saliva hit her thigh, staining her white nylon breeches.

He whipped his horse forward, bumping her as he passed. The Heckler leaped into full gallop. When she passed Mural's horse, Andy angled into his path, spraying dirt into the irate jockey's face. She could play childish games too.

The inquiry sign was flashing on the tote board as she pulled up.

"There is a stewards' enquiry into the running of this race." Jim Hannon's voice called out. "Please hold all tickets."

Pete looked even more nervous than he had in the saddling paddock. The moment she dismounted, he was down on his knees, inspecting the Heckler's leg "What happened at the gate? Did he outbreak you?"

"I don't know what happened. I'm sure I didn't grab him in the mouth."

"Didn't Jake get his head straight in time?"

"Candace said it wasn't Jake. It was some other guy. I had

to call to the starter to get him to straighten out his head. When the gate opened, we were ready, but Heckler went up instead of out."

She looked over at the tote board. The enquiry sign was still flashing.

Charlie appeared at a run, halter and lead shank in hand. "I thought we were doing the Knights of the Round Table, not hi ho Silver!"

She took a hold of The Heckler who was breathing hard, but still appeared sound.

"He's never run like that down the backstretch," Pete said, looking down at the bowed leg once again.

"I'm sorry, Pete, I tried to slow him down, but he was really pissed off about being left behind."

Charlie looked from Pete to Andy. "This is the first time I've heard a jockey apologize for getting a horse to run better than expected."

Even Pete had to smile. "Okay, come on, Charlie, we've got to get that leg into the ice tub."

Andy quickly undid the girths and pulled the saddle off. She watched as they headed off down the track. The Heckler was walking smartly, not a sign of a limp.

She turned her attention to the tote board. Liam's number was in the win position, but second and third were blank. The margin was too close to call without a photo finish.

She carried her saddle to the scales.

"They want to talk to you," Gerry informed her after checking her weight. He pointed to the wall phone that connected with the stewards' office.

She stepped down off the scale and reached for the receiver. She had no idea what the protocol was for speaking with the stewards during an inquiry and answered as she would any phone call. "Hello, Andy here."

"Andrea, what happened in the gate?" Arthur's voice was brisk and efficient.

"I don't know, sir. We were about to break, everything

was fine and then my horse reared."

"I've spoken with the gate handler. He thinks the horse slipped, hit the side of the gate and spooked himself."

"No way," Andy insisted. "I would have felt that. We were fine when the gate opened, all set to go. Suddenly we were in the air."

There was a long silence.

"Sir? Are you there?"

"Yes. We'll take a closer look, see if we can see something," Arthur said. "Good job, Andrea. Glad you stayed on."

"Yes, me too," she agreed wholeheartedly.

A roar erupted from the grandstand as the phone went dead.

"Congratulations," Gerry said, slapping her on the back. "You got the show. And look at your pay-off, it's a nice one."

"Holy crow, eighteen dollars for show. What did I go off at?"

"Fifty-to-one," Gerry told her. "Nobody bets The Heckler in a sprint."

She looked at the two numbers ahead of her. Liam had won and paid ten dollars, Wally finished second and paid twelve dollars. Mural was in fourth place.

"They'll be calling you the miracle worker after this one," Gerry predicted. "Watch out. You're going to be offered a lot of long shots. I know you're in a hurry to get more mounts, Andrea, but choose your horses carefully. You've got a long career ahead of you."

She smiled up at him as they walked out of the scale room. "You might have to remind me of that a few times, Mr. Marinick. I'm a lot like The Heckler. I go a crazy if I'm left behind."

Andy caught sight of Mickey the Mouse rushing into the clubhouse. She wondered if he'd made a bet.

"I hope you had a few bucks on me," she murmured as she headed to the jocks' room.

She stripped the soiled breeches off the moment she slipped inside and stuffed them into her duffle bag. That was her final race for the day. She had a long, leisurely shower, letting the hot water sooth her sore muscles. She thought about what the clerk of scales had said. He wouldn't have called her a miracle worker if he'd known she was trying to slow the horse down.

She wanted to watch the final race to see how the girls did, but she also wanted to beat the traffic out of the parking lot. She left the room and walked across the grandstand, her duffle bag slung over her shoulder. Bettors lined up to place their bets at the mutual windows. At their feet, a carpet of discarded tickets told the tale of past disappointments. Andy wondered how many thousands of lost dollars lay on the floor.

A whoop of joy caught her attention as a young man danced across the grandstand. Not everyone was losing money it seemed. Had he bet on her earlier? Heckler's payoff of eighteen dollars would have been an excellent return for a two dollar bet.

She shifted the duffle bag to the other shoulder as she opened the door and walked out into the parking lot. The bag wasn't quite as heavy as it was the day she rode her first race. Her racing tack was stowed in the jocks' room but she was in the habit of hand washing her tee shirts and breeches. They lasted a lot longer that way. When she became leading apprentice, she could afford to buy breeches by the dozens but for now, her three pairs were precious.

She suddenly stumbled over something lying on the ground.

"Damn it, Andy, pay attention," she chided herself as she regained balance and looked down to see what had caused the stumble.

She gasped as she saw a human leg sprawled out across her path. Her first instinct was to run. A drunken punter was not someone she wanted to meet in the parking lot. A bettor who'd had a bad day was a dangerous animal.

But the leg was eerily still. She gathered her courage and slowly walked around the parked car, holding her duffle bag in front of her as protection. She gasped again, gripping the bag tighter. The man's face was drenched in blood, both eyes were swollen shut. His lips were split and blood slowly seeped from the flatten mass that had been his nose. His right arm lay in his lap, twisted like a gnarled branch. Near the car was a duffle bag bearing the inscription, 'M Allen.

Tears stung Andy's eyes as she looked down on the battered body.

Her stomach heaved as she turned away. She could barely believe what she was seeing.

A moan from the still figure startled her. Her heart seemed to shudder as she gazed across the parking lot and called, "Someone help me here!"

The only response was a louder moan from Mural. When she looked down at him, one eyelid lifted partially. She squatted down beside him, but did not touch him. Even in his deplorable condition, he reminded her of a cobra, wounded, but still capable of a strike.

He shifted slightly against the bumper.

"Mural, who did this?"

One eye opened again and his lips moved as he struggled to speak. She leaned closer to hear him.

"Fook uff!" he growled, blood and saliva spraying the air between them.

She jumped back and lost her balance, landing on the pavement. As quick as a cat, she was up on her feet.

The sympathy she'd felt for him evaporated even as she stared at the mass of raw flesh propped against the car wheel, but she knew his situation demanded her help. She sprinted back to the grandstand and ran past the lines at the mutual windows to the first aid room. A nurse sat at a small table reading a book.

"I need help," she gasped. "A man, in the parking lot, in

bad condition."

"Someone had a little too much to drink, huh?"

She shook her head. "He's beaten, badly, can't get up."

The nurse's casual attitude changed immediately. She grabbed the phone and called for a security guard.

"He'll be here in a minute," she said, gathering blankets and bandages. "He'll walk out with you. I'll get the doctor down from the tower, but you show the guard where he is."

The nurse tossed the supplies to the uniformed guard as he walked in. "Follow her, there's been an incident in the parking lot."

The guard had to rush to catch up to Andy who was already sprinting across the grandstand. He was out of breath before he reached the door.

"Wait!" he gasped. "Slow down."

He followed her at a slow trot as she weaved among the parked cars. Suddenly she saw a trail of blood drops. She followed it until she found Mural lying prostrate on the pavement several feet from his previous position.

"There he is," she said, grabbing her duffle bag.

"Wait!" the guard called out as she headed off. "Help me lift him up."

"He's all yours," she called back over her shoulder. "I've done my good deed for the day."

PONY'S PRIVATE VIEWING

Mickey took advantage of the quiet room to put his strategy together. Thousands of dollars had been lost today, thanks to Mural's blunders and Andrea Crowley's determination. Tommy had been the one who had to break the news to Pony, an unenviable job. As he related to Mickey, only after he described how he had dealt with Mural did Pony settle down. But now he was insisting on seeing the replays.

Mickey knew that watching the races wasn't going to make the big man any happier. Somehow, he had to find a way to mitigate Pony's rage.

He held two reels of film in his hands, the first race and the third. If he could convince Pony of his plan by the end of the first race, there would be no need to suffer through the third.

Adept at the procedure, he set up the first reel on the super eight projector and had it ready just as Pony walked into the room.

"So where's the fuckin' retard now?" Pony demanded.

"At Mass General," Tommy replied from behind him, balancing a tray of drinks with one hand while he shut the door with the other.

"How come he ain't at the funeral parlour? Ya gettin' soft, Tommy?"

Pony yanked the table over towards his chair and set his bulk down. Tommy quickly placed a shot glass, a bottle of Johnnie Walker and a mug of beer in front of his boss. He ripped open a large bag of pretzels and poured them into a bowl within easy reach.

"Got your Glenlivet here, Mickey," he said, waving the bottle before setting it down beside the projector.

The frantic energy in the room set Mickey's nerves on edge. Contrary to habit, he poured himself a generous shot and gulped it down. He signalled to Tommy to turn off the overhead lights.

"I've got everything set up," he said as the room plunged into darkness and the film began to roll. The starting gate appeared on the screen.

"So where's the motherfucking retards?" Pony demanded.

"Mural is in number three post position," Mickey informed him, "and Wally's number five."

The latches opened. Without audio on the head-on view, the action was eerily silent, compelling the viewer to concentrate on every visual detail. The horse in the number three stall ducked to the right the moment he left the gate. The number five horse broke to the left. The two horses collided with such force that both jockeys were thrown off balance.

Pony slammed a fist down on the table, rattling glasses and bowls. "What do we have here, two fuckin' stooges?" He grabbed a glass and drank two shots of whiskey in rapid succession. "I'm paying the fuckin' pinheads to knock each others' balls off!"

"That might be the solution," Tommy suggested. "Geldings are easier to control."

This conversation was clearly going in the wrong direction. It wasn't the first time Tommy had suggested castration. He'd even offered to perform the operation himself.

"Cutting their balls off ain't gonna improve their brains, Tommy. How about ya do a lobot-tommie?"

Mickey glanced over to see if Pony was making a joke.

"I've done some research on that," Tommy replied. "You have to be precise, but I think I know which part of the skull to hit."

Mickey grabbed another shot. He'd known Tommy long enough to know he was serious. Even as a child, Tommy had relished a good fight. While Mickey had been watching Walt Disney matinees at the local movie theatre, Tommy was sneaking in at night to watch the gangster movies. Unlike his hero, Edward G Robinson, Tommy hadn't made it to the top of the pack, not yet.

"Do you want to see that again?" Tommy asked as Mickey stopped the projector.

"They break out of the gate one more time, they both fall off," Pony sneered. "Show me the rest of the race."

Mickey started the projector rolling. The horses were already out of the gate and picking up speed. At the half mile pole, Mural's horse suddenly swerved over to the rail sending the horse behind him into a cartwheel. As the jockey flew over the inside rail, Mickey looked away.

"I'd have given him a gun if I wanted him to snuff the guy," Pony bellowed, reaching for his mug of beer.

"It was really unfortunate he had to do that, but Leo wasn't backing off like he usually does," Tommy quickly explained. "Run that back, Mickey, so we can have a good look."

Mickey ran the film backwards, judging exactly where to pick up the action. The film began at the half mile pole.

"Who's the chump he ditched? Leo?" Pony asked.

"Yeah, Leo the Lamb," Tommy answered.

"So our fuckin' pinhead sends him to slaughter," Pony chuckled.

Pony's anger was mitigated by the sight of violence. It gave Mickey a sick feeling deep in his gut.

"Can ya believe that old geezer's still riding? Hell, he was around same time as yer nonno, Mick."

Mickey remembered his grandfather talking about Leo. He was one of his favourite jockeys. Very talented, grandpa Sheehan had said, and honest. Mickey turned back to the screen at the precise moment the girl's horse made his heroic leap.

Pony whooped and clapped his hands. "Hey, send that horse to England. We'll bet him in the Grand National!" He reached for another whiskey and the second bowl of pretzels. "Hell, this is more entertaining than the fuckin' movies. Show that again, Mick."

Mickey rewound the film, careful to avoid the gate scene. Pony whooped when the horse fell and clapped when the horse behind made his leap.

"Let's claim that hoss! We'll make a fortune in England."

"We did claim him," Mickey informed him.

"Smart move, Mickey," Tommy commended him. "Eddie says the horse has a couple of wins left in him."

"So we own the hoss? Great, we move him up a notch, put that jump rider back on and we make a killing. What's his name?"

"*Her* name is Andrea Crowley."

"What are ya talking about? That can't be no broad."

"That's the apprentice jockey I told you about," Mickey informed him, "the one from New York."

"What? The bitch that screwed up my trifecta?"

"We should have played her as part of it," Mickey insisted. "As you can see, they can't hold this girl back."

"But the fuckin' bitch screwed up my bet!" He glared in Tommy's direction.

"I had someone with her in the gate. He held her at the break, she got left seven lengths." Tommy threw his hands up in the air. "Like Mickey said, no one can hold her back!"

"Come on, she can't be that good, she's a fuckin' broad!"

Mickey poured himself another shot. "Take my word for it, she is that good. She was on a distance horse in a sprint," he explained pointedly. "She was left seven lengths behind the field and she hits the board."

"And this is the fuckin' broad ain't even broke her maiden?"

Mickey nodded. "That's her."

"It doesn't make any sense. If the broad's so good, why

ain't she won a race?"

"Because she's riding broken down nags that should have been in the glue factory a decade ago," Tommy said, fully on board with Mickey. "For some strange reason, the nags run the race of their life."

"She's our apprentice, Pony," Mickey assured him.

"My boys were riding races when the damn broad was in diapers," Pony mumbled as he drained his beer.

"And she's riding circles around them," Mickey added, his courage fuelled by the alcohol.

"God fuckin' damn!" Pony swore, wiping his mouth with the back of his hand. "I'm paying the fuckin' pinheads more than they've ever made and this broad comes along and whips their ass!"

Mickey shut off the projector and the room went dark. Tommy jumped up and turned the lights on.

"Never used a maiden jock before, and sure as hell not a broad!" Pony shoved the empty glass aside and glared at Tommy once again. "When's the Mule getting out of the hospital?"

"Tomorrow. He's got an appointment right here, twelve noon. He'll be whistling a new tune, I can tell you that."

"Kinda hard to whistle without yer front teeth." Pony laughed as he poured himself a shot of Johnny Walker.

Tommy laughed along with him, but Mickey didn't join in the laughter.

"I think you may be putting a little too much faith in Mural," He advised them.

The laughter stopped. Both men stared at Mickey.

"I know why he's not coming through for us."

Pony's expression turned dark and menacing. "Mule's two timing me?"

"No," Mickey replied quickly, averting the tide of rage that was about to erupt. "No one would dare interfere in your territory, Pony. And you're right about the boys having more experience than this girl. But think about it for a minute. That means they've had some serious spills, they've broken bones and knocked themselves senseless."

Pony eyed Mickey warily, leaning back in the chair until it groaned. "You saying my boys are chicken shit?"

Mickey knew he was about to tell Pony something he didn't want to hear, a dangerous proposition. He reached for the bottle, seeking reinforcement. "We've got to look at their lifestyle. Injuries aside, these boys have been dealing with a weight problem. They've been on stimulants and diuretics for decades. Their reflexes have slowed down and their brains aren't functioning at top speed." Mickey downed another shot. "That is, if they have any brain cells left."

Pony's chair groaned as he considered Mickey's theory.

"Shutting a horse off is no big deal to them," Mickey continued. "They know it's the guy behind who's going down. Like what Mural did to Leo. But in the end it doesn't help us. They take our number down. And then they give our boy a long vacation."

Pony's chair tipped forward and he grabbed the bottle. "Yeah, sure, he's got days, but what the hell, he got his point across. Leo chicken shit lamb won't be messing with him again."

Pony poured himself half a glass.

"Leo isn't our concern," Mickey said, his tongue loosened by the Scotch. "It's what our jocks do that matters. And they're missing golden opportunities. Let me show you what I mean."

He signalled Tommy to shut down the lights and started the projector rolling. The action picked up where they had left off at the half mile pole. The horses rounded the turn and headed into the homestretch.

"That's Mural behind the three leaders. You can see the horse directly in front of him is glued to the rail so he's not going to get through on the inside. Now, a horse is coming up on his outside. He's stuck."

As the action carried on, a small opening appeared

between two of the three leaders.

"There it is, a gift from heaven!" Mickey said dramatically.

"That hole's not big enough for a greyhound," Tommy argued.

Mickey kept silent as the action continued. Pony leaned forward and squinted at the screen just as the horse on the outside of Mural flew up into the narrow opening.

"He who hesitates loses the race," Mickey stated succinctly.

"Son of a bitch!" Pony swore, slamming his hand down on the table.

"I can't believe it!" Tommy exclaimed, rolling his shoulders and flexing his muscles as if he was about to step into the ring. "He told me he couldn't get through on the rail. Honest to God, that's what he said!"

"Chicken shit bastard!" Pony yelled.

"He said he got screwed up coming out of the gate and had to go to the inside to save ground, then he got stuck in traffic. Wally was supposed to look out for the girl, keep her out of the action."

"Looks like they kept each other out of the action." Mickey added a little more fuel to the fire.

"Son of a bitch!" Pony thundered again, knocking a glass over as he reached for the Johnny Walker.

Tommy quickly righted the glass and poured a generous shot. "Okay, the girl's got guts. We can't deny that. But really, Mickey, do we want another Smartalex on the payroll?"

Mickey shook his head. "We don't have to fly this girl half way across the country like we did with Alex. We don't have to give her a nice apartment and a kilo of blow every week. And we don't put her on the payroll. We simply get her on horses with some ability, tell the boys to run interference for her, and let her do what she does best, ride like the wind."

"What does she tack?" Tommy asked, sounding like he might be open to the idea. "If we put her on long shots, she'll be getting in pretty damn light."

"She can tack a hundred and five without coming anywhere near the sweatbox."

"Holy shit, she weighs about the same as my foot," Pony snorted. "Maybe the broad's got more guts than the Mule, but them lightweights ain't got no strength. They can't hold a hoss back."

"We don't want her to hold them back," Mickey said with a smile.

"Mickey's got a point." Tommy spun on his heels, as if on military parade. He took three steps and spun again. "I think we've got our next bug rider, Pony. Eddie told me she won't take guff from anyone."

"Your fratello says she's alright?" Pony asked, almost on board.

"Yeah, Eddie says she's the real thing."

"He can keep her in line?"

"No problem."

"I'm gonna have to trust ya on this," Pony said, reaching into an empty bowl.

"I'll get you some more." Tommy marched towards the door.

"Never mind the pretzels, get me a winner," Pony barked.

Tommy halted and turned in the same stride. He flexed his shoulder and neck muscles as he walked back.

Mickey began breathing easier.

"We'll get you a winner alright, a big one," Tommy promised, throwing a couple of punches.

"The show's all yours," Pony said, downing his whisky. "I'm going to Atlantic City tomorrow. I got some reliable boys there, kind that don't fuck up. So you two gotta take care of things here. Mick, ya get the broad on a long shot. Tommy, ya talk to the boys, get them lined up."

Tommy nodded. "The Boston boys will be back in a couple of days. And they won't be riding like the butchers from Rhode Island." He rolled his shoulders and hit his knuckles together. "This new head steward, Arthur Healey, is really laying down the law, watching every move the jocks make. But don't worry, the Suffolk boys will use a little more finesse to get the job done."

"They better. One more screw up and the Winter gang takes us all out," Pony grumbled. "Ya think Mural looked rough? Hell, he's still alive!"

"When you get back from Atlantic City, we'll have the job done right," Tommy promised. "Won't we Mickey?"

Mickey poured a shot and held the glass high. "Here's to the biggest bet of the year!"

PAHK THE CAH

Candace dropped the overnight sheet on Andy's lap. "I got ya named on four mounts, but only two of them drew in."

Andy stared at the list of races. She saw her name on horses in the first and second race. In races six and eight, her name was on horses on the also eligible list.

"Hey, you never know, someone could scratch from the later races and we could draw in. The weather forecast calls for rain. There's always scratches if the track's muddy."

"Yeah, and your hosses'll be the first to scratch. They don't like mud."

Andy shrugged her shoulders. "Okay, two mounts it is. So, who are they? I see one is named Little Miss and the other is Dundurn Dancer."

"Two hosses ya galloped for Emmett."

Andy was immediately suspicious. "What's wrong with them?"

"Why does something have to be wrong with them?"

"Because Emmett has his own apprentice. Why isn't Billy Feagin riding them?"

"The hoss in the first race is a first time starter. Billy's too green to be riding a hoss his first time out. Besides, he hasn't got the smarts. I told ya that you'd be riding for Emmett. Billy will get a few mounts but he won't last long. You'll be Emmet's bug rider like you were supposed to be."

When she arrived at Suffolk Downs, she would have been

221

thrilled to be riding for the leading trainer, but so much had changed in a month's time.

"You never know what a horse will do when they run in their first race. I'll bet Emmett's riding me so his apprentice doesn't get hurt."

"He's riding you because the owner said so. It's the Kentucky colt."

Andy's attitude changed immediately. "You're kidding? He's put me on the colt?"

"Yeah, best hoss in the barn...maybe. Not going to know for sure till he runs. Ya see what he's running for? Maiden special weights. That's top class not some cheap claiming race.

That hoss will carry you back to New York." Candace hung up the bridle she'd been holding, "Ya win that race and Emmett'll have ya on everything in the barn. Feagin'll be on the also eligible."

"Let's not get carried away," Andy warned her. "You said it was the owner who put me on. Al grooms Mickey's horses and he's only got three, the nice colt and two claimers."

"Mark my words, you do a good job on this colt and Emmett will name ya on everything in the barn. He'll make ya leading rider. Just remember to thank your agent at the big award's dinner."

"When I win the award, you'll be the first person I acknowledge in my acceptance speech." Andy pulled her helmet off and wiped the sweat from her forehead.

"Tomorrow I ride, today I'm a tourist."

"I hear you're taking Charlie out on the town. Don't be showing up with a hangover tomorrow. Ya need to be sharp."

"Don't worry about it, I'll be bright eyed and bushy tailed."

Charlie came down the shed row, Rupert and Jasper at her side. "Come on, time is wasting. Let's make the best of it."

They waved as they left and made their way to the parking

lot, piling the dogs into the car and enjoying a leisurely drive home. After a quick bath, Andy put on a pair of neatly pressed corduroy pants with small flared bell bottoms. A white blouse and hounds-tooth jacket completed the outfit. She glanced with satisfaction at the trim figure in the cheval mirror, formal enough for a restaurant, but still the functional horsewoman.

"How do I look, Dolly Button? Am I presentable enough?"

The tabby cat looked up from her roost on top of the book case. She yawned and stretched in response.

"Yeah, you're right, it's more comfortable than stylish," Andy agreed. "But I've never been able to keep up with the latest fashion."

"So, what do you think?" Charlie's voice called out from the hallway.

"I think we've got to install a shower," Andy remarked as she turned around. "This bath thing just doesn't d—"

She stared at the figure standing before her. Charlie was dressed in dark blue cotton loon pants, the wide bottoms completely covering her platform shoes. She was now a foot taller than Andy. Her voile shirt had what looked like a hundred tiny buttons, the sleeves ballooned out and tied at the wrists. A short fitted brown velvet jacket with silver buttons completed the outfit.

Andy turned and gazed at her own reflection in the mirror. "Oh my God, I'm completely under-dressed."

"Not at all. You're very spiffy, a true horsewoman. It suits you." Charlie held up a worn, camel hair coat. "This will spoil the whole effect, but summer isn't quite here. It's no use freezing for the sake of fashion."

She picked up a purse large enough to meet the demands of an Amazon and slung it over her shoulder. "We're off!" she announced, doing a much better imitation of Jim Hannon than Andy could.

The dogs watched them leave, whimpering in protest.

"I'll bring you a treat," Charlie promised, waving as she

stepped out the door.

"How glorious, a whole afternoon off! What shall we do? Where will we go?"

"Where it all began," Andy said, holding up a thermos of tea and two china cups. "Boston Harbour."

"You mean where it all ended," Charlie said in a very precise English accent.

"I guess it depends on your perspective," Andy laughed.

Within twenty minutes, and two wrong turns, they were in downtown Boston. Andy pulled over to the curb.

"I think we're safe here," she said, tucking the Volvo into a tight spot. "I hear Boston is notorious for towing cars away."

Charlie leaped out of the car, anxious to get going. "I'll stow the cups in my purse. You take the thermos."

Andy grabbed the thermos and they set off.

"Wait a minute, I don't want to do this again."

"Do what?" Charlie asked, confused.

"I parked in New York City once and forgot to check the street name. Took me two days to find my car. By then it had no wheels." They walked to the nearest intersection and looked up at the street signs. "Beacon and Park Streets. Commit that to memory."

"Information filed." Charlie took a deep breath. "Okay, history major, tell me the story of the Boston Tea Party."

"One of my favourites." She rubbed her hands together in anticipation. "I'll take you on the same tour my father gave me when I was in high school."

They walked amid a stream of afternoon shoppers and tourists, the spring sun warming their souls if not their bodies. Andy's sense of direction was much improved when she was a pedestrian. Soon they were on Washington Street at the Downtown Crossing.

"Here it is, the South Meeting House," she announced, thoroughly enjoying her role as tour guide. "This was built in 1729 and was the largest building in Boston during those early days. It was a Congregational Church then, a popular meeting place. It's gone through a few renovations. Back in 1775, during the revolution, *your* countrymen gutted the inside."

"Sorry," Charlie said with feigned contrition. "I'm sure they had a good reason."

"Yes, they used it as a riding arena," Andy explained, "for the Lighthorse 17th Regiment of Dragoons."

"My God, how can you remember all that?"

"History was my major at University. I was taking ancient history, Rome and Greece, but I love reading anything historical. And Massachusetts is *our* ancient history." Andy pointed to the building. "Anyway, back to the Regiment. Not only did they have horses but they installed a bar up in the gallery. Funny how horses and alcohol always go together."

"Don't forget gambling," Charlie reminded her.

"How could I. Without it, we wouldn't have a job." Andy stared at the tall steeple and ornate clock tower. "A very important meeting was held here on December 16, 1773. English parliament had imposed a tax on tea and the colonists were furious." She tapped her fingers against the thermos to make her point. "The Sons of Liberty disguised themselves as Mohawks. They made their way from the meeting house to Griffin's Wharf. If you'll follow me, please. "

In true tourist guide fashion, Andy led the way down Washington Street. "We're not on the exact route. Several tons of landfill have changed the landscape not to mention these high rise buildings. And to tell you the truth, the precise location of Griffin's Wharf has been disputed. But we'll be close enough."

There were no wrong turns as Andy found her way to the harbour. She avoided the few tourists who were braving the early spring weather to visit the historic site with its museum and souvenir shops. She found a secluded spot to continue her lecture.

"There were three ships here in the harbour, all loaded

with tea from the East India Company. The Dartmouth and the Eleanor were here at the wharf. The Beaver was anchored further out in the harbour. So, our band of mock Mohawks made it to the wharf and they quietly boarded the ships. They found the wooden crates of tea, hauled them on deck and hacked them open".

"And with great glee dumped them overboard," Charlie said, wincing as if in pain. "All that lovely tea!"

"All for a good cause," Andy assured her. "Your country-man, Admiral Montague, was the man in charge, so to speak. He saw the tired, but happy, Mohawks trudging by his house and called out, 'Fine job you've done with your Indian dis-guise, boys, but you have got to pay the fiddler yet!'"

Andy unscrewed the thermos and Charlie dug into her voluminous purse, holding up two slightly chipped cups. When the steaming liquid was poured, they gently clinked the fragile china cups together.

"Long live the revolutionary spirit," Andy toasted.

"To reconciliation and better days," Charlie added, taking a sip. "Oh my God, it's Earl Grey."

Andy grinned. "I splurged. I've got two new mounts tomorrow. That may not go down in history, but in my books, it's a big event."

"And it's just the beginning," Charlie assured her. "Every-one says you've got the talent to make it to the top."

"If I get the horses who can take me there, you bet I will."

"Come on," Charlie said, draining her cup. "It's time for Filene's. Everyone tells me you haven't experienced Boston until you've been to Filene's basement."

"Everyone except my parents." Andy finished her tea and handed the cup back to Charlie. "The Coop Bookstore is the highlight of Boston according to them. It sounds like my kind of place, but I'll need to win a few races before I dare step in there. Today, we do freebies."

As famous as Filene's was, it wasn't part of the Freedom Trail. Andy had to ask directions. Within minutes, they were at the famous department store. Charlie headed for the basement and Andy lost her in the crowd. When she found her, she grabbed a hold of her purse strap and hung on.

"Hey, what do you think?" Charlie asked, selecting a hat and putting it on.

Andy looked up to see a crocheted skullcap in shades of pink and mulberry purple with a floppy flower sewn on the side.

"I never realized you were so eclectic," Andy replied.

"Weird, strange, way out—is that what you mean?"

"I mean you're one of a kind."

"Okay, I'll take that as a 'go ahead and buy the hat, quipped Charlie'."

"Yes, buy the hat and let's get out of here," Andy insisted, elbowing her way through the crowd. "God, this is harder than trying to get by Carlo and Pedro."

When they were finally back on the street, Andy looked both ways trying to decide which direction to follow.

"What was the name of the restaurant Pete recommended?" Andy asked.

"It's called The Whistling Clam. They said it has the best seafood in town," Charlie replied.

They asked a passerby for directions and were given several left and right turns.

"I can't even follow simple directions like turn right at the corner and there it is," Andy complained. "Let's just walk down the street and see what we find."

"Alright, but we better find something soon. It's almost past your bedtime."

Andy elbowed her in the ribs and they set off. Several blocks later, they saw a sign for a seafood restaurant.

"The Smiling Oyster," Andy said as she read the sign, 'the finest seafood in town'.

"Smiling oysters, whistling clams, what the heck."

"Oh, oh, somebody's getting grumpy."

"I'm starving and my feet hurt. Come on, if we can't have

the best seafood I'll settle for the finest."

Andy opened the door and they walked in and looked around. "The decor is a bit drab. Maybe it's like some Chinese restaurants, shabby interior but great food."

Charlie looked at her, eyebrows raised. "If there's a cockroach in my soup, I'm leaving."

"If there's a cockroach in the soup, we get our meal for free. Come on, let's sit down and take a load off our feet."

They chose a booth and sank gratefully into the soft seat. In unison, they looked over at the bottles arranged over the bar.

"Where'd ya park?" the bartender called over to them.

"I pahked the cah at Hahvahd yahd," Andy replied, reciting the famous Boston line.

The bartender roared with laughter.

"Candace would be proud of you," Charlie said with a thumbs up.

"What'll ya have, ladies?"

"Do you think he knows how to make a pina colada?" Charlie whispered.

Andy looked back over at the bartender, his arm muscles rippling as he wiped down the bar.

"I wouldn't go for the exotic drinks if I were you. Try something simple."

"I'll have a gin and tonic," Charlie called out.

"Rum and coke for me."

"Ya got it," he replied, reaching for the bottles.

When he placed the drinks on their table, he handed them menus.

"My waitress is outta town. Holler when ya ready and I'll take the order."

"Okay," Andy said with a smile.

Charlie took a sip of her drink and grimaced. "I thought prohibition was over. This must be what they called bathtub gin. Here, try it."

Andy shook her head. "I hate any kind of gin."

"Oh, go on, try it," Charlie insisted. "Close your eyes and think of England."

"I'd rather drink my rum and think of Jamaica." Andy picked up her glass and took a sip before scanning the menu.

"Right, we'd better order soon or you'll be falling asleep at the table."

"It's only seven o'clock." Andy was about to hit her over the head with her menu when someone caught her eye. "Holy crow, this really is a seafood restaurant. You're not going to believe this but a whale is coming down the aisle."

"What?" Charlie turned and looked behind her before quickly turning back. "You're right, he's as big as a beluga. What do you think he weighs, four hundred pounds?"

"I'll bet five jockeys could weigh in together and not balance the scales with him. But hey, if he eats here, the food must be great."

"See ya, Pony!" the bar tender called out as the big man headed towards the door. "Ya have a good trip."

"Pony?" Andy repeated. "I think Clyde would be more appropriate."

She dropped her menu and slapped the back of her own hand.

"What's that about?" Charlie asked. "Some weird Irish superstition so you'll never get fat?"

Andy shook her head. "If my mother was here, she'd slap my hand for being rude. She never lets me make derogatory remarks about people."

"Derogatory? I'd call that the simple truth."

Andy watched the fat man as he headed towards the door. She inhaled sharply when the man walking behind him became visible.

"No way, surely there isn't someone bigger?" Charlie exclaimed, glancing back over her shoulder.

"The guy behind him, that's the man who was with Eddie Flaherty in the parking lot."

"He's an identical copy," Charlie said, "only twenty

pounds heavier. They've got to be twins."

"They're definitely brothers."

"He's a good looking fella. Maybe he's more available than his brother."

Andy shook her head vigorously. "No thanks, I've got other things to think about, like my career."

"Come on, you must have at least one romantic bone somewhere in that skinny body."

"I'm not skinny just wiry," Andy retorted. "Once I'm established, there'll be plenty of time for romance."

"Time," Charlie repeated, looking at her watch. "Better make your order quick. You'll be turning into a pumpkin in ten minutes."

DUNDURN DANCER

A ndy walked into the jocks' room just as Denise strolled
out of the bedroom.

"Had a good nap?" she asked, watching her stretch.

"It's was an early morning for me," Denise said before
yawning. "My agent had me up too early. I keep telling him
I don't want to gallop until the sun comes up."

"Sounds like you have about as much control over your
agent as I do," Andy remarked, sitting down on the couch
with the *Form*.

"You're riding a first timer, I see."

"Yes," Andy replied. "Two races in a row today. Won't
exactly get me an article in The Blood-Horse magazine but
it's a start."

"What post position did you get?"

"One."

"Oh, oh, that's the worst for a first timer. You're better
off with a horse on either side of you, to keep him going
straight."

"There's not much I can do about it except pray that he
comes out straight."

She opened the paper to the first race at Suffolk Downs.
There was no past performance record on her mount as he
had never raced but there was a list of his workouts, includ-
ing the quarter mile breeze she had done down the stretch.
His sire was Round Table and he was out of a mare named
Skyeworth who was by First Landing.

"My God, he has to be the best bred horse on the grounds," she exclaimed.

Denise walked over and took a look at the *Form*.

"Yeah, you don't see those bloodlines around here until the Mass Cap," she agreed. "M&M Stables, huh? They usually have a bunch of cheap claimers. Watch out, they can have some serious leg problems."

"I galloped one of his claimers and told him the horse was sore behind. The next time I galloped him, he was sound. His groom, Al, told me he has a magic liniment that'll cure anything."

"Don't trust those magic cures. They sometimes only last as far as the quarter pole."

"It's the least of my worries today, at least in the first race. There's nothing wrong with this colt, he's just inexperienced."

"Don't fall in love with him," Denise warned her. "If he runs good today, he'll be sold tomorrow. You can't fall in love with a racehorse, girl, it'll break your heart."

"It's impossible not to fall in love with him."

"If he's got any speed at all, you'll want to go to the front. Half of the field is first time starters. My mount has already had a start so I know what to expect. I'll be laying second until the eighth pole. Then it's see you all later."

"Not if I can help it."

Andy's cool demeanour was mostly an act. She'd watched enough two year old races to know that a young horse's behaviour was unpredictable. At Belmont, she once saw a two year old come out of the gate in the number one post position and jump the inside rail. The memory didn't fill her with confidence.

She forced the image out of her mind and looked for the positives. She was the only apprentice in the race. The other nine horses were being ridden by experienced jockeys. She didn't have to worry about another bug rider making a mistake. Having Juan anywhere near her would be cause for alarm.

Denise was on the number three horse and Eddie was on the ten. Pedro was in the race. He and Carlo were both back from serving their suspensions and had been warned they were under close scrutiny. The newly appointed steward, John Krikorian, was getting the hang of his job and was quick to point out any infractions. Arthur had his Lancelot.

The two women dressed for the first race and Andy spent some quiet moments visualizing a successful ride. When the call came for jockeys out, she followed behind Denise who gave her more pointers on keeping the colt straight coming out of the gate.

"Be ready to cock your whip first stride out. Give him a crack on the shoulder if he acts like he might duck out."

Andy nodded as she walked towards the number one stall. She wished Pete was waiting for her instead of Emmett. Reassuring him would take her mind off her own nervousness. And Charlie could always be counted on to make her smile.

She consoled herself with the fact that she'd be getting a leg up on the best bred horse in the race. The best horse on the entire racetrack, she told herself, boosting her own confidence. When she reached the number one stall, Emmett was talking to Mickey but he wasn't listening. His eyes were on his colt as Alonzo led him around the saddling paddock.

Andy looked at the young horse closely. He pranced nervously and spooked when a bettor waved his program. Alonzo spoke to him in Spanish and he calmed down. Good, she thought to herself, he's responding.

Denise's mount was anything but calm. He reared and knocked his groom down. Eddie was passing just at that moment and grabbed the horse's reins. When the groom was back on his feet, dusty but uninjured, Eddie walked beside him as they led the horse over to the trainer.

Mickey stepped out of the stall as she approached and signalled to her to follow

"You know this colt," he said when they were out of

Emmett's earshot. "He has natural speed. Use it. I don't care what Emmett tells you, go to the front and stay there."

Andy saw Emmett coming over. She didn't like the way this was going. She was about to get caught between opposing instructions from the owner and the trainer. With Mickey's brooding glare, she wasn't about to argue with him. She simply nodded and turned to hear what Emmett had to say.

Emmett Gibbons was nothing like Pete before a race. Rather than worry about his horse, he was looking at all the others. "I think that's Pete Kingsley's colt, he's the one to beat. And that three horse, he's had some really fast workouts. He'll go to the front for sure. You don't want to get into a speed duel with him so take back." Emmett's darting glance settled momentarily on Andy. "If you're too far in front and he can't see any other horses, he could start loafing. Colts have a tendency to do that. Keep a horse beside you as long as you can."

Mickey looked deliberately at Andy. He held a hand up, his fingers taking the shape of a gun firing straight ahead. Andy agreed with Mickey that they should take the lead, but she didn't like the gun metaphor.

Alonzo was beaming with pride as he led the colt and Andy was boosted into the saddle. She was relieved to be up on the horse's back and headed to the track.

"You break my maiden today," Alonzo said excitedly.

"Careful how you put that," she said, looking over at the people gathered along the fence. "Some people don't understand racetrack lingo."

"It no matter," he said with a grin. "They no touch him today, you win easy."

"I like that prediction, Al. I'll do everything I can to make it come true."

Alonzo kissed the horse before he turned him over to the pony rider. Andy was surprised to see Ringo in the saddle.

"What's this, you've got a new job?"

"Hey, I can always use a few extra bucks," Ringo replied with a grin. "And if it means taking Sandy Andy to the gate, that's a bonus."

"Ladies and Gentlemen, please note that there has been a name change on a horse in this first race," Jim Hannon's voice called out over the loudspeakers. "The number one horse, listed as Dundurn Dancer in today's program, has been re-registered."

"It better be a noble name," Andy said, crossing her fingers.

"The colt is now named Excalibur."

"Oh my God!" she gasped, every cell in her body tingling.

Ringo looked at her. "Hey, man, what's wrong? You don't like his new name? It's a bad omen or something?"

"I love it," she exclaimed, looking up to the sky. "We really are in Camelot!"

Ringo looked at her, a worried expression on his face. "Andy, you shouldn't be trippin' before a race. That's dangerous, man."

Andy laughed. "I'm not tripping, Ringo. When we gallop together tomorrow, I'll tell you the story of King Arthur and Camelot."

Ringo grinned from ear to ear. "Great, man, I love a story."

"Show them what you've got, Andrea Crowley!"

Andy recognized the voice immediately. She looked over at the grandstand. A tall, dark haired man waved at her.

"Uncle Michael! What are you doing here?"

"I'm here to watch my niece win a race," he called back. "That colt's got the pedigree to show them the way home."

"Sounds good to me," she said with a grin.

Excalibur suddenly bucked, tipping Andy over his shoulder. She quickly righted herself.

"Let's get a move on," she instructed Ringo. "We need to get his mind on business."

When the post parade was over, Ringo urged his pony

horse into a gallop. They did a brisk quarter mile and the colt finally settled into an even rhythm, taking a nice hold of the bit. Andy was happy with his behaviour.

Denise's mount was still rearing and almost had the pony girl out of the saddle. Eddie's horse, who was without a pony, balked as they lined up for the gate. One of the starting crew ran towards him, but Eddie waved him away. He sat quietly on the horse, allowing him to look around and take everything in. With a deep breath and a shake of his head, the little chestnut colt walked forward to join the others.

"This one is yours," Ringo said as he led her behind the gate. He gave her the victory sign as she was loaded into the number one stall.

She took a deep breath. It could be a long wait.

"You okay?" the handler asked. "We're one man short. I gotta help out."

She had no idea what the colt would be like, but the handler was gone before she had a chance to answer. Excalibur trembled.

"Easy, beautiful boy, don't you worry about a thing," she said softly, turning his head so he could see the other horses. "You're not alone."

The grey colt in the stall next to them swung his head violently and the handler yelped in pain. Andy quickly turned the colt's head in the other direction.

"This is a much better view," she said, keeping up a chatter to keep them both relaxed. "You have noble breeding, my dear Excalibur, you're a true blueblood."

"Last horse coming in! " the starter called out.

Andy straightened the colt's head. "Let's show them the way home, Excalibur."

The gate opened and she expelled her breath with a sharp yell of encouragement. The colt exploded into action. Andy scrubbed his neck with her hands, urging him on. In three strides, they were in the lead.

The excited colt ran with his head high, his front legs

climbing. Andy slowed her tempo. Time to coast.

The wind whistled by her ears, muffling the sound of the other horses. The colt continued at his frenzied pace, his breath caught deep within his chest. If he kept this up, he wouldn't last half a mile.

"Breathe, Excalibur, breathe," she called out to him.

The quarter pole slipped by.

"Excalibur, you've got to take a breath," she pleaded.

Finally, the colt responded. His head came down as his ribs expanded in a deep breath. His legs reached out in a powerful, even rhythm. The turn loomed ahead. Excalibur changed his lead smoothly. They hugged the rail around the turn, saving every inch of ground. They entered the home-stretch with a clear track ahead.

Andy lifted her elbow and looked back. Only one horse was in sight, a good three lengths back.

A thunderous roar erupted from the grandstand. The colt threw his head. Alarmed by the noise, he broke his stride. Andy cocked her whip and waved it furiously.

"Go, Excalibur, go! It's your fans cheering you on!"

Eddie's shrill whistle rose above the thunder as he caught up to them. The sharp sound sent Excalibur forward. He launched himself as if breaking from the gate once again. Andy reached out with his impulsion as the thunder continued to roll from the grandstand. Eddie disappeared from view.

Andy thrilled to the colt's effortless stride. She stretched out over his withers as the sound of hundreds of cheering fans urging them on. Without another horse in sight, they skimmed under the wire.

A hundredth of a second changed her whole life. Andy stood up in the stirrups, a winner.

"Yes!" she screamed, patting the colt before pumping the air with her fist.

"Yeehaw!" Ringo yelled out as she passed the starting gate.

She wanted to gallop around the track one more time, to thrill to the colt's extraordinary stride but it was time to pull up and let him have his well deserved rest. When he came to a halt, she wrapped her arms around his neck and kissed him. Still fresh despite his exertions, the colt spun around almost unseating her. She quickly gathered the reins and brought him under control. The other horses were just pulling up.

"Where the heck were you guys?" she asked with a grin.

"We were in the second race," Eddie quipped, admiration in his eyes as he looked at the colt. "I thought you'd be in New York by now."

Andy laughed as she stroked Excalibur's neck.

"Good ride," he congratulated her."

"I have you to thank for that win."

"What are you talking about, you beat me by a city block."

"The noise from the grandstand spooked him half way down the stretch. He lost his stride."

"You mean when I caught up to you?"

"Yes. It was your whistle that sent him off again."

"You're kidding!" Eddie gasped, sucking air into his depleted lungs. "Damn, why didn't I keep my mouth shut."

She laughed as the colt pranced off, breaking into a smooth, rhythmic gallop.

Mickey was waiting for her in the unsaddling area, his face beaming. Andy had never seen such a transformation in a man. He looked anything but sleazy as he led his colt into the winner's circle.

INITIATION

Mickey congratulated Andy on her ride. "A tense moment there in mid-stretch but whatever you did to keep him going was perfect."

She was about to explain when she heard her uncle call out to her, waving his mutual ticket. "Brilliant ride, Andrea. Even Shoemaker couldn't have done better."

Mickey glanced curiously in his direction.

"He's my uncle," Andy explained. "He drove here from New York. Can he come in the win picture?"

"Of course." Mickey waved at the security guard to let him in.

Bettors flocked around the perimeter fence to get a look at the handsome colt. Some of them congratulated her as Mickey stood the horse in position for the picture.

Andy looked out over the infield. The view was better than she had imagined when she stood here on her own two feet. From the back of a magnificent Thoroughbred, the view was spectacular.

The photographer called for everyone's attention. Emmett stood in the trainer's position at the colt's flank while Mickey stood near the colt's head. Alonzo held the reins, beaming with pride as he gazed at the horse. Michael Crowley's eyes were on the jockey.

Andy gave her biggest smile when the camera flashed. As everyone congratulated each other, she leaped from the saddle, landing as light and agile as a cat and put her arms around the colt's neck.

"You're the best, Excalibur. You and I could be back in your old Kentucky home next spring," she told the colt. "The first Saturday in May."

"I'll be there for that one," her uncle said with a laugh. "Meet me in the clubhouse after your next race. This calls for a special celebration."

"I'll be there."

Andy pulled her saddle off the colt's back as Al started to lead him out of the winner's circle. When he walked by her, she would have sworn the boy was taller.

"Has this kid grown in the past couple of hours?" she called over to Ringo as he arrived on his pony horse.

"Naw, it's just because he's walking on air," Ringo said with a grin as he followed the colt.

Andy laughed as she made her way to the scale room. It felt like she was walking on air herself as she stepped up on the scale.

"Good one," Gerry commended her. "You'll go far with that colt."

"You've got an eye for a good horse, Mr. Marinick," she replied, feeling giddy with success. "He's the best."

Mickey met her as she stepped off the scale. "You did exactly what I asked," he said. "I like a jockey who can follow instructions."

"Your colt made it easy to follow instructions. You've got a stakes horse there, Mr Amato. He's really something."

"Emmett will give you a lecture about being too far in front," he warned her. "Don't worry about it. You'll be back on the colt next time out."

"I appreciate that, Mr. Amato. Thank you. I'd be pleased to ride any horse for you."

"I'll keep you in mind for the others," he promised.

With that, he turned and quickly caught up with Al. Andy took a long look at the magnificent bay colt. This was the horse that would get her back to New York. She'd have to talk to Mickey about some stakes races at Belmont.

She suddenly remembered she was riding the next race. Half way across the saddling paddock, Andy looked around for the other jockeys. The paddock was strangely silent. There were no voices excitedly discussing the events of the race. She wondered just how long she'd been in the winners' circle.

As she reached the steps leading down into the hallway, whoops and hollers suddenly engulfed her. Ice water hit her in the face and chest as a force knocked her legs out from under her. She fell on her back as more water doused her, ice cubes slipping under her silks. Shaving cream filled her mouth, nose and ears.

As quickly as the attack began, it ended.

Andy couldn't see a thing as she spit the vile taste of shaving cream from her mouth and tried desperately to get it out of her eyes. Wiping her hands on her breeches did little to help as they were sodden. It was several minutes before she could actually see the grinning faces surrounding her.

"Hey kid, you're now officially a jockey," Leo Valente announced.

Andy tried to speak, but choked on shaving cream. The jockeys laughed, patting the one dry spot on her shoulder.

Eddie held a hand out and pulled her to her feet. "Congratulations. Great ride."

"Fanks," Andy spluttered, still choking as she slipped down the stairs.

"Careful, you don't want to break a leg on the way to the jocks' room," Eddie warned her, putting a hand on her sodden shoulder to balance her. "I just got a lecture from the trainer I rode for. He thinks I could take lessons from you. He wasn't too happy with second place."

"Tell him even Willie Shoemaker wouldn't have caught me today," she said, grinning beneath the foam."

Eddie opened the door to the women's quarters. "Better hop in the shower quick. You don't have much time before the second."

Andy dragged her sodden body across the room. Denise jumped out of her way.

"I thought I'd watch it all from in here," she said. "I've got the shower running for you. Congratulations, Andy."

"Thanks." She peeled the wet breeches and silks off and dropped them on the floor as she stepped into the shower. She wanted to linger under the hot water but had only minutes to get ready. By the time she was out and dressed in clean racing breeches, Darrell was bringing in the silks. Andy inspected the one she would be wearing. It had white initials, AD, set on a black background.

"Someone doesn't have much flair for design," she remarked, slipping into them. "But

that's okay, I'll blend into the background and you won't see me coming."

"You mean going," Denise corrected her. "You've got the speed in this race too. "

Andy took one last look at the *Daily Racing Form*. The owner's name was Aberto D'Addazio. His five year old mare, Little Miss, had raced fifteen times in her life and had won only one of them. According to her past performance chart, she had plenty of speed, but it didn't last the full six furlongs.

"At least I won't be getting dirt in my face till the last six-teenth," she sighed, putting her helmet on over her wet hair as she walked with Denise out the door.

A commotion was going on in front of the number six stall when she arrived in the paddock. It seemed like the main population of the paddock had gathered there. It sounded like a lively, Italian family reunion. As Andy approached, a big man grabbed her hand and shook it with bone crushing intensity. She assumed this was Mr D'Addazio. He introduced her to his wife, his son, several cousins and three mechanics who worked in his auto repair shop. In a loud and boisterous voice, he promised to do her car maintenance free for a year if she won the race.

"You win this one, you've got the mount on my Kentucky horse."

As much as she wanted to ride another Kentucky horse, she was relieved when Emmett took her aside to give her instructions.

"You went too far in front in that last race," he told her, just as Mickey had predicted. "Don't open up so much with this mare. She's got speed so you'll be in front but, gear her down. A length is all you need."

The call came for riders to mount up and Mustang led the horse over. Emmett hoisted her into the saddle and the D'Addazio's waved and wished her luck.

Mustang led the mare towards the track. "She's ready to roll so don't you blow it."

"Thanks for the vote of confidence," Andy replied drily.

When they stepped onto the track, she was surprised to see Candace and Bucky waiting for her. "You're a pony girl for hire now?"

"Naw, Emmett's pony horse blew a shoe on the way back to the barn. Kinda hard for me to refuse him when he's using my rider." She slipped the leather strap through the bridle. "Ya got a real speedball here. She can burn some rubber, but she's hard to rate. You'll need those magic hands of yours to get her to settle."

"I'll see what I can do."

Candace reached over and slapped her shoulder. "Congratulations, jock, you looked as good as the Shoe coming down the stretch."

Andy grinned. "Thanks, but the real credit goes to my agent. She got me the mount."

Candace smiled in acknowledgement of the compliment. "Your agent's happy with her twenty percent."

They both laughed as they walked their horses through the post parade.

"Emmett wants me to use her speed," Andy remarked, looking around at the other horses. "But Carlo's got a speed horse too. Pedro will come from behind. He'll coast by us if we run each other into the ground."

"Carlo won't want to get in a speed duel with ya. Never mind Pedro, Eddie's the one ya got to watch out for. His hoss has a late kick, could catch ya at the wire."

Andy used the warm-up to get a sense of the mare's way of running. When she took a strong grip on the reins, the mare fought her. When she lengthened the reins, the mare relaxed.

When they approached the gate, all horses loaded without incident. Andy had only a few seconds in the stall before the latches opened. Little Miss headed right to the lead. Carlo's horse started to go with her, but he pulled back. Little Miss galloped quickly to the lead. Andy let the reins dangle slightly and sat chilly. She glanced under her arm. She was two lengths in front of the pack.

She had to save the little mare for the final sixteenth of a mile. She kept her at an even pace throughout the backstretch and around the turn. She still had the lead coming into the homestretch. Her view to the finish was unimpeded, but it had never looked so far away. Andy struggled against the impulse to go to the whip. She had to save that for the final strides.

The roar from the grandstand deafened her to the sound of the horses behind. The closers would be making their move, but she didn't dare look back and risk throwing the mare off stride. Instead, she sat quietly, using as little energy as possible.

The sixteenth pole slipped by and she felt Little Miss begin to tire. Andy shortened her reins to give her more support. Still in front at the seventy yards pole, she could almost taste victory.

"Come on, Little Miss, you can do it!"

Suddenly the filly's stride shortened and her head dropped. As they neared the wire, Andy struggled to hold the exhausted horse up.

In a flash, two horses charged up beside her, their jockeys screaming, whistling and whipping. Andy grasped the reins in one hand and reached out with her whip, tapping the mare under the chin. Little Miss stretched out her neck and put her nose over the wire first.

Andy stood up in the stirrups, about to let out a cheer when Little Miss stumbled and unseated her. Without warning, she somersaulting over the filly's neck. Instinctively, her body curled into a ball and she landed rolling. Adrenalin had her up on her feet as horses flew by, missing her by inches.

Elation turned to grief as she saw Little Miss stagger, dilated nostrils struggling for breath. Tears welled in Andy's eyes as she ran over to her and leaned up against the mare's shoulder to keep her on her feet.

"I'm so sorry, Little Miss!"

A galloping horse slid to a stop beside them. Candace reached out and grabbed the reins.

"Quick, undo the overgirth," she ordered.

Andy flew into action, unbuckling the elastic overgirth.

"Okay, I'll walk her around and get her legs under her again. She's gonna be okay so stop your crying."

Andy wiped the tears from her eyes.

"Get over to the winner's circle, they're waiting for ya."

In a daze, Andy walked slowly to the winner's circle, struggling to get her emotions under control. How could winning a race feel so bad?

Excited voices greeted her as the D'Addazio family and friends cheered and laughed. They didn't seem to notice that the horse wasn't there.

Aberto embraced her in a bear hug, dragging her into the midst of the celebration. "You rode that horse perfect!" he congratulated her. More bear hugs left her gasping as much as the mare. "You've got the mount on my Kentucky horse, kid."

The photographer, Henry Carfagna, was trying to organize the rowdy group for the win picture as they continued to hug and cheer and wave at friends in the grandstand. Andy looked over to the mare who was breathing heavily, but didn't seem to be in distress. Candace handed the horse to Mustang who led her into the small oval.

"Think you can stay in the saddle this time?" Mustang teased her.

Andy grit her teeth as she allowed the groom to leg her up. The view wasn't as brilliant as it had been for the last race and Andy dug deep to find a smile for the camera.

After the flash of the bulb, D'Addazio flew into action again. When he grabbed Mustang in a bear hug, Andy leaped from the saddle, unbuckled the girth and rushed to the scale room.

"From a city block to a head," Gerry remarked as he jotted down her weight. "You don't care how you win, do you?"

"I don't care about the margin, but I don't like it when my horse almost dies to win."

"Yeah, it looked a little rough after the wire."

"Where's my jockey?" D'Addazio's voice called out.

Andy looked over her shoulder and saw the big Italian coming.

"Run," Gerry instructed her, "I'll head him off."

Andy leaped off the scales and ran. She didn't look back.

CELEBRATION

"Drink up, everyone, there's another bottle where this one came from." Andy spilled a few drops as she filled paper cups from a bottle of Baby Duck.

"Started your celebration without us, huh?" Candace teased.

"I just had one drink with my uncle Michael. He has to drive back to New York so it was a short meeting." She passed the cups around and held hers high. "When I win the Kentucky Derby on Excalibur next year, we'll be drinking real champagne."

"It's a hell of a long way from here to the Derby. The colt will need to win an allowance race against winners before ya know what he's got." Candace held her cup up. "To my twenty percent of today's win."

"I wanna make a toast ta ma agent," Andy said in an almost perfect imitation.

"Ah, quit it." Candace elbowed her, spilling her drink.

"Careful, every drop is precious," Andy laughed. "Okay, let's get serious now. I really do want to make a toast. To Candace, for convincing a stubborn, hard-headed know-it-all apprentice to put her opinions aside and ride for an obnoxious trainer with an amazing horse."

Everyone raised their cups high and touched them together.

"Not exactly the satisfying ring of crystal," Charlie remarked.

"Long stemmed, crystal glasses and Dom Perignon after one of our horses wins the Massachusetts Handicap," Andy promised.

"Never mind all these stakes races, let's just win a claiming race," Candace suggested.

Andy turned a bucket upside down and sat down on it. "Life is full of surprises, isn't it? Here I am trying so damn hard to win a race, rating my horse, waiting for the perfect moment to move, slipping through holes barely big enough for a whippet and the best I could do is third. Then I get on a beautiful colt who gallops around the track and wins for fun. Crazy!"

"Call it crazy but that's horseracing," Pete said.

"I knew Excalibur would be hard to beat but what was going on in Little Miss' race? She was almost on her knees the last seventy yards. Where were the other horses?" She looked from face to face but no one seemed to have any answers. "You don't think they put me on the lead, do you? I can't stand the thought of winning a race that way."

"They wouldn't put a girl on the lead, would they?" Charlie asked.

"Where was Carlo? What was he doing?"

"I told ya he wouldn't get into a speed duel with ya. He was waiting for ya to tire, only you didn't tire soon enough. He closed on ya, but came up a head short. That was a cute trick you did at the wire. Where'd ya learn to tap a horse like that?"

"Willie Shoemaker taught me that. I did a few workouts with him at Belmont."

Candace drained her cup. "I'm going to try that."

"You paid ten bucks on the colt," Pete informed her, "but the mare's race was the one to bet. Twenty-two dollars on a two dollar bet. And did you see the perfecta? Over six hundred dollars. I wish I was a gambler."

Andy took her first sip of wine and coughed. "Oh my God, this stuff is terrible!"

"Well look it the blue blood. Only drink Don Pearignom huh?"

Andy laughed. "I can certainly tell you don't drink champagne."

"Don't have much use for it." Candace held out her empty cup. "But I like this."

Andy poured her drink into Candace's cup. "This is all so surreal. Hard to believe I had two wins in one day."

"It's real," Candace replied, "and you'll be winning a lot more now."

"The next time I ride Little Miss, she'll be a lot fitter. I'm going to talk to Emmett about her. I'm going to get her into better shape."

"Forget it, you're gonna to be too busy to fool around with one hoss. Let Feagin have her. You're gonna be on good hosses now."

"Candace is right, you'll be getting a lot of offers." Pete smiled as he held out his empty cup and Andy poured what was left from the bottle.

"I'm ready to ride the winners," Andy agreed, "but I'm still going to work with Little Miss."

Jockey and agent glared at each other for several seconds before Candace shrugged her shoulders.

"Okay, as long as we can fit her in."

Pete waved his cup in front of Andy. "Come on, don't be so cheap, that's only half a glass. Maybe you don't like this stuff but the rest of us aren't so fussy."

Andy popped the cork on the second bottle and poured everyone a generous amount.

"Drink a toast to our new telly."

"What? You're spending your money on a new TV?" Candace exclaimed.

"It's not new. I'm buying it from The Salvation Army. They have a colour set that they put aside for me until I could come up with the cash."

Charlie rubbed her hands enthusiastically. "I finally get to watch Coronation Street."

"I like Happy Days," Andy said, tossing her paper cup in the garbage can.

"Right now, we better focus on happy horses," Pete suggested, finishing his wine. "Come on, time to get back to work."

Candace drank up and wiped her lips. "Let's go, PM team. That means you too, hotshot bug rider. Take Tim for a walk."

"Good idea. The two of you can plan your strategy for your next race," Pete suggested as he handed her a halter and lead shank.

Andy stared as they turned their backs and left the tack room. It seemed odd that she, the hot apprentice, was being ordered around by the stable crew.

She sighed. "At least there's no chance of becoming vain. Not with this crew."

ROTTEN APPLES

The sun peeked over the horizon just as Andy pulled up on the outside rail. She sat quietly in the saddle, letting Tim B Quiet catch his breath.

Denise breezed by in the middle of a set of four horses. Her agent had obviously let her sleep in a little longer this morning. Andy turned Tim around and began jogging back along the outside rail. She thought about how hard Denise must have worked to win the title in '74. Her own dream of being leading apprentice here at Suffolk was going to be a struggle.

"I thought it would be a piece of cake," she said to Tim, shaking her head at her own arrogance. "Education on the racetrack is a lot tougher than university. Instead of a B A in History I'm getting a Masters in the School of Hard Knocks." She reached up and fondled the gelding's ears. "You know about that, don't you Tim. You've got a Ph. D from that school."

She jogged back along the outside rail and slowed to a walk when she reached the gap. Carlo was riding towards the track on a tall, muscular colt. The colt shied and ducked sideways. Carlo whipped him several times on the flank and shoulder. The colt lunged forward into full gallop onto the track.

"Well that's a wonderful way to calm a horse down," she muttered. "Come on, Tim, we'd better get back to the barn. I can't dawdle today, I've got some extra horses to get on."

Pete's prediction of her being offered more mounts had come true, but they weren't the kind of horses she had hoped for. Trainers with long shots in their barn were lining up for her services. Candace was vetting them, as she called it. Bowed tendons like The Heckler's were okay, but some of the horses with knee and ankle injuries were tenuous.

"I don't know, Tim, when I first dreamt about becoming a jockey, I thought I just had to learn how to ride a racehorse. Horses rearing in the gate and jockeys trying to put me over the rail hadn't been part of it. I never imagined dealing with the likes of Carlo and Pedro. And Mural the Mule wasn't in my worst nightmare.

"It's no wonder so many people think horseracing is crooked. One rotten apple spoils the bunch, they say."

"Hey, you're looking a little plumper this morning. Had a big celebration last night?" Eddie waved and disappeared into a shed row before she could respond.

"And what kind of apple is he? One of the rotten ones?"

Tim shook his head vigorously. "You don't think so? I'm not so sure."

Charlie was waiting for her when she rode into the shed row. "Lili's tacked up and ready to go. There's only fifteen minutes left before the track closes."

Andy's feet barely touched the ground and she was up on Lili. The filly pranced all the way to the track with a strong hold on the bit. She didn't stop pulling for the entire two mile gallop. Andy's arms felt like they were five inches longer when she returned to the shed row.

Her work finished for the morning, she headed off to the jockeys' room, eager to watch the day's replays in the film room. She wanted to see what was going on behind her in both Excalibur and Little Miss' race. She had just enough time for a short nap before they were called to films.

When the replay of the first race was up on the television set, Andy leaned forward in her seat, eager to see the race. Her eyes were glued to the beautiful colt the moment the gate opened. She thrilled to his stride all over again as the camera focused on him in the lead. When the angle swept back to the horses behind, she was amazed to see that she'd opened up five lengths by the five-eighths pole. By the time she reached the turn, the lead had widened to nine.

The other jockeys whistled and cheered as she headed into the homestretch. Only one horse came into view by the sixteenth pole and she assumed that was Eddie. Suddenly, the colt's stride shortened.

"What happened there, Andrea?" Arthur asked.

"The noise from the grandstand spooked him," she replied as the film continued to roll. "When Eddie's horse came up beside him, he got his mind back on running."

The film showed the colt launching back into action. Andy whooped with the rest of them as Excalibur won by four lengths. Even the stewards applauded.

"I think you may have a stakes horse, there," Arthur said. "No steeplechase for that one."

Everyone laughed.

"Your horse set such a good example, everyone rode straight and clear," George Krikorian commented.

"I would like to commend everyone who rode in that race," Arthur said. "Half the field were first time starters and it was the cleanest race of the day."

He picked up the phone receiver and told Don to play the second race.

Andy watched closely as the gate opened. Little Miss broke straight while the seven horse, just outside of her, bumped the eight horse. The number twelve horse stumbled and almost lost her jockey. Ohhs and awhs reverberated around the room.

Little Miss pulled at the bit for the opening sixteenth of a mile before settling into stride. Andy scanned the field of horses. Billy Feagin was directly behind her on the rail with Carlo outside, blocking him in. Behind them, a pack of horses travelled in a huddle. Barely six lengths separated her in the lead and Eddie in last place. The rest of the field were almost running into each other. Leo Valente stood up straight in the saddle several times.

"What's happening, Leo?" Arthur asked.

"My horse wanted to go. The front runner slowed the pace down and I had nowhere to go."

"Carlo, what's happening with your horse?"

"He's running easy, I'm saving him for the stretch."

"Who's outside of you, Leo?" Arthur asked, searching through his program.

"That's Pedro," Leo replied. "He could see I was having trouble, but he wouldn't let me out."

"I'm three horses wide already," Pedro argued. "I'm not going to the middle of the track 'cause Leo can't hold his horse."

As the field entered the turn, the traffic jam continued. At the head of the stretch, only Andy was out of the fray. Billy's horse started to make a move, but Carlo kept him blocked in on the rail. They continued in that position along the homestretch.

"You've been riding a smart race up until here, Carlo," Arthur pointed out. "You've just passed the sixteenth pole and yet you're not making your move. Why not?"

"My horse is all cheap speed. I wasn't going to hook the leader in a speed duel so I sat back. But my horse is getting tired anyway. I know I'm only going to get a short run out of her. So I'm saving her."

With Carlo holding Billy in and Pedro causing a traffic jam behind, Eddie took his horse to the middle of the racetrack.

"Pedro, you're sitting pretty chilly back there," Arthur said. "You've been saving ground by holding everyone in, so where's your stretch drive?"

"The trainer told me not to hit my horse," Pedro replied. "She doesn't like the whip."

"That's Carmel Dixon's horse," Farrell said. "I won on her last year. I had to tan her hide to get her there."

Arthur signalled to John Baxter. "Make a note to talk to Ms Dixon about that."

He picked up the phone receiver and asked Don to replay the last sixteenth.

As Little Miss tired in the lead and shortened her stride, the traffic jam behind intensified. Only Eddie was making up ground on the outside. As he caught up to Carlo in the last few strides, Carlo went to the whip.

"Looks like you misjudged your move, Carlo," George Krikorian pointed out.

"What are you talking about? Anybody else rides that nag, she finishes last. I'm barely beaten a head for it all."

"I know timing is crucial in a race, but I'd expect a jockey with your experience to know exactly when to make your move," Arthur told him. He looked over to where Eddie was seated. "Eddie, what's your opinion?"

Eddie stood up and walked to the front of the room, his expression thoughtful. "I've been guilty of making my move at the wrong time so I'm not going to point the finger at anyone," he said pragmatically. "A smart jockey will always look for the shortest route home. That's smart riding, but when it means putting other jockeys at risk, it's time to forget about getting the advantage. We all know what it's like to hear the death knell of heels clipping. Every one of us has been in that position. We've all prayed what we thought would be our final prayer. But you know what's worse?" He looked from one face to another. "Watching your fellow jockey go down and never get up again."

Andy shuddered. She could never live with that. Carlo didn't seemed bothered by the idea as he leaned back casually in his chair. She had no doubt that he was playing his own game, but proving it wasn't going to be easy. Intent was the hardest thing to prove in a court of law. Out on the race-track, it was even more difficult. Jockeys bumped each other in every race. A thousand pound racehorse was not easy to control. The only way to catch Carlo at his game was to get him to admit it.

She looked over at him. His face was an impenetrable mask. Getting this man to admit anything would be as much of a challenge as winning the Kentucky Derby.

MICKEY'S MISSION

"Mornin' Mr. Amato. Hey, that's one hell of a horse you've got." The security guard peered into the car to see who was in the passenger seat.

"It's my cousin, Perry Sheehan," Mickey informed him.

"Of course." Howie waved them ahead.

"Okay, Perry, you know the plan," Mickey said once they were out of earshot. "We've got thirty minutes before the grooms show up to feed."

He found an inconspicuous area behind one of the barns and parked the car. Emmett's barn was several hundred feet away.

"You sure you want to do this Mickey?" Perry took a deep breath, as if he were about to plunge into ice water.

"I told you already, Rodale's eager to sign the cheque. He's coming by this morning to have one more look at the colt. When he sees him bouncing around the shed row, he won't care if Pony doubles the price." Mickey turned the engine off.

"You sure you don't want to think about this a little longer?" Perry pleaded. "Pony's counting the money already. And nobody lies to Pony Cantoni, not if they want to take their next breath."

"We do this right, Pony'll never know."

Perry's hands trembled as he adjusted his glasses. "I thought you really liked this horse, that he's the best."

"He is the best," Mickey insisted. "That's why I'm doing

257

this. Come on, Perry, this is our last chance. Get moving!"

Perry jumped out of the car and grabbed a duffle bag from the back seat, heaving it over his shoulder. Mickey turned on a flashlight, keeping the beam close to the ground to avoid spooking the horses. Several of them snorted as they passed by and made their way to Excalibur in the end stall. The colt jumped when Mickey appeared in the doorway.

"Easy, boy, easy big fella, it's just me," Mickey said in a soothing voice.

Excalibur approached, sniffing his sleeve curiously.

Once he had the horse settled, he looked over to check on his cousin. Perry had always been able to get around in the dark. With his poor eyesight, Mickey figured he was used to navigating by touch.

"Perry, get the kettle out and go plug it in."

"Give me a second, will you? I'm just getting organized."

"This isn't a tea party, hurry up!" Mickey slipped the halter on over the colt's head while he waited for Perry to take the kettle into the tack room. He clipped the horse to the tie chain at the back of the stall and inspected his legs. The colt had come out of the race as if he'd just had a morning breeze, his shins and ankles cold. He didn't need any kind of veterinary care. Normally, this would have thrilled Mickey but today, the colt needed a problem.

He peeked out of the stall down the shed row. "Perry," he said in a hoarse whisper. "Hurry!"

Within seconds, Perry appeared in front of him holding a steaming kettle.

"About time," Mickey berated him, grabbing it. "Here, hold the lead shank and don't let him jump around."

"You want me to come in there?" Perry stepped back rather than forward.

"For God's sake, we don't have time to argue."

Perry reluctantly stepped into the stall, keeping a distance of several feet between himself and the horse. He extended his arm as far as it would go to take the shank.

"Oh for Christ's sake, I'll do it!" Mickey shoved the kettle back in Perry's hands. "What did you do with the hot water bottle?"

Perry looked at him blankly as if he'd never heard of such a thing.

"Damn it, Perry, in the duffle bag, the hot water bottle."

Perry rushed out of the stall, startling the colt by his quick movement. Mickey's swearing was muffled by the sound of pounding hooves as Perry dug through the duffle bag. When he finally found the hot water bottle, his hands were shaking so much he had difficulty filling it. He re-entered the stall, once again keeping his distance.

"You have to get a lot closer than that, Perry. Come on, wrap it around his ankle and hold it there."

Perry squatted down, still half way across the stall. Mickey's intake of breath warned him a tongue lashing was about to follow and he crawled forward, pressing the rubber bag against the colt's ankle. Immediately, Excalibur jumped away, sending Perry sprawling into the straw.

"For Christ's sake, Perry, stop messing around!" Mickey snapped.

"I can't help it if he won't hold still."

Two more attempts produced the same results. On the fourth attempt, the colt leaned into the warmth of the hot water bottle rather than away.

"Feels good, doesn't it?" Mickey said in a soothing voice, stroking him.

After ten minutes, they heard a car drive up behind the barn.

"Damn it, it's the grooms! We've got to get out of here, Perry, now!"

Perry needed no urging. He was out of the stall in record time and threw the kettle and bottle into the athletic bag, hauling it half open down the shed row. Mickey took the halter off the horse, hurriedly hung it up in front of the stall and rushed after his jittery cousin.

The moment they turned the corner and were out of sight, Mustang's coarse voice rang out. "Get your heads back in there, breakfast isn't ready yet. This isn't a bucket I'm carrying, it's my pocket book."

Mickey pushed Perry up against the wall in the adjoining shed row where they hid in the darkness.

"Damn that little spick, he can't even hang a halter up properly!"

Mickey swore under his breath. He should have taken the time to put Excalibur's halter back exactly as he'd found it.

When he heard Mustang go into the tack room, he motioned to Perry to follow. With long, quick strides, they made their way to the safe haven of the track kitchen. Only when they were inside the brightly lighted room did he breathe freely. Perry looked like he was on the verge of collapse.

"Go sit down, I'll get you a coffee."

Perry literally fell into a chair, dropping the heavy bag onto the floor. When the coffee arrived, he gratefully took a gulp.

"I've got to get back there before his ankle turns ice cold. You take the bag back to the car but keep out of sight. Don't let anyone in Emmett's barn see you."

When he arrived back in the shed row, Al had joined Mustang in the early morning chores. Al smiled when he saw Mickey.

"Morning, Al, how's my big horse?"

"He good, very good. He come back A okay," Al said, trying very hard to be Americanized.

Mickey walked over to the colt's stall.

"Legs nice and cold?"

"Si," Al replied, ducking under the webbing and running his hands over the colt's right leg. "He very cold."

He reached over and touched the left leg. His expression changed drastically. "Caliente!"

"What do you mean, caliente?" Mickey said, deliberately

looking confused. He bent down and touched the colt's ankle. "My God, you're right. Quick, get some ice."

"Si, hielo."

Mickey smiled as the young groom rushed off to get the ice. This would foil the sale to Rodale. The man was savvy enough to know that a hot ankle in a two year old didn't bode well for his future. This would give Mickey enough time to find another suitable horse to sell to the wealthy landowner.

As soon as that was done, Excalibur would be miraculously sound and ready for his next race.

LORD WON'T
YOU BUY ME

Andy walked into Emmett's barn at five thirty sharp. This was now her daily routine and she wasn't happy about it. Emmett first, Pete second and the rest of the trainers got whatever time was left. This new schedule had created the first argument between jockey and agent. Andy wanted to begin the day galloping for Pete and Arley, but Candace insisted the top trainer took precedence. Candace argued that Pete and Arley weren't going to give her mounts away to another jockey if she didn't exercise them every morning whereas Emmett had no such loyalty. Which was Andy's point of contention. Emmett would give her mounts to another apprentice without a moment's thought, so why should he take precedence over all other trainers?

"All other trainers," she muttered. "Who am I kidding. We haven't picked up a single decent mount."

Mustang's shrill voice jolted her into the present.

"Al, it's bad enough I've gotta get your horse tacked up, but the least you could do is have his bridle on the right hook!"

Andy whipped around to avoid Mustang and headed towards Excalibur's stall.

"Hi, Al, how's the big horse? Ready to—"

She stopped in mid sentence when she saw the colt standing in a tub of ice water. "Oh my God, what happened?"

Al shook his head. There were tears in his eyes. He quickly wiped them away.

"Caliente, his ankle. I no unnerstand. He fine after the race."

"A hot ankle? It couldn't have happened in the race. Did he hit it on something jumping around his stall? He's like a dancing cat when he gets excited. I'm sure it's nothing serious."

"Si, si, he no cojo," Al said with a hint of a smile.

"He no what?" Without thinking, she used his speech pattern. "Cojo? What does that mean?"

Al walked around in a circle limping.

"He's not limping? Well then, it can't be anything serious." She sighed in relief. "You walked him this morning, did you?"

Al peeked out of the stall, looking up and down the shed row to make sure Mustang wasn't around. "Si, Mustang tell me to keep him in here, but he want to go out so I take him for leetle walk. He walk A okay."

"Eso es bueno," she said with a smile. "Don't worry, I'll keep your secret. And I'll bring him some extra carrots this afternoon, when everyone has their siesta."

"An hombre, he come to look at him."

"What hom—what man?" she asked, catching herself.

"A man, he wear funny clothes. I think he want to buy him. But he not happy when he see him in the hielo."

Andy plucked a piece of ice from the tub and held it in front of Al's face. "What's it called?"

Al thought long and hard. "It called... hice."

"Close enough," she said with a smile. "If it was somebody who wanted to buy the colt, then I'm glad he wasn't happy. I don't want Excalibur going anywhere, except Kentucky next May."

"Sandy, for Christ's sake, stop drooling over the pretty boy and get your ass in this saddle!" Mustang yelled from the other end of the shed row.

Andy dropped the piece of ice back in tub. "I'll see you this aft—nos vemos luego."

She walked to the next stall as Mustang led a horse out. When the horse was in full view, Andy gasped. "What? You claimed Judge?"

"Yeah, of course I did," Mustang smirked. "I didn't know what else to do with last week's pay."

"I can't ride him," Andy insisted. "Not for Emmett."

She turned away and started down the shed row.

"You don't ride this horse, you don't ride any horse in the barn."

The ultimatum froze her in her tracks. Andy stood motionless, her emotions at war. She couldn't betray Arley and yet she couldn't sacrifice Emmett's entire barn. Slowly, she turned back to face Mustang.

"I'll gallop him, but I have no intention of riding him in a race."

"Billy Feagin will be happy to hear that," Mustang replied. "And don't dawdle on the way back. I've got your next horse tacked up."

The moment Mustang's hand touch her leg, Andy propelled herself up into the saddle. Any kind of physical contact with the woman felt repulsive. She quickly caught up with Ringo.

"He's sure glad to see you," Ringo said as he watched them approach. "You should see his face, he's smiling."

"I adore this horse, but I can't ride him in a race, not for Emmett."

"It wouldn't be for Emmett. You'd be riding for the man who broke your maiden." Ringo suddenly giggled. "Man, that doesn't sound good, does it?"

In spite of her frustration, Andy had to laugh along with him. "No, it doesn't."

It took several seconds for the information to filter through her brain. "Wait a minute, are you saying Mickey Amato claimed Judge?"

"Yeah, BJ's all his."

"BJ?"

"Stands for Big Jumper. That's his barn name, BJ."

"That's not a name for a classy horse like Judge."

"He doesn't mind. I think he kinda likes it." Ringo reached over and patted the gelding. "And the Candy Man sure likes your riding, Sandy Andy. You're his main man."

Andy grew thoughtful. That definitely put a different spin on the situation. If Mickey wanted her to ride Judge, she couldn't refuse him, not unless she was willing to give up Excalibur.

"Dammit, Ringo, I know how to handle being shut off and slammed against the rail but all the politics? How am I supposed to deal with that?"

"You don't," he said simply. "Let your agent handle it. Let her earn her twenty percent and deal with the crap. That's all it is, man, crap."

There was real wisdom in Ringo's words. Andy looked over at her favourite galloping buddy. "I think maybe you should be my agent. You're a smart boy, Ringo."

He giggled again.

"Alright," she said, determination in her voice as she shortened her reins and prepared to gallop. "BJ Judge it is."

"Breeze them down the stretch!" Emmett called out to them as they passed the trainers' stand.

They were the first riders to set foot on the racetrack, jogging onto the freshly harrowed surface just as the sun peeked over the horizon. The first rays of dawn and the beautiful Thoroughbred beneath her lifted Andy's spirits. In that moment, she felt truly blessed.

"Sandy Andy's got a smile on her face," Ringo called over. "It's gonna be a good day."

"It's going to be a good gallop, but we'll have to start off at an easy jog. This guy is a little stiff for the first quarter."

To her surprise, Judge went immediately into a gallop.

"Hey, man, that's not what I call a slow jog." Ringo had

to hustle his horse to catch up.

Andy was amazed at the old gelding's strong, fluid stride. "That's one hell of a liniment Mr Amato has."

"The Candy Man knows what he's doing," Ringo said with a grin. "Okay, you pick the song today."

Andy chose the one song she could sing without music. "Oh Lord, won't you buy me a Mercedes Benz," she began.

Ringo joined in. "My friends all drive Porsches, I must make amends. Worked hard all my lifetime, no help from my friends, so Lord, won't you buy me a Mercedes Benz!"

When they reached the homestretch for the second lap, Andy could barely hold Judge back. Both riders squatted down into racing position as the horses flew into action. They stayed shoulder to shoulder until the last stride. Andy picked the Judge's head up and put it across the wire first.

"Damn, I don't know how you do that!" Ringo cried as they stood up in their stirrups.

"It's a trade secret," Andy teased as they slowed down.

When they returned to the barn, Little Miss was the next horse to go. Andy tried to get the mare to relax on her way to the track but she pranced nervously. She grabbed the bit the moment they were on the track. Only towards the end of the two mile gallop did she slow down.

"That's not exactly what I had in mind," Andy muttered as she rode back to the barn. "We need a quiet pony horse to keep you company and get you to settle. I'll talk to hot shot Emmett about it. I'm sure he wants another win."

Finally, she was back in Pete's barn. The routine here was much more relaxed. She didn't have to rush any of the horses. Lili, Tim and The Heckler all went to the track. She let each of them take their time getting there and even longer coming back.

"I want you to stop by ole man Morris' barn," Candace told her as she dismounted.

"God no!" Andy exclaimed. "Not that old miser."

"He's about due for a win and I want you on it."

"And if I finish off the board? Farrell finished tenth on one of his horses last week and they were arguing about the jock's fee the moment his feet touched the ground. I wouldn't give that old miser a dime."

"The old man's been here since the track opened," Pete said as he pulled the saddle off Tim. "Give him a break. He's a heritage piece around here."

"An old fossil, you mean. I'll bet he's never been in the top ten list."

"He might have been close back in the fifties but he's a better handicapper than trainer. I saw him walking away from the mutual window last week with a wad of bills."

"What? He bet against his own horse?"

"The old man doesn't have any illusions about his talent for training," Pete said with a shrug.

"And yet he dares to ask for the jock's mount back?" Andy exclaimed. "If I ever ride for him, I'm charging him double."

"Ya leave the charging to me and just keep your mind on your own business. I've got ya named on two hosses for Cecil and one for Arley. Stop by and have a chat with them."

"Arley," Andy sighed. It was the first time she didn't look forward to seeing him. She walked slowly around to the AM side of the barn.

Arley had finished galloping for the day and was raking the shed row.

"Well, good morning, Miss Andy."

"Good morning, Arley. All finished, huh?"

"Yep, just some rubbing and bandaging to do."

Andy was trying to think of how to break the news gently that Judge was in Emmett's barn but she couldn't find a roundabout way to tell him. "Arley, I galloped for Emmett this morning, a couple of horses—"

"That's just fine," Arley interrupted. "I know your agent has your mounts all planned out for you. She's just doing her job. Don't you worry, Miss Andy, I don't need you here when the rooster crows. If I have a horse for you to breeze, I'll send him out after the break."

Andy winced. His kindness and loyalty made this even harder.

"Thank you, Arley, I appreciate that but there's something else I need to tell you." The gentle words still wouldn't come. "Judge is in Emmett's barn."

Arley nodded his head. "Yes, he surely is."

Andy was both relieved and confused. "You knew that?"

"There's nothing that goes on in the backside that doesn't see the light of day," Arley said with a smile. "I knew within the hour that Mr Amato signed the cheque. I was hopin' he'd put you back on, especially after you sailed home on his Kentucky colt."

Andy nodded as she absorbed this. "He might regret that decision. He likes to give instructions before a race, but the only instructions I'll follow are the ones Judge gives me."

"That gives Judge at least one more good race." Arley put his rake aside and motioned to a horse in the closest stall. "This here is the horse you'll be ridin' for me."

"In a claiming race?" she asked tentatively.

Arley shook his head. "Allowance. This one's coming back to my barn."

THE MOUSE ROARS

Mickey walked down the familiar hallway and opened the door. The room looked bigger without Pony's towering hulk presiding over the meeting. Tommy sat on the long suffering wooden chair but today it wasn't creaking. Tommy's weight didn't put any strain on the wooden legs nor did his presence carry much weight with Wally the Weasel.

"What do you mean tomorrow's race is off ?" Tommy demanded.

"I just told ya, Mural's horse scratched. We don't have the bottom half of the perfecta."

"So, get him on another horse."

Wally laughed. "And how do I do that? Put a gun to a trainer's head and force him to ride Mural?"

"Okay, now you're thinking!" Tommy clapped his hands in approval.

Wally laughed again. "Yeah, sure. You've been watching too many Hollywood movies, Tommy. It don't work that way."

"Listen, you fucking little pinhead, if you don't want a gun put to your head, you'll get Mural on a horse, tomorrow night! What the hell, we've had horses scratch before. We replace them."

Wally shook his head. "No way. We look at another race. Me and Mural always rode the card so it was no big deal. But Mural lost a lot of mounts thanks to his little accident." Wally's direct glare let it be known whose fault that was. "I

269

sure as hell ain't got a line up of riders to use. I'm working on a new bug rider, but he's going to need some trainin'."

"What the fuck, you're telling me we don't have anything going tomorrow?"

Wally nodded. "You got it, Tommy. It looks good for Monday, if the right horses draw in."

"Monday!" Tommy leaped up from the chair and punched the air.

Wally stepped back out of the line of fire.

"For fuck's sake, it might as well be next year! You think I'm going to call Pony tomorrow and tell him everything's off till Monday?"

It was the first time Mickey had seen Wally with the upper hand. He no longer looked like a snivelling little weasel. There was even a hint of the young, cocky apprentice in his stance. As far as Wally was concerned, he was off the hook. He wasn't the one who had to give the news to Pony.

Beads of sweat broke out on Tommy's brow.

Mickey felt compassion for his boyhood friend. The machinations of fixing a race were beyond his control, but Pony wouldn't see it that way. The big man would only see that his plan was screwed up and someone had to be punished.

Tommy picked up the white envelope. "I guess there's no payment this week."

"That's for last week." Wally's voice returned to his familiar 'weasel whine'. "I came through for you on Friday night."

"Yeah? Well your fucking friend, Mule, almost blew it!"

"No way, he knew exactly what he was doing. He was on the hot favourite, I had the twenty-to-one shot. Mural held the speed horse back and let me beat him a neck at the wire. If he got beat five lengths, the stewards would call him in, ask a lot of questions. He did a hell of a job and no one's suspicious."

"If Pony saw the race, you'd have given him a heart attack."

"Yeah, well, Pony wasn't there and we carried it off. Come on, hand over the envelope, Tommy. I gotta be in the jocks' room in an hour."

Wally stepped forward to take it when Tommy lashed out viciously with an uppercut. It was an instant knock out.

"Tommy, let's just cool it down for a moment," Mickey advised him, walking over to the fallen jockey. "It's bad enough that the race fell through, but you don't want to be telling Pony his main Rhode Island jock is dead."

The little man moaned and rolled onto his side. Mickey helped him to his feet, keeping a grip on his shoulders until he had his feet firmly beneath him.

"Last week was a freebie, asshole," Tommy snapped. "To make up for your fucking screw up."

Wally wiped the blood from the corner of his mouth and walked unsteadily towards the door.

"Get it right on Monday!" Tommy yelled as the door slammed behind him. He punched the air to vent his frustration. "You're here to give me good news, right, Mick?"

Tommy had never called him that before. His metamorphosis into Pony was surprisingly quick.

"Right. The new claimer, Charming The Judge, drew into the race tomorrow."

"Great, something went right." Tommy fell into the wooden chair. "What's his odds?"

"The handicapper has him listed at eight-to-one but he'll be higher by the time they load into the gate. The horse is moving up in claiming price and the girl's on him."

"Carlo and Pedro draw in?"

Mickey nodded. "Carlo's on the second favourite, Pedro's fifteen-to-one. You can use Pedro, he'll give you a good payoff."

Tommy shook his head. "That fucking steward, Healey, is breathing down everyone's neck. He's got the pinheads under a microscope. If the girl's got long odds, we use her on top, Carlo on the bottom. Pedro can run interference, keep the

girl clear. He's being paid enough to get rough if he has to."
Tommy seemed to calm down. "Okay, now we go through
with the deal for the colt. Rodale's got his cheque ready?"

Mickey hadn't expected to be so nervous about this. His
heart pounded furiously. He stepped back, putting more distance between himself and Tommy's fists. "We've run into a
snag on that one."

"Jesus, Mickey, don't tell me that!" Tommy leaped out of
the chair. "It's something you can fix, right, Mick?"

"Yes," he replied quickly, keeping the fists at bay. "The
colt will be alright, but he has heat in his ankle. Nothing
serious, but it kills the deal."

"What the fuck! The horse came back perfect after the
race."

"It sometimes takes forty-eight hours for an injury to
show, Tommy."

"No way! Something's going on." Tommy stabbed the air
in Mickey's direction.

"Calm down, Tommy."

"A little sabotage maybe. Who else knows about this
deal?"

"No one," Mickey replied, shaking his head. "Injuries are
all part of the game, Tommy, you know that."

"Something's going on. The fucking pinheads in Rhode
Island can't find their assholes with two hands and now you
tell me the colt's finished. Someone's jerking us off!" Tommy
lashed out with a vicious kick, sending the wooden chair
careening across the room and against the wall. With a loud
crack, one of the legs flew off and landed several feet away.

"Listen to me, Tommy, I didn't say the colt was finished.
He'll be fine in a few days, but Rodale came by the barn, saw
him standing in a tub of ice. The groom told him about the
hot ankle." Mickey knew instantly that was a mistake and
tried to cover for Al. "There wasn't anything else the kid
could do. He sent Rodale to me in the kitchen and Rodale
and I had a chat."

"And you fixed it, right? Like you always do. The deal's going through, isn't it, Mick."

Mickey didn't like the desperation in his voice. "Listen, I'll come up with a plan."

"It better be one hell of a plan, Mick, or we're going down!" Tommy grabbed the shattered leg and held it up like a weapon.

"We both need a drink," Mickey said. "I'll go get them."

His mind reeled as he quickly escaped, closing the door behind him. This wasn't going as he'd expected. Tommy had always been able to switch directions, to adjust to a difficult situation without hesitation. But this screw up had thrown him off his game. Mickey wondered if he'd be able to carry off his plan. Somehow, he had to get Tommy on board. Delivering bad news to Pony wasn't going to be healthy for either of them.

The voices of the diners and the clatter of dishes disrupted his thoughts as he entered the restaurant. The tables were full, many familiar faces looking over in his direction. Mickey quickly skirted the room to avoid conversation and signalled Matt at the bar.

"Give us the usual," he called out over the din.

While Matt searched through the industrial sized cooler, Mickey tried to solidify his plan. It had to be iron clad and he had to present it with confidence. It wasn't only Tommy's life at stake. If Pony's top lieutenant went down, everyone connected with him went down.

Matt slid a tray across the bar with a bottle of Glenlivet and a couple of Millers. Mickey picked up the tray and started to turn around when he looked over at Matt. "Make that a six pack," he told him.

"Tough night, huh?" Matt took four more bottles out of the cooler.

Mickey took the tray and eyed the half dozen bottles of cold beer. He hoped by the time Tommy polished them off, he would be amenable to Mickey's strategy. Luckily, Tommy was one of those rare Irishmen who got mellower as he drank.

When he returned to the back room, Tommy's fancy footwork had turned into nervous pacing. Unlike Wally, he turned right instead of left.

"Here you go, Tommy, have a beer and relax." Mickey popped the cap off one of the bottles. He was determined to play flunky better than Tommy was playing boss.

"We're dead meat when Pony finds out about this." Tommy grabbed the bottle Mickey handed him and downed half of it in one gulp. "Our balls first, then our heads."

"We can deal with this, Tommy. I've got a back-up plan. "

"Like what, a one way ticket to Australia? Won't work. Pony'll find us inside of a month." Tommy drained the bottle in a second gulp and let out a loud belch. "There's no back-up plan when you're dealing with Pony Cantoni."

Mickey picked up the opener Matt had supplied and wedged off the cap of the second bottle. He handed it to Tommy.

"Listen carefully. This is what you do. You soften Pony up by telling him everything is in order for our race tomorrow. It's the 'Gansett boys who have screwed up. They're not your territory. Wally will take the heat for that."

"Like hell he will. Pony left me in charge of the whole business. As far as he's concerned, it's my screw up."

"But Wally screwed up when Pony was here, didn't he?"

Tommy stopped his pacing to think about that.

"You carried out the punishment exactly the way Pony would. Wally got a blow to the head instead of his favourite white powder. He knows he has to get it right next time or he goes the same way as Smartalex." Mickey reached for the Scotch. The thought of another murder sickened him. He poured himself a generous swallow while Tommy made inroads into the second bottle of beer.

"Okay, okay, maybe I can carry that off. But what about the colt? That's two hundred K down the drain. Pony isn't going to take that one lying down."

"I've got that one covered. Listen." Mickey threw back a double shot and poured another one. The liquid burned its way down his throat to his stomach and it was several seconds before he could speak. "There's another two year old in Emmet's barn."

"There's a lot of two year olds in Emmett's barn. How the hell does that help us?"

"There's a particular colt, Roadhouse Boy. He's by Round Table, the same sire as Excalibur, but he's out of a better mare, a proven mare. D'Addazio bought him from the Kentucky sales for three times the price of our colt."

Tommy drained the bottle and slammed it down on the table in true Pony fashion. "Three times? That's about a hundred k. So, what's your big plan, Mickey?"

"Listen to this." Mickey kept his tone steady as he opened the third bottle and placed it on the table in front of Tommy. "The colt's big and strong and sound."

"Sound, I like that, but I still don't get how it saves my ass."

"D'Addazio's got a serious cash flow problem—the cash is flowing out of his auto repair business into his bookie's pocket."

The deep creases in Tommy's forehead softened slightly.

"He's not privy to our inside information, you see. His tips come from the grooms."

Tommy almost smiled. "One sure way to lose your money. Okay, so the guy's in trouble and needs some serious cash. Sounds to me like this horse is the answer to his prayers. He sells him for big money, right?"

Mickey shook his head in the negative.

Three quarters of the bottle slipped down Tommy's throat and another loud belch split the air. "I'm not following you, Mick. If this wop is in over his head, why is he going to sell us the horse cheap?"

"Because I do his books." Mickey held his glass up in toast but didn't get the response he expected.

Tommy's eyes flashed with rage. "You're doing books for someone else in the business?"

Mickey was stunned at how quickly Tommy had taken on Pony's paranoia.

"D'Addazio's business is strictly auto repairs. The only one he's screwing is the IRS." Mickey took a deep breath as he poured himself another double.

As quickly as the rage had erupted, a grin spread across Tommy's face. "Alright, the picture's changing."

Mickey breathed easy for the moment. "What I know about D'Addazio's business is worth more than the price of his colt."

"Much, much more, I'm sure." Tommy nodded, motioning to the next bottle. "Okay, looks like we've got a replacement colt at a bargain basement price. But what happens when this wop hears that you've flipped the colt? When the scuttlebutt reaches him, they'll have the price up to a million bucks."

"By the time he hears the rumours, D'Addazio will be back in the hole just as deep. His gambling addiction isn't going to disappear overnight." Mickey held his glass up in a victory salute. "And he'll need the services of A&M Accounting to once again cover his ass with the IRS."

Tommy laughed. "You've got the smarts alright, Mickey. I knew we had you on the payroll for a reason." He took a quick swig of beer. "It's a good plan but

you've got to swing it in the next twenty-four hours. You don't want to fuck this one up, Mick. You do and I can tell you one thing for sure. Pony's new accountant will be a pallbearer at your funeral."

Tommy laughed heartily at his own joke. Mickey reached for the bottle. He didn't find it funny.

"Listen, there's another race you can use next week, in case the Rhode Island crew screws up again. I've been watching one of old man Morris's horses."

"Can't believe the old codger's still alive." Tommy shook his head as he twirled the bottle in his hands. "What's he got going?"

"An old gelding from Chile. The horse pops up every so often with a good one. The way he's breezing right now, he's ready. The old man was in the secretary's office this morning talking to Bart. There's at least a hundred horses on the grounds with the same conditions so I'm sure Bart will run the race. The old man's horse will be at least twenty-to-one."

"Now you're really thinking, Mick. A bonus like this gets us back in the good books for sure. I'll see to it our boy, Carlo, is in the irons."

As Mickey poured himself a final drink, his eyes turned towards Pony's ruined chair. "Now for our next problem. How the hell are you going to explain that?"

Tommy walked over to the fallen chair, the fingers of his right hand forming the shape of a gun. He snapped his thumb and made the sound of a gunshot.

Giddy in his relief, he turned to Mickey. "I'll tell Pony his old friend didn't suffer. I put it out of its misery quickly."

SIGNED, SEALED, NOT DELIVERED

"Sandy, Andy, we've got another set to go." Ringo's melodious voice carried down the shed row.

Andy looked out from a stall and sighed.

"Oh, Ringo, I've already galloped for Emmett."

"*Who can take a sunrise, sprinkle it in dew, cover it in chocolate and a miracle or two? The candyman, the candyman can, the candyman can.*"

Andy laughed. "Okay, okay, if it's Mr. Amato's horse, I can make an exception."

Charlie was about to lead The Heckler out of the stall.

"Sorry, Charlie, I've got to go back to Emmett's barn. I'll be back as soon as I can."

Ringo switched back to his favourite band, The Beatles, and sang a chorus from *Yesterday*. Andy had a smile on her face by the time she reached the barn. Ringo led her past Excalibur's stall to an unfamiliar horse who was tacked up and ready to go. Standing with the horse was Mustang, not Al.

"Who's this?" Andy asked, looking the horse over.

"Secretariat," Mustang replied curtly.

"Can't be, Secretariat's a chestnut, this one's a bay." Andy walked to the horse's head. "Hello, handsome fella."

"Come on, come on, they're waiting for you at the track." Mustang held her hand out to leg her up.

"I can do it myself," Andy said, hoisting herself into the saddle much like a cowboy in a western movie.

"Well, hot damn, aren't you the gymnast." The surprised look on Mustang's face held a hint of respect.

Andy rode off down the aisle and caught up to Ringo who was riding a tall dabbled grey gelding. Mickey was waiting on the road.

"This is a very important breeze," he told her, his voice more tense than usual. "I want you to get the colt warmed up, have him ready. Crack him once at the eighth pole and let him blow out down the stretch. Ringo, you stay with him, head and head, but I want you in front at the wire, Andy."

Instructions finished, Mickey headed off, his stride faster than the horses. Andy looked over at Ringo. "What's going on? Who is this horse? I've never seen him before."

"Billy Feagin's been galloping him, but you're the hot rider now, Sandy Andy. The big Italian likes you."

"Big Italian?" Andy asked, confused. "You mean D'Addazio? This is his Kentucky horse?" Andy liked the horse even more now. "But why is Mickey giving the instructions?"

Ringo shrugged his shoulders. "Ask no questions, you get no lies," he sang, making up his own melody.

"This is one crazy barn," she muttered. "Okay, let's give the man what he asked for. I'm happy to ride another Kentucky horse."

Ringo giggled as they jogged onto the track. Andy saw Mickey standing in the grandstand with a man dressed in a loud sports coat.

"Hey, that guy's must be Lucien Laurin's brother," she called over to Ringo.

Laurin, the trainer of Secretariat, was known for his eccentric wardrobe but this man far outdid him in a green and yellow checked coat with a lime coloured fedora.

"*We all live in a yellow submarine*," Ringo sang out.

Andy joined in the chorus as the colt zigzagged all the way down the stretch. He was extremely green and hard to steer.

He bucked when they broke into a gallop. Andy nudged him with her heels and urged him forward with a slap on the shoulder, hoping to get his mind off his antics.

"I'll take the outside," Ringo offered, pulling back and swerving his horse over to the other side of her. Once the path to the outside rail was blocked, the colt steered much better.

They stayed head to head during the gallop. When they approached the home stretch for the final time, Andy signalled to Ringo to come in closer. "He needs to get used to being bumped. It'll happen a lot during a race."

When Ringo's horse touched his side, the colt tried to suck back. Andy tapped his flanks with the whip and clucked to him. He shot forward, putting his head in front. Ringo's horse chased him throughout the final furlong, but couldn't catch him. As instructed, Andy was in front at the wire.

She laughed when she pulled up and saw the dirt on Ringo's face. He'd forgotten to pull his goggles down and his eyes were tearing from the sand and loam that had been flung at him.

"I'm sorry," she apologized. "I should have opened up five lengths instead of just one."

"Hey man, you owe me lunch for that one." He spit out a wad of dirt. "And a bottle of beer."

"You get two bottles for that," she promised. As they jogged back along the outside rail, she saw the two men in the grandstand shaking hands. Mickey looked in her direction and gave her the thumbs up. She didn't know exactly what it meant, but he was obviously pleased with the work.

By the time she was back in Pete's barn, the Heckler was dragging Charlie off her feet.

"His Highness doesn't like to be kept waiting, does he?" Andy remarked.

"Oh my God, I thought you'd never come back. Take this beast off my hands!" Charlie pleaded.

Pete rushed over and legged Andy up. "You're going to

have your hands full with him. He needs a breeze today, but you'll have to convince him to save it till the last eighth of a mile. Get him warmed up and get him ready."

"Looks like he's ready to breeze from here," Andy replied, quickly tying a knot in the reins as the anxious horse pranced off. He was so eager when he reached the gap that he lunged in the air, almost breaking her hold. Andy gripped the rubber coated reins in a full cross and gritted her teeth.

"Come on, Heckler, give me a break," she begged him. "Keep this up all the way and I'll be the one with bowed tendons!"

Her hands were numb from the pressure of pulling on the reins before they had completed the first mile. The powerful gelding didn't quite hit full speed in the last furlong, but he went faster than Pete wanted him too. When he pulled up and Andy turned him around, he tried to run off on the way back. Pete met her at the gap and grabbed a hold of the reins, giving her a much needed break.

"Now this is what you call a racehorse," he said with a big smile. "And your next winner."

"He better be after that!" she exclaimed, shaking her hands to get the blood pumping again.

She was relieved to hear that was the final horse for the morning and headed off to the track kitchen. Ringo signalled her from the line up. He had two bottles of Bud on his lunch tray. Andy quickly handed over the cash. "Enjoy. You deserve it."

She headed out the door and almost bumped into Mickey.

"Just who we were looking for," he greeted her, his smile almost as bright as it had been in the winner's circle.

"That was an excellent workout this morning, miss," the loudly dressed man commended her.

Mickey nodded, looking just as pleased. "Andy, this is Mr Rodale. He's interested in buying the colt you worked this morning."

She smiled as they shook hands. "You'd be getting yourself

a fine racehorse, Mr Rodale."

"Tell me one thing, miss, how does this colt, Roadhouse Boy, compare with Excalibur?"

That was a leading question if ever there was one. The smile on Mickey's face stiffened as he awaited her answer.

"That's the $64,000 question, isn't it?" she joked, referring to the old quiz show as she bided her time.

Mickey's expression turned ever more serious and Andy wondered just how much money was involved. She felt a heavy responsibility, too heavy. After several moments thought, she turned to Mr Rodale.

"I was on Excalibur for one of his workouts," she replied, "and I've got to say this colt has his stride though he may not be as precocious. Give him a little more time and I don't think you'll be disappointed."

That was the best she could do.

"Well, well, we'll just see about that," Mr. Rodale said, slapping her on the back almost hard enough to knock the wind out of her. "We'll just see about that."

He repeated himself several more times as he walked into the kitchen.

Mickey looked down at her, a relieved look on his face. He quickly handed her a bill. "Good answer."

With that, he disappeared into the kitchen. Andy looked down at the money in her hand and gasped. It was a fifty dollar bill.

She quickly stashed it in her pocket. If Ringo saw it, he'd be demanding a six pack.

THE JUDGE IS BACK

Andy looked at herself in the mirror. She didn't like the new red and yellow silks. They wouldn't suit her next mount. Judge should have been carrying the colours of Texas as he had in every other race.

"Riders out!"

She tried to smile as she headed out to the saddling paddock but could only manage a neutral expression as Emmett met her in the stall. He seemed more interested in the other horses in the race rather than the gelding that had been under his care for the past two weeks. Judge was running in an eight thousand dollar claiming race, double what he had been claimed for.

The horse was running under the M&M Stables, but there was no sign of Mickey. She wouldn't be getting conflicting instructions this time.

Mustang led Judge over and Emmett legged her up.

"Ride him just like you did in his last race," he instructed her, "without the steeplechase, of course. See you in the winner's circle."

Andy looked quickly over her shoulder to see if Emmett was joking, but there wasn't a hint of a smile on his face. Surely he wasn't under the illusion that she could win this race. If he was expecting Arley to claim the Judge back, that wasn't happening either. Arley had spoken to two of his owners who were quite wealthy but neither of them were interested in a horse who was at the end of his career.

"I love you dearly, Judge, and I know you've got a lot of ability. But we've got our work cut out for us with this company. You haven't seen this kind of competition for a couple of years."

Mustang turned her loose on the track. "Ride the hair off him!" she called out.

"I don't know how you deal with her, Judge. I sure as heck couldn't put up with her all day. I'll talk to Mickey and see if I can get you into Al's hands."

She trotted through the post parade and galloped at a leisurely stride into the backstretch. "Ready for your sprint?" she asked, turning him loose. Like the previous warm-up, he reached almost full speed for a sixteenth of a mile. But this time, he wasn't as easy to pull up. The outrider was about to come after her when she finally got him stopped.

"Oh my God, Judge, you're on your toes today. I thought we were going to run the whole race there."

While she caught her breath, she studied the other horses. Liam was on the favourite, a stout chestnut colt who certainly looked like a winner. Carlo was on the second choice, a well muscled gray gelding exuding health and energy. Eddie was on the third choice, a small gelding who had already washed out, lather covering his neck and shoulders. Eddie was using his whip to scrape the heavy sweat off. Pedro's horse, like Judge, was a long shot at fifteen-to-one. He had a dull coat and a short stride.

The remaining horses had looked better in the *Form* than they did out here on the track.

"Well, old fella, we have a chance to hit the board. I only see two horses who'll give us a race. Let's see if we can sneak up on them."

As she trotted towards the starting gate, her eye caught someone leaning over the fence from the groom's stand. She brought Judge to a standstill. Arley looked his old horse over, a sentimental smile touching his lips.

"He's never missed picking up a cheque," Arley said.

"Don't spoil his record."

Andy nodded as she rode to the gate. She felt a new confidence now that she had the big Texan's blessing.

The Judge stood like a gentleman in the narrow stall and broke sharply. She tucked in behind the three leaders, angling between the two horses directly in front to lessen the kickback of dirt. Even in this position, Andy had to reach up and pull off the top layer of goggles before the first turn.

Just as the horses switched leads, she heard a scream. She looked over to see Liam being squeezed out of his position. Whoever was just outside of him was cutting over and causing him to clip heels. As soon as she recognized the rider, she stiffened. Pedro was back to his cowboy tactics and he was headed towards her.

She braced herself for the collision. Just as his boot brushed hers, he straightened his horse out. He had her closed in on the rail, but he didn't interfere with her.

They entered the homestretch in the same position. Andy studied the jockeys in front of her. She recognized them by their style and the shape of their butts. Carlo was directly in front of her with Eddie just to the outside of him.

She wasn't going to get through on the rail. Carlo would be scraping paint all the way to the wire. Maybe Eddie's horse would tire and drift out, but that would give Pedro the advantage, not Andy.

Judge pulled at the bit, ready to make his run. Andy ground her teeth in frustration. She had to take a hold and steady him when she wanted to turn him loose and fly. The sixteenth pole loomed ahead and still no change. Judge pulled harder and Andy braced herself in the stirrups to hold him back. The leaders were slowing down.

Carlo went to the whip, hitting his horse left handed. After three hard slashes, his horse veered out. The rail suddenly opened.

The Judge reacted as fast as Andy, rushing through the narrow opening. Andy got down on her belly and rode for all she was worth. There was no room to swing the whip, but Judge didn't need any extra encouragement. He knew where the wire was and he was determined to get there first.

He skimmed by the leaders, reaching out with the stride of a two year old, gliding well clear of his rivals.

Andy stood up just past the wire and let out a whoop of victory.

"And here comes the Judge!" she called out to the wind.

MEN IN DARK SUITS

"Hey, Pete, what kind of cake do you want for your birthday?"

"Never mind the cake, I want to see you and Miss Lili Marlene in the winner's circle."

"Is that with or without gift wrap?" Andy teased as she dismounted from the little filly.

Her mood of camaraderie was dispelled as Candace approached, a deep frown etched into her face.

"What?" Andy sighed, tired already from her morning gallops. "I've already been to Emmett's barn. I galloped three sets for him. Surely he doesn't have any more?"

"It's not Emmett looking for you. The stewards want to see ya."

Her worry dissipated, but now Andy was confused. "Why would the stewards want to see me?"

"Ya must have done something in that race yesterday. Did ya clobber Carlo when ya snuck through on the rail?"

"I may have brushed his boot, but after what Pedro did to Liam, they couldn't possibly call that a foul. Besides, there wasn't an inquiry after the race."

"They're calling ya name all over the backside."

"What? Calling my name over the PA system?" Now Andy was worried. "That means everybody on the backside knows I'm wanted in the stewards office!"

"With your illustrious reputation, they probably think the stewards want to commend you on your latest wins,"

Charlie remarked from the nearest stall.

"Whatever. Go on, they're waiting' for ya."

Andy headed immediately in the direction of the grandstand. She went over the races she'd ridden the day before
and tried to think of what she could have done that would
have the stewards upset. After her win on Judge, she'd ridden
a horse for a trainer who had just arrived from Pennsylvania.
The horse had been last all the way and passed two horses
in the stretch to finish tenth. She hadn't been close enough to
anyone to incur a foul.

Her mind then leaped to another channel entirely. Maybe
there'd been an accident. Were the stewards going to inform
her that her parents had been in an accident? Or her brother?

Her heart was racing when she reached the stewards'
office. In her nervousness, she opened the door and walked in
without knocking. Two men in dark suits turned and glared
at her.

Arthur jumped up from behind his desk. "Andrea," he
announced. "We've been expecting you."

The two men immediately relaxed.

Andy realized her faux pas. "I'm sorry, I shouldn't have
barged in. I...I don't know what I was thinking. I'll wait out
in the hall until you call me in."

"No, Andrea, stay," Arthur said as she turned towards
the door. "Come and have a seat. These gentlemen have
a few questions for you." He motioned to an empty chair
facing his desk.

With unaccustomed trepidation, Andy sat down in the
chair between the two dark suits. She looked from one man
to the other. If their facial features hadn't been so different,
they could have been mistaken for twins. Both men had the
same build, similar dark hair, brown eyes and navy blue suits.
The one contrasting element was their ties. The man to her
left wore a royal blue tie and the one on her right a brown tie.

"Miss Crowley, we just need a few minutes of your time,"
the blue tie announced. "I'm agent Bob Morrow and this is

agent George Wismer."

"Agent?" she repeated, confused.

"FBI,"' he informed her.

Andy's whole body tensed.

"Call me Bob and this is George." He nodded towards the agent with the brown tie.

His attempt at familiarity didn't put her at ease.

"We'd like to ask you a few questions about yesterday's first race," George informed her.

"First race?" Shock had paralysed Andy's mind and all she could do was repeat their words like a well trained Myna bird.

"You rode a horse named Charming the Judge," Bob continued.

Memory flooded back. "Yes, that's right. An amazing horse. I didn't think he could win for eight thousand but he sure did."

"You didn't think he could win?" George asked, a tinge of suspicion in his voice. "Why not?"

"He's been running for four thousand. Eight is a big jump, a different class of horse."

"So why did the trainer put him in for double his price?" Bob asked.

Andy turned to face Bob on the other side. "Emmett claimed him in his last race so he was in jail for thirty days."

"Emmett Gibbons was in jail?" George demanded, looking at Arthur. "Why weren't we informed of this?"

"Andrea doesn't mean that literally," Arthur said, stifling a laugh. "That's racetrack lingo for a ruling regarding horses that are claimed. For thirty days after the claim, the trainer has to run the horse for a higher price. So it's the horse that's in jail not the trainer."

"Sorry," Andy apologized. "I'll refrain from using race-track vernacular."

George turned back to Andy. "So, you said the horse won eight thousand dollars."

"No, that was the claiming price. The purse was three thousand dollars but the winner's share is only sixty percent of that."

"And the jockey's share?" Bob asked.

"The jockey gets ten percent of the winner's share." She swivelled towards Bob. "So that's ten percent of sixty percent. That works out to a hundred and eighty dollars for that particular race." Andy was beginning to sound more like a math teacher than a jockey but the FBI agents didn't seem to know anything about the workings of the racetrack.

"And maybe a little bonus? Did the trainer slip a mutual ticket in your boot when he legged you up?"

Andy laughed as she turned back to George but stopped the moment she saw his irritated scowl. She thought he'd meant it as a joke.

"Sorry," she apologized. "I thought that only happened in movies."

George looked her directly in the eye as if he were trying to see into her soul. It seemed more of a learned technique than a natural talent. Andy sensed this was a man who could only see what was on the surface.

"Did you notice anything unusual during the race?" George demanded.

"No, nothing out of the ordinary. Everything went well in the gate this time."

"This time?" George repeated, turning it into a pointed question.

"I had a horse rear in the gate not too long ago," she explained. "He'd never acted up before. We don't know exactly what happened, but the handler was someone new."

George looked questioningly at Arthur, as if information had once again been withheld.

"He was a replacement for one of the crew who was off sick that day," Arthur explained. "The starter fired him immediately after the incident."

George's pen was poised over his notebook. "What's the

horse's name?"

"The horse's name is The Heckler. The race was last Wednesday."

Andy was glad Arthur had answered the question. The past few weeks were all blurring together.

George finished his note taking. "No funny business in the gate yesterday?"

She shook her head. "We broke clean. I was exactly where I thought I'd be in the backstretch. I managed to save ground on the turn."

"What do you mean, save ground?"

Andy was beginning to wonder why this agent had been assigned to this case, whatever the case was. He was totally clueless about horseracing.

"I stayed close to the inside rail, to cover the shortest distance of ground from the gate to the wire. For every horse width you move out from the rail, that's how many lengths you lose. I wanted to save as many lengths as possible. I wasn't riding the favourite. I had two horses to beat."

"Two? But there were twelve horses in that race, weren't there?" George's tone insinuated she was holding back on him.

Andy sighed. "Yes, there were twelve horses in the race, but only two had a *Form* good enough to beat us."

He opened his mouth to ask another question, but Andy beat him to the punch. "A *Form* means the horse's past performance record. It's published in the *Daily Racing Form*. We study all the horse's past performances before a race, not just the one we're riding. We need to size up the competition. To me, there were only two horses that looked tough. Liam had the best horse in the race and he might have beaten me if he hadn't been shut off. "

"Liam was on one of these tough horses?"

"Yeah, the toughest. He was on the favourite."

Both men began scribbling furiously in their notebooks.

"Who shut him off?" George asked, still writing.

"Pedro. I couldn't believe he was back to his old tricks."

"Tell us about Pedro's old tricks," Bob said, leaning back in his chair.

Andy was beginning to think the questioning was more about the other jockeys than about he, only a partial relief. She wasn't a squealer by nature. Even though it was Pedro and Carlo, she still felt like a fink.

"Before Mr Healey became head steward, the riding around here was pretty rough. I knew the jocks would test me out, make sure I know what I was doing. Race riding is dangerous enough without having an incompetent rider in the middle of the herd. Whenever the riding got rough, Pedro and his buddy Carlo always seemed to be involved. That is, until Mr Healey cracked down on them." She nodded at Arthur in acknowledgement. "Pedro and Carlo both got suspensions and only returned a few days ago. They've been riding fairly clean. But yesterday, Pedro was back to his old tricks. He cut Liam off pretty bad. I thought he was going to shut me off too but he didn't touch me."

"We'll be reviewing that at the films today," Arthur assured them.

"And then what happened?" Bob asked, still sitting back casually as George took notes.

"Pedro cut half way across the racetrack and I thought he was going to slam me up against the rail. But he straightened out before he hit me. He kept a straight path the rest of the way so I started to concentrate on Carlo in front of me."

"Carlo Gessani?"

Andy nodded. "He was hugging the rail, like he always does. He'd been setting a slow pace in front on the second favourite so I figured he had plenty of horse left. Eddie was beside him. I was hoping Eddie's horse would tire and drift out so I could get through. Then, all of a sudden, the rail opened." She snapped her fingers. "Like magic."

"Like magic?" Both George and Bob echoed in stereo.

"Carlo's horse drifted off the rail, just like magic?" Bob

asked.

"No, it wasn't like he got tired and drifted out. Carlo was hitting him left-handed, hard, and his horse veered out. Carlo is pretty vicious with the whip. He leaves welts on the poor horses."

"So, you slipped through on the rail and won," George said, snapping his fingers. "Like magic."

Andy shook her head vehemently. "Lady Luck may have been smiling on me when the rail opened but she wasn't going to ride the race for me. I had to get down on my belly and do that."

George reviewed his notes. "You said Carlo was hugging the rail 'like he always does'. Didn't it seem out of character for him to open the rail and let you through?"

"*Let* me through? You've got to be kidding. Carlo would never give me that courtesy. He hates me."

"Maybe he can put his feelings aside if the payoff is big enough," George suggested.

"No way, not Carlo. He can't control his temper for a second."

"Hold on a second, you said a jockey loses lengths when they move away from the rail," George said, flipping through the pages of his notebook as though they were a deck of cards. "So why would he take the chance of his horse going out by hitting him left handed?"

"It's only on the turn that you lose lengths from drifting out. Once you're in the stretch and coming down to the wire, you ride as hard as you can. Carlo couldn't hit his horse right handed because he was blocked on the outside by Eddie." She pointed to his notebook to let him know he should write this down. "That's a strategy we use. Most right handed jockeys can't hit as hard with their left hand so you crowd them, come in so close they have to switch the whip to their left hand. You have to do that without dropping the reins or interfering with the horse's rhythm. It's a lot harder than it sounds."

George took note of that while Bob picked up the interview.

"What did Carlo do after you slipped through?"

Andy shrugged her shoulders as she once again turned back to Bob. "I have no idea. Horses don't have rear view mirrors."

Neither agent laughed. A sense of humour didn't seem to be one of their qualities.

"I wasn't paying any attention to Carlo or anybody else at that point. I just got down on my belly and rode like crazy. Judge is an awesome horse when he's in full flight, one of the most honest horses you'd ever want to meet."

"And he had an honest jockey," Arthur said pointedly.

"When there's gambling involved, honest people can start making bad decisions," George replied emphatically. "It's not easy to turn down a few thousand bucks when your pay cheque is chicken feed."

"Chicken feed!" Andy exclaimed. "I've won three races this week. That's not chicken feed!"

"I think we could do with a short break," Arthur announced. "Coffee anyone?"

CLYDE

They reassembled in the stewards' office, coffee cups in hand. This time, the FBI agents sat on different sides of Andy, brown tie on the left, blue tie to the right.

Bob looked over his notes as he twirled the pen in his hand. Satisfied, he held it up like a conductor's baton and opened with the first question. "Did anyone approach you before the first race yesterday?"

Andy glanced to her left, not totally certain of his meaning.

"Did anyone talk to you about your chances in the race, maybe somebody you'd never seen before, someone off the track?" he further explained.

She shook her head. "I'm here at five am every morning, seven days a week. By the end of the day, all I want to do is go home, eat and go to bed. There's no time to socialize with people off the track."

"Did anyone on the track make an offer of payment?"

"You mean to lose the race? Absolutely not," she said, offended by the idea. "I've never been asked to lose a race, with or without payment."

George joined in the interrogation. "Why would a trainer ask you to lose a race without payment?"

Andy took a second to formulate her answer. "Some trainers like to bet on their horses." She held her hand up as George was about to interrupt. "It's totally legal to bet on your own horse. It's betting on other horses in the race that's frowned on."

"Is there a lot of that going on?"

"I don't know. The trainers don't tell me what they're betting." She had to stop and think for a moment to remember where she was going with this. "So a trainer will sometimes tell a jockey to make a decision in the homestretch. If it looks like you're not going to win, the trainer may want you to finish off the board. A horse that finishes worse than third will always have higher odds in his next race."

The frown this time came from Arthur.

"None of the trainers I've ridden for have ever asked me to do that," she quickly explained to the steward. "But I've heard from other jockeys that it happens."

"Has Emmett Gibbons ever suggested that he wanted you to lose a race?"

The question came from Bob. George was busy writing down her latest tidbit.

Andy shook her head. "No, but Emmett doesn't say much to me at all. The only time he talks to me is when he gives me a leg up before the race, to say something like, 'she's got speed, use it'. Everybody in his barn is close lipped."

Both men wrote that down.

"Except for Al."

"Who's Al?" George asked.

"Alonzo, one of the grooms."

"The young Mexican groom?" Bob asked. "So what does Alonzo talk about? Does he give you information on the horses in the barn?"

"Only the ones he takes care of. He's the best groom Emmett has, a hell of a lot better than Mustang."

George actually flinched at the mention of her name. Andy wondered if he'd already questioned her. Her abrasive manner would make anyone flinch.

"Never mind Mustang, let's talk about Alonzo," Bob intervened. "What does he tell you about the horses?"

"How they're feeling, if they're eating properly, which stakes races they'll win."

"He knows which races they'll win?" George's suspicion reared once again.

"Of course not. It's the dream, the one everyone on the racetrack has, the dream of owning or training or riding the next Secretariat. That's why we get up at four o'clock every morning, rain, snow or sleet. "

George didn't look convinced. "Come on, you need a hell of a lot more than a dream to get up at four a.m. and slog around the racetrack in the mud. Promise of a little extra bonus, maybe?"

"You're really fixated on money, aren't you, George?" she said testily.

"Hey, you can't eat a dream, or smoke it," he added with a snide grin. "So why don't you tell us about this exercise boy, Ringo. He needs a hell of a lot more than a dream to feed his habit, doesn't he?"

Immediately on the alert, Andy reined herself in on this one. She wasn't about to get Ringo into trouble. In her mind, she took three deep breaths to steady herself.

"George is referring to his addiction," Bob said, keeping his tone neutral as if it carried no judgement.

"You mean his obsession with the Beatles? Ringo buys every album, tee shirt and memorabilia he can get his hands on."

"Come on, you know damn well what we're talking about," George egged her on. "After all you *know* him better than anyone."

"*Know* him?" The insinuation was unmistakable. "You think two people can't get along without hopping into bed?"

"You're a healthy young woman." George leaned closer to her as though they were about to share something intimate. "You need a little male companionship some nights, right?"

"Wrong." She leaned away from him.

"Really? He hasn't come on to you?" George shook his head. "Maybe he's just too stoned to make his move."

"Ringo has never come to the barn stoned," she insisted. "And if you'd ever ridden a racehorse, you would know that was impossible. You have to have lightning reflexes. If you were stoned, you wouldn't make it one lap around the track." She pointed to his notebook. "Mark that down in your notes."

"Richard Skyler is one of the most popular exercise riders on the grounds," Arthur informed them. "There's never been a complaint against him."

"He may be clean when he's in the barn, but how about off the track?" Bob asked, taking over the interrogation.

"I've never seen him off the track. Like I said, when I leave here there's no time or energy for socializing. The only person I see off the track is my roommate, Charlie."

"So you do have a boyfriend." George appeared vindicated.

"That's short for Charlotte," Andy said without looking at him.

"You're referring to Charlotte Middleton, Pete Mackenzie's groom?" Bob once again.

Andy nodded in his direction. "That's right."

"Charlie is the one you socialize with the most, correct?"

"You could call it that. I mean, we live in the same house."

"And go shopping together."

It took Andy a few moments to realize what he meant.

"You were watching us downtown?" she asked, remembering their day off. "Why would you do that?"

"We'll ask the questions," George insisted. "Tell us why you went to The Smiling Oyster?"

"The Smiling what?"

"Come on, you know the place, serves the *finest* seafood in town." His tone was facetious.

"I don't know what you're talking about." The idea of being watched everywhere she went had knocked Andy off balance. She tried to piece together everything they had done that afternoon. "You're talking about our day off, when we went downtown... a tour of the Freedom Trail, Filiene's basement. Charlie bought a hat...then we were looking for the restaurant, the one Candace had suggested...the Whistling Oyster."

"The Whistling Clam," Bob corrected her. "You missed that one by about three blocks. You went to the Smiling Oyster."

"Right." The sequence of events was coming back to her.

"So you hadn't planned on going to the Smiling Oyster?"

She shook her head. "And I certainly don't plan on going back. The food was awful."

She found it easier to stay focused if she looked in Bob's direction.

"Are you trying to tell us you didn't go there specifically to meet some friends?"

The mere sound of George's voice was enough to make her grind her teeth. "I don't have friends in Boston. I've only been here a month."

"Make that thirty two days," George corrected her.

She spun in her chair to face him. "You've been watching me since the day I arrived?"

"That's right, we've got eyes everywhere. We wouldn't need to watch you if you weren't hanging out with the wrong crowd," George informed her. "Birds of a feather..."

"I'm not hanging out with anyone! This is my job, I ride for these people."

"We know what a jockey's job is, we're just trying to find out what kind of a job you're doing." George rapped his notepad with his knuckles. "And you're not being very helpful."

"I believe Andrea is being extremely helpful," Arthur said, using the stern tone that he employed during film replays.

"No one's accusing Andy of anything." Bob's calm tone was meant to smooth ruffled feathers but Andy wasn't falling for it. She'd had enough of the good cop, bad cop act.

"I've got races to ride," she said, standing up and pushing

her chair back. "I'm supposed to be in the jockeys' room."

"I'm sure Arthur here can give you a note," George said, motioning her to sit down.

"Just a few more questions and you can be on your way," Bob assured her. "Did you talk to anyone in the restaurant?"

Andy tried to take a deep breath but it came out more as sigh. "Just the bartender. He served the food. He said the waitress was out for the day, but I'm sure she quit. No one with an ounce of dignity would want to serve that crap."

"Was the place full of customers?" George asked.

"You should know, you were watching." Andy was determined George wouldn't get another piece of information out of her.

"Was there anything or anyone that caught your eye?" Bob asked, still the voice of reason.

She was about to shake her head when a vision of the big man sprang to her mind.

"There was someone, he was impossible to miss. The man was as big as a whale."

"What was this whale's name?" George asked, his pen ready.

"I don't know. It's not like we were introduced."

"Did someone call him by his name?" Bob asked.

"Well, it must have been a nickname. The bartender said something to him as he went out the door, something like..." She struggled to remember. "Clyde..."

"He called him Clyde?" Bob prompted.

"No, sorry, that was me, I called him Clyde. The bartender called him Pony. He said, 'have a nice trip, Pony.' I thought he looked more like a draft horse than a Shetland."

Bob and George began writing furiously.

"Where was he—"

"I don't know where he was going," she replied impatiently, figuring that would be George's next question.

"Where was he sitting?" George asked pointedly.

"He wasn't sitting anywhere. I saw him walk across the

room and out the door."

"Could he have been sitting in one of the back booths?" Bob asked.

"I don't think he would fit in a booth," she assured him.

"So he appeared, like magic." George snapped his fingers.

"I don't know where he came from, but I can give you a guess." She continued to ignore George and spoke to Bob. "I went to the bathroom just before we left. There was a hallway that led to the back of the restaurant. He may have come from there."

"Nothing suspicious about the restrooms?"

"No but I just saw Minnie's room not Mickey's."

Bob nodded. He was obviously familiar with the icons on the bathroom doors.

"Anyone else?" Bob asked without lifting his eyes from his notebook. "Was there anyone with this guy, Pony?"

The face of the man behind Pony appeared in her mind's eye, the man who was the spitting image of Eddie. Her memory replayed the argument in the parking lot. She knew she should give them this information but she hesitated. She didn't want to lie but neither did she want to implicate Eddie.

"You're thinking hard again, Andy. You need us to repeat the question?" George taunted her.

To hell with him. She shook her head. "I only saw the big man."

Bob finished his scribbling. "We need to keep this conversation private, Andy. We're at a very critical point in our investigation."

"Yeah, so keep it under your hat," George warned her. "Or maybe I should say, under your helmet."

Andy got up to leave.

"One more thing," Bob said as she started across the room. "Is there anyone else who strikes you as odd? Anyone in Emmett's barn that seems unusual?"

The face that came immediately to her mind was one of the greatest enigmas of the racetrack, Mickey Amato. But his face blurred as an image of Excalibur formed.

"Here we go, thinking awfully hard again. Come on, spit it out" George demanded.

She nodded slowly. "There is one person in that barn I'd call suspicious, someone who seems to know a lot, but won't come clean."

George's pen was poised. "And his name is..."

Andy let out a big breath.

"Mustang."

COWBOYS AND JOCKEYS

A ndy opened the door to the jockey's room, ruminating
on all that had been said in the stewards' office. She
couldn't believe the agents suspected her of any foul play,
even George. His irritating attitude had to be an act. He must
have been purposely egging her on. People tended to spit out
the truth in a moment of anger.

Obviously, something bigger than just Carlo and Pedro
was going on. The stakes had to be higher. It crossed state
lines if the FBI was involved.

"I heard the stewards calling you," Denise remarked,
dressed and ready to ride. "What was that all about?"

Andy had to think quickly. She hadn't prepared an answer.

"Ah, the stewards just wanted to make sure I understood
the apprenticeship rules," she replied, formulating the answer
as she went along. "You know, I only have the apprentice
weight allowance for a year after my fifth win. So I've got
two more to go and then the clock starts ticking."

"You'll have those two wins in no time, the way you're
going. That gives you the bug till next spring. You're on your
way, girl," Denise predicted.

Andy took her racing clothes out of her cubicle. Her mind
was still on the interrogation. She couldn't be sure exactly
who the agents suspected, but Emmett's barn was definitely
under the microscope.

The PA system crackled to life, calling riders out just as
she slipped into the silks.

"Damn, I haven't read the *Form*."

She grabbed her whip as Denise held the door open for her. "Go get 'em, girl."

Andy walked quickly out to the saddling paddock. She smiled when she saw her petite mount prancing beside Charlie. Miss Lili Marlene was raring to go. Pete was his usual bundle of nerves.

"Don't let Eddie's horse clobber you at the break. He's just outside of you," he instructed her, all in one breath.

Andy smiled. "It's okay, Pete, Lili and I can handle whatever they throw at us."

"So you know Carlo picked up a mount, then."

She was instantly alert. "What? When did that happen?"

"It was announced twenty minutes ago. He's on old man Morris' horse."

"You're kidding." She scanned the riders and saw Carlo walking across the paddock to the number three stall. She quickly looked the horses over to find the one with the number three saddle cloth. The chestnut horse looked familiar.

"I've seen that horse somewhere," she said, searching her memory. "What's his name?"

"Fortune Hunter."

It instantly came back to her. "Right, that's the horse from Chile, the one who likes to gallop without stirrups. He's got speed, right?"

"Yeah, plenty of speed. Let him go to the lead. Lili likes to come from just off the pace."

"There's something else." Andy tried to remember what Candace had told her about the horse.

"He's a steam engine out of the gate. He'll be in front," Pete said before turning his attention back to Miss Lili Marlene. "Stay within striking distance. Lili can only make up so much ground."

Andy scanned the faces of the other jockeys. Carlo's side-kick, Pedro, was on the number eight horse. "What about Pedro's horse?"

Pete looked the horse over as she walked by. "She's only had one win in her life. This isn't her conditions. Don't worry about her."

Andy glanced at the tote board. Fortune Hunter was fifteen- to-one, Pedro's horse was thirty-to-one.

"Surely they won't try to pull off that perfecta," she muttered. "I hope Bob and George are watching."

"Who?" Pete asked.

"Nothing," she said quickly, catching herself. "Don't worry, Pete, I know where I need to be at the wire. That's all that really matters, right?"

"Right," he agreed.

Charlie brought Lili into the saddling stall and Pete legged her up, a good two feet higher than the saddle. She had to grab mane to pull herself down.

"Sorry," he apologized as Miss Lili Marlene pranced excitedly beside Charlie.

"I heard the announcement about Carlo picking up a mount," Charlie said as she quickened her step to keep up with the excited filly. "You don't think the boys are up to their old tricks, do you?"

"If they are, they've picked the wrong day."

"They certainly have," Charlie agreed, smiling up at her. "Let's give Pete the best ever birthday present."

Charlie didn't quite understand her meaning, but Andy just smiled. "Yes, let's do that."

When the filly was turned loose on the track, she broke into a canter and Andy took a strong hold to slow her down. Once she had her at a controlled prance, she studied the silks. Carlo wore black and tan. The earth tones wouldn't stand out, but if Fortune Hunter ran true to *Form*, he would be in front. Pedro would be easy to spot in his red and white silks and Eddie in blue and yellow. She didn't know if she had to worry about him, but she filed the information anyway. The apprentices, Benito and Billy Feagin, didn't have any speed. Aidan Odahl's horse had a little speed out of the gate, but usually ran out of gas by the turn. She'd make sure she wasn't stuck behind him.

She watched Fortune Hunter warm up. By the second gallop down the backstretch, he looked like he was raring to go. She tried once again to remember what Candace had said about the horse, but it wouldn't come to her.

She turned her attention back to Lili as they galloped off into the warm-up, keeping a strong hold on the reins as Lili pulled hard. She was relieved when they were called to the gate. One of the handlers led Fortune Hunter by. The gelding was at least two hundred pounds heavier than Lili. Andy didn't want to get into a shoving match with him.

"To hell with the boys and their little games, Lili, this is our race."

She headed towards the gate with a determination she had never felt before. The little filly sensed her resolve and dragged the gate handler into the padded stall.

"Easy now, the race hasn't started yet," the handler gasped as he climbed up on the ledge. "Hey, Andy, watch out for this horse of mine," Eddie told her from the stall just outside of her. "She lugs in."

Andy debated whether or not to believe him. He might be saying that to get her to pull back and let him have the inside rail. It was a common tactic.

She took deeper breaths than usual and focused straight ahead.

The latches sprang open and Lili exploded into action. For the first three strides, she had the lead until Billy Feagan passed her on the inside and Fortune Hunter flew by on the outside. Eddie followed right behind him, bumping her as he passed. He was pulling hard on the outside rein. He'd obviously been telling her the truth.

Andy turned her attention back to Carlo. He was two lengths in front and had a hold on his horse. He was saving some run for the finish.

She looked around to see where Pedro was and spotted him about one and a half lengths behind her, blocking horses in on the rail.

She turned her attention back to Carlo. She had to stay within striking distance. Her plan was to catch him when he least expected it, on the crest of the turn. Most horses slowed down to balance for the change of leads, but Lili was so agile, she picked up speed.

Andy resisted the urge to go to the inside rail. She wanted a clear path when it was time to make her move. She stayed one horse width off the rail and caught up to Billy. His horse tired at the three eighths pole and faded out of Andy's vision. Eddie's horse dropped in on the rail in front of her. Perfect. She wanted to pass him on the outside.

She was now in the perfect position. Suddenly a horse appeared on her outside. Aidan Odahl galloped up beside her and angled in, pushing her closer to the rail.

She was trapped behind Eddie as the turn loomed ahead. Andy tried nudging Aidan's horse out, but he held his ground. Just as the horses switched leads, Eddie smacked his filly on the left shoulder. Daylight appeared on the rail as the horse moved out. Lili instinctively started to go for the hole, but Andy pulled her back. Eddie's horse swerved in the moment she changed leads.

"Not yet, Lili, you'll get us killed," she called out as they narrowly missed clipping heels.

At the crest of the turn, Eddie hit his horse again, forcing her out. The sliver of daylight was a little wider and Lili leapt forward into the narrow opening. Eddie's horse swerved back in, hitting her hard.

"What the hell!" he shouted as Lili bounced against the rail and stumbled. Andy pulled on the reins with all her strength to keep the filly on her feet.

Eddie stood in the irons and yanked his horse out. The hole opened and Lili scrambled through.

Andy let out a breath of relief as they got back into rhythm. She set her sights on Carlo, now three lengths in the lead. She had plenty of horse left, but so did Carlo. He was still hand riding, confident that no one was going to pass him.

Andy knew if she closed the gap, stride by stride, he would have plenty of warning and go to the whip. She had to unleash Lili at just the right moment.

The roar from the grandstand drowned out her hoof beats as she held Lili back. She stayed directly behind him, out of his view. Lili pulled on the bit, raring to go, but Andy waited until the sixteenth pole slipped by.

"Now!" she called out, releasing her hold.

Miss Lili Marlene sprang forward like a cat pouncing on its prey. Within three strides, she was at Carlo's boot. It was then that she remembered what Candace had told her.

"Look him in the eye!" she called out as Carlo went to a vicious right hand whipping. Andy reached forward, stretching out over Lili's neck. "Come on, Lili, look him right in the eye!"

The filly gained inch by inch as Carlo's whip cut cruelly into the gelding's flesh.

Finally, they were head to head. The wire loomed in front of them.

Fortune Hunter conceded.

HAPPY BIRTHDAY PETE

Andy pumped the air. "Little but mighty!" she called out into the wind.

Lili continued to gallop at a furious pace. They were well into the backstretch before Andy could pull her up. Just as she came to a trot, she heard screaming behind her.

"You stupid son of a bitch! What the hell were you doing? You were supposed to take care of the bitch!"

Andy turned Lili around to see what was going on.

"What the fuck you talking about!" Pedro yelled back at Carlo. "I had everybody jammed in on the fucking rail. All you had to do was stay in front of her!"

"You stupid motherfucker, you were supposed to get her! Never mind the rest of those bastards, you were supposed to get the girl!" Carlo lashed out with his whip, hitting Pedro on the side of his face.

Pedro yelped in pain. "I did what I was supposed to do. You fucked it up!"

"Oh yeah! Thanks to you, we're dead, asshole, we're dead!"

Carlo raised his whip, ready to strike again when suddenly, his arm froze. He was staring in Andy's direction.

"Come on, Lili, we better get out of here." She turned Lili around, ready to gallop off down the backstretch when she noticed two men on the outside rail. A quick glance over her shoulder told her they were the ones Carlo was staring at.

Bob and George were watching them from the groom's

stand. In their dark suits, the FBI agents looked like hovering vultures, their intense concentration focused on the two jockeys.

"Go, get the fuck out of here!" Carlo screamed.

The two jockeys set off at a full gallop as the agents jumped over the fence and landed on the track. Lili leaped in the air as the two agents ran by.

Andy quickly turned her in a circle to keep her from running off. She caught glimpses of the agents chasing the horses towards the starting gate chute.

The horses had several lengths on the agents as they galloped by the chute. Both jockeys launched themselves from the saddle. Pedro landed on his feet running. Carlo rolled in a ball for several yards before getting his feet under him.

The gate crew stood shocked as the two jockeys made a mad dash towards the back fence. They scrambled up the chain link fence and through the top barb wire strands, neither shredded silks nor torn flesh slowing them down. They landed on the other side and sprinted off into the streets of east Boston.

Bob was a dozen lengths in front of George and tried to scale the fence. Unlike the fleeing jockeys, he wasn't oblivious to barb wire. When the sleeve of his jacket became entangled, he gave up the chase. George didn't attempt the climb.

"Loose horses!" the outriders called out as the two riderless horses flew around the clubhouse turn and into the homestretch.

Andy galloped back, barely in control. All of the returning horses were in an excited state and the jockeys had their hands full trying to pull up. Andy couldn't get Lili stopped until she passed the unsaddling area. She had to jog back.

"What the hell's going on?" Charlie asked as she reached for the excited filly's reins.

"Looks like Pedro and Carlo didn't finish in the right order," Andy replied. "I think Carlo was supposed to finish in front of me."

"Bloody hell!" Charlie laughed. "They weren't going to beat you today."

Charlie led the triumphant horse and jockey into the winner's circle where Pete was waiting for them. Andy smiled down at him.

"Happy birthday, Pete."

"That was the best present anyone could give me," he said, patting his horse and shaking his jockey's hand. "Brilliant, ride, Andy. Willie Shoemaker himself couldn't have done any better."

"Thanks, Pete, but Willie's the one I have to thank. He taught me how to wait for the right moment."

"Looks like Carlo and Pedro weren't so impressed. I've never seen two jockeys so upset about losing."

Andy grinned down at him. "They lost more than the race."

Candace rushed into the winner's circle. "I've got to pony in the next race, but I'm not going to miss this win picture."

Lili stopped her prancing just long enough for everyone to take their places for the picture. After the camera flashed, Andy jumped off and removed her saddle.

"I'll spring for the champagne and it's going to be a heck of a lot better than Baby Duck."

"Sounds good to me," Pete said as he and Charlie led the filly off down the track.

"We've got offers coming in already," Candace called over her shoulder as she rushed off towards the pony horse. "And they're not all long shots."

"Good, maybe I won't have to work so hard," Andy replied as she headed to the scale room.

The clerk of scales was looking out towards the back fence as she stepped up on the scales.

"I don't think Carlo and Pedro will be weighing out, " she quipped.

Gerry shook his head as he turned to her. "I've been here for twenty years and I've never seen anything like it."

"With any luck, we'll never see it again," she said as she handed her saddle to a valet and headed across the paddock. Eddie fell in step beside her.

"That was a foolish move you made on the turn," he reprimanded her. "I understand taking a chance to win, but you need to choose your risks more wisely in the future—if you want to have a future."

"It was more Lili's idea than mine, but I hear you." She looked at him and smiled. "And yes, I do want a future."

IT'S IN THE BOOKS

Mickey pushed open the front door of his apartment building and stepped out. The breeze had a warm, dry smell. There would be no rain today. The racetrack would be perfect for Excalibur's first gallop.

There was almost a spring in his step as he walked to his car. He was looking forward to seeing how much the colt had matured from the experience of the race. Would he be more focused? Would his stride be stronger and more confident? If he was too racy, would the girl be able to hold him?

"Mickey, hey Mickey."

He stopped as he reached the curb. He couldn't be sure if someone was calling his name or if it was the breeze rustling the leaves of the laurel bushes.

"Psst, Mickey, over here."

The branches of a bush parted just off to his left. He stared for several seconds before recognizing Tommy.

Mickey looked around quickly, to see if anyone was following. He moved quickly towards the bushes.

"Tommy? What the hell are you doing?"

"We're in trouble, Mickey."

Again, Mickey searched up and down the street for sight of anyone following them before concealing himself in the bushes. "What do you mean, we're in trouble? What's going on?"

"They've busted Pony!"

Mickey was sure he hadn't heard him correctly. "Busted?

Pony? "

"Clean out your ears, Mickey, we haven't got much time. We've got to think fast."

"Hold on a minute." Mickey pushed a branch out of his way so he could see Tommy's face clearly. "Slow down and tell me what happened."

"It was one of the pinheads at Atlantic City. The chicken shit bastard spilled the beans. They jumped Pony at the motel. He's behind bars, Mickey, they've got Pony. And they've got a witness. Now the FBI are snooping around the restaurant. They want to see the books." Tommy grabbed a handful of leaves and crushed them in his fist. "We're all going down, Mickey."

"Tommy, for God's sake, just tell me what they said to you."

"They haven't said anything to me. You think I'm crazy? I'm not showing my face."

"Then how do you know about the FBI?"

"Matt called me. He said they showed up last night, demanding to see the accounts. They want the books, Mickey. That means they're coming after you."

"All right, give me a minute to put this together."

"What's to put together? They're probably on their way to your office. We've got to get the hell out of here, now."

Mickey shook his head. "Just hang on and let me think. Nobody's going anywhere."

"Maybe you aren't, but I'm blowing this place. I'm headed out of town." Tommy tried to step out of the bushes but Mickey pulled him back.

"Leaving town is a sure sign of guilt, Tommy."

"So what, there's nothing they can do about it if they can't find me."

"They'll find you , they've got agents in every state." Mickey kept a grip on Tommy's arm. "That's not how we're going to handle it. Nobody's leaving town. There's nothing in the books, Tommy. The only way they can get anything on us is if we panic. And that's exactly what you're doing."

"But Mickey—"

"Listen to me." Mickey tightened his grasp. "This is what you do. You show up at the restaurant, on time and you act like it's just a normal day, same old routine. You're just there to do your job."

"What the hell, you want me to walk into a trap?"

"I want you to walk into the restaurant and do your job." Mickey took a hold of both shoulders. "What's your job, Tommy?"

"You know what I do."

"What's your job, Tommy?" he demanded in a more forceful tone.

"My job, hell, I'm Pony's lieutenant, I'm his number one—"

"What's your job at The Smiling Oyster, Tommy?" Mickey shook him roughly.

"I'm...I'm..."

"It's in the books."

"Hell, I'm a bouncer," Tommy blurted out.

"And? What else are you paid to do?"

Tommy struggled to think.

"What did you do as a kid, Tommy, at McDonalds?"

"I was a cook."

"Exactly." Mickey released his grip. "So what do you tell the FBI when they start asking you questions?"

"I tell them I'm a bouncer and a cook."

"And when they ask about the books?"

"I don't know anything about the books, that's your job!"

"Exactly." Mickey patted his shoulder. "You've got it all straight. There's nothing to worry about."

"Christ, I need a drink."

"That would be perfect, the bouncer shows up shit faced. That'll impress them."

"Where the hell do you get these nerves of steel?" Tommy demanded.

"From dealing with the likes of you all my life." Mickey straightened Tommy's collar. "Okay, what you need to do is go somewhere quiet and get your act together."

"Yeah, you're right, Mick, that's what I need to do. There's a joint on Revere beach that's open all night."

"No way! None of your usual hangouts, Tommy. They'll be waiting for you. You've got to go some place where they'd never think of looking for you. A nice, quiet coffee shop, somewhere in Malden."

"Malden? I don't know any coffee shops in Malden."

"Exactly, that's why it's perfect. Have some breakfast, go for a walk, clear your head. Then you show up at the Smiling Oyster ready for the lunch crowd."

Tommy nodded. "Yeah, Mickey, good thinking. That's what I'll do, a coffee shop in Malden."

"And don't worry about a thing. There's nothing in the books they can use. You just keep your cool, don't go slugging an FBI agent. You lose your temper or you'll be sharing a cell with Pony."

"Okay, Mickey, I'll take your word on this."

"You remember how to handle the grill, right? You know how to turn it on?"

"Of course I know how to turn it on." Tommy stepped out of the bushes and brushed himself off. "And I know how to flip burgers."

"And I know how to keep books," Mickey said decisively.

"That's good because they'll be coming to talk to you. Matt told them you're the accountant."

"I'll take care of my business, you take care of yours. Have a good breakfast, Tommy."

"Yeah, okay, Mickey."

There was still a note of uncertainty in his tone, but Tommy's stride was purposeful as he

disappeared into the darkness. Mickey sighed as he walked in the opposite direction.

AGENTS FINISH THIRD

The track kitchen was filled to capacity as grooms and trainers took advantage of the mid-morning break to grab breakfast.

"Holy crow, Carlo and Pedro got away!" Andy exclaimed, reading the headlines of the Boston Globe as she sat down at a table. "'*Jockeys First and Second, FBI a distant Third.*'"

Candace carried a tray with a plate of bacon and eggs and three cups of coffee and a cup of tea and placed it on the table. "Of course the jocks won, they were on hossback."

"What else does it say?" Pete asked, sipping his coffee.

Andy continued. "*Jockeys Carlo Gessani and Pedro Vargas were last seen scaling the back fence of Suffolk Downs Racetrack. The starting gate crew watched in disbelief as the jockeys ran down Waldemar Street.*"

Charlie shook her head as she reached for her cup of tea. "Surely somebody noticed two jockeys in bright silks running down the street."

"Maybe they hopped on the subway," Pete suggested.

Candace broke into song. "*Will they ever return? No they'll never return and their fate is still unlearned. They may ride forever 'neath the streets 'a Boston. They're the jocks that never returned.*"

Andy had to laugh along with of them. "Okay, now for the rest of the article. '*No eye witnesses have come forth with information. It is believed the jockeys were involved in a country-wide race fixing scheme run by Anthony Cantoni*

*who was arrested yesterday in Atlantic City. The FBI have
had him under surveillance for the past three years.'"*

Andy turned the page and her expression changed from
interest to shock. "Oh my God, it's him! Look, Charlie, it's
Clyde, the fat man at the The Whistling Clam."

"The Smiling Oyster," Charlie corrected her. "You never
get that straight."

"You just said his name was Anthony," Pete countered.

Andy turned the paper so Candace and Pete could see
the picture of the enormous man. "The bartender called him
Pony, but I thought Clyde was a better name." She turned
her attention back to the article. "Listen, the plot thickens.'
*'Anthony Cantoni, more commonly called Pony Cantoni, is
believed to be connected to the Winter Hill Gang. Several
reputed members have been brought in for questioning,
including Howie Winter and Whitey Bulger. No other arrests
have been made."*

The enormity of the situation stunned her. "That means
Carlo and Pedro weren't playing their own little game, it was
big mafia business."

"And you tried to mess it up for them," Charlie reminded
her. "Do you realize that could have been you beaten to a
pulp in the parking lot?"

"More like cement shoes and dumped in the harbour,"
Pete suggested. "Your guardian angel must have been
working overtime."

"I told ya not to be a hero, didn't I?" Candace said pointedly. "It's not over yet. A lot of guys are going down on this
one. I got all the dope before those newspaper guys did. Way
I hear it, our top trainer's going to the slammer. Lots a guys
going behind bars when all the rats start singing."

"I think the Boston Globe is more accurate than backside
gossip," Andy insisted.

"Newspapers have their bias too," Pete reminded her.

"Arley's got it right," Candace insisted. "He says Carlo'll
turn himself in, just to save his skin. He'll start singing and

fry Cantoni, send him to the electric chair."

"The electric chair is for first degree murder, not race fixing," Andy informed her. "And I can't see Carlo turning state witness. He isn't the type to work with the FBI."

"If he doesn't, then they might want to send him to the electric chair. He deserves it. Poor Fortune Hunter's finished. He's got a bow bigger than Heckler's."

Andy felt a pang of guilt. "I wish I'd remembered what you told me a little earlier in the race. I could have caught him at the head of the stretch and the poor horse would have chucked it in before he got hurt."

"Just be grateful you didn't get hurt," Charlie remarked. "If the FBI hadn't been waiting in the backstretch, Carlo would have come after you. You never would have made it back to the winners circle."

"That would have been a real shame. Then Pete wouldn't have received his birthday present," Andy joked, reaching for her coffee. She suddenly noticed Candace's plate piled high with eggs, bacon, fried potatoes and toast. "I know you don't have to count the ounces anymore Candace, but you may want to watch the pounds."

"Hell, if I'm hanging up my racing tack ta be your agent, I've got twenty years of starvation to make up foah."

"Fine, but don't do it all in one day," Charlie remarked reaching for the newspaper. She shuddered when she looked at Pony's picture. "Ignorance is bliss."

"Yeah, but ya ain't ignorant anymore. Those boys are going to bring a lotta folks down. The backside'll be half empty by the time they've finished talking."

"And now, on to brighter topics," Charlie said, quickly changing the subject. "How's the birthday boy? Did you have a big celebration last night?"

"It's hard to get a lot of celebrating in before eight thirty," Pete replied, leaning back in his chair with a sigh.

"Now that you're forty, bedtime will be an hour earlier," Andy teased.

"I feel more like sixty. Look, two more grey hairs." He pointed towards his forehead. "That's thanks to you and Lili. Next time go to the front and stay there. I'd rather you get beat on the front end than have her try another little stunt like she did on the turn. You came within my two grey hairs of going down. Eddie saved your skin on that one."

"Yes, dear Eddie, I wonder how he figures in all this?"

"Why would Eddie have anything to do with it?" Pete asked.

Andy hadn't meant to say that aloud. She glanced across the table and met Charlie's eyes. They had made a pact not to talk about Eddie's brother being with Pony in the restaurant. Andy wanted to find out just how Eddie was connected to this whole business before she made any further statements.

"Eddie's the Jockeys' Guild representative, so I was just wondering how he would handle defending jockeys who are obviously guilty."

Charlie winked, to let her know she had squeezed out of that one. But then Andy's mind flew off in another direction. How was Mickey involved in this? If anyone fit the bill of a gangster, it was Mickey Amato.

"With Pedro and Carlo gone, maybe Arthur Healey can get this place cleaned up for once and for all," Charley remarked. "Wouldn't it be nice to have some clean, honest racing?"

"The shit just started hitting the fan," Candace assured them. "It's gonna go a lot deeper than Carlo and Pedro. Those two retards couldn't have been the brains behind the whole thing, they were taking orders from someone."

"Of course, the brains would be Pony Cantoni," Andy replied.

"Pony gives the orders, sure, but he doesn't carry them out. Ya saw *The Godfather*, his lieutenants and the crew do the dirty work. They'll be calling more names to the steward's office, ya can bet on that."

"You don't think any more jockeys were involved, do

you?" Charlie asked.

"Carlo and Pedro were the main guys, for sure," Pete said, "but they'd probably call on a few pinch hitters when they needed back up."

Andy stared at him from over the paper. "Part time gangsters? Is there really such a thing?"

"Nobody here at this table is an expert on the mafia," Pete admitted, "but it would make sense for Carlo to call on some of his buddies to help out."

Andy thought about that for a moment. "If there are some pinch hitters, the FBI will be flushing them out so they can have witnesses in court to convict Carlo and Pedro."

"If they get to them first," Candace pointed out. "If it's true the Winter Hill gang is behind Cantoni, they'll get to them first. They know where to look."

"Okay, that's enough sleuthing," Pete informed them, getting to his feet. "Time to do some real work. Come on, the morning's half over. Let's get the rest of the horses out to the track."

Andy sighed as she folded up the paper, her mind a jumble of questions. Her mental jury was ready to convict Carlo and Pedro, but they were still undecided about Eddie.

What was going on between him and his brother? She vividly remembered seeing them together in the parking lot on her first day headed to the jockeys' room. She knew for certain that his brother was connected to Cantoni. The real question remained.

Was Eddie connected to his brother?

OPERATION BISCUIT

Andy struggled to hold back the eager horse. "Whoa, Heckler, this isn't race day!"

She had just finished a two mile gallop and was trying to jog back on the outside rail. The big gelding hadn't let up during the entire gallop and was still pulling.

"Andrea!" someone called out from the grandstand.

Andy didn't dare take her focus off the exuberant horse.

"Yes, Mr Healey?" she called out, recognizing his voice.

"Andrea, please come to my office, as soon as possible."

Andy groaned. She had a good idea who would be waiting for her.

"Yes, sir, I'll be right there."

Tim was tacked and ready to go when she returned to the barn, but when she told Candace Arthur wanted her in the office, she was sent on her way. Andy ducked into Emmett's shed row on the way.

"Hey, Al, is Excalibur going to gallop today?"

Al shrugged his shoulders. "The Mouse, he not show up."

She stood with her hands on her hip in her best school teacher imitation.

Al took a deep breath. "Mr. Mouse, he no...he did not come this morning. I walk... I am walking Excalibur."

"Eso es bueno," she commended him. "Is Ringo here?"

"He down...no, he is down there, in tackroom."

"*The* tackroom," she corrected him before rushing down the aisle. "Hey, Ringo!"

He poked his head out of the doorway, coffee cup in hand.

"Listen, if Mr Amato shows up and wants Excalibur galloped, would you get on him? I don't want anybody stealing my best mount."

"Over my dead body," Ringo promised.

Andy felt a chill run along her spine. "No Ringo, don't go that far."

She rushed off to the stewards' office without further delay. When she arrived at the door, she knocked and waited for permission to enter. The door opened and Arthur showed her in. George and Bob were there, as expected, still in their dark suits but the monotony was relieved by a change of ties. She heard a cough and turned to see Eddie Flaherty standing next to a coffee urn.

The jury was about to deliver their verdict.

"Let's make this as comfortable as possible," Arthur said, pulling out chairs and arranging them in circular fashion in the middle of the room. "After all, this is more of a fact finding meeting than an interrogation."

Andy liked the fact that Arthur was taking control today. Eddie was the first to sit down. Andy sat beside him.

"Feels like an AA meeting," he remarked, glancing at the circle of chairs.

"You're familiar with AA meetings, are you? " George remarked.

Eddie nodded. "My dad took me to his weekly meetings when I was a kid. He wanted me to hear all the horror stories so I wouldn't end up like him."

"And you didn't, right?" Andy asked.

"I didn't have time. I had my jockey's license before I reached legal drinking age. Besides, too many calories in alcohol."

George and Bob sat down facing each other rather than side by side. Andy figured it was easier to play good cop, bad cop that way. There was a knock at the door and once again, Arthur answered it. The man who entered looked vaguely familiar, but Andy couldn't quite place him. Only when he spoke did she recognize his voice.

Gone was the blue and orange checked sports jacket, the lime fedora. Mark Rodale greeted the FBI agents by name as he walked to the coffee urn.

"Hey, George, Bob, how's it hanging?"

"I guess we'll know pretty soon," George replied.

"Everyone, this is Agent Marcus Wright," Bob introduced him. "Or Marker as he's known. Las Vegas is his usual haunt, but we were fortunate enough to borrow him for this operation."

"Good morning, Mr Rodale," Andy greeted him.

Marker laughed. "You're a quick one, Andy. What was the giveaway? My nose?" He pointed to his bulbous nose.

"No, your voice."

"Of course, the hardest thing to disguise. I'm lousy at accents." Marker poured himself a cup of coffee and sat down facing Eddie. "We haven't been formally introduced. Eddie Flaherty, right?"

"Right."

"Okay, let's get on with Operation Biscuit," Bob announced.

"Operation Biscuit?" Andy repeated. "You named this after Seabiscuit?"

"Right again," Marker commended her.

"I would have thought you'd call it Operation Pony."

"Tell us what you know about Pony," Marker asked, settling into a chair with a cup of black coffee.

"Only what I read in the Boston Globe this morning. It said you arrested a man you've been watching for three years, a Pony Cantoni."

"Goddamn squid, he always jumps the gun!" George hissed. "Asshole reporter could have kept it under wraps at least forty-eight hours."

"Okay, so that part is public knowledge, but whatever else we discuss in here is not to leave the room. Everyone understands that?" Bob looked at everyone in turn, his gaze lingering a little longer on Eddie. "We've moved in on the big players, but we need to do some clean up to get a tight case."

Andy felt a sudden pang of regret. Mickey hadn't shown up at the barn this morning. Did that mean he was one of the big players?

"You've caught Carlo and Pedro?" Eddie asked.

Bob shook his head. "No, but we're closing in."

"So, Andy, I want to know the truth." Marker's unflinching gaze made Andy feel as if she had been hiding vital information.

"Is Roadhouse Boy as good as Excalibur?"

She expelled her breath in relief. "Only the racing gods know the answer to that one."

"What do you say we get down to business," Bob intervened. "Andy, you were about to tell us what you know about Pony Cantoni."

She shrugged her shoulders. "I know he weighs about as much as a racehorse and he's been arrested for race fixing. And he must have lousy taste in restaurants if he eats at the Whistling...no, the Smiling Oyster."

"He eats there because he owns it," Marker informed her, "at least, on paper. All that dough from race fixing has to go somewhere."

"Well he's not using it to pay top chefs," Andy quipped.

"Maybe Eddie can fill us in on that department." Marker turned to Eddie. "Your brother is one of the chefs there."

Eddie looked surprised to hear that. "Tommy, a cook? You could have fooled me. He's always worked as a bouncer. I can't see anyone hiring him as a chef. He didn't last a month at McDonald's back in high school."

"You trying to tell us you don't know what your twin brother's up to?" George demanded. "Come on, Eddie, that's hard to swallow."

Andy shifted in her chair. She wasn't on George's side, but if they were twins, it was heard to believe they wouldn't be connected.

"You swallow it when our state representative, Billy Bulger, denies knowing anything about *his* brother."

Eddie had a point there, she had to agree.

"Let's move on," Bob suggested. "It's Pony's family we're interested in. Tell us what you know about Mickey Amato, Andy. We know you've had a lot of contact with him."

"I know he owns the finest racehorse I've ever been on."

"Finally, the truth," Marker said with a grin. "I knew Roadhouse Boy didn't hold a candle to Excalibur. Mickey was trying to sell me a hundred thousand dollar dud."

"A hundred thousand!" Andy exclaimed. "Is that what Roadhouse Boy is worth?"

"I've been waiting for you to tell me."

"I didn't know they were asking that much. The colt has potential, but who knows what kind of horse he is until he runs a race."

"The Keeneland auction records show that he was purchased by D'Addazio for eighty thousand," Bob informed her. "But we have no record of when Amato bought him. Can you enlighten us on that?"

Andy shook her head. "The morning I worked him was the first time I'd laid eyes on the colt. I won a race on Mr D'Addazio's mare, Little Miss, and he promised to put me on his Kentucky colt. I thought that's what was happening."

"Then why was Mickey the one giving you the instructions?" Bob asked.

Andy shook her head. "I thought Mickey was helping Mr. D'Addazio out."

"Why would Mickey be helping him out?" George demanded. "Emmett Gibbons is the trainer."

Andy didn't need much time to think about that question. "I'm sure even Mr. D'Addazio has figured out that Mr. Amato has more talent for training than Emmett Gibbons. He only knows how to claim horses not train them."

"So you're saying Emmett Gibbons is just a front."

George leaned back in his chair, satisfied with his conclusion.

"No, that's not what I'm saying," Andy insisted. "All I'm saying is what everyone around the track believes, that Emmet runs horses off of everybody else's training. He has a knack for claiming but that's where his talent ends."

"Talent," George scoffed. "You don't think maybe he gets inside information?"

"From where, the racing gods?" She shook her head. "Emmett's a good poker player. He watches everybody else's horses galloping in the morning. When he knows a horse is about to peak, he reaches into the claiming box for him. He also knows which trainers like to make a bet and run their horses below their claiming price. So he gets them for a deal."

"How does Excalibur fit into this theory of yours?" Marker asked.

"He's not really trained by Emmett. Mickey Amato trains him."

"The accountant?" George asked. "Where does an accountant get his training ability?"

"From his grandfather, Broedy Sheehan. I looked him up in the records book. When Broedy was assistant trainer for Will Ricci, they were at the top of the trainers' list. Backstretch rumours can't always be believed but I've heard from just about everyone that Ricci was a drunk. Sheehan did the hands on training. So it doesn't surprise me at all that Emmett gets the credit while Mr Amato does the training."

"So you're saying Mickey Amato is the brains behind the outfit?" George's brusque style was in complete contrast to Marker's conversational tone.

Marker motioned George to back off and rephrased the question. "Do you think Mickey Amato influences Emmett Gibbons?"

"As far as his own horses are concerned, yes, but I've never seen him get involved with any other horse. Well, except D'Addazio's colt."

There was a loud knock on the door. It opened before

Arthur was on his feet and Mustang strode into the room. Andy stared in disbelief. Gone were the skin tight tee-shirts and grubby jeans, replaced by a navy blue suit and white shirt. There was no tie.

"Christ, I thought I'd finally get to sleep in and you guys go and call an early morning meeting. Where's the coffee?"

Marker laughed, pointing in the direction of the urn. "Come on, Hanna, we let you sleep an extra two hours. And don't say I didn't warn you about track life."

"You call rubbing horses and shovelling shit a life? Jesus, up before dawn, in bed before sunset—that's no life!" She made her way towards the urn. "You said I'd love it. You were way off your mark there!"

"Mustang, an FBI agent?" Andy exclaimed. "I wouldn't have believed it in a hundred years."

"Thanks," Hanna replied, filling a cup to the brim. "Guess that means I did a good job."

"Your disguise had us all fooled," Eddie remarked. "I have to admit, I miss the tee-shirts."

"I'll bet you do, Casanova." She sat down beside Marker, spilling coffee in her lap.

"You can dress the girl up but you can't take her out," Marker teased.

"Give me a break, I haven't had a decent night's sleep for eight months."

"So who's coming through the door next?" Andy asked, glancing in that direction. "Is Ringo an agent too?"

Marker shook his head. "Ringo seems to be the genuine article."

"He's the real article alright, a pothead," Hanna agreed. "We may have to turn him in."

"You can't do that!" Andy blurted out.

Eddie put his hand on her shoulder and gave her a look that said, keep cool. Try as she might, Mustang always seemed to press her buttons.

"So what if he smokes a little grass?" she said in a

level tone. "It's not like he's a dealer. Ringo minds his own business."

"How can you be so sure of that?" Mustang challenged her. "If you're such a good judge of character, how come you didn't have me figured out?"

"You had us all fooled," Eddie added. "You should get a promotion, Mustang."

There was another knock at the door and the valet, Johnny Ryerson, entered. Eddie sat bolt upright.

"No way, not you, Johnny. FBI?"

"Relax, lover boy," Hanna told him. "Your valet just did a little information gathering for us. He'll still be polishing your boots. Unless, of course, you come up on the tapes."

She held out her hand and Johnny gave her the tape cassettes.

"Have a seat, Johnny," Bob instructed him, pointing to the empty chair beside him.

Andy turned to Eddie. "Are you and I the only ones not in on this?"

Eddie nodded in Arthur's direction and she turned to look at him.

"I'm the genuine article too," he replied. "I didn't know about this until the same morning you were informed."

"Okay, getting back to Operation Biscuit," Marker continued. "As the Boston Globe article stated, we've been watching this guy, Pony Cantoni. Does the name ring a bell, Eddie?"

Eddie shook his head.

"Come off it, Casanova, you know Cantoni, your brother works for him!"

"I have no idea who he is."

"Tommy tells you when something's going down, we know that for a fact," Hanna insisted. "What we don't know is how much *you* tell Tommy."

"You've got your facts all wrong. I don't know who Tommy works for and I don't want to know. I told him that right from the beginning."

"Right from the beginning," Hanna echoed triumphantly. "The beginning of what, lover boy?"

"The beginning of high school. Tommy got mixed up with some local guys. It was petty stuff, stealing off the trucks as they were unloading, grabbing some bottles at the local package stores. He spent a night in jail back in grade eight. I don't know what happened. I was rubbing horses by then, I didn't have a life off the track."

"You expect us to believe that?" she demanded.

Eddie returned her glare. "You said it yourself, there's no life outside the track."

"Come on, you don't expect us to believe you'd turn down thousands of dollars, tax free? You'd rather pick up the thirty dollar jock's fee?" George was now playing tag team with Hanna.

"Try multiplying that by thirty, forty times a week," Eddie calculated, "and throw in ten percent on the wins. It makes for a nice weekly pay cheque."

Hanna stared him in the eye. "I've got a witness who says you give your brother information that isn't available in the *Daily Racing Form*."

Eddie didn't flinch. "Then your witness is lying."

There were several moments of silence as they stared at each other.

"We can get into that later," Bob intervened, ending the stand-off. "Johnny, how did the tapes turn out?"

"It worked perfect," Johnny replied. "I put it above Pedro's locker. That's where he and Carlo always talk. Picked up their conversation beautifully. They were in a huddle before yesterday's race, talked about who's going to be where. Carlo even asked Pedro if he'd be carrying. Pedro said yes."

"Carrying?" George asked.

"A battery, " Johnny explained. "So he could zap the horse, give her added incentive. Works like a charm."

"Not always," Eddie informed them. "Some horses will

go over the rail when they get hit with an electrical device."

"You talking from experience?" Hanna challenged him.

"You're even meaner when you're dressed up," he retorted. "Yeah, I carried a battery, once, back when I was an apprentice on the fair circuit. The horse bolted and went over the outside rail. I never tried it again."

"Johnny, does Pony or Tommy's name come up in any of the tapes?" Marker asked.

Johnny shook his head. "Sorry, no names."

George and Hanna groaned in unison.

"Goddamit! We need names!" George shouted.

"You'll find it incriminating enough as far as Carlo and Pedro go," Johnny assured them.

"Fine, but we've got to catch the bastards first," Hanna reminded him.

"If either of you could help track these guys down, we'd appreciate it." Marker looked from Eddie to Andy. "Any ideas?"

They both shook their heads.

"We travel in different circles," Eddie replied as Andy nodded agreement. "I've never seen either of them off the track."

"Anything else you can tell us?"

Andy glanced at her watch. "Yes. Eddie and I were supposed to be in the jocks' room ten minutes ago."

"Okay, you'd better take off." Marker reached into his pocket and handed her a business card. "I can be reached at that number day or night. If you think of anything else, no matter how minor it may seem, give me a call."

Hanna also gave her a card.

Andy was excused, but Eddie was asked to stay for more questioning. When she left the office, she glanced at the two cards. Walking to the nearest garbage can, she dropped Hanna's in it. Marker's card went in her pocket.

She walked slowly across the grandstand trying to digest all that had been said, or more importantly, unsaid. She tried to put all the facts together, but some of the most important piece was missing. What were Eddie and Tommy arguing about?

Andy remembered her first foggy morning here at Suffolk Downs. Mustang had served as an omen of all the negative things that had happened since that first day. And then Eddie had appeared, smiling, friendly and quick to give good advice. If he too was mixed up in this mafia scheme, she would pack her tack and head back to New York.

She made her way across the grandstand and stopped when she came to the stairs leading down to the men's quarters. She would wait here for Eddie. The jury hadn't presented its verdict on his guilt or innocence as far as she was concerned. She didn't want to believe that Eddie was mixed up with the race fixing scheme, but she knew what she saw in the parking lot. If Johnny's duties went further than cleaning tack and shining boots, was it possible Eddie wasn't quite who he seemed to be?

"Still trying to get into the boys' room?"

Eddie's voice startled her out of her reverie.

"Oh, they let you out, did they?" she said.

"You make it sound like I've just been released from prison." His tone inferred he was only half joking. "Go ahead, you have questions to ask me too."

She took a deep breath and jumped in. "I saw you that first day I rode, out in the parking lot arguing with your brother."

The muscles in his neck and jaw tightened, but he remained silent, waiting for her to say more.

"Then, in my second race that day, you came up on my outside. You purposely stayed there and boxed me in. It was like you didn't want me to win."

"That's right, I didn't want you to win."

His direct answer shocked her. She couldn't believe he was admitting it.

"But not for reasons you're thinking right now."

"I don't work with my brother, Andy. That's the question you really want to ask me, isn't it?"

"Yes," she admitted, not knowing what else to say.

"I've never been involved in Tommy's business and never will. He showed up that day in the parking lot to tell me he was desperate. He said I was supposed to be his link to the jocks' room. I knew nothing about it. That was the first I knew about him being a runner for the mob." His gaze was unflinching as he kept steady eye contact with her. "Tommy and I have travelled different paths since high school. He's gone down one road, I've gone down another. I told him whatever predicament he was in, it was his own choosing. I wasn't going to sacrifice my career to get him out of a jam. That's when I walked away." He searched her face, looking for a sign that she believed him. "What you saw was the first and last time Tommy ever approached me at the track."

"So you knew something was going on in that race?"

He nodded. "I didn't hang around to hear any details. I didn't want to hear any names, but it didn't take a genius to figure out Carlo and Pedro were involved. When I saw them jamming everyone in on the rail and you got your horse in gear, I knew you were headed for trouble. And I knew what the consequences would be."

"How could you know that if you aren't part of Tommy's business?" she demanded.

"I put the pieces together. When I read the article about that bug boy in Rhode Island, Alex Munsey, I knew something was fishy. Then I started to hear rumours. The scuttlebutt on the backstretch is usually more fiction than fact, but they all begin with a grain of truth. I was sure the kid didn't die of an *accidental* overdose. I didn't want you to be the next casualty."

Andy needed time to let that sink in.

His face softened. "I had no idea Tommy was involved with them at that time. I thought he was still doing the small time stuff. But I guess he's supplementing his income as a runner." He leaned his arm against the wall and gave her that same smile that had appeared through the darkness of the shed row on that foggy morning.

"I owe you big time, Andy. If you'd mentioned the parking lot incident in there, those agents would have been all over me. Mustang is dying to nail me. She never liked me, right from day one."

"Mustang doesn't like herself," Andy retorted. "She and George should get married. They're a perfect match."

"I wouldn't want to live in the apartment next door," he said and they both laughed.

"Me either," Andy agreed before turning serious once again. Andy leaned back against the wall, not relishing what she had to tell him. "There's something else you need to know."

Eddie braced himself, knowing instantly it wasn't good news.

"I don't know how the mafia works, but I think the guys that are runners are at the bottom of the totem pole. I think your brother's a lot higher up. When I saw the fat man in the restaurant, that Pony Cantoni, Tommy was with him."

"Shit!" Eddie swore. "God damn shit! So he's in deep. That's why he was desperate enough to come to me."

Andy watched him as he turned one way and then the other. She felt his distress as surely as she sensed a Thoroughbred's unease. She had no doubt it was genuine.

"No wonder Mustang's after my ass," he muttered between clenched teeth. "She smells blood!"

"They can't blame you for your brother's crimes," Andy insisted.

"They need someone to blame and they'll grab anyone they can."

"Well, they haven't had any luck with the Bulger brothers, have they? If they can't prove there's a connection between them surely they can't convict you for your brother's crimes."

Eddie slapped the wall with both hands.

"If it's any consolation, Eddie, I believe you. I don't think you're involved in any way with your brother."

Eddie expelled his breath as he slumped against the wall. "At least I have one person on my side."

DON'T LEAVE TOWN

Mickey paced back and forth along the sidewalk, going over the details in his mind. Had he covered his tracks thoroughly? The IRS hadn't found any proof of wrong doing when they audited his books, but the FBI agents would not resemble the myopic accountant from the IRS. They were ruthless hunters who made their own rules and enforced them in creative ways.

Just keep cool, he told himself as he stopped to take a breath. He glanced over at the store fronts that were elbow to elbow with his office. On one side was a pawnshop that boasted a trio of enormous brass spheres suspended above it's door. On the other side was a Chinese restaurant guarded by a brilliant green neon dragon. Snuggled in between was his office window which proclaimed 'M&A Accounting Ltd' with his name and title, 'Michael S Amato, Certified General Accountant' in gold letters outlined in solemn black.

He unlocked the door and stepped into his outer office. A small brightly coloured oval rug was a cheerful island amid the darker tones of the office. Muddied footprints emphasised it's need for a good vacuuming. That was Perry's job but today he was in Maine on a creative writing course. Arrangements for the course had been completed several weeks ago, but the FBI might still suspect Perry had skipped town to avoid questioning. Perry's nervous temperament would not be useful in an interrogation room where his guilt would be presumed.

Mickey looked around the room to see if anything had been disturbed. A large mahogany desk and matching chairs took up most of the space. Surrounding the electric IBM typewriter on the desk were several lined notepads, boxes of paperclips and a colourful St Patrick's day ceramic stein bristling with pens and pencils. The walls were covered with prints of famous racehorses of yesteryear—Man O' War, Seabiscuit, Citation, Twenty Grand and Regret, the only filly to win the Kentucky Derby.

Mickey went into the backroom, his private office, and tried to see it through the eyes of an FBI agent. Everything was tidy—too tidy. They would think he'd cleaned it up because he was hiding something. They wouldn't know that he had to be organized to function properly, that he always kept files and papers neatly stacked. He spread pencils, erasers and a stack of bills haphazardly across the green blotter on his desk to make it appear less suspicious.

Next, he looked over at the file cabinet. He had checked Pony's file to be sure the most minute detail would hold up under scrutiny. The 'Special Editions' had been turned to ashes in the back room of The Smiling Oyster. He was sure his tracks were well covered. Anything he didn't want the FBI to know was safely tucked away in his mind. Nothing short of torture could pry that information out of him.

He shuddered at that thought. To keep himself busy, he began straightening the pictures on the wall. He lingered over a photograph taken in the spring of 1955. A slender boy with intense dark eyes and a serious expression looked out at him. Mickey was seven years old when the picture was taken. He stood close to his grandfather who held the reins of the winner, Shy Boy. A craggy looking man of advanced years stood at the horse's flanks. Will Ricci, Racing Hall of Fame trainer.

Mickey shook his head and moved on to more recent pictures of horses that he had claimed over the past three years. All of these had moved on to other stables, except for one.

Excalibur.

Mickey glowed with pride as he stared at the sleek colt he had picked from all the others at the Kentucky sales. Even to the untrained eye, this horse stood out amongst all the rest. A grand colt, his grandfather would have said.

"My colt," he said aloud, with deep satisfaction.

No one could argue with that now. It was his name on the receipt from the Kentucky sales, his name on the Jockey Club registration papers. The only man who could contest Mickey's ownership was behind bars, thanks to one of his Atlantic City boys.

The reliable kind, Pony had said in their last meeting, the kind that don't fuck up. "Well, one of them fucked up royally," he muttered as he smiled at the picture.

The agents would be here any minute. Mickey looked for something to keep himself busy. He decided to prepare a pot of coffee. He had just plugged in the percolator when the front door opened.

One last look around the room, a deep breath and he headed towards the door. He saw three men in dark suits enter the outer office.

"Good morning," he greeted them.

"Michael Amato?" one of them asked.

He nodded.

"I'm Agent Bob Morrow and this is Agent George Wismer and Agent Mark Lehman."

"That's Marker," he offered, stepping forward.

Mickey recognized him immediately.

"Mr Rodale, I believe we've met." He kept his face emotionless as he nodded acknowledgement, deliberately keeping his tone even to cover his surprise.

"Seems my disguise didn't fool anyone," Marker said.

Marker moved aside and a woman appeared from behind him.

Mickey felt his heart constrict.

"Hi Mickey," she said. "The name's Hanna Fazzolari."

"I never would have guessed," he admitted.

"She's one of our best," the man named George commented.

"We need to ask you some questions about one of your clients," Bob explained.

"Yes, I think I know which one," he said. He stepped into his inner office and went straight to the file cabinet in the far corner. "There's fresh coffee if you would like some."

He opened the top drawer and searched through it as Hanna and Marker helped themselves to coffee. Pulling a file he placed it on the desk, his composure back. "Anthony Cantoni."

Bob immediately picked it up and began reading.

"There isn't another file hidden away in a safe place, is there?" George asked facetiously.

Mickey shook his head. "No reason for that. There's nothing to hide."

"You don't really expect us to believe that," George argued, pointing to the pictures on the wall. "Cantoni's horses, right?"

"No, these are my horses," Mickey insisted.

"And my name is Annie Oakley," Hanna cut in, spilling her coffee as she placed it on the desk.

Mickey quickly looked for something to clean it up. He grabbed a tissue from the Kleenex box on the far side of the desk and mopped up the spilled coffee.

"Come on, M&A Accounting can't afford a stable of racehorses," she insisted.

"Not without a little help," George added, "from your friends."

"The only help I get is from my trainer," Mickey insisted, dropping the soggy tissues in the wastepaper basket. "As I'm sure you know, Emmett Gibbons' talent is for claiming horses. He's taught me everything he knows."

"Maybe it was Pony Cantoni who taught you everything he knows," Hanna insisted. "After all, his payoffs are a hell of lot better."

"Anthony Cantoni was ruled off the racetrack two years ago. To my knowledge he hasn't been within ten miles of the track since," Mickey insisted.

"He doesn't need to be on the track when he's got you at his beck and call," Hanna insisted. "We know you're the front man, Mickey, so don't bother denying it."

"I do deny it," Mickey insisted.

"Really? Then where did you get the twenty grand to pay for the big colt?" she demanded, nodding toward the win picture of Excalibur. "That's a little beyond M&A Accounting, *Limited*," she added pointedly.

Mickey walked back to the filing cabinet and pulled a file.

"Year end, 1975 A&M Accounting." He handed her the file.

She passed it over to George. "This is your field, take a look."

"With a microscope," George remarked, sitting down at the desk.

"It's all there, every penny," Mickey insisted.

"We know you're the brains behind the money laundering, Mickey," she stated. "You know how to cook the books. But it isn't going to work. We've got people ready to talk."

"Including the big man himself," Marker added, stepping close to him. "When Pony sings, you're all going down, the whole rotten crew."

This was an angle Mickey hadn't expected. He clasped his hands behind his back to conceal their sudden trembling Could it be true, Pony was going to talk?

"The game's up, Mickey, better start answering some questions now and make it easier on yourself." Marker leaned in until Mickey could smell his acid breath. "We can make a deal, you talk to me and I talk to the DA, get you a reduced sentence."

Hanna closed in from the other side. "Go for it, Mickey. The big man's going to tell all and your precious colt is gone."

Mickey's confusion turned to anger. No one was taking his colt away.

"Take a look at the file, it's all there," he stated firmly.

"Oh, for fuck's sake, give me a break!"

The frustration in Hanna's voice strengthened Mickey's resolve.

"You're wasting your time. I own the colt." He brushed past the two agents and strode into the outer office.

"Come on, Mickey, we've got a witness who saw you with Cantoni at the auction." Hanna was right at his heels.

"Your witness needs glasses. Mr. Cantoni wasn't anywhere near the auction ring.

I was there *by* myself and *for* myself."

"By yourself, were you?" Marker strode into the room and folded his arms across his chest as he cornered Mickey once again. "What about Aberto D'Addazio?"

"He wasn't there with me. I bumped into him in one of the barns. He asked my opinion about a Round Table colt."

"Roadhouse Boy. Yes, I know the horse, you tried to sell him to me, remember? So when did you buy him?"

"*Why* did you buy him? That's the real question," Hanna interceded. "You smelled a rat, didn't you? You knew we were on to you and you needed to hide the trail that led to Cantoni."

Mickey shook his head. "D'Addazio needed some cash flow. His business had a slow winter. He offered me a deal I couldn't refuse."

"You mean you offered a deal *he* couldn't refuse." Marker raised his voice so George could hear him in the next room. "Hey, George, pull D'Addazio's file."

"We trotted Excalibur around the barn," Hanna informed him. "There's nothing wrong with him. Funny how the heat in that ankle disappeared right after you switched horses. What happened? Did you and Pony have a disagreement?"

"The groom discovered the heat. Have you questioned him?"

"You were right there when Al discovered it. So why didn't you send for the vet, have the ankle x-rayed? That's the normal course of action, especially for a future stakes horse."

"I don't need a vet to tell me what's wrong with my horse." Mickey's voice was cool. Hanna was fishing and he wasn't about to seize the bait.

"So you've got x-ray eyes, do you?"

Mickey held out his hands. "I've got these."

"Oh, there's some kind of special magic in those, is there?" Hanna laughed. "And where did you get these magic hands?"

"My grandfather, Broedy Sheehan."

"You mean the Broedy Sheehan who never got beyond assistant trainer?" Marker scoffed. "The man who rode on the coattails of Will Ricci, Racing Hall of Fame trainer?"

Rage began to ignite in Mickey's eyes. "The Broedy Sheehan who trained horses while Will Ricci drank himself to death," he declared. "My grandfather got those horses to peak condition and kept them there. He knew when to run a horse and when to rest him." Mickey looked from face to face, meeting their eyes directly. "And he taught me never to sell a lame horse."

For once, Hanna stood speechless while Marker shifted from one foot to the other.

Mickey grabbed the upper hand while he had it. "Now, if we're done here, I have some work to attend to."

"Not so fast." Hanna returned to the office. "What has your microscope picked up, George?"

George tossed the files aside. "These have been through the washer at least a dozen times."

"Yeah, well bring them along. We've got a few more people to question at the Smiling Oyster. I'm sure the accounts won't jive with what they tell us. And we're not done with you," she assured Mickey as she headed to the door. "Don't leave town."

"Not until next spring," he replied with a smile. "First Saturday in May."

She laughed as she stepped out the door. "Yeah sure, see you at the Kentucky Derby."

MISSING IN ACTION

"Take a look at this," Pete said as he walked into the track kitchen. He dropped the Boston Globe on the table.

Andy reached over and picked up the newspaper. "Look at that, we're front page news!"

She held the paper up so Charlie and Candace could read the headlines.

"*Race Fixing Scandal Hits New England*," Charlie read aloud. "That's not exactly news to us, is it? Read us the article."

Andy spread the paper out in front of her. "'*The largest race fixing scam in history has been successfully shut down. Anthony 'Pony' Cantoni, was arrested earlier this week in a motel a few blocks from the Atlantic City Racetrack after the dismal performance of the favourite in the fifth race. Racing officials became suspicious when the two-to-one choice, Monkey's Joy, finished in last place. The stewards called in jockey Keith Barnhart to question him on his lacklustre ride. The tale Keith had to tell led directly to Mr Cantoni at the Blue Star Motel where he was waiting for his runners to appear with the payoffs.*

The Federal Bureau of Investigation and the U.S. Department of Justice Organized Crime Strike Force have been working on race-rigging since 1973. Mr Cantoni has been their prime suspect and FBI agents have been watching him closely. A break came in the case on Sunday, April fourth,

344

right here at Suffolk Downs. In the second race, the heavy favourite, Houseboy, ridden by Liam Brady, finished off the board after being severely shut off in the backstretch. Charm the Judge, ridden by apprentice Andrea Crowley, conveniently slipped through on the rail to win at fifteen-to-one odds.' "

Andy dropped the paper and sat bolt upright in her chair. "My God, they think I'm one of the gang!"

"They didn't say you were involved," Pete corrected her. "They just said you won the race."

"*Conveniently slipped through on the rail,*" she stated emphatically. "That sounds like I knew what was happening and played my part to perfection."

"Keep reading," Pete told her.

Andy shook her head. "I don't think I want to read anymore. My name has been linked with race fixers!"

"Have Bob and George arrested ya?" Candace asked.

"Not yet," she replied.

"If they thought ya were part of it, they would have slapped handcuffs on ya before ya left the jocks' room."

"That's right," Pete agreed, digging into his scrambled eggs. "Keep reading."

Andy reluctantly picked up the paper. " '*FBI agents were watching the race from the backstretch. The two jockeys who allegedly set up the race spotted the agents watching them. Carlo Gessani and Pedro Vargas leaped from their mounts and scaled the back fence, disappearing into the streets of east Boston. The agents set chase, but were unable to catch them. Both jockeys have not been seen since and are believed to be hiding out in Mexico.'"*

"Sounds better than riding the MTA forever." Candace laughed before stuffing a piece of sausage in her mouth.

"That'll be the end of their racing days," Charlie surmised.

"And mine too," Andy insisted. "Everyone on the track has read this by now. They'll think I'm part of the set-up."

With a sigh, she continued reading. "*Several members of*

the notorious Winter Hill Gang have been called in for questioning. It is believed that the gang's leaders, Howie Winter and James Bulger, have been bankrolling Cantoni. Several members of the gang have been questioned but none have been arrested at this time.' "

"*At this time*," Andy repeated in an ominous tone, throwing the paper down.

"Why are you so worried?" Charlie asked. "Do you have a record that we don't know about?"

"Of course not."

"Ya didn't have a big bet on the Judge, did ya?"

"No. You know I don't bet."

"Then, ya got nothing to worry about. With your squeaky clean background, no one's gonna suspect you're part of the gang."

"That's right," Charlie agreed. "Carlo knew you'd go through the eye of a needle if you had to. It was easy enough for him to give you some space on the inside. They used you as part of their bet."

" '*Several people from the backside of Suffolk Downs have also been called in by the FBI,*'" Pete continued reading the article. " *A trainer is presently being held in custody.* "

"A trainer," Charlie pointed out, "*not* an apprentice jockey."

"That's got to be Emmett. He wasn't at the barn yesterday," Candace surmised. "Those stupid FBI guys don't know they're ass from their elbow. Emmett can't even get his hosses out to the track on time, how's he gonna set up a race?"

"They've got the wrong guy, all right," Pete stated as he folded up the paper. "They should be questioning one of his owners."

This remark elicited a groan from Andy. "I think they are questioning his owner. Mr. Amato hasn't been at the barn the past couple of days."

"It's Mr Amato, now? I thought he was Mr Sleazy," Candace teased.

"That was before I knew what a good horseman he is. Sure, he looks like a wiseguy, but with his talent for training, he doesn't need the mafia to help him win races."

"He's only got one good horse," Pete pointed out. "Lots of brilliant two year olds are running for a tag by the time they're three. If his colt doesn't pan out, Mickey will be back to claiming cheap horses. "

"One thing is for certain," Charlie said. "If he doesn't show up, you won't be winning the Kentucky Derby next year, Andy."

"Never mind all this talk about the Derby. We've got races to ride here at Suffolk." Candace pushed her empty plate aside. "Carlo and Pedro are gone so there's all kinds of hosses to pick up. Those boys rode a bunch of winners."

"Sure, but they had a lot of help, didn't they?" Charlie pointed out, nodding in the direction of the newspaper.

"Those retards needed a lot of help. My rider can ride circles around those boys and still win by a city block." She patted Andy on the shoulder as she stood up. "Come on, jock, we've got mounts to pick up."

"You've got to be kidding." One look at Candace and Andy saw that she was serious. "I don't want to ride for trainers who used Carlo and Pedro."

Candace glared down at her. "And ya didn't want to ride for Emmett Gibbons either."

Andy tried to think of something to say in her own defence but nothing would come to her. She surrendered. "Alright, you've got a point."

"I'll see ya at the barn after the break."

"Yeah, we'll plan our strategy." There was little enthusiasm in her voice.

"Don't get discouraged, Andy, your career is just beginning," Pete assured her as he got up and followed Candace out of the kitchen.

"Pete's right, you'll be getting lots of mounts from now on," Charley agreed, sliding her chair away from the table.

"I'll go and tack up Tim. He'll cheer you up."

"Good idea. I'll be there as soon as I finish my coffee."

Andy leaned back in her chair and sighed. She had spent the last two days trying to figure out where her career was going. She was being offered a lot of mounts, but not the one she really wanted to ride. There wasn't a horse on the grounds that could touch Excalibur. If Mickey had been arrested, the colt would soon be in the hands of a new owner and a new trainer—and a new jockey. Her dream of returning to New York and winning the two year old Futurity Stakes was a fading dream. The Kentucky Derby was completely out of the question.

"There you are."

The voice shook her out of her reverie. It was a voice she would recognize anywhere.

Andy spun in her chair as he approached. It was Mickey Amato, but something had changed. A navy blue sweater broke the pattern of his usual sombre black attire. His manner was business as usual, but a smile hovered at the upturned corners of his mouth.

"I've got two sets to get out to the track. I want to be the first one out after the break."

"Yes sir," she said eagerly, jumping to her feet.

"I hope you're feeling strong." The slightly curved lips turned into a full blown smile. "Excalibur is raring to go."

"I'm ready," she said, returning his smile as she reached for her helmet.

"I'll send him out in the first set."

Mickey looked over his shoulder and nodded to someone before briskly heading for the door.

"Hey, Sandy Andy," Ringo greeted her with his puppy dog grin. "Time to saddle up. The Candy Man's back."

ACKNOWLEDGEMENTS

This book has been a labour of love but without the help of several people, it would never have come to completion. My partner, Bobbie, has supported me in every way while I toiled at the computer. Frances, my editor, honed and sharpened my prose, and gave me gentle shoves when my enthusiasm waned. Crystal, a fellow writer, knew when to encourage and when to challenge me. Diane, a talented artist and photographer, shared her creativity, enthusiasm, and a good laugh when it was most needed. Pat, a friend and one of my readers, gave me helpful, critical reviews. A special thanks to Don Cress for recreating his role for the novel.

My family have always been there for me. My deepest love and gratitude go to my mother, Frances, my sister, Terry, my brothers, Steve and Frank, my aunt Mary and Kathleen, and my uncle Michael, who has a cameo appearance in the novel. Every one of them encouraged my childhood imagination and asked daily about my invisible horse, Silver. (Terry didn't really go along with that one but has been my big sister in every other way). Thanks to their love and acceptance, I have remained a free spirit well into adulthood.

My four legged family, both past and present, have been an integral part of my life. (I can't imagine life without them.) Cats and horses have been my most intimate lifelong friends. Thanks to their guidance, I have honed my skills as an animal communicator and have facilitated a conversation between animals and their human companions. Two of my wisest and most loving soul mates, Harry, my wonderful ginger cat and Aphra Behn, my beautiful Thoroughbred, guide me from the other side. On this side, Mayah, Roxanne, Lilibet, Isanna, Princhessa and Shug share their equine knowledge daily. Dolly, Harriet, Zoomer and BillyBob inspire me with cosmic feline wisdom. And Clancy keeps me grounded with canine common sense.

All of the characters in this novel are fictional. Some of the racehorses, however, are horses that I rode at Suffolk Downs. Each of them has given me permission to use their names and re-create the exciting races that we had together.

Visit my website to meet
these amazing Thoroughbreds.

www.paddyhead.com